"What are you doi

She grinned and tipped
I live here."

"I mean, why aren't you at the hospital?" He tried to ignore the rush of happiness that filled his chest.

"Sophie is doing better, and I needed to come home and get some things done. I've been wearing the same dress since we took Sophie to the hospital. It was time for a change."

"That's great. How are you?" She looked fine to him. Better than fine. She looked wonderful.

He studied her lovely face. A light blush colored her cheeks, and her eyes had dark circles under them but they sparkled now as she gazed at him. A soft smile curved her lips. She was happy to see him.

Clara wasn't his type, so why was he so delighted to see her?

After thirty-five years as a nurse, **Patricia Davids** hung up her stethoscope to become a full-time writer. She enjoys spending her free time visiting her grandchildren, doing some long-overdue yard work and traveling to research her story locations. She resides in Wichita, Kansas. Patricia always enjoys hearing from her readers. You can visit her online at patriciadavids.com.

With over seventy books published and millions in print, **Lenora Worth** writes award-winning romance and romantic suspense. Three of her books finaled in the ACFW Carol Awards, and her Love Inspired Suspense novel *Body of Evidence* became a *New York Times* bestseller. Her novella in *Mistletoe Kisses* made her a *USA TODAY* bestselling author. Lenora goes on adventures with her retired husband, Don, and enjoys reading, baking and shopping…especially shoe shopping.

PATRICIA DAVIDS

His New Amish Family

&

LENORA WORTH

Their Amish Reunion

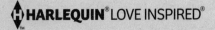

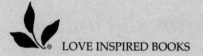 **LOVE INSPIRED BOOKS**

Recycling programs for this product may not exist in your area.

ISBN-13: 978-1-335-47013-3

His New Amish Family and Their Amish Reunion

Copyright © 2019 by Harlequin Books S.A.

The publisher acknowledges the copyright holders of the individual works as follows:

His New Amish Family
Copyright © 2018 by Patricia MacDonald

Their Amish Reunion
Copyright © 2018 by Lenora H. Nazworth

CONTENTS

HIS NEW AMISH FAMILY

Patricia Davids

This book is dedicated with love and respect to my daughter, Kathy. Thanks for all your help and the two wonderful grandkids. Mama loves you.

If any man among you seem to be religious, and bridleth not his tongue, but deceiveth his own heart, this man's religion is vain. Pure religion and undefiled before God and the Father is this, To visit the fatherless and widows in their affliction, and to keep himself unspotted from the world.
—*James* 1:26–27

Chapter One

❧

"This is what you spent our money on?"

"It's *wunderbar, ja*? What a beauty." Paul Bowman grinned as he wiped a spot of dirt off the white trailer bearing his name in large black letters on the side. It might look like a big white box with windows but it was his future. It sat parked inside their uncle's barn out of the weather.

His brother, Mark, shook his head. "Beauty was not my first thought."

Paul stepped back to take in the full effect. "Paul Bowman Auction Services. Has a nice sound, don't you think? A friend did all the custom work. He found this used concession stand trailer, stripped it to a shell, then installed the sliding glass windows on each side, rewired it for battery power as well as electricity, installed the speakers on the roof and customized the inside to fit my needs. It did smell like fried funnel cakes for a while but the new paint job took care of that."

Mark sighed heavily. "This is not what I was expecting."

Paul walked around pointing to the features he had

insisted on having. "It is mounted on a flatbed trailer with two axles and radial tires for highway travel. The front hitch is convertible. It can be pulled by horses or by a truck if the auction is more than twenty miles away."

"What were you thinking?"

Paul didn't understand the disapproval in his older brother's voice. "I told you I needed a better sound system. People have to be able to hear the auctioneer."

Mark gestured toward the trailer. "I thought you wanted a new speaker. This thing looks like a cross between a moving van and the drive-up window at the Farley State Bank. It's huge. And white. Our buggies must be black."

"The bishop won't object to the color. It's not like it's sunflower yellow and it isn't truly a buggy. It's my place of business. It has everything I need."

"Everything except an auction to take it to."

"The work will start rolling in. You'll see." He pulled open the back door. "You have got to hear this sound system. These speakers are awesome. It all runs on battery power, or I can plug it in if there is electricity at the place where the auction is being held. The bishop allows the use of electricity in some businesses so he shouldn't object to this."

"You will have to okay it with him. It isn't plain."

"I'll see him soon. I'm not worried."

"And if he says *nee*, can you get your money back?"

"He won't." Paul stepped up into what was essentially an office on wheels.

The trailer was outfitted with two desk spaces, two chairs and a dozen storage bins of assorted sizes secured to the walls. Sliding windows on both sides opened to let him deal directly with customers and call the auction without leaving the comfort of his chair. A third window at the front with an open slot beneath it served as a windshield so he could drive a team of horses from inside.

The feeling of elation that it all belonged to him widened Paul's smile. Mark didn't understand how much this meant. No one in the family did. They thought being an auctioneer was his hobby and nothing more. Maybe that was his fault.

He was the joker in the family. He was good at pretending he didn't take anything too seriously. He was a fellow who liked a good joke even if the joke was on him. He enjoyed light flirtations but avoided serious relationships at all costs. Auctioneering was his one true love.

This trailer was the culmination of three years' work to fulfill his dream of becoming a full-time auctioneer.

Detaching the microphone from the clips that held it in place while the vehicle was in motion, he flipped a switch and began his auctioneer's chant. "I have two hundred, um two, two, who'll give me three hundred, um three, three, I see three. Now who'll give me a little more, four, four, do I hear four?"

He slid open the window and propped his elbows on the desktop as he looked down at Mark. "What do you think?"

"It's mighty fancy for a fellow who has only been a licensed auctioneer for a couple of months."

Paul wanted his brother to share his enthusiasm, not dampen it. "I completed the auctioneer's course and served my year of apprenticeship with Harold Yoder. He's one of the best in these parts. I have called twenty auctions under his supervision. I have earned my license, and I'm ready to be out on my own."

"There's a difference between going out on your own

and going out on a limb. How much did you spend on this?"

"Enough." All he had saved plus the money he had borrowed from Mark and a four-thousand-dollar loan from the bank on a short-term note. Paul kept that fact to himself. He didn't need a lecture from his always practical older brother. Sometimes life required a leap of faith.

It was true he had expected to be hired for several major auctions by the time his custom trailer was finished but he'd had only one small job so far. His commission had barely covered his expenses for that one. He'd been forced to borrow the money to pay the builder when his trailer was ready. No Amish fellow liked being in debt but sometimes a man's business required it. Paul closed the window, switched off the microphone and stepped out.

Mark shook his head. "I hope you know what you're doing."

Paul grinned. "I talk fast. That's the secret. You'll see. This is a *goot* investment. You'll get your money back soon."

"I hope so. I'll need it to pay for the new ovens we're putting in at the bakery. Have you told Onkel Isaac about this purchase?"

"Not yet. I hope he approves but I know this was the right decision for me even if he doesn't." They both walked out into the early morning sunshine.

"He will support your decision but if you fail at this business venture, don't look to him to bail you out. Or me. Lessons learned by failure are as valuable as lessons learned by success."

"I know. It's the Amish way." Paul had heard that many times in his life but it never meant as much as it meant now. When his loan came due in two months, the bank could repossess his van if he didn't have the money. He was starting to worry.

Maybe he could get an extension on his loan. His uncle did a lot of business at the bank but Paul's finances were what they would look at.

He crossed the farmyard with Mark and headed toward their uncle's furniture-making business, where they both worked. As they entered the quiet shop, they went their separate ways. Mark went out back to start the diesel generator that produced the electric power for the numerous woodworking machines, lights and office equipment. When Paul heard the hum of the generator start up and the lights came on, he raised the large door at the rear of the building so the forklift operator could bring in pallets of raw wood and move finished products to the trucks that would soon arrive for the day's deliveries.

He saw a car turn into the parking lot and stop but he knew Mark would be up front soon to deal with any customers. A man got out of the car and walked toward Paul instead of going to the entrance to the business. He was dressed in khaki pants and a blue polo shirt. Definitely not an Amish fellow.

"I'm looking for the Amish auctioneer?"

Paul grinned and clapped a hand to his chest. "You found him. I'm Paul Bowman."

"I'm Ralph Hobson. I recently inherited a farm and I am no farmer. The place is a pile of rocks and weedy fields fit for goats and not much else. I've been told that an auction is the easiest and fastest way to get rid of the property."

"Auctions are very popular in this part of the country. The buyer can see he's getting a fair deal because he knows what everyone else is offering. The seller gets his money right away, and my auction service takes care of the details in between for a ten percent commission. Does that sound like something you're interested in?"

"It does. How soon can you hold an auction?"

"That depends on the size and condition of the property and the contents of the home if you are selling that."

"I am. The farm is a hundred and fifty-five acres. How much can I expect to get for it?"

"Farmland in this part of Ohio sells for between five and six thousand dollars an acre depending on the quality of the land."

Ralph's eyes lit up. "It's a good thing I didn't take the first offer I had. That weasel was trying to cheat me. So roughly seven hundred and seventy thousand, give or take a few thousand?"

Paul wondered who the weasel was and how much he had offered. It wasn't any of his business so he didn't ask. "Minus my commission. It could go higher if there is a bidding war."

"What's that?"

"That's when two or more bidders keep upping their bids because they both really want the item."

"That sounds interesting. What keeps the seller from putting someone in the crowd to drive the price up?" Ralph slipped his hands into the front pockets of his pants. "Hypothetically, of course."

"I won't say it never happens but the bidder is taking a chance he could get stuck with a high-priced item he doesn't want or can't afford if the other bidder quits first."

"I see." Ralph smiled but it didn't reach his eyes. "I guess we can both hope for a bidding war since you earn more if I make more. Right?"

"Right. Are there outbuildings? Farm equipment?

Livestock? I'll need to make an accurate inventory of everything."

"A few chickens, three buggy horses and a cow with a calf are the only livestock. A neighbor has them for now. The rest is a lot of junk. My uncle rarely let go of anything."

Paul tried not to get his hopes up. "One man's junk is another man's treasure. I'll need to look the place over."

"I can drive you there now."

This was too good an opportunity to pass up. To handle an entire farm and household sale could bring him a hefty commission. Enough to pay back Mark and the bank loan plus get his business off to a good start. "Who owned the farm before you?"

"My uncle, Eli King."

"I think I know the place. Out on Cedar Road just after the turn off to Middleton?"

"That's right."

Paul had gone there last year with his cousin Luke looking for parts to fix an ancient washing machine. Ralph was right about his uncle collecting things but not all of it was junk. There were some valuable items stashed away. "Let me tell my uncle where I'm going and I'll be right with you."

"Great." The man looked relieved and walked back to his car.

Paul found his uncle, his cousin Samuel and Mark all conferring in the front office. Paul tipped his head toward the parking lot. "That *Englisch* fellow wants to show me a farm he plans to put up for auction. Can you spare me for a few hours?"

The men looked up from reviewing the day's work schedule. "Can we?" Isaac asked.

Samuel flipped to the last page on the clipboard he held. "It's not like he does much work when he is here."

Mark and Isaac chuckled. Paul smiled, too, not offended in the least. "Very funny, cousin. I do twice the amount of work my brother does these days. Mark spends more time at the bakery than he does here."

Mark's grin turned to a frown. Isaac patted his shoulder. "That is to be expected when he and his new wife are getting their own business up and running."

"That's right," Mark said, looking mollified. "It takes a lot of thought to decide which type of ovens we need and where they should be placed, what kind of storage we need—a hundred decisions have to be made."

Isaac's wife, Anna, ran a small gift shop across the parking lot from the woodworking building. Mark's wife, Helen, had been selling her baked goods in the shop and at local farmers markets but the increasing demand for her tasty treats and breads made opening a bakery the next logical step for them.

A month ago, the church community held a frolic to help Mark and Helen finish building their bakery next to the gift shop. The couple would live above the bakery until they could afford to build a new home. They were currently living with Helen's aunt, Charlotte Zook, but her home was several miles away, making it impractical to stay there once their business was up and running.

"When is the grand opening?" Isaac asked.

"The dual ovens we want are back-ordered. We can't set a date until they are paid for and installed." Mark gave Paul a pointed look. It was a reminder that he needed his money back soon.

Paul winked at his brother. "Mark's interest isn't in the

new ovens. Sneaking a kiss from his new bride is what keeps him running over there."

Mark blushed bright red and everyone laughed.

Paul turned to Isaac for an answer. "Can you spare me today? I'm trying to get my own business up and running, too."

Isaac nodded. "We will do without you. Any idea when you'll be back?"

"I can't say for sure." He opened the door and saw his cousin Joshua and Joshua's wife, Mary, coming across from the gift shop. Mary carried her infant son balanced on her hip. The happy, chubby boy was trying to catch the ribbon of her *kapp* with one hand and stuff it in his mouth with little success.

Mary called out, "*Guder mariye*, Paul. Is Samuel around?"

"Good morning, Mary. He's inside."

"*Goot*, I need to speak to him. Don't forget about Nicky's birthday party two weeks from Saturday. You can bring a date if you like."

"I won't forget and I won't bring a date. Meet the family. Bounce the cute baby. That would be a sure way to give a woman the wrong impression," he called over his shoulder.

"You can't stay single forever," Mary shouted after him.

"I can try." He hurried toward Ralph Hobson's car. He didn't want to keep a potentially profitable client waiting.

On the twenty-minute ride, Paul did all the talking as he outlined the details of the auction contract and his responsibilities, including advertising and inventory, sorting the goods and cleaning up after the sale. Hobson listened and didn't say much.

Paul hoped the man understood what he was agreeing to. "I'll send you a printed copy of all I've told you if you agree to hire me. A handshake will be enough to seal the deal."

"Fine, fine. Whatever." The man took one hand off the wheel and held it out.

Paul shook it. He was hired. It was hard to contain his joy and keep the smile off his face.

When Ralph turned into the lane of a neat Amish farmyard, Paul noticed a white car parked off to the side of the drive. Ralph stopped beside it. A middle-aged man in a white cowboy hat got out. He tossed a cigarette butt to the ground and came around to the driver's side. Ralph rolled down his window.

"Good morning, sir. My name is Jeffrey Jones. Are you the owner of this property?"

"I am," Ralph said.

"I understand this farm is for sale. I'd like to take a look at the property and maybe make an offer on it."

Ralph frowned. "Where did you hear it was for sale?"

The man shrugged and smiled. "Word gets around in a small community like this."

Ralph shook his head. "Your information isn't quite accurate. There will be a farm auction in the near future."

"Ah, that's a risky way to get rid of the place. You should at least hear my offer. You've got no guarantee that an auction will top it."

"I'll take my chances," Ralph said. "Keep an eye out for the date of the sale. You might get it for less."

Mr. Jones stepped back from the vehicle. "Do the mineral rights go with the farmland or are they separate?"

"I'm not selling the mineral rights."

"Smart man. I imagine leasing those rights to the local

coal mine will bring you a tidy sum for many years. My offer for the farm expires when I get in my car. No one is going to want this place except maybe a poor Amish farmer. You'll have trouble getting a decent price."

If Ralph sold the land now, Paul wouldn't get a dime but he had to put his client's interest before his own. "You should at least hear what the man had to offer."

"I have my heart set on an auction. Besides, I thought we had a deal. We shook on it."

Paul grinned. It seemed his new client was an honorable man. "It's up to you but he is mistaken if he thinks all Amish farmers are poor. You'll get a fair price at auction. You can put a reserve on it if you want. If the bidding doesn't reach your set price, it's a 'no sale' and you are free to sell it another way."

Ralph smiled. "I'm going to hope for a bidding war."

Mr. Jones appeared more puzzled than disappointed but he got back in his car and drove away.

Paul leaned forward in his seat to get a good look at the farm as they drove up. Both the barn and the house were painted white and appeared in good condition. He made a quick mental appraisal of the equipment he saw, then jotted down numbers in a small notebook he kept in his pocket.

"What is she doing here?" The anger in Ralph's voice shocked Paul.

He followed Ralph's line of sight and spied an Amish woman sitting on a suitcase on the front porch of the house. She wore a simple pale blue dress with an apron of matching material and a black cape thrown back over her shoulders. Her wide-brimmed black traveling bonnet hid her hair. She looked hot, dusty and tired. She held a girl of about three or four on her lap. The child clung tightly to her mother. A boy a few years older leaned against the door behind her holding a large calico cat.

"Who is she?" Paul asked.

"That is my annoying cousin Clara Fisher." Ralph opened his car door and got out. Paul did the same.

The woman glared at both men. "Why are there padlocks on the doors, Ralph? Eli never locked his home."

"They are there to keep unwanted visitors out. What are you doing here?" Ralph demanded.

"I live here. May I have the keys, please? My children and I are weary."

Ralph's eyebrows snapped together in a fierce frown. "What do you mean you live here?"

"What part did you fail to understand, Ralph? I… live…here," she said slowly, as if speaking to a small child.

Ralph's face darkened with anger. Paul had to turn away to keep from laughing.

"You can poke fun at me if you want but that is not an explanation." The man was livid.

Clara sat where she was, seemingly unruffled by his ire. "Eli invited us to live with him last Christmas. We moved in six months ago."

"No one told me that. I didn't see you at the funeral."

"We have been in Maryland visiting my mother for the past month." She stroked her little girl's hair. "Sophie became ill and was in the hospital briefly. Eli's friend Dan Kauffman called me to tell me about Eli's passing. He knew Mother and I couldn't return for the funeral. Surely he told you that, for I know he attended."

"I don't speak to the Amish and they don't speak to me. You'll have to find somewhere else to live. Uncle Eli left the farm to me."

Her eyes widened with astonishment. "I don't believe it. He told me he had amended the farm trust and made me the beneficiary months ago."

Ralph looked stunned but he quickly recovered and glared at her. "Even if he did, he revoked that amendment three weeks ago when he made me the new trustee. He said nothing about you or your children. That's why they call it a revocable trust, Clara, because a man can change his mind anytime. It's irrevocable now that Eli is gone and this farm belongs to me."

Paul wished he knew more about how such things worked.

"You're lying, Ralph. Eli wouldn't turn over his farm to you."

"You make it sound like we weren't on speaking terms. I came to visit the old fellow at least once a year."

"Only to see if you could beg money off him."

"I admit my motives weren't always the best but things have been different lately. I cared about the old guy."

"Cared about what you could get from him. Open the door at once."

Ralph crossed his arms and leaned back. "You haven't changed, cousin. You're still trying to boss me around. I'm not going to let you in my house."

"You *have* changed. You've gone from scamming Amish folks out of a few hundred dollars to stealing costlier things, like this farm."

"If you feel that's the case, cousin, call the cops. You can use my phone."

Her lips narrowed into a thin line. "You know it is not our way to involve the *Englisch* law."

"Yeah, I do know that. The Amish don't like outsiders. Suits me."

"Is that what you were counting on? You're a man without scruples. You are a blemish on our family's good name."

Her biting comment surprised Paul. She might look small but she was clearly a woman to be reckoned with. She reminded him of an angry mama cat all fluffed up and spitting mad. He rubbed a hand across his mouth to hide a grin. His movement caught her attention, and she pinned her deep blue gaze on him. "Who are you?"

He stopped smiling. "My name is Paul Bowman. I'm an auctioneer. Mr. Hobson has hired me to get this property ready for sale."

Her angry gaze snapped back to Ralph. "I would like to see the document Eli signed giving you the farm that he had promised to me and my children."

"That document is none of your business. My attorney has it." He turned and walked toward the car.

She stifled her anger. Paul saw the effort it took and felt sorry for her. She drew a deep breath. "Ralph, please, search your heart and find compassion for us. You know Sophie will need medical care her entire life. I will be hard-pressed to pay for that care without the income this farm will provide."

Ralph stopped but didn't look at her. "The church will take care of you. Isn't that what they promise? Eli and I mended our difference. You should be happy about that. The Amish are all about forgiveness."

"I wish I believed you." Clara turned to Paul. "You can't auction off this farm. It doesn't belong to him."

Paul held up both hands and took a step back. "This is clearly a family matter, and I don't think I should get involved. Do you have a place to stay? My aunt and uncle will be happy to welcome you to their home."

Her tense posture relaxed a little. "I'm grateful for the offer but we have to stay here. My daughter has Crigler-Najjar syndrome. It's a rare liver disease. She has a special blue-light bed she must sleep in at night. It is upstairs in the front bedroom."

Paul had heard of the blue-light children but he'd never seen one. Clara's daughter was a pretty child with white-blond curly hair and a golden hue to her skin. Her bright blue eyes regarded him solemnly. The boy shared the same blond hair and blue eyes. He glared at Ralph but didn't speak.

Ralph gave his cousin a falsely sweet smile. "I don't have the keys to the house with me but you're welcome to sleep on the porch."

Clara's scowl deepened. "My child can't be without the lights. She needs to be under them for ten hours a day or risk brain damage. I have a set we travel with but I left them with my mother to be shipped here later. You must let us stay."

Paul heard the desperation in her voice. He caught Ralph by the arm. "This isn't right. Let her in."

Ralph jerked away. "You heard her say I'm a liar and a thief and you think I should help her? I'm going to call the sheriff and report her for trespassing. A night in jail might change her tune. Get in the car. I'm leaving."

Paul cringed. He was about to lose a sale that would have paved the way for his future business. He glanced around and picked up a rock twice the size of his fist. "Do you have the key, Mr. Hobson? If not, I'm going to owe you for a new padlock and a smashed door. I'm not leaving here until she and her *kinder* are safe inside."

Ralph pulled out his cell phone. "Go ahead. The sheriff can arrest both of you."

Chapter Two

Clara's jaw dropped in shock. Ralph was just the kind of man to make good on his threat. Would the *Englisch* law put her in jail? What would become of her children? Sophie had to have her light bed. Would the sheriff allow her to use it?

She had no wish for the young auctioneer to suffer because he was standing up for her and her children. She met the young man's gaze, ready to give in and leave if she could take Sophie's bed but Paul didn't look the least bit concerned. He winked at her, a sly smile lifting the corner of his mouth. What should she make of that?

He leaned toward Ralph and pointed to the phone. "The sheriff's name is Nick Bradley. Be sure to tell Nick it's Paul Bowman you want arrested. Nick's daughter, Mary, is married to my cousin Joshua. Oh, and tell him Mary is planning a birthday party for Nicky two weeks from Saturday. The picnic will be at Bowmans Crossing at six o'clock. You know what? Never mind. I'll just wait here with Clara and tell Nick myself."

With an angry growl, Ralph put away his phone, pulled a set of keys from his pocket and threw them at

Paul. He caught them easily. "You'd do well to remember you work for me now. Get her out of here as soon as you can."

"*Danki*. I'll finish looking the place over and let you know in a couple of days when I think I can schedule your auction. Off the top of my head, I estimate six weeks. Maybe less."

Ralph nodded once. "Make it less. I need to get rid of this place as soon as possible. Inventory it from top to bottom and get me a copy of the list. Don't make me regret this. I can easily find another auctioneer."

"I'll do my best for you but if you're in a rush to get rid of the place, why did you turn down Mr. Jones without even hearing his offer?"

"I didn't like the look of the fellow." Ralph pointed at Clara. "I don't want her removing things she claims are hers without checking with me first but I want her gone as soon as possible. If she's not out of here in a few days, I will call the sheriff."

Paul glanced at her and then nodded. "I understand."

Ralph opened the car door. "Are you coming?"

"I can find my own way home."

"I'm staying at the Swan's Head Motel in Berlin until the sale is over." Ralph pulled out a business card. "This is my number. Don't believe a word that woman says. She's crazy. She imagines all kinds of things." Ralph got in, slammed the car door and sped away.

"I guess I won't need this after all." Paul tossed aside the rock and walked up the porch steps.

Clara stood and pulled a crowbar from behind her. "I reckon I won't need this, either."

He threw back his head and laughed. Clara settled Sophie on her hip as a smile twitched at the corner of her lips. Her son, Toby, was chuckling. It was a wonderful sound. It had been a long time since they had anything to laugh about.

"I reckon your cousin Ralph didn't think to padlock the toolshed." Paul grinned at her as she handed him the crowbar.

"He did," Toby said, putting the cat down. "Mamm boosted me up to the window and I climbed in to get it."

Toby was so pleased that he had been able to help her. Ever since her husband's death two years ago, Toby had been trying to be the man of the family. A big undertaking for a boy of only eight.

Paul's face grew serious as he gazed at Toby. "Your *mamm* is blessed to have a son who is both agile and brave."

This stranger's words of praise to her son raised him another notch in her estimation. Toby stood a little straighter. "It didn't take much bravery. The spiderwebs were pretty small."

Paul smiled. "Agile, brave and modest, too. Just as a *goot* Amish boy should be. Your *daed* will be pleased when he learns of this."

Toby's shoulders slumped. He looked down. "Daed is in heaven."

Paul laid a hand on the boy's shoulder. "My *daed* is in heaven, too. God must have needed two strong Amish fellows to help him up there. I'm happy Daed is serving our Lord even though I miss him. I never forget that he is watching over me just as your father is watching over you. We must always behave in a way that pleases them, and I'm mighty sure that you pleased your *daed* by helping your mother today."

"You helped Mamm, too. Cousin Ralph would have made us leave if you hadn't been here."

Paul looked at Clara over Toby's head. "I think it would take a tougher man than your cousin Ralph to move your mother if she didn't wish to go."

Clara felt a blush heat her cheeks. She couldn't remember the last time a man had complimented her.

"Do you suppose your *daed* and mine are friends in heaven?" Toby asked. "I think he might be lonely without us and without his friends to talk to."

Clara bit her lip as she struggled to hold back the tears. Toby had a tender heart. He worried about far too many things. Adam had been a good husband but an indifferent father, preferring to spend his free time with his unmarried friends rather than the children.

Paul crossed his arms over his chest and then cupped his chin as he considered Toby's question. "Did your *daed* enjoy a good game of horseshoes and did he like baseball?"

Toby's eyes widened in surprise. "He liked both those things."

Paul turned his hands palms-up. "Then I reckon they must be friends 'cause my *daed* liked horseshoes and he loved baseball, too. Would you do me a favor and take a quick look at the barn. I need to know if Ralph put padlocks on it."

"Sure." Toby took off at a run.

"You were very kind to my son," Clara said softly.

"Losing his father is hard for a boy that age to comprehend." Paul watched Toby for a moment and then turned to Clara. "And for his mother, too."

"How old were you?"

"Six. I'll get the door open. I almost wish you had produced the crowbar in front of Ralph. I would have given a lot to see his face."

It seemed he didn't want to talk about a painful time from his childhood and she respected that.

After unlocking and removing the padlock, Paul pushed the door open and stood back as she carried Sophie inside. The cat darted in and bolted into the living room. Clara set her daughter on a chair by the kitchen table, then turned to get her suitcases but Paul was already inside with them in his hands. "Where would you like these?"

"The black one can go on the bed in the room at the top of the stairs. The gray one goes in the room at the end of the hall. That door leads upstairs." She nodded toward it as she untied her black traveling bonnet and took it off. He opened the door and she heard him going quickly up the steps.

A quick glance in the mirror by the front door showed her *kapp* was on straight but her hair had frizzed at her temples. She smoothed them as best she could.

Paul Bowman was a nice-looking young man. He smiled easily, defended her right to enter the house and spoke kindly to Toby. She appreciated all that but even after hearing her say Ralph's trust had to be a fake, Paul was still going to work for her cousin. She wasn't sure what to make of that. Would he ignore her claim and auction this farm in six weeks? She couldn't let that happen. A handsome face and a few kind words weren't enough to blind her to the fact that he was helping Ralph cheat her children out of their inheritance.

She settled Sophie in the living room with one of her favorite books. The cat curled up at her side. Sophie had missed her pet while visiting her grandmother but happily, the bishop's wife liked cats and had taken care of Patches while they were away. Sophie was pretending to read the story to the cat but she looked ready to nod off. A nap would be just the thing for her. None of them had managed to get any rest on the long bus ride here. Toby came in to report everything was locked up tight. She told him to stay with Sophie when she heard Paul coming downstairs.

She joined him in the kitchen. "I appreciate your help, Mr. Bowman but I need to know your intentions."

He grinned. "My intentions are to stay single for as long as possible. Sorry."

She wasn't amused. "I'm talking about your intentions with regards to this farm."

"I'm an auctioneer. My intention is to inventory the property and ready the place to be sold." He quickly covered his head with his arms as if expecting to be hit.

She clasped her fingers tightly together. "Even after hearing that Ralph's claim to this farm is false?"

He opened one eye to peek at her. "That did give me pause but Ralph seems certain that he owns this place." He put his arms down and leaned one hip against the kitchen counter. "Is it possible your uncle changed his mind?"

"I don't believe Eli would do that to me. I will not let you and Ralph sell this place. I don't know how I can stop you but I will."

"Don't get riled at me. As an auctioneer, I have a responsibility to preform my due diligence by making sure that everything I sell is legal and as represented."

She crossed her arms. "What does that mean?"

"It means I won't sell a horse as a five-year-old if he has ten-year-old teeth in his mouth. I'll thoroughly check

Ralph's claim of ownership. It may take a few days. In the meantime…"

"In the meantime, what?"

"I need to begin an inventory of the property."

"Why?"

"Because I have given my word to Ralph Hobson that I will handle the details of the sale for him. It's part of my job, and I have a reputation to consider. I can't say I hold much respect for the man after his actions today. No one should treat a woman and her children with such callousness. Unfortunately, he is my client."

"I'm sorry you have been placed in an awkward situation."

"*Danki*. Have you thought about where you will go?"

She planted her hands on her hips. "I'm not going anywhere. I'm staying here. This farm belongs to me."

"If you prove to be the rightful trustee, what are your plans for this place? Will you farm it? Rent it? Sell all or part of it?"

"I will sell most of the land but I plan to keep a few acres and the house to live in." Her uncle's death wasn't unexpected—he had been in poor health—but it still came as a shock. Maybe if she could make Paul understand how much was at stake, he would stop Ralph from selling the farm. It was worth a try.

"Crigler-Najjar syndrome is a fatal disease. I won't bore you with the medical details but a liver transplant is my daughter's only hope of living beyond her teens. A few months ago, I learned that I am an excellent match to donate part of my liver to Sophie. It's called a living donor transplant but it is a very expensive surgery. With all the testing and follow-up care, it will easily reach five hundred thousand dollars."

His eyebrows shot up. "Half a million?"

"*Ja.* Staggering, isn't it?"

"Won't the Amish Hospital Aid pay for most of that?"

Amish Hospital Aid was a form of insurance that depended on contributions from a pool of members each month. She was a long-time member and paid a modest monthly amount since before Toby had been born. Not all Amish approved of the method, preferring to rely on the alms contributed by their church members in times of need.

"Amish Hospital Aid has helped pay for Sophie's hospitalizations in the past. I paid the first twenty percent of each bill and they paid the rest. However, a liver transplant is not an emergency hospitalization. They won't pay for disability-related costs like her doctor's visits or her special lights. I have already sold my house and my mother sold her home to help pay for Sophie's future medical care. All I have to live on is the rent from my husband's harness-making business back in Strasburg, Pennsylvania, and the charity of church members. Eli's offer to come and live with him was a Godsend."

She blinked back unshed tears. "When we learned I could be a donor for my daughter, Eli altered the trust to leave the farm to me. He knew he didn't have long to live. He had cancer of the blood. The doctors told him a year or less."

"Why didn't he sell the farm outright and give you the money?"

"He was planning to do that once his crops were harvested this fall. Making me the beneficiary of the trust was a safeguard in case he died before that happened. Sophie needs a transplant before she gets much older. Every year, her skin gets thicker and that makes the blue lights less effective at breaking down the toxic chemical in her blood. Even a simple cold can put her life in jeopardy or cause serious brain damage because the toxin builds up faster when she's ill."

Would he help her or was she wasting her breath? She couldn't tell. She was exhausted and couldn't think straight anymore.

Paul rubbed a hand over his chin. "Unless you want Ralph to come back here with the sheriff in a day or two, you'll need to give me some idea of how long it will take you to move out."

Her hopes sank. He didn't care. "I told you I'm not moving."

"I heard you but we need a way to stall Ralph. He sounded adamant about calling the sheriff on you. We don't want that to happen and certainly not before I have his story checked out. I will insist on seeing a copy of the trust he claims to have and make sure it's real. I have no idea how long that will take."

Relief made her smile as she reached out and grasped his arm. "Then you believe me."

Paul didn't reply. His gaze remained fixed on her face. When she smiled, it changed her appearance drastically. The lines of fatigue and worry around her eyes eased, and she looked years younger. She was a pretty woman but more than that—she had a presence about her that was arresting and made a man look closer. She probably wasn't much older than he was.

She let go of his arm and clasped both hands together as a faint blush stained her cheeks. He liked to flirt with women and make them smile but he knew Clara wasn't in the mood to enjoy a little banter. He looked away and took several steps to put some distance between them.

It was surprising that he found her so attractive. She wasn't the kind of woman he was normally interested in. He liked to go out with girls who knew how to have fun. A widow with two children didn't make the list. He cleared his throat. "I believe you feel certain that you own the land. However, feelings aren't proof."

Her smile vanished. "At least you are willing to investigate Ralph's claim. It's a start. I'm not lying about Eli's intentions. My uncle kept all his important papers in his desk. I'm sure the trust papers are there."

Paul turned to face her. "You have them here?"

"I do. This way."

Paul followed her down the hall to her uncle's study at the rear of the house. The moment she opened the door, she stopped. "Someone has been in here."

"Are you sure?"

She looked around. "Every piece of furniture in this room has been thoroughly dusted. Eli didn't like me to clean in here and he wasn't this neat."

"I imagine the women of his church came to clean the house before the funeral." It was a common custom among the Amish to prepare the home for the service.

Obviously feeling foolish, she avoided meeting his gaze. "Of course. I should have thought of that. You must think I'm crazy to suspect someone has tampered with my uncle's possessions because the room is clean. The women wouldn't have disturbed the papers in his desk."

She opened the drawers one by one and went through them. Not finding what she was looking for, she went through each drawer again more slowly. "The trust document isn't here."

The trust wasn't there because Ralph had it. Paul kept that thought to himself. Ralph had warned him not to believe her. He hated to think Ralph was telling the truth about Clara's unbalanced state of mind.

She pressed a hand to her forehead. "What do I do now?"

She looked lost and desperate, as if she had reached the end of her strength. Paul fought the desire to put his arms around her and console her. It was highly unlikely that she would welcome such a move but he was compelled to offer a sliver of hope even if it was false hope. "Could your uncle have moved it?"

"I don't know why he would."

"If he wasn't feeling well and you weren't here, he might have given it to the bishop, his attorney or a friend for safekeeping so that someone would know what his final wishes were."

"Perhaps." She didn't look convinced. "I'll speak with the bishop and his friend Dan to see if they know anything about it. I don't know who his attorney was."

"I hate to suggest this but Ralph may be telling the truth. Your uncle might have changed his mind."

She shook her head, making the ribbons of her *kapp* flutter. "I can't believe that. Eli wouldn't leave us with nothing. Besides Ralph and my mother, the children and I are Eli's only family. He loved my children."

"I'm sure he did." She was vulnerable and sad. Paul wanted to comfort her but he didn't know what else to say. He chose to retreat. "I need to look around the property if that's okay with you."

"It seems I have no right to stop you." Her eyes filled with tears and one slipped down her cheek. She brushed it away.

Not tears. He hated to see a woman cry. He wanted her to smile again. He stepped closer. "Don't give up. Things will work out. You'll see. Maybe Ralph will have a change of heart and share the proceeds of the farm sale with you."

Her weary expression changed to a look of fierce determination. She squared her shoulders and rose to her feet. "I'll be very old and gray before that happens. Go and do my cousin's evil bidding. Make an inventory. Find out how much this place is worth so I'll know how much the two of you are stealing from my babies."

"I'm not stealing anything." Her sudden change of mood took him by surprise. Angry mama cat was back and spitting mad.

"You are if you help him! Get out!"

He made a hasty retreat to the front door and out onto the porch. He turned back to her, hoping to make her see reason. "I have a job to do."

"Then do it without my blessing." She slammed the door shut in his face.

Clara leaned her back against the closed door and took several deep calming breaths. Her heart hammered in her chest. She could feel the blood pounding in her temples. Allowing herself to become so upset served no purpose.

"What's wrong, Mamm?" Toby asked from the living-room doorway.

"Nothing." She moved to peek out the kitchen window. Paul was standing on the porch looking stunned. She wished she knew what he was thinking. One minute, he seemed compassionate and caring, tempting her to trust him. In the next breath, he said he was going to sell the property for Ralph as if that was the way things had to be.

It wasn't. She would find a way to stop them.

Her actions today ran contrary to her Amish upbringing and she was ashamed of that, ashamed her children had witnessed her behaving like a shrew. She had made a serious accusation against Ralph that she couldn't substantiate. Not unless she found the papers she knew had to exist.

Ralph possessed few, if any, scruples. This wasn't the first time he'd tried to trick or cheat an Amish family member out of money. This time it wasn't just about money; it was about Sophie's life.

Eli had wanted Clara to sell the farm when he was gone and use the funds to help Sophie. He had been a dear, kind man and she missed him deeply. She folded her hands together and sent up a quick prayer that God would be merciful to her and her children and allow her to grant Eli his final wish.

She went to search her uncle's bedroom next. She found a suit of clothes and his straw hat hanging on pegs. His work boots were sitting beside the bed on a blue oval rag rug, where he always kept them. It was hard to imagine he would never put them on again and tromp mud across her fresh-scrubbed floors. Brushing away a tear, she searched the single chest of drawers without success.

There was nothing in her bedroom or the children's rooms. She searched the kitchen and finally the large ornate bible cabinet in the living room. It contained only the family's oversized three-hundred-year-old German bible and a few keepsakes. There was nowhere else to look unless she got a ladder and went up to the attic. She couldn't imagine her uncle putting important papers where they would be so hard to access.

"Mamm, I'm hungry. Can I have a cookie?" Sophie asked.

"I don't have any cookies but I think I can find a Popsicle for you and Toby." Eli always kept a large box of assorted flavors in the freezer for the children.

The freezer compartment of the kitchen's propane-powered refrigerator turned out to be completely filled with frozen meals in plastic containers, all neatly labeled. The members of the church had made sure that she and the children would be taken care of when they returned. Clara took a moment to give thanks for the wonderful caring people in her uncle's congregation.

She found the box of Popsicles and gave each child their favorite flavor, then put out a container of spaghetti and meatballs to thaw for supper.

A knock at the door sent Toby rushing to open it. "Hi, Paul. You don't have to knock. You can just come in. Want a Popsicle? Grape ones are the best."

Paul stood on the porch with his straw hat in his hand. "*Danki*, Toby, but not today. I wanted to let your mother know I was leaving. I checked the generator and it's got fuel."

Clara moved to stand behind Toby. *"Danki."*

She had forgotten to do that. Because the Amish did not allow electricity in their homes, Eli had gotten permission from his bishop to use a generator to supply the electricity for the blue lights Sophie needed. Eli had taken charge of keeping it running but she would have to do that from now on. She battled with her conscience for a moment but knew she couldn't lie. "The generator belonged to Eli. You should add it to the farm equipment inventory."

"I'll try to remember but I'm a forgetful fellow. It

might not make the list. I'll be back tomorrow. Is there anything you and the children need before I go?"

She hated to ask him but Sophie's health was more important than her false pride. "Would you start the generator so I can make sure the lights come on?"

"Of course." He started to turn away.

"May I come with you?" Toby asked.

Paul looked over his shoulder. "Sure thing. I can always use an extra hand. Come on."

The two of them had the generator started in a few minutes. Upstairs, Clara was relieved to see the lights come on when she flipped the switch. Eight blue fluorescent-light tubes were suspended above Sophie's bed by a wooden canopy that could be raised and lowered with a chain. Mirrors on the headboard, footboard and one side of the bed reflected the light all around her. Sophie hated sleeping under the lights. Clara let her go to bed with her favorite blanket each night but once she was asleep, Clara had to take it away so the light touched as much of her skin as possible.

After she was sure the lights were all working, Clara went downstairs. Paul was standing outside the kitchen door again. "Does it function as it should?"

"The lights all came on. Thank you for making sure the generator would run."

"You're welcome." He looked down at Toby. "I'll see you tomorrow. I might need someone to help me list all the machinery on the place. That is, if your mother doesn't mind."

Toby turned pleading eyes in her direction. "You don't mind if I help Paul, do you?"

She didn't want Paul coming back but he would in

spite of her wishes. Telling her son he couldn't help would only hurt Toby.

"You can as long as you finish your own chores first," she conceded.

"I will." The happiness in her son's eyes relieved some of her reservations. He had taken a liking to the auctioneer.

Paul patted the boy on the head and smiled at her. "See you tomorrow then."

The man had a smile that could melt a woman's heart. Unless she kept a close guard on it, and Clara always kept a close guard on hers. Her life was filled with complications she wasn't sure she could manage. Adding one more was out of the question. She closed the front door as he walked away and then began sorting through the pile of mail waiting for her.

Paul did have a nice smile. She remembered the sound of his laughter when she produced the crowbar and how gentle he had been when he talked to Toby about losing his father.

And this absurd line of thinking only proved how tired she was when a man's simple act of kindness had her thinking he was someone special. After a good night's sleep, she was sure she wouldn't find Paul Bowman half as attractive the next time she saw him.

Chapter Three

Early the following morning while the children were still asleep, Clara walked down the road a quarter of a mile to the community phone shack shared by the Amish families who lived in her uncle's area.

The small building that housed the phone and message machine was only six feet by six feet. It was painted a soft blue color and had large windows on two sides to let in the light. A solar panel on the roof provided electricity for the message machine. Inside was a narrow counter across one wall, where writing utensils and paper sat along with a copy of the local phone book.

A red light was blinking on the machine. She listened to the three messages. None of them were for her so she didn't erase them. Sitting on the single chair in the room, she placed a call to her mother's phone shack. She hoped her mother would be there to answer the phone. They had agreed on this time the last time they talked.

Her mother picked up on the second ring. Clara's throat tightened. It was wonderful to hear her mother's voice. "We made it safely back to Eli's farm. It was a long bus ride."

"How are the children?"

"They are doing fine. There was a letter from the Clinic for Special Children waiting for me when I got here. They did some lab work at her last visit. Sophie's bilirubin levels are holding steady with ten hours of light but we might need to increase her to twelve hours soon."

"Then the surgery can't be put off much longer, can it? Have you decided what to do with my brother's farm? It's hard to believe he is gone but what a blessing he has left for us."

Clara hated to share this news but saw no way to avoid it. "Ralph is here. He says Eli left the farm to him and he plans to sell it."

"What? Eli wouldn't do such a thing. He and I agreed you should have it."

"We know that but I can't find the papers Eli signed. Ralph claims to have them."

"That boy broke his mother's heart with his sneaking ways. I pray for him all the time. What are you going to do?"

"I thought I would speak to Dan Kauffman and see if he knows anything about this."

"The Lord has placed a heavy burden on you, dear. I wish I was there to help."

"I wish you were here, too. I miss you. The children miss you."

"As I miss them. Give them my love."

After hanging up the phone, Clara blinked back fresh tears. She had needed to hear her mother's voice, but it made her miss her even more.

Her mother, a widow, had moved from her home in Pennsylvania to live with a dear friend in Maryland after selling her house to help Clara pay Sophie's mounting medical bills. The two older women were like peas in a pod and got along famously. They made and sold quilts to a local tourist shop and enjoyed living by the sea.

When Clara had her emotions under control, she phoned Dan Kauffman next but no one picked up and he didn't have an answering machine. She hung up and decided to visit him as soon as possible. She needed to know where her uncle's trust papers were. They might not prove that Ralph's document was a fake but it would prove that she wasn't lying.

Let down because she hadn't accomplished anything, Clara started back to the house. She had only gone a short distance when she heard the clop-clop of a horse coming up behind her. A farm wagon drew alongside and stopped. Paul held the reins. He tipped his straw hat. "Good morning, Clara. May I offer you a ride?"

"I enjoy taking my morning strolls alone." She looked straight ahead and kept walking. She had managed to avoid thinking about him until now. He didn't pass her. Instead, he held the horse to a pace that matched hers.

"I think we got off to a bad start yesterday," he said after a long moment.

She chose not to reply, hoping he would get the message that she didn't wish to converse with him. He didn't.

Stopping the wagon, he got out and took the horse's rein to lead it as he fell into step beside her. "I hope you will accept my apology if I offended you yesterday."

"Are you still planning to auction my uncle's property for Ralph?"

He didn't say anything for a long moment but finally nodded. "I am until I have proof that he doesn't own the place."

She turned to face him and saw he had a horse and

buggy tied to the back of the wagon. "Then I have no reason to accept your apology, for clearly you will continue to offend me. It's a wonder you can sleep at night knowing you'll be putting two small children out of their home."

She wasn't as angry with him as she was with herself. A night's rest hadn't lessened his attractiveness. She couldn't shake the annoying feeling that she liked him.

"Your sharp tongue slings some pointed barbs. Do you practice or is it a skill you were born with?"

She stared at him with her mouth open. No one ever talked to her like that. She snapped her mouth shut. "Perhaps you should move out of range."

"Can't."

She glared at him. "Do you need directions? Let me help. Get in your wagon and tell your horse to trot on. Within a minute or two, you will be beyond the sound of my voice."

To her amazement, he burst out laughing. "I admire your sharp wit even if I am the target of your jabs."

"Clearly, I have to be more direct. Mr. Bowman, go away."

"It's Paul. You must call me Paul because I'll be spending a lot of time at your place for the next few weeks. I need to finish my inventory of all the possessions, take measurements of the house, barn and outbuildings, inspect the fencing and determine the condition of all the fields. It could take me as much as three to four weeks to sort through everything. After that, it will take me at least another week or so to organize the items into lots for sale and tag everything."

She gave him an icy stare. "If my sharp wit offends you…leave. I am a woman with a serious and distasteful mission. The future of my children, Sophie's very life depends on proving that my cousin Ralph is a liar."

"Now you are wrong about one thing."

"You don't believe he's a liar?"

"I was raised to believe the best of every man until proven wrong and then such a man needs forgiveness and prayers. You're wrong if you think your sharp wit offends me. It doesn't. It's rather refreshing. You remind me of a mother tabby cat, all claws and hiss with her tail straight up and her back arched ready to defend her kittens at all cost."

Clara had absolutely no idea how to answer him except to say, "I don't like being compared to a cat."

"Sorry. I'll make a note of that. Is tigress or lioness a better comparison? Maybe not. I can see you're about ready to claw my eyes out. Should I stop talking?"

"*Ja*, stop talking," she said dryly, trying to maintain her anger but it was slipping away. His roguish grin and the twinkle in his eyes made it hard to resist his teasing charm. The most annoying thing was that she suspected he was well practiced at charming women.

He leaned toward her. "I predict we are going to be friends. You know why?"

"I don't have a clue."

"Because everyone likes me. I'm not bragging, just stating the truth. I'm a likable fellow."

She rolled her eyes. "And one who is in love with the sound of his own voice, I gather."

"Absolutely. See how well you know me already?"

He launched into the singsong chant of an auctioneer selling an imaginary hand-painted antique china teapot to an eager crowd of imaginary bidders. By the time they reached her uncle's lane, the price was over two thousand dollars. She had to wonder how he managed to take a breath while he was calling.

"Sold, to the bishop's grandmother for two thousand two hundred dollars and two cents. Please pay the clerk at the end of the auction." He grinned at her and Clara found herself smiling back as they stopped beside the hitching rail in front of her uncle's house.

She quickly regained her common sense. This handsome, smooth-talking man wasn't going to distract her from what she had to do. "Sadly, I don't have a valuable antique teapot so I won't need your services."

"Are you sure about that? Have you done an inventory?"

Paul saw the indecision flash across her face before she composed herself. "I have not. After I prove the property is mine, I do plan to sell the farm and equipment along with some of the contents of the house."

"I'm sure you'll want an accurate inventory in that case. Why have it done twice? There's no reason I can't give you a copy of the lists I'm making now."

"I will need one, won't I?"

"Absolutely. If you want to ensure that my assessment is correct and complete, then perhaps you would like to assist me while I go through your uncle's possessions."

"While I hate to agree with you, you may have a valid point."

"And if we work together, you can be sure I won't hide the documents you need if I should find them."

Her eyes narrowed. "What makes you think I haven't already found them?"

He leaned close. "If you had, you would be shouting for joy from the rooftop."

A hint of a smile curved her lips. "I guess I would, at that."

He grinned. "See? I'm getting to know you better all the time. Where do you suggest we start our inventory?"

"You're going to let me decide? Aren't you the expert?"

"I will give you my opinion if you want. We should start in the attic and work our way down in the house."

Paul suspected that Clara was someone used to taking charge in whatever situation arose. He was willing to give her enough leeway to make her feel comfortable. He hated that he would be party to selling her home out from under her if Ralph did own it. He wasn't quite sure why it was important but he truly wanted her to like him.

There was something about her that touched him in a way no other woman had. He was afraid to examine his feelings too closely.

"I have no idea what is in the attic. I've never been up there," she said.

"I'm going to guess we will find cobwebs, spiders and maybe a mouse or two."

"If you are trying to frighten me, it won't work. I'm not afraid of spiders or mice."

"*Wunderbar.* Spiders give me the heebie-jeebies. I'll let you deal with any we find."

She tipped her head as she regarded him. "I thought all men were tough and brave when it came to squishing insects."

"Nope. I never said I was a tough guy. I'll let you go first."

She stared at him for a long minute. She had something other than cobwebs on her mind. He said, "You might as well ask me whatever it is."

"Before we tackle this project, may I borrow your buggy for a short trip today?"

"I see you noticed that I brought one along. I did plan to leave it for you to use. I noticed Eli had one in the barn but the front wheel has a broken spoke and I don't know if Ralph will okay the repair. Do you want to borrow my horse, too?"

Her smile was brief but genuine. "*Ja*, I would like to borrow the horse, too. I looked but I couldn't find a harness to fit Patches."

He cocked his head to the side. "Patches?"

"Sophie's cat."

He laughed. "That's a *goot* one. My horse's name is Frankly."

"Frankly, not Frank?"

"*Nee*, it's Frankly and he's a bit high-strung. I'm sure you can manage him if you know ahead of time that he likes to try and turn left at every intersection."

"Why?"

"Frankly, he has never bothered to tell me that."

She cocked her head to the side. "Are you ever serious?"

"Not unless I have to be. Are you going to leave the *kinder* with me?"

She shook her head. "*Nee*, I'll take them with me."

"*Goot*, *kinder* are scarier than spiders."

Clara went to collect the children, leaving Paul waiting outside. She might have thought he was kidding about looking after the children but he wasn't. Toby he could manage but the needs of a girl Sophie's age were far outside his level of comfort. Paul was still standing beside the buggy when she came out with the children.

"*Danki*, for the loan of the horse and buggy, Paul. We

should be back in an hour or two. Why don't you start downstairs and save the attic until I return?"

He hung his head and tried to look downcast. "You think I'm not brave enough to go into the spider's den alone."

She chuckled. "That's right."

"Paul is plenty brave," Toby insisted.

"Not as brave as your mother," he replied, meaning what he said.

He opened the buggy door and handed her up. He held her fingers a moment longer than necessary because he liked the way they felt in his hand. His eyes met hers and he saw them darken with some emotion before she looked away and pulled her hand free.

Clara blamed her fast pulse on the importance of talking to Dan Kauffman. She wasn't willing to admit Paul had such an effect on her. He was nice-looking, with his sincere brown eyes and light brown hair. In a way, he reminded her of her husband, Adam, but she wasn't looking to marry again. She needed to put all her time and effort into seeing that Sophie stayed well and providing for both her children.

She picked up the reins. "Frankly, walk on." As the horse headed down the road, Clara resisted the urge to look back and see if Paul was watching her.

When she reached the highway, Frankly tried to turn left, forcing her mind back to the task at hand. Once she straightened out the horse, she headed down the highway at a steady clip. Frankly had a high-stepping gait that made the miles fly by. He was the kind of horse young men wanted to pull their courting buggies so they could impress the girls. Was there someone Paul hoped to impress? She quickly dismissed the thought as none of her business.

Four miles from her uncle's farm, Clara allowed the horse to make his preferred turn to the left and entered the driveway for Dan Kauffman's home. She had only been to the place twice when she was younger but not much had changed. His wife still cultivated an extensive rose garden, and there was a large shaded pool with water lilies where gold and white koi fish made their stately rounds waiting for a handout.

She secured Paul's horse and allowed the children to go look at the fish while she walked up the graveled path to the front door. If anyone knew why her uncle had changed his mind, or if he hadn't, it was Dan. Although he wasn't Amish, he had been her uncle's closest friend since their boyhood days.

She raised her hand and knocked on the brightly painted red door.

Paul decided he would spare Clara the task of climbing into the attic with him. He was glad he did the minute he opened the trap door leading to the space. It was as dusty and cobweb-filled as he had suspected it would be.

An hour later, he hauled the last box of odds and ends down the ladder and carried them into the kitchen. Eli King had stored very few things in his attic. There were some books and a set of dishes with three chipped plates. There was a shoebox full of newspaper clippings. As an appraiser, Paul knew they were worthless but he set them aside for Clara to look through.

The final box contained a dozen carved wooden toys. They were dark with age but all in good condition. These were the kind of small items that usually sold well at an auction. He would have to ask Clara if there was a story associated with them. *Englisch* auction-goers particularly enjoyed purchasing an item with a history.

Paul made a list of every toy and noted the condition in the margin beside the description. When he was finished, he wasn't sure if he should wait for Clara's return or if he could go ahead and inventory the kitchen without her. As he was making up his mind to wait, he wandered into the living room and noticed a tall, beautifully carved bible stand in the corner.

It was made of dark oak and deeply carved with vines and leaves in the elaborate German style popular hundreds of years before. The sides and front of the cabinet were panels carved with bible chapters and verses in three-inch-high letters. On the front was Genesis 1:1. Below that one, a panel bore the inscription Isaiah 26:3. On the left side three panels were inscribed with John 3:16, Matthew 5:44 and Philippians 4:13. On the right side was Proverbs 22:6, Daniel 6:22 and Romans 12:2. Paul drew his fingers along the carvings. The verses must have held a special meaning to the cabinetmaker or the person he made it for.

Paul lifted the lid and stared at the huge antique German bible inside. The book was at least six inches thick and bound with red calfskin. He opened the cover and saw the publication date of 1759 on the yellowed page. Clara's family must have brought this bible with them when they immigrated to America with the first Amish families. This wasn't going to be sold. This heirloom belonged to Clara to be passed down to her children and her children's children no matter what Ralph Hobson thought should be done with it.

Paul heard the arrival of a buggy and glanced out the

kitchen window. Clara had returned and his heart gave an odd little skip at the sight of her.

He pulled back from the window. This wasn't normal. He had dated plenty of young women and none of them had triggered a jolt of happiness, or whatever this was, when he saw them.

He walked outside, intending to take care of his horse but Clara was already unhitching Frankly. Should he take over or allow Clara to finish? He wasn't used to watching a woman do his chores while he stood idly by. "Did he behave for you?"

"He tried several times to turn without permission but once he understood what I wanted, we didn't have any trouble." She unhooked the last strap and led him out from between the buggy shafts. "But you will have to get a new buggy whip."

"What? You whipped my horse?"

"I'm teasing, Paul. Does he look like I beat him?" Frankly was nibbling at her black traveling bonnet. He pulled it off and tossed his head with it between his teeth.

Paul snatched it from the horse and handed it to Clara before he took the lead rope from her. "He doesn't look whipped but he looks like he is developing more bad habits. Maybe I should cut his ration of apples. Is it okay if I turn him out in your corral?"

"I don't see why not. I walked him the last mile so he should be cooled down. Good fellow. Thanks for the lift." She patted the horse's neck as he walked past her.

Toby and Sophie both had to pat the horse, who put his nose down to them before Paul turned him loose.

"Children, I want you to go play in the backyard."

"But I want to tell Paul about the fish," Toby said.

"Me, too," Sophie said. "They were gold and white and this big." She held her arms wide.

"You can tell Paul about them another time." Clara gave them a stern look. They walked away without arguing.

Paul unbuckled the harness and lifted it from Frankly's back. The tall black gelding shivered all over, happy to be unburdened. After hanging the tack on the wooden fence, Paul opened the gate and let the horse loose. Frankly trotted to the center of the corral. He put his nose to the ground and turned around in a tight circle several times before he laid down and rolled onto his back. He wiggled like an overgrown puppy scratching in delight. Paul would have to groom him again before putting him in a stall for the evening.

When the horse finally got to his feet, he shook all over, sending a cloud of dust flying about him. Paul realized that Clara had followed him to the fence and stood watching the horse, too. "Was your trip successful?" he asked.

"The man I went to see wasn't home. I left a note asking him to come and see me."

"Have you tried calling him? Almost every *Englisch* fellow has a cell phone these days."

"I did call his home but no one answered. He doesn't have a message machine. I don't think he has a cell phone."

She sounded depressed. He wanted to lift her spirits but he wasn't sure how. She believed the farm belonged to her but Paul didn't see how she could be right. The Amish, like many *Englisch*, took great care to make sure their property passed legally into the hands of their heirs.

She pushed back from the fence. "What did you find in the house?"

"Twenty-two spiders, six mice, a box of newspaper clippings, several bags of material scraps and a box of old carved wooden toys. I decided to tackle the attic and show you how brave I am."

"I'm rather glad you did. I wasn't looking forward to it. Were the toys horses, cows, sheep and a collie dog?" she asked with a sad smile.

"That's exactly what I found."

"I remember playing with them as a child…" Her voice trailed away as a car turned in the drive. It was Ralph.

He and another man got out of the car. Ralph looked over the property with a heavy frown in place. "I don't see that you have gotten much done, Mr. Bowman."

"I have finished the inventory of farm equipment and I've started in the house. I'll begin moving the machinery out of the buildings and into the open tomorrow."

"I see you're still hanging around, Clara. Maybe this will hasten your departure." He turned to the man with him. "This is my attorney, William Sutter."

A distinguished-looking man with silver hair wearing a fancy *Englisch* suit stepped forward. "Good afternoon, Mrs. Fisher. I have here the signed and notarized trust document with the amendment attached naming Mr. Hobson as your uncle's heir, also signed and notarized. I hope this lays to rest any question about the validity of Mr. Hobson's ownership of this property. I was present at the signing and I assure you that your uncle executed this change of his own free will."

He handed the papers to Paul. Paul glanced over the documents and handed them to Clara. "It looks legal to me but I'm no expert."

"Fortunately, I am," William Sutter said without smiling.

Clara studied the documents and handed them back to Mr. Sutter. "This is not my uncle's signature. This is a forgery."

Hobson threw his hands in the air. "Unbelievable."

Paul stepped closer to Clara and spoke in Pennsylvania *Deitsch* so the two men could not understand what he was saying. "Be reasonable, Clara. A notary must have proof of the person's identity before affixing their seal. Without a driver's license, your uncle would have needed two people who knew him to vouch for him in front of a notary."

"I don't care what you say, that is not my uncle's signature." She switched to English. "Who vouched for him? I want to speak to the notary. Where can I find him or her?"

"I was one of the people who vouched for Uncle Eli." Ralph shoved his hands in his front pockets. "The other doesn't matter. Now you've seen the amendment and now you know the place is mine."

"I will never accept that my uncle deeded this property to you." She turned pleading eyes to him. "Paul, can't you see that he is lying? Tell me that you believe me."

Chapter Four

Clara desperately wanted Paul to say he believed her. Someone had to believe her.

He didn't. She saw it in his eyes. Ralph and his attorney were too convincing.

She was right and that was what mattered. But how could she prove it? She prayed God would show her the way.

Paul folded his arms over his chest and turned to Ralph. "I noticed an antique cabinet that contained a very old bible in the living room. I won't sell a family bible at auction."

"I want everything sold," Ralph stated firmly.

"If you don't want to keep it, then it rightfully belongs to Clara and her children. I will not sell it."

"It's mine and I want it sold!"

Paul shook his head. "I won't do it."

The attorney held his hands wide. "Gentlemen, is it worth squabbling over?"

His resolve evident, Paul said nothing. Ralph gave in. "Fine. It's hers. It's in German anyway."

Paul was confusing her again. He didn't believe she

owned the farm but here he was standing up to Ralph over her family bible. She honestly didn't know what to make of him but she was thankful he understood the importance of keeping the bible in her family.

Paul pulled a notebook and a pen from his pocket. "I need to know who you want to do the land survey for property boundaries."

Ralph glanced at his attorney. Mr. Sutter smiled. "The sale of farm property doesn't require a new survey. The historical boundaries of the farm are adequate."

Paul looked skeptical. "Are you sure? It's unusual."

"Let the new owner pay for a survey if he wants one," Ralph said. "I'm spending enough to get rid of this place as it is." He pointed at Clara. "When is she leaving?"

"Never," she said.

"As soon as she can locate a suitable home for herself and the children," Paul said quickly. "Her situation is unusual given her child's special needs. Having her live here a while longer won't make any difference to our sale date."

Ralph looked ready to argue but his attorney forestalled him. "He's right. There's no point making waves. We want this sale to go smoothly."

Ralph's scowl deepened. "All right. Have it your way."

The attorney bowed slightly to Clara. "If you will excuse us, we must get going. We have another meeting." The two men went back to the car and drove away.

Clara stared at Paul. "That's it? You are just going to stand there and let Ralph get away with this?"

"I don't have a choice. He is the legal owner."

"The document they showed you is a forgery and I'm going to prove it." Her shoulders slumped as she realized he was looking at her with pity in his eyes.

"I'm sorry, Clara."

"*Nee*, you aren't. You wouldn't get your commission if I prove he's lying."

"I'm sorry you believe I would let that cloud my judgment."

She wasn't sure what to believe about him. Was he working with her cousin to steal her inheritance or was he the innocent party he appeared to be? She had no way of knowing. She stiffened her spine. "Where are the items from the attic?"

"I left the boxes in the kitchen and put some things in the rubbish bin."

"I want to go through it all." She didn't meet his gaze.

"Of course."

If he sounded defensive, she could live with that. Sophie's life might depend on her making the right decisions here. She liked Paul but she had no way of knowing if she could trust him.

Two days later, Paul took a seat at the table in his uncle's kitchen while his family gathered around. His uncle, his brother, Mark, and his cousins Samuel and Joshua were present. His aunt Anna finished filling everyone's cups with fresh hot coffee and then took a seat at the foot of the table. Paul looked at them and took a deep breath. "I need some help and I'm not sure where to turn."

"This is about the auction you are holding soon?" Mark asked.

Paul nodded. "Ralph Hobson asked me to sell the farm he inherited from Eli King. Onkel Isaac, did you know the man?"

"Can't say that I remember him."

"He was Millie King's husband," Anna offered.

Paul turned to her. "Did you know the family well?"

"Not well but Millie and I served on a few committees together. The Haiti relief quilt-auction drive was one we both served on for several years. I think Millie passed away about five years ago. She never had any children, poor soul."

"Did she talk about her nephew or niece?" Paul asked.

"Let me think. I believe she said she had one *Englisch* nephew and an Amish niece who married a fellow from Pennsylvania. That's all I recall. Why?"

"Hobson thought the house was empty but his cousin, a widow with two children, has been living there for some time. She was away when Eli died so Hobson didn't know it. They each claim to be the rightful heir."

Isaac added a lump of sugar into his coffee. "This sounds like something the *Englisch* law must settle. Is there a will?"

Paul shook his head. "A trust. That's the real problem. Hobson and his lawyer have what they claim is a legal document making Hobson the new owner but Clara says her uncle's signature on it is a forgery. The papers that prove she gets the place are missing."

"What do you know about Clara?" Mark asked.

"Not much. She belongs to Gerald Barkman's church now. Her little girl has a genetic illness. She has to sleep under blue lights at night."

Anna pressed both hands to her cheeks. "Oh, how sad. My cousin Sarah in Pennsylvania had two boys who passed away from the same thing years ago. Children with the disease all die before they are grown. Such a hard burden for a young mother to bear. I will pray for her and her child."

"Actually, her daughter can live for many years if she gets a liver transplant," Paul said.

"Really?" His aunt smiled. "Then praise God for the doctors who do such work."

"Clara was counting on the sale of her uncle's farm to pay for the surgery. Now you can see why I'm sorry I accepted this job. It doesn't seem right to put her and her *kinder* out of their home and take away her daughter's chance to be well."

"We must care for widows and orphans as the Lord has commanded us to do. Is her church helping her?" Isaac asked.

Paul stirred his coffee. "I don't know. I assume they are but none of them have been around when I've been there."

Isaac pulled on his beard as he often did when he was deep in thought. "That doesn't sound like Gerald or Velda Barkman. They are good and generous members of the faith. I'm sure they will help her."

Joshua leaned back in his chair. "I think this woman needs an *Englisch* attorney but if this man has the law on his side, she will have to leave."

Paul turned to him. "Do you know an attorney who might help an Amish widow with limited funds?"

"What you need is an estate planning lawyer," Samuel offered. He was the oldest of the Bowman brothers and a thoughtful man.

Paul's hopes rose. "Do you know one?"

Samuel shook his head. "I don't. Sorry."

"Anna and I have worked with one to set up our wills," Isaac said. "His name is Oscar James. He has an office in Berlin. He might help. I will ask and let you know."

Paul looked at all their faces. "I guess the real question I want to ask is should I resign from this contract?"

"Did you accept it in good faith?" Isaac asked.

"I did but that was before I knew the situation," Paul said.

Isaac leaned forward. "Do you believe the man has the legal right to sell the property?"

"After the papers I saw and after hearing from his lawyer, I think he does but something about Ralph Hobson is off. He keeps stressing that he's in a hurry to get rid of the property but he could sell the place tomorrow if he wanted. It's *goot* farmland. So why did he hire me to set up an auction that will take weeks of work? Clara is his cousin. You would think he would help her instead of throwing her off the property."

Mark folded his hands on the tabletop. "Is the widow a pretty woman?"

Paul felt everyone's eyes on him. The heat began rising in his cheeks. "I hardly noticed."

Joshua nudged Samuel. "A telling answer if I've ever heard one. Paul notices every woman from sixteen to sixty."

"This isn't a laughing matter," Paul said. "Besides, I've only known her a few days."

His aunt laid her hand on top of his. "You must ask yourself if you truly distrust Mr. Hobson or if your dislike stems from the way he is treating his cousin. He has known her far longer than you have."

"He warned me not to believe what she said because she is crazy. She is a determined desperate woman but not a crazy one."

"A man's word is his bond. You must honor the contract you made with Hobson unless you have irrefutable evidence that he is cheating this woman," Isaac said. "Every man is a child of God and innocent until proven otherwise, even those we dislike. We cannot judge him. We can and will aid this young mother in whatever way is necessary to make sure she and her children do not suffer because of this situation."

All the men around the table nodded. It wasn't something they said; it was the way they lived their lives.

Paul sighed with relief. He knew this was what his family would say. Together they would find a way to take care of Clara and her children.

"Paul is here and he has the biggest horses I have ever seen." Toby left his place at the window overlooking the lane and ran to the front door.

Clara was busy drying Sophie's hair with a towel. "I want to see," Sophie said, trying to wiggle off the kitchen chair.

"You may go see after I am done with your hair. Toby, do not run near the horses."

"I know. I wonder if Paul will let me drive them."

"Don't pester him," Clara cautioned. "He has work to do. He is not here to entertain a curious boy."

"I'll behave," he said, shutting the door behind him on his way out.

Sophie crossed her arms in annoyance. "Toby gets to do everything."

"He gets to do more because he is older. When you are older, you will do more things, too." Clara closed her eyes and prayed that God, in His infinite mercy, would allow Sophie to grow old.

"How come boys get to do things that are so much more fun?"

Clara laid aside the towel and began the task of combing Sophie's long thick curly hair. "What kind of things do you mean?"

"Toby used to milk the cow and you never let me do it. He can throw hay out of the loft with a pitchfork and I can't."

Clara chuckled. "Most boys would consider those things chores and not fun."

"Then boys are silly."

"Sometimes they are." Clara tied Sophie's hair back with a ribbon and patted her shoulder. "Go outside now and let the sun dry your hair. You can watch but I don't want you to get in Paul's way. Is that understood?"

"Yup." She hopped off the chair and headed for the door.

"And stay away from the horses," Clara cautioned but Sophie was already out the door.

Clara finished cleaning up then moved to the sink and looked out the kitchen window. Both her children were standing on the fence at the corral watching Paul unhitch his team from the wagon. The huge caramel-colored Belgians, with their blond manes and tails, stood quietly as he worked around them.

She found herself as eager as her children to see Paul again but she resisted the urge to go outside. Her mind was in a constant state of turmoil where he was concerned. Such giddy foolishness over the mere sight of a fellow was better suited to a teenage girl, not a widow of twenty-eight with two children.

For the past few days, she had tried to sort out her feelings about him with little success. He was a hard worker. It was easy to see that. He enjoyed the children and took special care when they were around. He made them laugh. That was certainly a point in his favor. Once, she caught him enjoying a game of hide-and-seek with them. He would make a good father one day but why wasn't he married already? She had married at nineteen and was a mother by twenty. She guessed Paul's age to be twenty-four or twenty-five. Most Amish were married by the time they were twenty-two or twenty-three. Was he interested in someone? If she knew more about him perhaps she could decide if she should trust him.

She noticed him watching the house and she stepped away from the window. No point in letting him think that she was interested in him. She wasn't. She had better things to do than gawk at him while he worked.

Her steadfast resolve lasted less than an hour. Before she realized what she was doing, she was back at the window watching him work and entertain her children.

She was relieved when he left in the early afternoon without speaking to her but she was quickly regaled with stories about him from Toby and Sophie when they came in. Paul was nice and funny and he knew everything about the machinery Eli had collected. Whatever his flaws, he knew how to endear himself to children.

The following morning, she left her uncle's ancient propane-powered washing machine chugging away on the back porch and walked around the house to check on her children. They were both sitting on one of Paul's draft horses. Their short legs stuck out straight from the horse's broad back. Sophie giggled when the horse reached around to nibble at her bare toes.

Paul was using the second horse to pull a broken wagon out into the sunlight from her uncle's shed. He had a dozen various pieces of equipment lined up along the side of the barn. She could see it was hard work. His shirt was already damp with sweat. He had his sleeves rolled up and he stopped to mop his brow with them.

She went back into the house and made a pitcher of fresh lemonade. Stacking a few plastic cups together, she carried her offering to the corral fence. Paul had the wagon positioned where he wanted it. He dropped the lines when he saw her and came toward her. "I hope some of that is for me."

"It is. I see you found a way to keep my children out from under foot."

He leaned against the board fence, took off his hat and wiped his forehead with his shirtsleeve. "At least they won't get stepped on up there and Gracie is as gentle as they come."

"Mamm, see how high I am?" Sophie called out.

"I see. That's very high. How are you going to get down? I don't think I can reach you."

Sophie bent over to look at the ground. "I'm going to stay up here forever."

"Me, too!" Toby shouted.

"Then I reckon my fresh lemonade will have to go to waste."

Sophie held out her hands. "Paul, get me down. I'm thirsty."

He walked over and turned his back to her. "Come on, Goldilocks, change mounts."

She clasped her arms around his neck and slid off. Carrying her piggyback, he brought her to the fence and allowed her to step off beside Clara. Sophie grinned. "I like riding Gracie."

"So do I," Toby said from the horse's back.

Sophie looked at her brother and then at Paul. "Can we leave Toby up there forever?"

"That is a tempting thought but I imagine he is as thirsty as I am." He went back and lifted the boy off the horse. Carrying Toby under one arm, Paul toted the laughing boy to the fence and set him down.

Smiling at their antics, Clara handed them each a plastic cup full of ice-cold lemonade through the fence. She held up a cup to Sophie, who was straddling the fence but the little girl hesitated. "Will it make me turn yellow, too?"

"It won't make you turn yellow," Clara assured her. "It's good for you. It has lots of vitamin C."

Toby looked up at his sister. "Do things look yellow to you because your eyes are yellow?"

Sophie frowned as she considered the question. "The lemonade looks yellow but you don't."

Clara looked closely at the whites of Sophie's eyes. Whenever she had an episode of high bilirubin, Clara noticed the change in her eyes first. They were slightly yellow. More so than yesterday. Was her skin getting too thick for the light therapy to work?

Paul seem to notice her worry. "Is she okay?"

"I think so. Sophie, does your tummy hurt?"

"Nope. Can I have some more lemonade?" She held out her cup.

Clara relaxed. "You may."

Toby pointed toward the lane. "Mamm, I see the mailman. May I go get the mail?"

"I want to come, too," Sophie added, climbing down from her perch after leaving her cup on top of the fence post.

"You can both go. Make sure to watch for cars. Toby, hold your sister's hand."

"I will." The two of them took off together.

Paul finished his drink and handed the glass to Clara. "Exactly what is wrong with Sophie? Or does it distress you to talk about it?"

"It doesn't. You already know she has a rare genetic disease called Crigler-Najjar syndrome. Blood cells in our bodies are replaced constantly by new ones when the old ones die. As the old cells break down, they release a substance called bilirubin. That isn't a problem for people like you and I because we have an enzyme in our livers that turns bilirubin into a form that can easily be removed. Sophie was born without the ability to make this enzyme in her liver. When her cells break down, the bilirubin remains in her body and that leads to jaundice. We see it as a yellow color in her skin and the whites of her eyes. What we can't see is the damage high levels of bilirubin do to her brain, nerves and muscles. It can cause permanent brain damage and even death in a short period of time."

"How did this happen to her? Do you know?"

"Like her blue eyes, she inherited the defective gene from me and from her father. We were both carriers but neither one of us had the disease. It takes two genes to make the liver defective. It's very rare but it is seen more often among Amish and Mennonite children in Pennsylvania."

"How is it that Toby doesn't have it?"

"The doctors told us we had a one-in-four chance of having another child with the disease. God decides…as with all things in this world."

"Why do the blue lights help her?"

"That is the mystery of God's mercy. Light, particularly blue light, causes a reaction in the bilirubin in her blood beneath her skin. It changes it into a harmless product her body can get rid of easily. She needs to be under those lights for a minimum of ten hours every day. As she gets older, her skin will get thicker and it will take more hours to keep her level normal, and it will be less and less effective until it won't do her any good at all. At that point, she will die. Any stress, like a bad cold or the flu, can cause the bilirubin to rise high enough to turn her brain yellow. If that happens, the damage is permanent."

"What do you look for when she gets worse?" Paul asked, glancing down the lane at the children walking back from the mailbox.

"I must sound like I am an expert. I'm not. I only repeat the things they tell me. I don't truly understand the science. When her bilirubin goes up, she gets a yellow cast to the whites of her eyes first. She gets sick to her stomach and very tired. Sometimes she complains of pain in her stomach. When she does, I know it's time to take her to the doctor right away. If I wait too long, she can have seizures."

"What do the doctors do for her?" He sounded genuinely interested.

"They use plasmapheresis to quickly lower the levels of bilirubin in her blood."

He frowned slightly. "What does that mean?"

"It means they connect her to a machine that removes some of her blood and separates it into blood cells and plasma—that's the fluid in between our blood cells where the bilirubin stays. Then they replaced her plasma with some from other people, added back her own blood cells and transfused it all back into her. It takes a long time because they can't remove a lot of blood all at once. It helps but the effect doesn't last for long."

"It must be frightening to live with such a sentence hanging over your child."

"God is good. He is our protector and our salvation. I

will do whatever I can for my baby girl but I know she is always in His hands. I grieve for what she must endure. I wish I could take the burden from her and carry it myself but that is not possible. I accept that."

"Isn't a transplant a cure?"

Clara took a deep breath. "A liver transplant will cure the syndrome. She will never need the lights again if the transplant works but she will need to take medicine to prevent her body from rejecting the new liver for a lifetime. The medicine is expensive. There can be serious complications. We may simply be trading one illness for another but I have to believe it will help her."

"I admire your strength in the face of such sadness."

"I look for the bright spot in every day. I try to teach my children to do the same. God is with us. Today, the bright spot was seeing Sophie up on your horse and her smile when you gave her a piggyback ride. To you, it might have been be a little thing. To me, it will be a memory to treasure for a lifetime."

The children came back from the mailbox with a single letter. It bore the return address of Clara's mother.

Clara took it from Sophie. "Toby, why don't you and Sophie go feed Patches. I forgot this morning."

"Okay." The children went up to the house.

Clara opened the letter. It contained a note from her mother and another envelope.

Her head started to swim at the sight of a familiar scrawl on the enclosed envelope. She grasped the fence behind her.

"What's wrong?" Paul bounded over the boards to stand beside her.

She looked at his concerned face. "It's a letter from Eli."

Chapter Five

"A letter from your *onkel*? How is that possible?"

Clara heard Paul's voice coming as if from a long way away as she stared at the envelope in her hand. A cold chill ran down her spine, making her shiver.

"Are you okay?" he asked, his voice stronger now.

She shook her head to clear the cobwebs from her brain. "I'm okay. It's just something of a shock. It's post-marked two days before he died and addressed to me at my mother's house."

Clara quickly skimmed her mother's note. "Mamm was as startled as I am to get the letter. She didn't mention it when I spoke to her on the phone. It must have come later."

"See what your uncle has to say."

Clara's fingers trembled as she tore open the envelope. She read his brief letter. "He asks about Sophie and goes on to say he had several visits from *Englisch* fellows wanting to buy his land. I can't believe this. He says he came home and found a man going through his papers. The fellow asked Eli his plans for the place after he was dead. He told the man his plan was to watch his crops grow from heaven." She looked up at Paul. "Why would anyone be that interested in this farm?"

"I have no idea. Does he mention anyone by name?"

"Nee."

"Don't you think he would've said something if one of them had been Ralph?"

"I believe you're right about that. He goes on to say he was concerned enough that he placed his extra cash, the deed and his trust document with Daniel for safe-keeping."

She sprang to her feet and held the letter up to Paul's face, tapping it with her finger. "Do you see this? He says he placed some of his important papers, including the trust document, with Daniel. Not with Ralph and not with Ralph's attorney. This is proof that I wasn't making it up. I have to see Dan Kauffman right away. I can prove Ralph is lying. Now do you believe me?"

"It doesn't matter what I believe. It's what you can prove that matters. He doesn't say in this letter that he was leaving the place to you."

"Nee, he does not." Her elation drained away.

"Why did he think it was important to give the trust document to someone else? It has no value if someone were to steal it."

Clara shrugged. "I don't know. Maybe he knew it would be needed soon if he thought he was dying."

"Shall I hitch up the buggy and drive you to the Kauff-man place?"

"Ja, that would be fine."

Clara clutched the letter to her chest. For the first time in days, she had hope, real hope that she could prove the truth about her uncle's intentions even if he didn't mention them in the letter. She hurried up to the house to get her bonnet and her purse.

Toby and Sophie were both in the kitchen. "Come on, children, we are going to see Dan Kauffman."

"We just went there the other day," Toby reminded her.

Sophie patted her hands together. "Can I see the fish again? I like them. Can I feed them?"

"Dan wasn't home so we are going to try to see him again today. Why don't you take some bread for the fish? Let me put your hair up right quick. Is it dry?"

Sophie ran her fingers through her hair and nodded.

Clara put up the child's hair and secured her *kapp* with several white bobby pins. Sophie grabbed two slices of bread from the table and then Clara hustled both children outside.

Sophie stooped to gather up Patches on the front porch. Clara shook her head. "The cat isn't coming with us."

"But she wants to see the fish, too," Sophie said hopefully.

"*Nee*, she stays here."

"Okay." Sophie put her down and the cat headed for the barn.

Paul sat in the driver's seat of the buggy with the reins in his hand.

"You don't need to come with me." It surprised Clara just how much she wanted his company. The thought was quickly followed by a mental reminder that she shouldn't depend on him. He would be gone from her life soon enough.

"I'd like to see how this mystery ends. I'm not staying here while you do all the great detective work."

Could she trust him? She wanted to but was that wise?

Maybe not but she was going to anyway. "Very well. I'm not in the mood to argue with you."

"I figured you'd tell me to mind my own business."

"I almost did." He chuckled as he helped the children in and then moved over so Clara could sit beside him. He clicked his tongue to get the horse moving and before long they were on the highway. He set the horse to a fast pace and for that she was grateful.

"What prompted you to let me come along?"

She looked down at her hands clasped together in her lap. "I'm not sure. I want to believe that you are not a willing accomplice to Ralph's plan."

"I will not aid him to do something illegal. I hope you find your proof."

She cast him a sidelong glance. "Why are you helping him? You have to know he isn't being honest."

"I gave him my word. I can't go back on that because I have learned to dislike him. What good is a man if he only keeps his word when it is convenient?"

It was an honest man's answer. She felt a growing respect for Paul. He was in an uncomfortable position because of her.

"You stand to make a lot of money from the sale, don't you?"

"I charge the standard amount for the industry in this part of Ohio."

"What will you do with your windfall if Ralph succeeds?"

"Most of the money will go back into my business. However, if we find proof that Ralph is lying and his documents are a forgery, I will not handle the sale. My reputation as an honest auctioneer and my scruples don't have a price."

"I'm sorry that you may lose money over this." She hadn't considered that her right to the property might cause Paul harm.

"Don't be sorry. The health of your *kinder* far outweighs any risk I am taking."

Feeling better about her decision to trust him, Clara settled back and waited impatiently to reach their destination.

When they turned into the Kauffman farmstead, Clara's heart began beating so hard she could hardly draw a full breath. She scrambled down from the buggy without waiting for anyone else and rushed up to the door and pounded on it. No one answered.

"Maybe he is out doing chores," Paul suggested.

Sophie tugged on Paul's arm. "Want to come see the fish?"

"Okay. Try the barn, Clara. I'll keep an eye on the kids."

"Danki." She scanned the farmyard for activity and started toward the large red barn.

Paul allowed the children to lead him to the koi pond at the side of the house. It was an impressive structure, made of concrete, and at least fifteen feet wide and twenty feet long. Water lilies in the center spread their large leaves and blooms on the surface and gave the fish a place to hide if they felt threatened.

"See the one with the white spot on his head, I like him best." Sophie tossed a piece of bread toward him but a quicker solid gold one got it.

"Stay back from the edge, Sophie. It's deeper than I thought it would be." He heard chickens cackling at being disturbed. Glancing past the trees around the pond, he spotted a woman coming out of a henhouse.

"Toby, watch your sister."

"I want to feed the fish, too."

"Okay, take turns." Paul saw the woman spot him and change direction to come toward him. He walked out to meet her. Clara saw her, too, and joined him.

"Are you looking for the Kauffmans?" The *Englisch* woman was tall and stout with short gray hair. She held a feed bucket in her hand.

Clara nodded. "*Ja*, I'm Clara Fisher. I need to see Dan. It's important."

"You are the one who left the note. I'm sorry I haven't been able to stop by. I guess you haven't heard. Dan suffered a stroke a week ago. I'm Opal Kauffman. Dan is my father. He's in the hospital in Millersburg. I just came by to take care of the animals, water my mother's plants and check on the house."

"I'm so sorry," Clara said. Paul heard the disappointment in her voice. It had to be frustrating for her to encounter another roadblock.

Would Opal allow them to search the house for the document Clara needed? "When do you think he will be home?"

Sadness filled Opal's eyes. "To be honest, his doctors give him only a slim chance for recovery. We are all having a hard time accepting the inevitable. What did you want to see him about? Maybe I can help you."

Clara clutched the sides of her skirt. "Your father was great friends with my uncle, Eli King. In his last letter to me, Eli said he placed an important document with Dan for safekeeping. Do you know anything about it?"

Opal slowly shook her head. "I don't remember seeing anything with your uncle's name on it but I haven't gone through Dad's things yet. I will ask my mother if she knows anything about it."

"Perhaps we could look for ourselves?" he suggested.

Opal's eyes narrowed. "I don't feel right about letting you search the house. I will see Mom later today and ask her what she knows about this."

Clara folded her hands in a pleading gesture. "Couldn't you call her? It's vital that I find these papers as soon as possible. If you could just look for me, I would be eternally grateful. I wouldn't impose on you at such a difficult time without good reason."

The woman set down the feed bucket and pulled out her cell phone. "Okay. I'll see if Mom answers her phone. Sometimes she keeps it off when Dad is sleeping." She turned and walked a few feet away with the phone to her ear. Clara couldn't hear what she was saying.

Finally, Opal put away her phone and came back to Clara. "Mom didn't know anything about Eli bringing over papers for Dad. She said to tell you how sorry she is about your uncle's passing. He was well-liked by my family. She gave me permission to let you go in the house. I'm to help you if I can. What are we looking for?"

"The document is a trust, like a last will and testament but it leaves the control of the farm to the trustee named without having to go through probate court."

"Sounds like something that he would keep in his safe. I have the combination. Let's go check." Opal opened the door and stood aside as Clara and Paul went in.

The safe in Dan's office held only a few items—a pocket watch and several pieces of jewelry. The only documents were insurance policies and the deed to the Kauffman property. A search of Dan's desk proved fruitless, as well. If he had Eli's trust, it wasn't in an obvious place.

"I'm sorry," Opal said as she showed them to the front door. "Mother and I will ask Dad about it when he comes around." Her voice cracked slightly. Paul suspected Opal was worried that might never happen.

"We appreciate your help," Clara said as they stepped outside. "Let us know if we can do anything."

"Mamm! Come quick. Sophie fell in the fishpond and I can't reach her." Toby skidded to a stop in front of them. "Hurry."

Paul bolted past Clara and reached the koi pond first. He jumped in and grabbed Sophie as she was flailing to keep her head above water. "I got you. You're okay."

He lifted the soaking child in his arms. Sophie clung to his neck, coughing and gasping for air. The water was only waist-deep on him but it was over her head. He slogged to the edge and handed Sophie up to Clara. She sank to her knees and held her daughter close.

"Is she okay? Do I need to call 911?" Opal asked, her cell phone at the ready.

Clara pushed Sophie's wet hair out of her face. She had a slight bluish tinge to her lips and she continued coughing. "I don't think so."

Paul plucked Sophie's *kapp* from among the lilies and heaved himself out of the pond. Water cascaded down his pants and pooled in his boots. It was going to be a cool ride home. He looked around for Toby. The boy was sitting a few feet away with his face buried in his lap and his arms wrapped tightly around his knees. His little shoulders were shaking.

"I'll get some blankets and towels." Opal hurried away.

Paul walked over to Toby and sat down cross-legged beside him. "Want to tell me what happened?"

Toby shook his head but didn't look up.

"Toby pushed me," Sophie said between coughing fits.

"It was an accident!" Toby shouted, looking up. His cheeks were stained with tears.

"Of course it was." Paul put his arm around the boy's shoulders and the child burrowed against his side.

Opal came running out with several blankets and towels. She and Clara swaddled Sophie. Paul accepted a towel and spoke softly to Toby. "Why don't you tell me what happened."

"She wouldn't share. I wanted to feed the fish, too. I was only trying to take the bread out of her hand. I didn't mean to push her so hard. She stumbled and fell in. I tried but I couldn't reach her."

"You did the right thing by coming to get help," Paul assured him.

"Is Mamm mad at me?"

"*Nee*, she isn't. She's happy you are safe."

"Will Sophie have to go back to the hospital? Mamm is always worried that Sophie will get sick. I never get sick."

Paul heard the unspoken part of Toby's statement. The boy believed his mother cared more about Sophie than she did about him. "Your mother depends on you a lot, Toby. She needs you to be strong because Sophie can't be. Let's go tell Sophie you are sorry."

"Okay." The boy rose to his feet and walked over to kneel beside his sister. "I'm sorry, Sophie. I didn't mean for you to fall in the water."

"That's okay. I forgive you. You can still be my friend." Her speech brought on another fit of coughing.

Clara looked up at Paul. "We should get her home and out of these wet things as soon as possible."

He helped Clara to her feet and soon they all climbed into the front seat of the buggy. Clara kept Sophie in her arms while Toby squeezed in between the two adults. Opal stood beside them. "Let me know how she is. I've told my mother a hundred times that pond is too deep not to have a fence around it. My parents aren't used to having small children around here."

"She'll be fine," Clara said. "Don't worry your mother with this. Let her concentrate on helping your father get well."

Paul put the horse in motion and kept the animal to a fast trot once they reached the highway.

Sophie continued to cough. Paul thought her breathing was starting to sound labored. He exchanged worried glances with Clara. "She sounds worse."

"I know. I can feel a rattle in her chest. She must have gotten some of the pond water in her lungs. Stop at the phone shack and call for an ambulance. It's just ahead."

Paul stopped and got out. He made the call and then returned to the buggy. "They are on their way. Toby is welcome to stay with me and my family if that is okay?"

"That will be one less worry, *danki.*"

"She's going to be fine. It's going to be okay." He didn't know what else to say except to reassure her and Toby.

It wasn't much more than fifteen minutes until they heard the siren in the distance but it was the longest fifteen minutes of Paul's life. He didn't understand how Clara stayed so calm.

Once again, he was reminded of what a strong woman she was. As the ambulance approached, Paul stepped out into the road to flag them down. Ten minutes later, Sophie was strapped to the gurney with an oxygen mask on her face. Clara sat beside her holding her hand. One of the ambulance crew closed the rear doors. Paul knew the man from his work as a volunteer firefighter. "Have Clara call me at my uncle's shop when she can."

"Sure. I'll let Captain Swanson and the guys at the fire station know. You'll have a driver when you need one."

"Thanks. That will help."

The man nodded, returned to the front of the ambulance and the vehicle sped away with red lights flashing.

Toby looked at Paul. "What's going to happen now?"

Paul pulled the boy against his side. "That is up to God. He has some fine men and women waiting at the hospital to help Sophie."

Clara's fears were realized in the emergency room as the doctors and nurses tended to Sophie. After looking at her X-rays, the physician in charge called it aspiration pneumonia.

"Depending on how much inflammation develops, this could be very serious. It wasn't clean water, it was more like a germ broth. She will likely get worse before she gets better. She's on oxygen now but her breathing is still labored. We've got her on some strong antibiotics and breathing treatments that will help. I understand she has Crigler-Najjar syndrome. Type one."

Clara nodded. "She does."

"I'd like to speak to her pediatrician. The syndrome is rare. I have not personally treated a case. I'm hoping her doctor can tell me how and if her syndrome will affect her treatment. Is she on phototherapy at home?"

Clara wrote out the name of Sophie's doctor and his

phone number. "She stays under the lights for ten hours at night but I received a letter from her doctor telling me to expect to increase it to twelve hours a day before long."

"Is she on a liver-transplant list?"

"We are planning a living donor transplant. I am a match for her."

"I understand they've been doing wonders with this new technique since there are so few cadaver donors available. I wish more people would consider donating their organs but I understand why not everybody wishes to do that."

She could hear Sophie crying for her in the other room. Her daughter was too young to understand much English. The family spoke *Deitsch*, a German dialect at home. Most Amish children didn't learn English until they went to school.

"How long do you think she will have to be here?" Clara squeezed her fingers together.

"That's difficult to say. Forty-eight hours of antibiotics should show us an improvement. I will want her to have a two-week course to make sure this doesn't come back on her but the last week of that won't need to be intravenous. She'll be able to take pills. If you'll excuse me, I am going to try to have a conference call with her physician and several of the doctors on the staff here."

"Can I go back in with her?"

"Absolutely." He smiled for the first time. "We are going to take good care of her."

Instead of going directly back in, Clara called the phone number the ambulance driver had given her. It was Paul's uncle's furniture-making business. A woman named Jessica Clay answered the phone and identified herself as the secretary. As soon as Clara gave her name,

Jessica said, "Hold on. Paul is right here waiting to hear from you."

"Clara? How is she?" The breathless concern in his voice was almost her undoing.

She fought back the tears. "As we suspected, some of the pond water went into her lungs and has caused pneumonia. They are going to keep her in the hospital. She could be here for two weeks. Less if she improves with the antibiotics they are giving her but it is too soon to tell how well they will work. I'm worried about her bilirubin. Anytime she gets sick it gets worse. How is Toby?"

"He's fine. Don't worry about him. He's playing catch with my cousin Joshua's daughter, Hannah, at the moment."

Clara was suddenly so tired she had trouble standing up. "I have to get back to Sophie. I will call you again tomorrow."

"Is there anything I can do? I feel awful. I should have been watching her."

She heard the deep regret in his words and knew how badly he must feel. "You are not to blame any more than Toby is. We must accept *Gott*'s will and pray for the strength to endure. If you need to do something, let Bishop Barkman know what has happened. He'll need to contact the district treasurer for the Amish Hospital Aid and tell him to expect a bill from the hospital. I will be fine. Take care of my boy for me. He likes a story at night before bedtime."

"I think I can manage that. I know some really scary ones."

"Paul, don't you dare."

"I'm kidding."

"I hope so but I wouldn't put it past you." She smiled

as she hung up. He had a way of making her smile when she needed it the most. She thanked the nurse at the desk for the use of the phone and went back to sit with Sophie while they waited to move her out of the ER to a room.

"What did she say?" Jessica asked.

Jessica was the only person in the office with Paul. He repeated the information Clara had shared. "I wish I could do something. I feel terrible. I'm selling her house out from under her and now her little girl is in the hospital because I wasn't paying attention."

"Coulda, woulda, shoulda isn't helping." Jessica closed down her computer. "Think about what the woman needs and do it."

"Like what?" Paul asked.

"Really? Are all men so clueless?"

Annoyed, Paul sought to defend himself. "I can't stop the sale of her home."

"So, what's the next step?"

What was the next step? "She will need a new place to live."

Jessica smiled. "Now you're thinking."

"I'll let her bishop know her situation so her church can help."

"Good. What are her immediate needs at the hospital?"

"Clara can't stay awake around the clock to take care of Sophie but I know she will try. She doesn't have any family here to help her. Samuel's wife, Rebecca, has experience in caring for the sick. I wonder if she could help?"

Jessica took him by the shoulders and turned him toward the door. "Wondering is not doing. Go ask Rebecca.

You're right, she has experience and she is the perfect person to aid Clara. Do Anna and Isaac know what has happened?"

"Not yet. I've been waiting to hear from Clara but I'll let them know after I've spoken to Rebecca. *Danki*, Jessica."

"Tell them I'll be happy to drive anyone who needs a lift. Consider me on twenty-four-hour call until further notice."

"You are a blessing to this family."

She winked at him. "And don't I know it. Get going."

On the short walk to Samuel and Rebecca's house, Paul pondered what else he could do for Clara. Without the money from the sale of her uncle's farm, she would have to delay Sophie's liver transplant. The Amish communities across the country were well-known for their fund-raising to assist with the special needs of their members. Paul had been an auctioneer for several such charity events. His cousin Timothy Bowman was currently the cochairman of the annual county fire department's fund-raiser. Timothy would be the one he should ask about setting up something to help with Clara and Sophie's medical bills.

After crossing the parking lot, he passed the new bakery and noticed Charlotte Zook standing in front of it, staring at the building. Her brown-and-white basset hound, Clyde, sat beside her. Charlotte's pet raccoon scampered toward Paul. He sidestepped her as she made a grab for his pant leg.

"Naughty girl, Juliet. Come here at once." Charlotte held out her hand. The raccoon raced back to her and climbed onto her shoulder. Mark was married to Charlotte's niece, Helen. They lived with Charlotte across the river. "I'm sure Helen and Mark have gone home by now."

"I know." She and the dog continued to stare at the building. Charlotte was known for her eccentric ways as well as her unusual pets.

"Is something wrong?"

Charlotte tipped her head one way and then to the other side. "Juliet has decided this is a nice place to visit but she doesn't want to live here. I am trying to decide if she is right. I think she is."

Charlotte turned to him. "What has you so worried, Paul?"

He had no idea how she knew but she was right. "A friend's little girl is in the hospital with pneumonia."

"How sad. Do I know them?"

"The mother's name is Clara Fisher."

Charlotte shook her head slowly. "I don't believe we've met."

"She isn't from our church and she has no family here. I'm on my way to ask Rebecca if she can sit with little Sophie so that Clara doesn't have such a heavy burden to bear alone."

"That's very thoughtful of you. How old is her daughter?"

"I think she is four. Clara's son is eight."

"Such delightful ages. What do you think, Clyde?" She stared at the dog, who barked once. "I agree." Charlotte smiled at Paul. "Please tell Rebecca that Helen and I will be happy to help, too."

"I will, and thank you." He left her still staring at the building and headed toward Samuel and Rebecca's house.

On the way, he stopped to watch Toby and Hannah playing catch in front of Joshua's home. Hannah was a few years older than Toby and enjoyed taking care of younger children. Toby caught sight of Paul and raced toward him. He skidded to a halt a few feet away. "How is Sophie?"

Hannah came to stand behind him.

Paul kneeled to be on the boy's level. "Sophie is going to have to stay in the hospital for a while. That means your *mamm* will be staying with her. I hope you don't mind bunking with me until she goes home."

"I guess not." He didn't sound excited at the prospect but Paul wasn't offended.

"I know it's hard not to feel sad but this wasn't your fault. It was an accident. Sophie doesn't blame you and your mother doesn't, either. Remember how I said your *daed* and mine are watching over us?"

"I remember."

"Then you remember that it pleases them when we are brave and do the right thing."

"What's the right thing for me to do?"

Paul swallowed the lump in his throat and laid a hand on the boy's shoulder. "Keep on being the kind and helpful young man your mother expects you to be. Pray for your sister and your mother. Can you do that?"

"I guess. I wish I could do more."

"That will be enough. I'll make sure you get to talk to your *mamm* on the phone and I'll even take you to the hospital to visit her and your sister."

"Is the hospital far?"

"It is but my friend Jessica has a car and she has offered to drive us."

"Really?" Toby looked up from contemplating his feet.

"Really," Paul assured him. "I need to speak to my

cousin Samuel and his wife. Hannah, why don't you show Toby the new kittens in the barn."

She grinned. "Okay."

"Toby, I'll need you to help me later with Isaac's horses. They need grooming."

"Even Gracie?" Toby asked eagerly.

"Even Gracie. Wait for me at the barn. I won't be long."

The two took off and Paul heard Toby telling Hannah about Patches. He rose to his feet. Somehow the boy had wiggled into a place in Paul's heart that he didn't know was vacant. The Lord had given Clara great challenges but He had given her great blessings, too.

Paul had never given much thought to having children. That was someday way off in the future but if he ever had a son like Toby, he would be blessed, too.

Four hours after arriving at the hospital, Sophie was finally asleep in her bed in the pediatric ICU. There were several small banks of phototherapy lights over her and a blanket-type fiber-optic light pad underneath her. She had IVs going in one hand and an oxygen mask on her face that she kept knocking aside while she slept. Clara finally ended up pulling her chair close enough to hold her hand. The wonderful nurses did everything they could to make sure they were both comfortable.

Clara realized she must've dozed off when she heard Paul's voice close beside her calling her name. She sat up and blinked several times to clear her vision. The clock on the wall said it was nine thirty in the evening. "Paul, what are you doing here?"

"I brought some help for you." He gestured to a tall, blonde Amish woman standing beside him. "This is my cousin Samuel's wife, Rebecca. She has had nursing experience. She will spell you so that you can get some sleep and if Sophie wakes up, she will have someone here who understands her *Deitsch*."

"Have you had anything to eat?" Rebecca asked. She had kind eyes and a gentle smile.

Clara shook her head. "Not since breakfast."

"Then my first nursing order is for Paul to take you down to the cafeteria and get you something hot to eat. You need to keep up your strength. But I don't really need to tell you that, do I? You've been through this before. You must let me know if there is anything I need to do."

Clara hated to leave but Rebecca was right. "Make sure that she keeps her oxygen mask on. She has a tendency to knock it aside."

"I will do that. We have also brought a pager. It has fresh batteries in it. If I need you, I or the nurse can call the number from the phone in here."

Paul moved to the door. "The pager will buzz no matter where you are. It will even reach outside for several hundred yards."

"How do you come equipped with a pager?" Clara glanced between Paul and Rebecca in astonishment.

"The Bowman men are all volunteer firefighters and have pagers to notify them when they are called out to fight a fire. This is one of the extras they keep on hand. Paul thought of it. He's not usually so bright." Rebecca smiled at him with a twinkle in her eye, taking any sting out of her words.

"I'm actually smarter than I look," he said in a hurt tone.

The women shared a speaking glance. Clara rose from

her chair and walked past him. "I reckon I'll have to take your word for that until I see some solid evidence."

Paul held the door open for her and glanced back at Rebecca. "I'll see that she eats something."

They stopped at the nurses' station to let the staff know Clara had a pager and then they took the elevator to the lower level of the building. The cafeteria was almost empty. Clara chose a salad and a bowl of hot vegetable stew. Paul carried two cups of coffee to an empty table and settled across from her.

"How is she doing?" he asked.

"Her bilirubin level is climbing but the doctor believes the lights can keep it under control. I'm not so sure."

"They are prepared for that other treatment you mentioned if the lights don't work?"

"They are. Thank you for bringing your cousin's wife with you. That was very thoughtful."

"I had to. She insisted. If you don't know anything else about Rebecca, know that she gets her way when she sets her mind to something."

"I don't know how I can thank you for everything."

"We'll work something out. I like peach pie but apple will do in a pinch if there is ice cream."

She smiled at his teasing tone. "Why is it hard to get a serious answer out of you?"

"Because I don't have a serious bone in my body."

"I find that hard to believe. How is Toby?"

"He's worried. He feels badly but I put him to work taking care of our horses and that helped. He needed to be busy. He fell asleep on his cot before I had a chance to tell him a scary story tonight. My aenti Anna is keeping watch in case he wakes up while I'm gone."

"I'm thankful for that."

"I promised he could call you tomorrow and that I would bring him along when I come to visit. That should make him feel better."

It would make her feel better, too.

He pointed at her bowl. "Eat before your stew gets cold."

She did, only realizing after her bowl was half-empty just how hungry she'd been. She gazed at Paul and tried to separate the emotions swirling through her. There was gratitude but there was something else. Something more. Having him with her was comforting. She liked him. Maybe more than she should. Twelve hours ago, she had been wondering if she could trust him. Now, she couldn't imagine going through this without his help.

"Paul, I want you to know how much—" Her words were cut off by the sudden vibration of the pager in her pocket. She pulled it out and read the message that scrolled across the small screen. Fear clutched her heart.

Come to Sophie's room right away.

Chapter Six

Clara rushed toward the elevators with all thoughts of food forgotten. Paul was close behind her. She managed to catch the elevator door as it was closing. It opened revealing two nurses inside with trays in their hands.

"What floor?" one of them asked.

Clara couldn't recall the number.

"Three," Paul said, holding the door until she was inside and then stepping in beside her. "Clara, what's wrong?"

"The message said come to the room right away. I shouldn't have left."

When the elevator opened again, they hurried out and down the hall. Rebecca was waiting just outside the ICU doors.

"What is it? What's happened?" Clara pressed a hand to her heart, trying to stem her panic.

"Sophie spiked a fever and that led to a seizure. They were able to stop the seizure with medicine but they are concerned about her rising bilirubin levels."

"They will need to start plasmapheresis. Does the doctor know that?"

"Is that the blood exchange?" Rebecca asked. "That's what they are getting ready now."

"Can I go in?" Clara had been kept out of the ICU before when Sophie was ill in the past but she needed to be with her baby girl.

"You can go in. I just wanted to prepare you for what was happening. The doctor is pretty busy right now."

"Danki." Clara drew a deep breath to compose herself, pushed the button on the wall and went inside when the doors swung open.

Feeling helpless and useless, Paul watched the doors close behind Clara. He turned to Rebecca. The grim look on her face wasn't reassuring. "Will Sophie be okay?"

"That is up to *Gott.* Only He knows the answer. We must pray for the strength to accept His will no matter what it is."

"That's what Clara said but it doesn't seem fair that Sophie has to go through this. She is such a sweet child."

"All children are gifts from Him and precious in His sight. We are not meant to understand His plan in our time on earth. You are very concerned about them, aren't you?"

"Of course I am."

"It's a little surprising. You've only known them a few days."

"It seems like I have known them for ages. I can't explain it."

"She's not your usual type, Paul."

He gave her a puzzled look. "What is that supposed to mean? What's my usual type?"

"Lighthearted. Very pretty. Intent on having a good

time by sneaking off to see a movie or going to a barn party."

"So?"

"Clara is anything but lighthearted. She has her hands full with the two children she has. She doesn't need another boy. She needs a serious and steadfast man as a helpmate."

"Now see, that's where you have it wrong. You think Clara and I have some kind of relationship going."

"Don't you? You practically insisted that I come here tonight. You went out of your way to provide her with the pager. You are looking after her son since she can't. That sounds like the actions of someone who cares very seriously about Clara and her children. Are you thinking of courting her?"

"Rebecca, stop trying to make this into something it's not. I'm glad that you and Samuel are happily married but not everyone is meant to wed. I'm working at the farm where Clara lives and that's it. I happened to be with her when Sophie fell in the water. I know the kind of trouble Clara is having so I'm trying to be a friend."

"There isn't anything wrong with showing someone how much you care or admitting how you feel."

He gave a dismissive wave with one hand. "This is the thanks I get for being responsible for once in my life? My family is ready to plan a wedding for me. Well, don't set the date because I won't be there."

"No one is planning a wedding for you. Samuel and I simply noticed you seem to be settling down and becoming more serious lately and we thought maybe Clara is the reason. Mark says you talk about her all the time."

Paul sighed. "If I don't seem as carefree as usual it's because I have troubles of my own and Mark is speaking out of turn. If I talk a lot about Clara it's because, through no fault of my own, I'm selling the property she believes is hers. How would you feel in my shoes? I wish the place did belong to her." He walked a few paces away and then came back. "I'd rather not talk about this now. How soon do you think we can see Sophie?"

"You should ask at the nursing desk. They will know."

Paul left Rebecca and went down to the nurses' station. Two nurses rushed past him and entered Sophie's room. He walked to the main desk and spoke to a woman with clouds and rainbows on her pink scrubs. "How is Sophie Fisher doing?"

"Are you a family member?"

"I'm not."

"I'm afraid I can only give information to her family. I'll have her mother come speak to you. There is a waiting room outside the doors. It could be a while."

"Don't bother Clara. I'll check back later." There was nothing he could do for her or Sophie now anyway.

He returned to Rebecca in the waiting area. "They won't give me any information. I'm not a family member. Tell Clara I decided to go on home. Will you be okay?"

"I'm fine. I will get word to you if anything changes. Jessica has agreed to be our messenger."

"Tell Jessica I appreciate her help." He left the building and found his driver, one of his fellow firemen, still waiting outside.

Later that night, as Paul lay in bed watching Toby sleeping across the room instead of sleeping himself, he kept replaying Rebecca's comments in his mind. Were others seeing something in his friendship with Clara that he didn't see himself? How did Clara feel about him?

He knew she couldn't stand him at first because he

was working for Ralph but that wasn't where things stood
between them now. For his part, he wanted to help her
and the kids. She deserved her uncle's farm. She didn't
want it for selfish reasons. She was trying to save her
daughter's life. His need to pay off his trailer, repay Mark
and improve his business paled in comparison to her goal.
He needed the money the commission would bring but
he would lose a lot less sleep over defaulting on his loan
than he would over selling the farm with Clara's big, blue
eyes watching his every move.

Early the following morning, he and Toby went down
to his uncle's office to call the hospital. The operator rang
him through to Sophie's room.

"Hello?"

The sound of Clara's voice dispelled the gloomy mood
he was in. "Clara, it's Paul. How are things?"

"Sophie is resting well and her fever is down. The antibiotics are doing their job and the blood exchange lowered her bilirubin level." There was relief in her voice
as well as an underlying weariness. Was she happy to
hear from him?

He wished he could see her face. "That's the best news
I could hear. How are you holding up?"

"Trying to sleep in this recliner is like trying to sleep
on a bed of rocks. They won't put a cot in here for me.
Some sort of hospital regulation in the ICUs. I'm more
grateful than you can know for Rebecca's company. I was
able to go out and get some rest on the sofa in the waiting room while she sat with Sophie."

It pleased him that his actions had eased her way even
a little. "I'm glad. Is there anything else I can do? Anything?"

"Sophie is worried about the cat. Can you check on Patches?"

"Sure. Toby and I'll be working at the farm most of the day. Tell Sophie not to worry, and tell her I miss her and…" He almost said "I've missed you" but stopped himself just in time.

"And?" she prompted.

"And I want her to get well quick," he added lamely. "Toby wants to say hello."

He handed the boy the phone and shoved his hands in his pockets while Toby chatted happily about his new friend, Hannah, the kittens and standing on a stepladder to brush Gracie's back. After a few minutes, Toby held out the phone to Paul. "Mamm wants to talk to you again."

Paul took the phone. "Toby's grinning from ear to ear. It did him a world of good to talk to you."

"You have no idea how much good it did me to hear his voice. Paul, I don't know how to thank you."

"I told you, peach or apple pie."

"You always find a way to make me smile."

"Then I'm doing my job. With all that is going on, don't forget to take care of Clara."

"I will try. I have to go, Paul, the doctor just came in. Goodbye."

"Goodbye," he said but the line was already dead.

He walked back up to the house with Toby skipping beside him. "What are we going to do today, Paul?"

"We're going back to your great uncle's farm."

"Are you still going to sell it?"

"I am."

Toby cast a sidelong glance at Paul. "I wish you wouldn't. It makes my *mamm* sad."

"Ah, Toby, I wish I wasn't the man Ralph hired for the job but I am. I must honor my commitment."

"Is it the right thing to do?"

Out of the mouths of babes. "I'm not sure, Toby. Sometimes it's hard to know what the right thing is. Why don't you fetch Frankly from his stall. I'll get him hitched to the buggy in a few minutes."

"I can harness him. I know how. Onkel Eli let me harness his horse."

Frankly was a docile fellow. He would be safe for the boy to work around. "Okay but be careful."

"I will." He took off at a run but before Paul could caution him again, he slowed to a walk.

Paul entered his uncle's house to find his aunt packing a basket with food. His cousin Timothy's wife, Lillian, was helping her. Anna glanced his way. "You look the worse for wear, Paul."

"I didn't sleep well."

"Worried about Clara Fisher?" Lillian asked in a lilting tone that suggested she already knew the answer.

"Is that so unusual?" He glared at the women in the room.

"Of course not," Anna said. "Lillian and I will relieve Rebecca and give Clara a chance to go home today if she wants. We are on our way to the hospital as soon as Jessica is free to drive us."

"Clara won't want to leave her daughter." Paul thought of the panic in her eyes when the pager had gone off.

"We will be there to keep her company and to provide whatever help she needs. It will be a wonderful opportunity for us to become acquainted."

"I appreciate you doing this."

The outside door opened and his cousin Luke Bowman came in with his wife, Emma. Behind Emma came her youngest brother, Alvin Swartzentruber. Luke and his wife ran a hardware store not far from Bowmans Crossing.

"We heard about the little Fisher girl," Emma said. "What can we do to help?"

Paul looked at them in astonishment. "How did you hear about it?"

Emma moved past him into the kitchen. "Janice Willard, the midwife, ran into Rebecca at the hospital last evening. Janice stopped at our hardware store to get some lamp oil on her way home and shared what she knew. Anna, what do you need me to do?"

Anna looked over her supplies. "I've made sandwiches for Isaac and the men but if I am not home by supper time, they will need something. They're not very good at fending for themselves."

Luke chuckled. "They are much better than you think. As long as you believe they can't fend for themselves, they don't have to, and you will rush home to cook for them."

Anna looked taken aback. "In that case, I may stay away for a week."

Luke's smile vanished as he realized the implications of that statement. "Please don't."

All the women laughed at his discomfort. Emma walked over and patted his cheek. "Never fear. I won't tell them it was your idea if she makes good on her threat."

Luke looked relieved. "Paul, are you going over to work on your farm-sale property?"

Paul nodded. "I have to do it. I like the idea less and less but I'm stuck. The man owns the farm even if I wish he didn't."

Alvin stepped forward with a cell phone in his hand. "Luke says I should help you today. Anna, I'm going to write down my number for you. That way you can call me and give us information without our having to stop work to run down and check the message machine at the phone shack."

Anna patted his face. "I do not approve of young people having their own phones. You know that but since you are not yet baptized I cannot forbid you to use it. In this case, I'm actually grateful that you are willing to share this with Paul. Please put it away before Isaac sees it. He has stronger feelings on the subject. Emma, could you run the gift shop while I'm gone today?"

"I can. Luke will manage alone at the hardware store."

"Paul, if you see Mark tell him I have the plate glass windows he wanted installed. We'll get them put in tomorrow."

Alvin kneeled and slipped the phone in his sock. He adjusted his pant leg and stood up. After writing down his number for the women, he followed Paul outside. Toby had Frankly tied to the corral fence and was nearly finished with the harness.

Paul walked around and inspected his work. "You did a fine job, Toby. *Danki.*"

Toby beamed with pride. Alvin finished harnessing the horse to the buggy and they were soon on their way.

An hour later, they turned into Eli's lane and stopped in front of the house. There was a car sitting beside the barn. It was empty. Paul scanned the area and saw a man in a white cowboy hat walking around the machinery that had been pulled out. It was Jeffrey Jones, the man who had offered to buy the farm from Ralph the day Paul met him.

Jones saw them. He flipped away his cigarette and walked toward them with an unhurried pace. "My dad used to use a corn planter just like the one out here. I knocked at the house but no one answered. Thought I'd look around a little while I waited."

"Waited for what?" Paul asked.

"Thought maybe I'd see if the owner has changed his mind about selling at auction. Will he be around soon?"

"I have no idea when he'll show up. He doesn't live here." Paul had an uneasy feeling about the man. He didn't look or act like a farmer so why was he so interested in buying this land? He turned to Toby. "Go open the corral gate for me."

The boy jumped out of the buggy and walked to the corral.

Jones pushed his hat up with one finger. "The young woman with the kids, she lives here, right?"

"She does."

"She is the old fellow's niece. I heard one of her kids is sick. I'm surprised the old man didn't leave her the farm. That would make more sense than giving it to a fellow who isn't Amish and who doesn't farm."

Paul didn't say anything. He nodded to Alvin. They both turned away and began unhitching the horse.

Jones chuckled. "I see you're going to give me the Amish silent treatment. I've had it before. I know when I've worn out my welcome. It's in my nature to ask questions. Sorry if I offended you." He tipped his hat and walked to his car.

After he drove away, Paul left Alvin and Toby to take care of the horse and crossed to the house. Like most Amish, Clara didn't lock her home. Paul stood in the kitchen doorway trying to remember how the room had looked the last time he was in it. A loaf of bread was still on the table. There were a few dishes in the sink. The room looked undisturbed. Patches was sunning herself on the back of the sofa.

Alvin peered over his shoulder. "What's wrong?"

"He was in the house."

"How do you know?"

He gestured toward the cat. "Sophie put the cat outside yesterday. She wanted to take Patches with her but Clara said no. Now the cat is over there by the window. She must have slipped in when he opened the door."

"That's creepy. Who is that guy?"

"I wish I knew. Where is Toby?"

"I put him to counting wrenches and arranging them by size."

"Okay. Let's finish the inventory of tools in the shed and then call it a day."

"Are you going back to the hospital?"

"I thought I might."

"To see the child or the child's mother?"

Paul scowled at Alvin. "What's that supposed to mean?"

"Nothing." The boy gave him an innocent grin.

Paul was eager to see Clara. She hadn't been far from his mind since he met her and that was starting to scare him.

He avoided serious relationships and with good reason. He had a hard time being serious about anything. He enjoyed being free to date whomever he wanted and whenever he wanted. He used to think being tied down to one woman was like having an auction without a loudspeaker. It was possible but it didn't make much sense.

He had five sisters at home, all younger than he was.

He and Mark had grown up in a house full of women. The squabbles and petty arguments had been almost more than Paul could bear. Sure they all loved each other but they seldom got along. What did they argue about the most? Boys.

When Mark wanted to serve an apprenticeship with Isaac for two years, Paul had jumped at the chance to go along. Not only did it get him away from the foolishness of his sisters but it also gave him a chance to start earning enough money to begin his career as an auctioneer.

He liked women, he just didn't like the idea of being stuck with the same one for the rest of his life. What if she turned out to be boring or a nag? He had watched his sisters act coy and shy until the fellow they hoped to impress was out of sight. He always thought some poor fool was in for a rude awakening after he married one of them.

Paul vividly remembered some of the loud and scary arguments his parents had before his father's death. After retreating from the house following one of them, his father had laid a hand on Paul's head and said, "Don't be in a hurry to marry, son. There is no telling who your wife will become once you say 'I do.' Divorce is forbidden to us. One miscalculation and a fellow could end up regretting his choice for a long, long time."

Paul had a self-imposed limit of three dates with any given girl. More than that and they would start talking about weddings and babies. It would be a few more years before he was ready to have that conversation, if ever. So why was he in a rush to spend time with a woman who already had children?

The more he thought about it, the more he realized he'd spent too much time with Clara already. They hadn't been dating but they had seen each other almost every day for almost a week. He had no real reason to go to the hospital to visit her. He could send Toby with someone else. Clara had the women in his family to keep her company and support her. She didn't need him. That was a good thing. Wasn't it? So why didn't it feel right?

Paul turned and walked toward the toolshed. "You get started in here. I'm going to check the fences and the condition of the fields."

"Can I come with you?" Toby asked.

Paul shook his head. "Stay here and do what Alvin tells you."

A long walk alone was exactly what he needed to clear his head and gain some perspective.

He followed the perimeter of Eli's farm to make sure the fences were intact and in good repair. He found one place that needed to be mended and made a note of its location. It wasn't until he was on the far side of the property in the pasture on a rocky hillside that he came across something odd.

A new chain-link fence had been installed recently. Based on the fragments of the old fencing down the hill, the new fence was inside the farm's property line by nearly three hundred yards. Had Eli sold some of it to the mine? If that was the case, the land had to be surveyed even though Ralph didn't want it done.

Paul noticed a pile of rocky rubble near the fence. A closer look proved it was a drill site, and a recent one. Someone had been test drilling on Eli's land. The spot was on the far side of a steep ridge at the very end of Eli's property. The area was pasture and not farmed. It wasn't visible from the house.

"Can I help you, mister?"

Paul turned to see a man in a hard hat approaching

from the mine buildings down below. He wore the uniform of a security guard for the New Ohio Mining Company.

"I'm not sure if you can help or not. I think this fence may be inside the property line of Eli King's farm."

"So what if it is?" The man stood with his arms akimbo, frowning at Paul.

"If it is, it will have to be taken down and moved back to the property line."

"Maybe you should speak to Mr. Calder. He's the boss."

"I'll be happy to. Shall I wait here?" Paul managed a pleasant smile.

"You'll need to call and make an appointment."

"Fine. Can you give me the number?"

"I'm not at liberty to give out personal information about the boss." The man turned and walked down the hill toward a cluster of buildings.

"I guess you're not at liberty to be friendly, either," Paul muttered.

He left the newly fenced area and followed Eli's old fence to the crest of the hill. A lone hickory tree marked the far corner. Paul caught the scent of cigarette smoke and stopped. There was no one about but there were several dozen cigarette butts littering the ground at the base of the tree. He picked one up.

Why would someone come out into the middle of nowhere to smoke? There was nothing here but a nice view of Eli's farmstead to the west and the mining company buildings to the east.

A feeling of unease made the hair at the back of Paul's neck prickle. Had someone been watching the farm? A gravel road ran along the other side of the fence. Paul assumed it wound around back through the hills to the mine but he wasn't sure. He'd never been on it.

Should he tell Clara about this? He didn't want to worry her. She had enough on her mind already. He didn't know for certain someone was watching the farm—they could as easily have been watching the mining company.

Most likely there was a simple and innocent reason someone had been waiting here. It wasn't unusual for a group of Amish teens on their *rumspringa* to meet at such an out-of-the-way place to smoke and enjoy music where their parents wouldn't see them. He decided not to mention it to Clara.

He finished walking the remaining fence lines and didn't find anything else out of order. When he reached the gate beside the barn, he saw a shiny black SUV turn into the drive and stop beside the house. A man in a gray suit got out and walked toward him.

"I'm Alan Calder. I understand you wish to see me. I own the coal mine you were snooping around today."

"I wasn't snooping and I didn't expect to see you so soon." Paul closed the gate behind him.

"I don't like to waste time. What can I do for you?"

"I think the fence you put up between your property and this one isn't on the property line."

"We didn't put up that fence."

"You didn't?"

"Eli King had the fence installed."

Taken aback, Paul wasn't sure he'd heard that correctly. "It would be unusual for an Amish farmer to install a chain-link fence across his pasture, not to mention expensive."

"I have no idea what is usual for an Amish farmer. I

understand this land is for sale. I'm willing to make a reasonable offer."

"It's going to be sold at a public auction. You are welcome to bid alongside anyone else who is interested."

"I doubt the new owner will get much for it. The place is a pile of rocks and weedy fields fit for goats and not much else."

Paul tipped his head slightly. That was the exact phrase Ralph had used when he first described the property. "Do you know the new owner, Ralph Hobson?"

Alan Calder frowned and crossed his arms over his chest. "Never met the man. Why?"

"Just wondering." Something wasn't right. There was no reason for the mine owner to rush over and speak to him. The man's demeanor seemed wrong. He looked ill at ease.

"Tell this Hobson fellow that I'm willing to make him a generous offer for the farm today as long as the sale includes the mineral right."

"I can give you his contact information."

"What is it?"

Calder immediately dialed the number Paul gave him and walked away speaking on his cell phone. The conversation quickly became heated by the sound of Calder's raised voice but Paul was unable to hear what was actually said. After a short time, the man returned to his car and sped away.

"Who was that?" Clara came out of the house and down the steps.

Had the sun come out from under the cloud? There wasn't any other explanation for why Paul's day suddenly seemed so much brighter. "What are you doing here?"

She grinned and tipped her head to the side. "Paul, I live here."

"I mean why aren't you at the hospital?" He tried to ignore the rush of happiness that filled his chest.

"Sophie is doing better and I needed to come home and get some things done. I've been wearing the same dress since we took Sophie to the hospital. It was starting to smell like old pond water. It was time for a change. Jessica drove me. She promised someone will be here at seven to take me back."

"That's great. How are you?" She looked fine to him. Better than fine. She looked wonderful.

He studied her lovely face. A light blush colored her cheeks, her eyes had dark circles under them but they sparkled now as she gazed at him. A soft smile curved her lips. She was happy to see him.

Rebecca's comment came back to him. Clara wasn't his type, so why was he so delighted to see her? He'd never felt this way around any other woman.

Suddenly uncomfortable, he hooked his thumbs under his suspenders. "I made a check of all the fences."

"Were there any problems?"

"What do you know about the mining company on the east side of this farm?"

"Not much. They wanted to buy or lease the mineral rights from Eli but he wasn't interested in selling. It seems they own the mineral rights under most of the land around here. People sold them ages ago. Dan Kauffman didn't know his grandfather had sold the rights in 1929 until underground blasting woke him up one night and he tried to get it stopped."

"Did Eli give someone permission to test drill out in the pasture?"

"Not that I know of. Why?"

"Because it looks like a test site has already been dug. That was the mine owner who just left. He wants to make Ralph an offer for the farm as long as it contains the mineral rights."

"One more thing he is taking from my children."

One more thing I'm helping Ralph Hobson take from them.

Paul pressed his lips together tightly. He wanted to beg Clara's forgiveness and promise he'd break his contract with Hobson. It might make her look more kindly on him but it wouldn't solve her troubles and it would only add to his. He had his brother to think about, as well. Mark and Helen couldn't open their business until Paul repaid them. Even knowing all that, Paul was ready to seek out Hobson and end their bargain.

His feelings for Clara were getting out of hand. He needed to put some distance between them.

The door of the house opened and Toby came out. "Mamm, can I stay with Paul again tonight?"

"I reckon that's up to Paul."

He rocked back on his heels and pasted a big grin on his face. "Sure. I'm glad to hear Sophie is doing better. I'd love to stay and visit but I've got work to do." The words came out sounding more abrupt than he intended.

A look of disappointment flashed across her face but it was gone before he could be sure. Her smile slipped a little. "Don't let me keep you."

She turned around and went in the house ushering Toby in front of her.

The letdown was massive. Paul didn't want to hurt her feelings. He didn't want her to be disappointed in him.

He wanted to see her smiling again. At him. He took a step toward the house and stopped.

No, it was best to leave it this way. If she was unhappy with him, so much the better. That way she wouldn't harbor unrealistic romantic expectations.

Who was he kidding? Why would Clara harbor any romantic feelings about him? He was the joking auctioneer who was getting ready to sell the roof over her head. They barely knew each other. He should keep things professional and get things done as soon as possible. The less he saw of her, the less likely he was to open his mouth and say something stupid.

He found Alvin finishing up in the toolshed and said, "The barn is next. Let's go."

"I thought we were quitting early?" Alvin hurried to keep up with him.

"I have to get finished here before I make a fool of myself."

Chapter Seven

Paul was already hard at work in his uncle's shop when Mark came in the next morning. Paul continued sanding the top of a dresser while he waited for his brother to say something but all Mark did was raise one eyebrow and then get to work himself.

After about ten minutes, Paul couldn't take the silence any longer. "Aren't you going to ask me what I'm doing here so early?"

"It looks to me like you're working. That's what you get paid to do, right?"

"Right." He blew the sawdust off the piece he was working on and ran his fingers over it to test the smoothness. It would pass even his uncle's stringent quality requirements. "I'll go bring in some more particleboard and finish putting the backs on these dressers."

"Where is your little shadow?"

"Onkel Isaac took Toby and Hannah fishing this morning. I don't know which one of them was more excited."

"I'm going to say Isaac. When was the last time you knew him to take a day off?"

"Never. How is the bakery coming along?"

"Helen and I are moving into the upstairs tomorrow. We are still trying to convince Charlotte to come with us. She's decided Juliet doesn't want to move. I love the woman but she can be a trial. We are still waiting on the ovens before we set a date for the grand opening. Any idea when you can repay me? I hate to ask but I need to pay for the new picture windows that were installed and order baking supplies soon."

Sighing deeply, Paul faced his brother. "I'm sorry I'm holding you up. It was foolish of me to spend so much money on a fancy wagon that should have waited until I was actually making money at auctions. I let my wishful thinking override my common sense, if I ever had any common sense."

"Have you finished getting Eli King's farm ready to sell?"

Paul started sanding again. "I have a few things left to take care of."

"Such as?"

Paul threw down his sanding block. "Why is everyone so curious about Clara Fisher and me?"

Mark stopped work on the piece he was carving. "I didn't ask about Clara Fisher. What makes you so touchy on the subject?"

Running his hands through his hair, Paul struggled to find an answer. "I don't know. I can't get her out of my mind."

Mark crossed his arms and leaned against the corner of the unfinished desk behind him. "What makes you think you have to get her out of your mind?"

"I feel like I can't think straight. What's wrong with me?"

"Offhand, I would say you are smitten with the woman."

"I can't be."

Mark shook his head. "You're going to have to explain that one to me."

"She's not anything like the girls I go out with."

"Okay, right there is your difference."

Paul frowned at his brother. "What do you mean?"

"Clara Fisher isn't a girl. She's a woman. She's been married and widowed. She has children and one of them may die from a disease inherited from her mother. She might have been a girl at one time but she has been forged in the fire of life since then."

Paul thought of all Clara had been through and wondered how she could still face life with such a stalwart attitude. "Rebecca said Clara needs a strong and steady man as a helpmate, not another boy."

"Rebecca is probably right about that. She was widowed at a young age, too. She and Clara have a lot in common. Rebecca found love again and maybe Clara will, too. Paul, have you considered that you are looking at your feelings the wrong way?"

"How do you mean?"

"Instead of wondering if you are the right fellow or the wrong fellow or even if you should think about her as a potential mate, why don't you just be her friend."

"A friend?"

"Maybe she doesn't want a strong and steady help-mate to replace the man she loved. Maybe she just needs a friend to lean on until things improve. Stop trying to make sense of your emotions. Stop making this about you. Instead, concentrate on helping Clara through this rough time. If she is meant to find a new husband, the Lord will provide that man for her when the time is right. Until then, I think she could use your help without worrying if there are strings attached."

"But Rebecca said—"

Mark cut him off. "Rebecca is a wonderful person but she does have a tendency to meddle in other people's business. Don't let what she thinks influence you."

Paul considered his brother's words. "You're right. I don't have to make a decision about the rest of my life. I just have to help Clara when I can."

"That's right. I've known you to give a helping hand to a lot of folks. You're not as frivolous as you like people to believe."

"I appreciate you listening to me." Paul picked up the sanding block he had tossed aside and handed it to Mark, then headed for the door.

"Where are you going?" Mark called after him.

"To finish my work at the King farm before Sophie comes home. Clara doesn't need to see me counting each hammer and nail that should have been hers. Toby says it makes her sad, and that's the last thing I want to do."

Sophie improved slowly but steadily. Three days after her seizure, she was moved to a regular room on the pediatric floor. Clara was given a cot so that she could be with her daughter around the clock. It was a huge improvement over the uncomfortable recliner she'd been trying to sleep in.

On the morning of the fourth day, Clara woke to the sound of Sophie giggling. Clara lay still savoring the wonderful sound and giving thanks to God.

"Shh, we don't want to wake your *mamm*," a woman whispered.

Clara sat up and saw an older Amish woman standing next to Sophie's bed. The two of them had on hand puppets. Sophie's puppet was a raccoon. The woman held a long-eared dog puppet.

Sophie giggled again. "I'm quiet."

"It's too late—I'm awake." Clara sat up and stretched.

"It's about time," the woman said. "Juliet and Clyde are hungry for some breakfast. Clyde is so hungry he is going to eat Sophie's nose. Woof, woof, woof." The dog puppet scaled Sophie's arm, tweaked her nose then raced down her arm again.

The woman clapped her free hand to her cheek. "Oh, dear, what will you do without a nose, Sophie? You will never smell pancakes and bacon again."

Sophie tentatively touched her face. "My nose isn't gone, Charlotte. It's right here. Mamm, see my puppets? Charlotte brought them for me to play with."

"I hope you have thanked Charlotte." Clara folded her blanket and tidied the cot.

"No thanks are necessary, dear. I am Charlotte Zook. My niece, Helen, is married to Paul's brother, Mark. He was Clyde's choice and a good one."

Charlotte held up the dog puppet. "This is Clyde. Of course, it's not the real Clyde but it does look something like him. However, my Clyde is much more beautiful and so very smart. This is the only dog puppet I could find with the long ears. Isn't that sad? I must write a letter to the manufacturer and insist they add a basset hound. I wanted to bring Clyde—the real Clyde, not the puppet— but I couldn't think of a way to get him into the hospital without being seen. They have the most ridiculous ideas about dogs not being clean enough to visit sick people. Why, they let people into animal hospitals all the time. Where is the sense in that?"

"I don't know." Clara had no idea where the conversation was going.

"Juliet would be much easier to smuggle in but I knew she didn't want to spend the day away from Clyde. They get very unhappy if they are apart. Clyde has been known to howl all night long when she is gone. Have you heard about the time Juliet went missing and then Mark married Helen and Juliet returned with her new family so Clyde didn't have to howl under Mark's window anymore?"

Clara stared at the odd little woman wondering if she was quite all right. "I have not heard the story."

"I must tell you all about it from the beginning."

"Not now, Aenti Charlotte," a young Amish woman said as she came in the door with a fast-food paper bag in one hand and a tray of coffees in the other. "I hope you like sausage biscuits, Clara. I'm Helen Bowman and you have met my aunt."

"Oh, I love sausage biscuits," Charlotte said. "Not as much as your croissants, of course. My niece is an excellent baker. She and Mark are starting their own bakery at Bowmans Crossing. I'm positive it will be a success. The smell alone will be wonderful in the mornings. I do miss those yummy aromas now that you and Mark have moved into your new home above the shop."

"I thought you were going to move in with us soon. We talked about it, remember?" Helen set the food and coffee on the bedside table.

"Juliet has made up her mind. She wants to live near the woods on our side of the river. I rather like the blue lights Sophie uses, don't you? They are very pretty. I understand you have to move out of your home, Clara. I have a tidy place two miles from Bowmans Crossing on the far side of the river. You are welcome to move in with me as long as you like dogs and raccoons. I think we will get along wonderfully well, don't you?"

Clara wasn't sure what to make of the woman's offer. "I'll have to think about it."

Until now, Clara had refused to contemplate moving

out of Eli's house but she was being stubborn and foolish. She had to have a plan.

"Does Clyde like cats?" Sophie asked. "I have a cat named Patches. I miss her a lot."

"Clyde loves cats and so does Juliet. How does Patches feel about raccoons?"

Sophie shrugged. "I don't know."

One of the nurse's aides came in carrying a tray. "Good morning, Sophie. I hope you're hungry this morning."

Clara translated. Sophie shook her head. *"Nee."*

The aide sighed heavily. "I guess I'll leave it here. Perhaps she will feel like eating later."

Clara crossed to stand by Sophie and pushed the bank of blue lights aside. "Is there anything that sounds good?"

"Dog food with a side order of raccoon food, please." Charlotte winked at the young woman and waved the puppet's paw.

The aide chuckled. "I'll speak to the kitchen right away."

"Sit down, Clara, and eat your breakfast. The *kaffi* smells *goot,*" Charlotte said. "Helen and I are here to look after you today. Although I must say you look perfectly capable of looking after yourself. I'm not sure why Paul is so worried about you."

Clara began to straighten her daughter's bed. "Paul is worried about me? I think you mean he is worried about Sophie."

"Nee, he particularly said Clara Fisher has a heavy burden to bear and we must help her carry it. That's not at all like Paul. He has never asked me to help him carry anything before."

Helen cleared her throat. "Aenti, you should eat your breakfast."

"Not until after we feed Clyde and Juliet. They love eggs."

Charlotte handed a spoon to Sophie and then positioned the dog puppet in front of her face. "It's your turn to feed Clyde, Sophie."

Sophie put a small amount of egg on the spoon and held it toward the dog. Charlotte moved the puppet aside, ate the offered egg off the spoon and then whipped the puppet back in front of her face. "Yum. Yum. Yum. This is *wunderbar,*" she said in a deep voice. The puppet rubbed his tummy.

"My turn." Charlotte picked up a fork.

Sophie giggled and held the raccoon in front of her face. Charlotte offered a bite of egg to the puppet. Sophie moved Juliet aside and ate the egg then made the puppet nod. "This is fine food for a raccoon," she declared in a high voice.

Clara, amazed at Charlotte's successful strategy, took a seat beside Helen on the cot. She ate her biscuit and sipped her coffee as Sophie and Charlotte continued the game until all the scrambled eggs and half the oatmeal was gone.

Clara looked at Helen. "Your aunt is quite remarkable."

"You have no idea. Wait until you meet the real Clyde and Juliet."

"Did Paul actually say he wanted to help carry my burdens?" She tried to sound indifferent.

"I'm not sure those were his exact words, were they, Charlotte?"

Charlotte used the puppet's paw to tap her temple. "Perhaps not his exact words but you know I often hear what people mean instead of what they say."

Helen nodded slowly. "I thought that might be the

case. Paul is concerned about you and about Sophie. He has had Toby helping him at the farm almost every day. The two of them are becoming inseparable."

A warm glow settled in Clara's chest. She tried to convince herself it was because she was thankful for the wonderful new friends she was making among Paul's family but she finally had to admit the truth. It was because Paul cared.

Clara leaned closer to Helen. "Was Charlotte serious when she offered to let us live with her?"

"This is the first I have heard of it but I think she is. Would you consider it?"

"Only as a last resort. I don't want to give up on Eli's farm."

The long days and nights at the hospital continued as Sophie gradually improved. Her biggest complaint was not getting to see Patches. She was convinced the cat was sad and crying for her. The time would have been unbearable without the cheerfulness of Anna, Charlotte's nonsense, Helen's kindness and the steady good sense of Rebecca and Lillian. Twice Anna brought Toby for a visit. He regaled her with stories of his time with the Bowman family. Paul let him help at the farm. Isaac took him fishing with his new friend Hannah, who could throw a ball as good as any boy. Paul let him harness Frankly and take care of Gracie.

Clara was happy Toby was enjoying himself but she wondered if her boy wasn't headed for a heartbreak. After Sophie was dismissed and the farm sale was over, Paul wouldn't have a reason to see the boy. Or to see her again. She didn't dare examine why the thought brought her to the verge of tears.

Clara enjoyed meeting everyone from the Bowman

family but as the days wore on, the warm glow in her chest faded. She was left to wonder why Paul hadn't been back to visit.

Perhaps it was silly to want to see him but she couldn't help herself. She missed his cheerfulness and his teasing ways. It would be nice if she and Paul could resume their friendship once she was home again.

It was just friendship they shared. Clara refused to admit her feelings were stronger than that. She had known the man for less than two weeks. Any dependency that she felt was only because of the unusual circumstances they were both in.

It made a convincing argument, so why wasn't she convinced?

Perhaps Paul was seeing someone. Someone younger and without children. Without a complicated life. It was hard to imagine that an attractive and charming fellow like Paul didn't have a girlfriend. Who was she? What was she like? Was she pretty?

Clara shook her head at her own foolishness. It was none of her business if Paul had someone special in his life or not. The best thing she could do was stop thinking about him.

On Friday morning, eight days after Sophie's seizure, Clara received word that her child was being discharged. As much as she wanted to take her girl home, Clara was worried that Sophie's bilirubin level would rise. She could try to keep her child under the lights longer at home but she knew she would have a fight on her hands once Sophie started to feel better.

There was a knock at the door and a young woman in street clothes came in. She was dressed in a modern style, in a simple gray skirt and a white blouse with a touch of gray lace at her throat. Her blond hair was cut short and danced in springy curls around her face. "Good morning. I'm Debra Merrick, one of the public health nurses in this county. I was asked to stop in and visit with you about meeting Sophie's needs at home. I understand your daughter uses home phototherapy."

"She does."

Debra approached Sophie's bed and introduced herself in halting *Deitsch*. She looked over her shoulder at Clara. "That's almost the extent of my entire Amish vocabulary."

"That's not bad."

"I work with many Amish families in the Bowmans Crossing area. One thing I do fairly often is help Janice Willard, the local midwife, to get blue lights into homes for infants with jaundice. Amish homes without electricity present a unique challenge."

"I have a generator that runs through the night."

"That's good to know. I have not worked with a child Sophie's age. How does she do with her lights? Does she turn them off or get out of bed to avoid them?"

"Not often but I know she'll resent having to spend time under them at home when she feels like playing outside."

"Since I began working with Amish mothers, I have developed a particular interest in alternative treatments. There is some new research out on this topic. One study in particular caught my interest. It was done in Nigeria, where many people have little or no access to electricity. The study found that jaundiced babies who were placed in filtered sunlight did as well or better than babies under traditional blue lights."

"What do you mean by filtered sunlight?"

"A tent was constructed of a special clear plastic film that blocks the harmful rays of the sun and allows the blue light to come in. The babies didn't get overheated or sunburned."

"You think Sophie would benefit from this filtered light?"

"I do. As far as I know, studies haven't been done on children her age but I think it is worth a try. Is it something you would like me to look in to?"

"What does the doctor say?"

"Truthfully, he scowled and said he didn't know he was working in a third-world country. He hasn't been out of school very long. He'll learn that sometimes new ways aren't always better. The good thing is that sunlight doesn't require a doctor's prescription."

"How do we get this special film and how much will it cost?"

"I'm not sure. Do you want me to find out?"

"Would this replace her blue lights at night? What about in the winter?"

"It won't replace the blue lights but if it helps keep her levels lower longer, she might not have to spend as much time under the lights at night. We want to reduce the chance of brain damage until she can have a liver transplant."

"So we are only stalling for more time."

"That's one way to look at it. A transplant is still Sophie's only hope of a cure but we want to keep her brain healthy until that happens."

How long before Sophie suffered a bad cold or the flu or had another accident that would lead to her death? How long could she keep her beautiful baby girl before she had to return her to God?

Sophie's illness was God's will, and Clara accepted that. Determination was His gift to Clara. She used it to see that Sophie lived every day that He allowed. "Find out how we can make a special tent."

"Okay. I will be visiting Sophie at home once a week to see how things are going. I will also draw her blood for the lab studies if you agree to have a visiting nurse."

"I do and *danki*."

"When would be the best time for me to visit you next week?"

"Monday before noon, I think."

"That sounds great. It will take at least an hour to get her paperwork done before she is discharged so don't be in a rush."

"We've waited this long. We can wait a little more."

"Do you have a ride home?"

"I will need someone to drive us."

"The hospital has a list of people who volunteer to drive Amish patients. I'll have the nurse make arrangements."

After Debra left, Clara tried to keep Sophie entertained but she quickly grew bored. "Mamm, can I have a Popsicle? My throat hurts." It was her most frequent excuse for needing one. It was amazing how many sore throats had been cured by a single strawberry Popsicle.

"I will check in the kitchen to see if they have them. If not, will some orange sherbet make your throat feel better?"

"*Ja*, it will."

Clara walked down to the small kitchen on the pediatric floor and checked for Popsicles but didn't find any. She took a container of orange sherbet out of the freezer instead. When she walked out into the hallway she came face-to-face with the man she had decided not to think about again. "Paul."

* * *

"Hey. Hi." Being taken aback by Clara's sudden appearance before he was sure of what he wanted to say to her left Paul tongue-tied.

Clara seem to be suffering from the same malady. She looked down at her hands. "Hello."

Her voice broke the logjam in his brain. *Keep it light. Make it friendly.* "Did I catch you sneaking to the kitchen for a snack?"

He was rewarded with a fleeting smile. "Sophie has become addicted to the orange sherbet."

"I can't say I blame her. I like the stuff myself. How is she?"

"She's getting crabby. I think it's time we went home."

"Samuel mentioned that Sophie might be released soon."

"And how did Samuel know this?"

"I would say the Amish telegraph but half the participants in the chain aren't Amish."

She tipped her head to the side "Explain."

He smiled, amazed at how happy he was to be with her again. How had he managed to stay away this long? "Your doctor told Debra, Debra told Janice, Janice told Rebecca, who told Samuel and Samuel told me."

"I'm surprised you didn't mention Clyde in there somewhere."

"I try to avoid that dog."

"I don't know the dog but his mistress is a very unusual woman."

"That's one way of putting it. Charlotte is unique."

"Sophie adores her. She invited us to move in with her. Was that your doing?"

"It was not. I thought she was going to sell her house and move in with Mark and Helen."

"Apparently, the raccoon doesn't want to move."

"She did mention that when I saw her last. Charlotte, not the raccoon. What do you think of the idea?"

"I will have to go somewhere if I can't find Eli's trust document but I haven't given up."

"I didn't imagine you would. Have you had any word from Opal Kauffman about Dan's condition?"

"He's here in the rehabilitation unit. I don't know more than that."

"Are you ready to go? I have a very excited boy waiting in the car with Jessica."

"Why did you leave him in the car?"

"Because of the surprise for Sophie. Can we go now?"

"You take this sherbet to Sophie and I'll check with the nurses."

Paul took the cup and peeked around the door into Sophie's room. She was sitting on the couch with puppets on both hands. A dog and a raccoon. If he had to guess, he would say that meant Charlotte had been in to visit.

For the first time, he noticed a yellow tint to the whites of her eyes. Would it go away or did it mean her condition was getting worse? The thought that she might die soon hit him like a felled tree. He blinked back tears, determined to present a cheerful face.

"Does someone in here want orange sherbet?"

Chapter Eight

"**P**aul!" Sophie's face lit up with a bright smile. "Come see my friends." She made the animals wag their paws at him.

He swallowed hard and walked over to her. "Clyde and Juliet are old friends of mine. Which one of them is going to eat this treat?"

She laid them aside. "Me."

He sat down on the sofa beside her. To his surprise, she climbed in his lap and cupped his cheek with her hand. "I've been missing you."

His heart swelled with emotion. "I've been missing you, too. Are you feeling better?"

She nodded. "I had a seezmure."

Paul looked up to see Clara watching them from the doorway. "She means a seizure," Clara explained as she sat on the arm of the sofa.

Sophie nodded solemnly. "I didn't like it."

He pulled her close in a tender hug. "I'm sorry you had a seizure, little one. That must have been very scary."

"Mamm was crying and I got scared of all the people

staring at me. I thought it would happen again. Will it happen again?"

"I don't know. I pray it won't."

"Want a bite of my sherbet?" She offered him a spoonful.

"You finish it. You're going home today. Toby is waiting downstairs."

"I'm going to ride in a car?" Her eyes widened with glee. "Can we go really fast?"

"As fast as the law allows," Clara said. "Eat up, the nurse will be here soon to take us down to the car."

When the nurse came in, Sophie happily hopped into the wheelchair for the ride down to the car. Clara and Paul walked behind her. Several nurses waved goodbye as she passed the main desk. Paul hung back while they got her wheelchair into the crowded elevator. "I'll catch the next one," he said as the doors closed.

A nurse walking past stopped. "Was that Sophie going home?"

He smiled. "It was."

The woman patted his arm. "Your daughter is a special little girl. We are all praying for her."

Rather than explain that he had no claim to the child, he simply nodded and got on the next elevator that stopped.

Sophie and Clara were already out the front door when Paul arrived in the main lobby. He watched Toby get out of the car and run to hug his mother. "I missed you."

Paul had a moment to wish her smile for him had been as radiant as the smile she bestowed on her child. The thought was quickly followed by a hearty mental shake. There was no comparison between a mother's love for her children and her feelings for a friend.

* * *

Thrilled to have both children with her again, Clara hugged them until Toby complained that she was crushing him. When he and Sophie were settled in the back seat between Clara and Paul, Jessica turned around after lifting Patches out of a pet carrier on the front seat. "I think someone has been missing Sophie."

"Patches!" Sophie took the cat and cuddled her close. "I missed you so much."

Clara smiled at Jessica. "Thank you. She has been worried sick about her pet."

"Don't thank me. It was Paul's idea."

Clara turned to Paul. "It was a wonderful idea."

"Solid evidence that I'm smarter than I look," he said with a grin.

"I have to agree."

Clara caught sight of Opal Kauffman coming toward the hospital's front doors. She motioned to Paul and they both got out to greet the older woman.

"Opal, how is your father?" Clara asked.

Opal looked tired but happy. "He is doing amazingly well. His stubborn streak is finally paying off."

"I'm so glad to hear that."

"Do you think it would be possible for us to speak to him?" Paul asked.

Opal shook her head. "He isn't able to speak and he tires very easily. The rehabilitation staff are working with him, trying to teach him to write again. They are having some success. I have asked him several times about Eli but I'm afraid I couldn't get him to understand what I was asking. I'm hoping in time he will recover enough to communicate with you but I'm just so thankful that he has made it this far."

Clara hid her disappointment. "We must give thanks for every little blessing. Do let me know when he is able to answer my questions."

Opal smiled. "I will and I have convinced Mother to have a decorative fence put around the koi pond so what happened to Sophie can't happen to another child. Do you have a date for the farm sale yet?"

"If a date has been set, I haven't heard." Clara glanced at Paul.

"It will be four weeks from tomorrow."

Clara prayed that Dan recovered enough to tell her where the trust documents were before that fateful day arrived. What if she discovered them later? Did she have a right to the farm even after it had been sold? Maybe Paul knew the answer.

He decided to ride up front with Jessica so Clara wasn't able to ask him about it on the way home. As helpful as Jessica had been, she wasn't Amish and Clara was loath to discuss her personal business in front of an outsider.

When they reached Eli's home, Paul sent Jessica home and said he would find his own way when he was ready to leave. Clara quickly dismissed the surprising surge of joy his words brought as a combination of her own weariness and her happiness at having Sophie home. It didn't take long to get Sophie settled into bed for a nap with her lights on in spite of her resistance to being under them. Paul was able to coax her into taking a nap by promising a ride on Gracie when he came to work on Monday.

Back in the kitchen, Clara sighed as she sat down at the table. "It's good to be home. At least for a while. Would you like some coffee?" She started to rise again but he stopped her.

"You sit. That's an order. I'll make coffee."

"I can follow orders. I'm sitting. See me sitting?"

"I see you're about to fall asleep."

"I'm fine. Really."

"I'm going to scatter some pillows around your chair anyway."

She chuckled. "In case I pass out and fall out of my chair? That's not a bad idea."

Closing her eyes, she put her head back and listened to the sounds of Paul moving around her kitchen. It was a homey, comfortable sound. Like he somehow belonged in her home.

"Cream or sugar?"

"Just black, *danki*."

She rested until the aroma of fresh-brewed coffee grew stronger and she realized he was waving a cup of it under her nose. "I'm awake, I'm awake."

"Not so as anyone would notice."

She took the cup in her hands and savored her first sip. "Mmm, you make good coffee."

"Glad you like it."

"What do you have left to do here?" She wanted to know how much longer she could count on his company.

"Not much outside until right before the sale. Everything needs to be tagged and set up for people to view. I have an awning, tents and tables for that. I'll need to get auction announcements into the papers and farm journals as soon as I can. Four weeks isn't much notice for the general public. Most of what still needs cataloging is in here."

"And you can't do that while the kids and I are living in the house."

"Something like that. I'm sorry. This isn't something we have to talk about today. Get some rest. I'm going."

"Don't go." She didn't want him to leave. Tired as she was, she wanted to share these quiet moments with him but she didn't know how to explain it.

"Okay." He seemed to understand. He sat down across from her and sipped his coffee. For several long and soothing minutes, Clara relaxed and let the tension of the last weeks fade from her muscles.

When he rose to carry his empty cup to the sink, Clara decided to ask about the property. "What happens if the house and farm are sold and then I find the real trust papers?"

He shrugged, then folded his arms over his chest and leaned against the counter by the sink. "Honestly, I don't know but Isaac has an estate lawyer who should be able to answer that. I'll check with him."

"You've done so much for me already."

"That's not the way I see it." He stared at the floor for a short time and then looked up. "Is Sophie going to get over this illness, or has it caused damage that won't improve?"

"You mean to her brain?" Clara wanted to reassure him but she couldn't.

"I guess."

"I don't know. I assume she is going to get better until I see signs that show me she isn't."

"What signs?"

"Does she stay irritable? Does she have trouble re-membering her numbers or how to button her coat? Those are the kinds of things I watch for."

"How do you do it? How do you live with this uncer-tainty and not fall apart?"

"I do fall apart. I try to do it behind closed doors with the windows shut, that's all."

"I'm serious."

"And I am being flippant. How is that for a role reversal? Do you use your teasing remarks and jokes to keep from answering serious questions?"

"You mean like you are doing now?"

She sighed. "I reckon I do. I don't fall apart because my children need me. I must be the one thing in their world that doesn't change. God is my rock and I am the rock of my family."

"I admire you tremendously."

"*Danki*, Paul. That means a lot to me."

"I'm glad. I'll be back on Monday. You know how to contact me if you need anything." She nodded, and he walked out the door.

On Sunday morning, Sophie felt well enough to go to church. Clara thought she was eager to tell the tale of her fall in the pool and her stay at the hospital to her friends. Clara drove the horse and buggy Paul had loaned her to Leonard Miller's farmhouse and arrived twenty minutes before the church service was due to start. Paul's thoughtfulness was one reason she had a hard time putting him out of her mind. Once the farm sale was over, it was doubtful she'd see him again. She would do well to remember that whenever she started looking forward to his arrival tomorrow. At least she knew she wasn't going to see him today. It was a relief knowing she didn't have to guard her emotions for a few hours.

As she turned her buggy over to the young men parking them and stabling the horses, she knew there would be plenty of questions to answer from those who hadn't seen her in weeks. She was greeted warmly by the women of the congregation in the kitchen when she carried in her basket of bread, jars of church spread and two fresh-baked apple pies. Although the congregation had not yet voted to accept her as a member, she had been treated with kindness by everyone from the first day she arrived.

Sophie clung to her side but Toby had already taken off to play with some of his friends outside.

"We hadn't heard that Sophie was out of the hospital." Velda, the bishop's wife, was slicing the pies at the counter. She put down her knife and came to kiss Clara on the cheek. "How is she and how are you?"

"We are both doing well."

Velda pressed her hands together. "God be praised. I know this is the news we were all hoping to hear. Paul Bowman notified us about the accident. Gerald has already contacted the Amish Hospital Aid treasurer. Are you able to pay the first twenty percent of the bill? If you can't, we will raise the money for you with a special alms collection."

"*Danki*, I will need help. I know I have the prayers of you and many more people to thank for Sophie's recovery. Perhaps Eli put in a good word for us, too."

"I am sorry for your loss," Velda said. "Eli was a dear friend to my husband. Many times Gerald sought Eli's counsel when he was troubled and he always came away feeling at peace. Eli is with God now and we must draw comfort from that."

"I haven't asked but was anyone with him when he died?" She hated to think he had been alone in his final hours.

"Gerald and two of our sons went to check on him when he didn't come to the worship service that morning. They found him in bed. He was weak and couldn't stand. He didn't wish to go to the hospital so they stayed with him until he passed away quietly at about six o'clock in the evening."

"I'm so glad that he wasn't alone."

"I know you wished to be with him. He was grateful for all you did these past months. Was there anything missing when you arrived home?"

"Missing? Why do you ask?"

Velda's eyes filled with sadness. "The house was a mess when we returned from the burial. A few of us came back to straighten up before you got home. It looked as if someone had gone through the place looking for valuables. It is a sad testament to our times when a funeral published in the newspaper is an invitation for someone to ransack a house. I know it happens other places but this was the first time it has happened to someone in our church."

So Eli had been right to move his valuables. "Do you know if Eli visited with the bishop while I was gone?"

"Gerald and our daughter took supper to him the Sunday before he died. They stayed and visited for a while. Why?"

Clara heard footsteps on the stairs and turned to see the bishop and two preachers coming down. The men normally met about thirty minutes before the service began and decided on the theme of their preaching for that day. None of them used notes. They preached as the spirit moved them, taking turns during the three-hour service. Their return from the meeting signaled the start of the preaching. Clara whispered, "I will tell you why it's important after church."

Like many Amish homes, the Miller house had walls on the lower level that could be moved back to make one large room for the preaching service. Amish prayer meetings were held in the homes of church members every other week. Backless wooden benches brought to the house in a special wagon were arranged in rows with the men sitting on one side of the room and the women sitting on the other. Some of the most elderly members were allowed to sit in cushioned chairs at the perimeter of the room. It wasn't unusual to see them nodding off. The youngest children sat with their mothers, who often had two or more under the age of three to keep quiet.

Clara took her place near the front among the married women with Sophie beside her. Toby was old enough to sit with the men. Before Eli's passing, Toby sat with him. Today, he and one of his friends sat near the back of the room with the unmarried boys. She hoped that he would behave but she wasn't above leaving her place to take him outside and admonish him if he was being inattentive. She had a moment of worry that Toby would find it difficult growing up without a man in his life but she gave over that worry to God and lifted her voice in song when the first hymn began.

Three and a half hours later, the final notes of the last hymn died away. The bishop addressed the congregation. "As many of you know, our little sister Sophie Fisher was in the hospital with pneumonia for more than a week. We give thanks to *Gott* that she is making a recovery. Her mother, our sister Clara Fisher, is a widow and dependent on us to help her with the burdensome cost of Sophie's hospital care. I ask that you give generously. Our deacons will now pass around baskets."

When the collection was finished, the congregation filed out of the house. The young boys and girls darted outside as fast as they could to start a game of volleyball. The men rearranged the backless benches into tables for the noon meal. The limited seating meant the congregation ate in shifts, starting with elders and ministers. The unmarried boys had to wait until the married men and married women had taken their turns. The unmarried girls were the last to eat.

Clara waited impatiently until the bishop finished eating. Before she could approach him, he began what turned out to be a lengthy conversation with one of the church members, who had a grievance against another member. When the bishop was finally free, Clara quickly moved to his side. "May I speak to you for a few minutes?"

He smiled at her. "Of course. It is good to see you. I'm told we raised several thousand dollars for you today. I will see that the hospital gets paid and what is left will be sent to you. How are you managing without Eli?"

"Well enough except for a problem brought about by my cousin Ralph Hobson."

"Ah, that one. Eli was always disappointed with his nephew. He felt that Ralph had great potential but that he chose a material path rather than a spiritual one."

Clara explained Ralph's claim to the farm and her doubts about the validity. "Did Eli ever mention the farm trust he had created?"

"We talked about it years ago. I believe he wanted the farm to go to his sisters."

"That was the original arrangement but not long ago, he told me that he had changed the trust and left the farm to me so that I might care for my children. I take it he didn't discuss this with you?"

"*Nee,* he did not, although it sounds like something he would do. He was extremely fond of you and of little

Sophie. He wanted to do everything within his power to help her."

"I believe Ralph's claim is a fake but I can't prove it unless I can locate the real trust."

"I wish I could help you. The only thing Eli mentioned recently that was unusual was that some strangers wanted to buy the farm. They were making a nuisance of themselves because they wouldn't take no for an answer."

"Do you know who they were? Do you have a name?"

"He was an *Englisch* fellow, that's all Eli said about him."

"*Danki*, Bishop Barkman." She tried not to let her disappointment show.

"Let us know if you need anything, Clara. You have only to ask."

Clara thanked the bishop and went to find her children. At the barn, she told the boy looking after the horses that she was ready to go. He brought up Frankly and proceeded to hitch him to her buggy.

"Isn't that Paul Bowman's horse?"

Clara looked over to see Beverly Stutzman getting into her father's buggy. Clara had met the pretty young woman several times but they weren't really friends. "*Ja*, this is Frankly. Paul was kind enough to loan the horse and buggy to me until Eli's buggy can be fixed."

"I hope you don't mind a word to the wise. Paul Bowman is a fun, friendly fellow but he's not husband material."

"Since I'm not looking for a husband, perhaps that is a good thing," Clara replied with a stiff smile. She wasn't about to engage in gossip about Paul.

Her ride home was long and quiet. Sophie fell asleep

for most of the way but woke with a start before they reached the house. "Mamm?"

"I'm here, sweetheart."

Sophie leaned against her side. "Where are we going to live when Mr. Hobson makes us leave our house? Will we live in a hollow tree?"

"A hollow tree? Where did you get that idea?"

"Charlotte said Juliet lived in a hollow tree."

"I'm not sure where we will go but it will be a lovely home because I will have my daughter and I will have my son and they will have their cat."

"Maybe we could live with Paul," Sophie said.

"That's a great idea, Sophie." Toby smiled from ear to ear. "Then maybe he could be our new *daed*."

"We are not going to live with Paul, and I forbid you to mention such an idea to him. Do you understand me?" If her voice was too sharp, at least the children got the point.

"*Ja*, Mamm," Toby said softly.

Sophie nodded but didn't say anything. Her eyes glistened with unshed tears. Clara was sorry she hurt her child's feelings but she would die of embarrassment if Paul heard the children plotting to make him their new father.

"Paul said he was going to take me fishing," Toby said. "Can I still go with him?"

This was the first Clara had heard of the offer. Sophie scowled at her brother. "I'm not going to the fishpond anymore."

"We're not going to the fishpond. Those are tame fish. We're going to go fishing in the river. Paul has a boat and everything. We might catch a fish as big as a hog."

Sophie eyed him skeptically and then looked at Clara. "There aren't fish as big as an old hog, are there, Mamm?"

"There are, too, fish that big. Bigger. Fish in the ocean can be as big as our house. Hannah told me so."

"Who is Hannah?" Clara asked.

"My new friend. She's going to be in the sixth grade. Her *daed* is Paul's cousin. She has a baby *brudder* who is going to be one and they are having a party for him." He leaned toward Sophie. "Her grandpa is a sheriff with real handcuffs and everything. He could throw me in jail if I didn't mind Hannah. I was very good."

Clara smothered a chuckle. It was an unusual babysitting technique but it sounded like an effective one. "I'm sure glad you didn't end up in jail."

He sat back and nodded. "Me, too."

Paul will enjoy hearing this story. Clara sobered. Paul shouldn't have been the first person she thought to share the story with. It should've been her mother or even one of the Bowman women. The sad fact was, she spent far too much time thinking about Paul Bowman. How could she change it when she was going to see him almost daily?

The answer was painful, too. She would have to leave the farm and find somewhere else to live. She didn't want to do that but staying in the house was becoming pointless. It hadn't deterred Ralph's plans for the property. All she had accomplished was to fall for a handsome, smiling, smooth-talking fellow who liked her children and her cat. She wasn't normally a foolish person but she was turning into one where Paul Bowman was concerned.

That needed to change.

Chapter Nine

Paul harnessed his mare before daybreak on Monday morning and was soon on the road. Clara and the children were at home, and he was excited to see them again. He hummed a happy tune as his horse's rapid trot ate up the miles.

Clara was outside hanging her wash on the line. He pulled the horse to a stop in front of the house. "Did you finally get rid of the pond water smell?"

She laughed. "It took some scrubbing but I did. Go say hello to the children. *They* are looking forward to seeing you today."

An intense joy filled him at the sight of her smile. He longed to see her happy and the fact that he had made her smile filled him with a sense of accomplishment. "Where are they?"

"Putting a puzzle together in the kitchen."

He got out of his buggy and started for the front door but stopped when he heard the sound of car tires on the gravel lane. Ralph's car came into view. Paul's good mood faded.

Clara moved closer to him. "Just when I was beginning to enjoy the day. I know Ralph. He's going to start yelling about my still being here. That was his style even when he was a boy. Attack first."

Ralph brought his car to a stop beside Paul's buggy. There was no question that the man was angry as he stepped out of his vehicle. "I thought I told you to get her moved off my property. That was over a week ago. Why is she still here? If you can't get the job done, I will find someone who can."

Clara stepped forward. "You can't have known that Sophie spent the last week and a half in the hospital. She had pneumonia. She had a seizure. She was very ill. I didn't have time to look for somewhere new to live."

Some of Ralph's bluster faded away. "I'm sorry the girl was sick. That's not my fault. You can't keep staying here rent-free. And don't tell me you'll pay rent. I don't want a renter."

Paul tried to defuse the situation. "We have someone who has offered to let them live with her but there are no electric lines there and it would take some time to have them installed even if the bishop would give his permission."

"Use a generator. I thought that's what the Amish did."

"They are expensive to purchase," Clara said softly.

Ralph gestured toward the house. "You already have one."

Clara stared at the ground with her hands clasped in front of her. "Eli purchased that generator so it actually belongs to you, cousin."

Paul almost laughed at the honeyed meekness in her tone. Ralph threw his hands in the air. "Take the generator. I give it to you. Just get off this land. People will be coming to view the farm and I want them to be able to walk through the house without tripping over your kids or your cat."

"That's very generous of you." Clara inclined her head slightly. "It would be even more generous to return the farm to me."

Ralph ignored her and stepped up to Paul. "You have been dragging your feet, too. This place should be ready to auction today. Is it?"

"Advertising a sale this size takes time. The notices have gone to all our local papers. I have proofed the flyers and handbills with the printer in town. We are on schedule."

"Cut that schedule by two weeks."

Paul shook his head. "I can't. Not if you want it done right. The more people who hear about it and can plan to attend, the better."

"Plus it gives me more time to find my uncle's legitimate trust documents," Clara added, to Paul's chagrin.

Ralph's eyes narrowed. "I've made some inquiries about you, Bowman. You need this sale more than I do. Don't let your sympathy for my conniving little cousin sink your new business. Did you know that your loan can be purchased from your bank by someone else? I'm friends with a few people who have enough capital to do just that. Once that happens, any chance of getting an extension or refinancing goes out the window. I want you to think about that."

There was no mistaking the threat in Ralph's words. "I told you it would take six to eight weeks to be ready. I am pushing things to have it done in six weeks as it is."

"I'm not seeing the progress."

Paul took a deep breath so he wouldn't say something he'd regret. "I know you didn't want a new survey done but I think the coal-mining company that owns the land east of here is encroaching on your property."

"I don't need a new survey and I sure don't need you snooping into things that are none of your business. Don't make me sorry I hired an Amish auction service."

Paul regarded him steadily. "Given your obvious dislike of the Amish, I have to wonder why you did hire me."

Ralph took a step back and held his hands wide. "Did you think I picked the first auctioneer I ran across? I did my homework. You're young and your business is new. You've invested a good chunk of capital in getting it up and running. You stand to lose a lot if you can't get some money flowing in. I thought you'd be eager to do a great job for me as fast as possible. Don't jeopardize your future to impress my cousin."

Coming closer, Ralph smiled but it didn't reach his cold eyes. "There's an old Amish saying that goes something like this—'a man's good reputation is easy to lose and hard to recover.' What if I told folks things have been sold under the table or important items have come up missing? It would be your word against mine. Some of the Amish will believe you but not all your customers are going to be Amish, are they? Do you get my meaning?"

Paul understood but he didn't say anything.

"I see that you do." Ralph got in his car and drove off.

Clara moved closer to Paul as she watched her cousin drive away. She felt a chill in the air that hadn't been there before. "What did he mean?"

"He believes he has leverage he can hold over me to ensure I won't back out of our deal. If I try, he'll ruin my career."

"Can he?"

"A word here or word there about how I failed to carry off my first big auction, or how I took advantage of his lack of knowledge about farming to cheat him, and people will think twice about hiring me. All he needs to do is tell a few people I sold some of the best items before the auction even got started and my reputation will be in shreds. A man's reputation is everything in this business. In any business."

She laid a hand on his arm. "Are you in financial trouble?"

He lifted his straw hat and raked a hand through his hair. "Not yet but if I don't earn a hefty commission on this auction, I will be. I made some poor choices because I had too much confidence in myself and now I may have to pay for it."

She admired his honesty. "What are you going to do?"

He settled his hat low on his brow. "What can I do except hold the best possible auction and pray he lives up to his part of our bargain."

"I told you he wasn't trustworthy. You have seen how he conducts business. Do you still think the papers he holds are legitimate?"

He reached out to brush back a loose strand of her hair and tuck it behind her ear. The gesture was oddly tender and endearing. Her breath caught in her throat as she gazed into his eyes. A hint of a smile curved his lips. "You are brave to confront him. I admire your tenacity, Clara."

"I'm sorry I suspected you were helping my cousin rob me. Ralph has taken advantage of your honesty the way he has always taken advantage of Amish people in the past."

He grew somber as he stared at her. "Clara, I hope you know that you can count me as a friend."

"It's heartening to know I have a true friend at my side. I shall give thanks for that no matter how this turns out."

"It doesn't feel good knowing Ralph picked me to be his dupe but he is underestimating me because I'm Amish. It's true the Amish forgive those who have wronged us instead of reporting them to the authorities. I think he is counting on the fact that we won't report his actions to the law."

"You aren't suggesting we do that, are you? My bishop would not sanction such action."

"If you won't consider it, I understand, but you should know that Ralph Hobson isn't the only one with influential friends."

"Do you think your friends will help me?"

"I'm sure of it."

She closed her eyes and breathed a prayer that it might be true.

"Clara, my family is giving a birthday party for my cousin Joshua's son, Nicky, on Saturday. I thought perhaps you would enjoy spending the afternoon with us."

His abrupt change of subject puzzled her. "You are inviting me to a party? Like a date?"

Toby and Sophie came rushing out of the house. "Hi, Paul. When did you get here?" Toby was grinning from ear to ear.

Sophie took hold of Paul's hand. "You promised I could ride Gracie soon."

He picked up her daughter. "I don't have Gracie here today."

"Then can I have a piggyback ride?"

Paul lifted Sophie over his head and settled her on his shoulders. She squealed and knocked off his hat in the process.

"Just a little bit ago, I was asking your mother to come to a birthday party. There will be games and other *kinder* to play with. I'm pretty sure there will be cake and ice cream. It should be a fun day. Do you think we can convince her to come?"

Toby looked at her with pleading eyes. "Please, can we?"

"It's very kind of you to offer, Paul, but I don't think we should. We aren't members of the family. It would be awkward."

"You already know my aunt, my sister-in-law and the wives of all my cousins. The men of the family are barely of any importance. Just ask their wives."

She smiled. "I think my time would be better spent looking for somewhere to live. I'm sure Ralph will have me evicted if I delay much longer."

"I thought you were considering moving in with Charlotte Zook?"

"She asked but I'm not sure she was serious."

"That's how most conversations with Charlotte go. If you are serious about looking for somewhere to live, then that is the perfect reason to come for a day. My aunt knows everyone. She'll help you find a place."

Clara nodded. "Okay, tell me how to get there, what time does the party start and what should I bring?"

"You don't need to bring anything."

"I am not showing up empty-handed."

"Then bring some treats that your own children enjoy and I'm sure the other children will, as well."

"Okay. We'll come."

The kids hopped up and down and clapped their hands. Paul favored Clara with a beaming smile. She felt a little bit like a kid herself. It was exciting to think about going to a party when her life had been bouncing from one crisis to another. It was exciting to think Paul would be there, too.

When Clara's buggy turned into his uncle's lane on Saturday, Paul was unprepared for the jolt of happiness that hit him. He ignored the warning bells that went off in the back of his mind. He was becoming much too involved with Clara. His idea of strictly being friends could become a problem if he couldn't keep his feelings for her under control. In spite of that fact, he walked out to greet her. "I see you found us."

"We didn't have any trouble following your directions," she said as she gathered her picnic basket.

Toby jumped down. "Where's the cake?"

Sophie gazed at Paul with her bright blue eyes. "Where are Clyde and Juliet? I want to meet them. I have their puppets." She held the toys up for him to see.

"Clyde and Juliet aren't here yet but I know where there is some cake and ice cream just waiting to be enjoyed. Shall I tell you? It's a secret."

Sophie giggled and put both hands over her mouth. "I like secrets."

He leaned in the buggy and whispered, "So do I. Want me to tell you where the ice cream is?"

She nodded. He cupped a hand to her ear and whispered directions. He helped her out of the buggy and she took off at a run.

"No fair," Toby said. "I'm hungry, too."

"Better follow your sister."

Paul settled his hands on his hips as he watched Toby race to catch up with Sophie.

"You are good with *kinder*. My two are quite fond of you."

He grinned at her. "That's because I'm a kid at heart. Besides, I told you everyone likes me."

"Everyone except the string of Amish maids with broken hearts you've left behind you." Jessica Clay came up behind him. She was wearing a pink polka-dot dress. No one would mistake her for an Amish woman.

"You are simply jealous because I wouldn't go out with you, Jessica."

"Ha. I'm too smart to fall for the likes of you. I meant what I said about him, Clara. He never dates anyone more than three times."

Clara liked the outgoing *Englisch* woman. "I must thank you for your generosity in driving people and passing phone messages while Sophie was in the hospital. Don't worry that I will fall for Paul. I have already been warned that he isn't husband material."

"Warned? Who has slandered my good name?" His expression of pretend outrage was comical.

Clara arched one eyebrow. "Beverly Stutzman is a member of my church."

"Oh." His teasing manner vanished as a red flush crept up his neck.

"Busted," Jessica declared and walked away.

Paul helped Clara step down. "Beverly is a sweet woman but she's in a hurry to get married. I'm not."

Another buggy pulled up beside them. Charlotte sat in the front seat with a large brown-and-white basset hound beside her. A raccoon with a pink collar sat on top of the buggy making chittering sounds. Charlotte lifted the dog's front foot and waved it at Clara. "Clyde is delighted to meet you at last," she called out. "I have told him all about you and your daughter. We are looking forward to meeting your son."

The dog looked at Paul and woofed loudly. "Watch out for the dog," Paul said under his breath. "I meant to warn you about him."

"Is he vicious?" Concern for her children instantly took over Clara's mind.

"Not vicious but he does lack manners. He has a tendency to jump on people. I'm just warning you."

"He's certainly big enough to knock over Sophie or Toby."

"Don't ask me why but he likes to pick on adults. I'd never seen him misbehave around children."

That was a relief. Charlotte got out of her buggy and held her hands up to the raccoon. The animal jumped to her and quickly climbed to the top of her head. She lay down on Charlotte's *kapp* and began patting her owner's face with her little paws. Clyde lumbered ahead of them, occasionally stepping on his own ear in the process. He didn't seem to mind.

At the back of the large house, Clara saw lawn chairs had been set up in the shade of a hickory tree. The wide, well-kept lawn sloped down from a lush flower garden outside the back door of the house to the banks of the wide river. Downstream, she could see where a faded red–covered bridge gave access to the far bank.

Near the tree, a picnic table covered with a blue checkered cloth held a birthday cake with a single candle and several dozen gifts. She added her own offering for a one-year-old—six pairs of sturdy socks.

Anna waved and rose from her lawn chair amidst the group of women. A shout rose from the men in the horse-shoe pit. Most of the men were either engaged in the game of horseshoes or watching and shouting encouragement to the participants. The exception was an *Englisch* fellow who lounged in a chair near the women. Clara noticed several of the partygoers weren't Amish.

Anna steered Clara toward an empty chair. "Let me introduce everyone you haven't met." She gestured toward an *Englisch* couple. "This is Nick Bradley and his wife, Miriam."

Clara was sure she had heard the name before but she couldn't recall where. Anna gestured to the young mother with a toddler on her lap. "You have met Mary but this is our birthday boy, little Nicky."

Mary smiled fondly at her child and then looked at Clara. "Nick and Miriam are my parents and the reason my children are spoiled. My husband is the one who just made a ringer."

Clara glanced that way. "They all look like they are enjoying the game."

"The Bowman brothers manage to give every competition their all," Nick said.

It was fairly easy to pick out the brothers, for they looked alike with some variation in their hair color. She was finally able to match the husbands to the wives she had met except for one. Noah wasn't in the game but another man was. Clara hazarded a guess. "The tall, burly fellow is not a Bowman."

A woman with a baby about six months old in her arms laughed softly. "That one is my husband. You are right—he is not a Bowman."

"That is John Miller," Anna said. "He is a good friend

as well as a good neighbor and a fine blacksmith. This is his wife, Willa, and his mother, Verna."

Willa shifted the sleeping baby in her arms so Clara could see him. "And this is Glen, who arrived last Christmas morning."

"A precious gift any day."

"You are so right," Willa said.

"And no party would be complete without the twins," Verna declared as a pair of girls raced up to her chair. "Lucy and Megan, this is Clara Fisher."

"Hello," they said in unison.

Clara smiled at them. "Are you enjoying the party?"

"Yup," one of them said.

The two blonde, blue-eyed girls were carbon copies of each other. Clara couldn't tell them apart. They kneeled on a blue-and-white patchwork quilt spread on the grass in front of the chairs. Sophie sat shyly to one side with her arm around Clyde. The dog seemed well-behaved to Clara.

"Toby said you have yellow eyes," one of the twins said and moved closer to Sophie.

The other twin leaned in, too. "They don't look yellow to me. They look blue."

"They only get yellow when I'm sick," Sophie told them.

Another Amish woman came out of the house with a pitcher of fruit punch and one of iced tea. Her gaze settled on Paul standing behind Clara. "Go away, Paul. We women want to talk about the men and we can't do that if you are standing here."

Paul swept one hand toward her. "This is Fannie Bowman. If you couldn't guess, she is the wife of another cousin. Noah Bowman."

"It's good to meet you, Clara. I've heard a lot about you and your children. Now scram, Paul. Men are not welcome until we are done gossiping."

"That includes you, Nick," Anna said.

Nick heaved his tall frame out of the folding lawn chair. "Come on, Paul. Let's see if we can get in the horseshoe game. I've been waiting to settle the score with you since Hannah's birthday."

"Where is Hannah?" Miriam asked.

"Noah has taken her and some of her friends riding. He promised to have them back before we cut the cake."

"Here come some more of our friends," Willa said. Clara turned to see Debra Merrick and another woman approaching.

"Clara and Sophie, how nice to see you again," Debra said. "Let me introduce Janice Willard, the midwife who delivered Glen and Nicky, Rebecca's Benjamin and many other babies in our community."

Two nurses were soon peppering Clara with questions about Sophie's illness, her treatments and the planned liver transplant. Clara could tell that they were genuinely interested in her daughter's well-being.

"I am still researching how to make a filtered light tent. I had hoped to have the information for you today but there isn't a lot of literature on the subject. I still haven't found what type of plastic film is best."

"Are you talking about the window film that blocks UV light?" Helen asked.

"Yes." Debra looked hopeful. "Do you know anything about the different types of film?"

"I know a little," Helen admitted.

"Luke knows a lot more," his wife, Emma, said.

Helen nodded. "Mark and I purchased the film for our

new display windows in the bakery from Luke's hardware store. Luke said it would reduce the amount of heat coming in during the summer and keep our furnishings from fading. Would you like to talk to him about it?"

Debra and Janice looked at each other. "Yes, we would," Janice declared.

"I'll get him," Emma said.

A few minutes later, Luke approached the group of women with an apprehensive look in his eyes. "I don't know what it was but I'm pretty sure I didn't do it."

They all laughed. Debra pulled a sketchbook from her bag. "We are investigating the use of UV-blocking film in the treatment of jaundiced infants."

"How can I help?"

Debra opened her sketchbook. "This is a tent made of plastic film. Would you be able to obtain the materials to build something like this?"

He took the sketchpad from her. "Do you want the frame to be wooden or metal?"

"I'm not sure it matters."

"The cheapest would be a wooden frame. How big do you want it?"

Debra looked at Clara. "What do you think?"

"Six feet by six feet. Large enough to cover her sandbox." If Sophie had a place to play and to keep her occupied, she was more likely to remain outside in the light.

"Sure, I can order that for you but I thought you wanted something for babies?"

"I do," Janice said. "I have several pictures in my car if you would like to see what we have in mind."

The two of them walked away. Debra grinned at Clara. "It seems there aren't many problems that the Bowmans can't solve."

Clara caught sight of Paul watching her. "They are a remarkable family."

Before long, Sophie and the twins were busy playing with the puppets and with Clyde. Charlotte looked on with Juliet. As the women around her chatted happily, Clara was amazed at the number of people gathered for a one-year-old's birthday party and at the number of non-Amish people who had been welcomed. It seemed that Bowmans Crossing was more than a group of houses near the bridge over the river. It appeared to be a gentle and welcoming community.

Miriam Bradley came over and sat beside Clara. "I understand you are facing some problems with your uncle's estate. Paul has told us about it. My husband, Nick, would like to ask you a few questions. Do you mind?"

It clicked in Clara's mind where she had heard the name before. "Your husband is the sheriff."

He and Paul came up behind her and settled in chairs on either side of her. "I am off duty today," Nick said. "Today, I am the proud grandpa of a darling little boy and nothing else."

Clara glared at Paul. "Is this why you invited me?"

"I did know that Nick would be here and I hoped that you would speak to him but that wasn't the reason I asked you to come. I invited you because I wanted you and your children to have an enjoyable afternoon. You have all been through a lot lately. I thought you deserved a little cake and ice cream."

"If you don't wish to speak to me, I understand," Nick said. "I would like to say that Ralph Hobson is well-known to my department. We have had many complaints about him in the past, mostly from the Amish. He takes advantage of their reluctance to report him. I would be interested in hearing what you have to say about him and this forged revocable trust and amendment he showed you."

Paul leaned forward with his elbows on his knees. "Clara, I believe you when you say your uncle would not leave the farm to Ralph. I'm asking you to trust Nick. He may be able to help you."

"In what way can he help me?"

"You said that your uncle used an attorney to draft the original trust."

Clara nodded. "I don't know his name."

Nick met Clara's gaze without flinching. "There are not many attorneys that work with Amish clients in this area. I can easily check to see which of them had your uncle as a client. If they have a copy of the original, it will be easy enough to compare signatures on the two documents. Let me do some checking for you. You don't have to file a complaint unless you want to."

Clara glanced to where her children were lining up to get a piece of cake. She wasn't doing it for herself; she was doing it for Sophie. She looked at Nick. "I don't want to file a complaint unless I have to but I can't stop you from asking questions."

"Fair enough. I don't want you to go against your beliefs. I see the riders returning." He rose and walked toward a half dozen young girls riding Haflinger ponies. The girl in the front waved to him and galloped up to him.

Charlotte came and sat in one of the empty chairs. "Have you made a decision, Clara?"

"About what?"

"Moving in with me. You said you would consider it."

"You truly want us to live with you?" Clara glanced

at the women sitting around her. Was Charlotte being serious?

Charlotte's smile widened. "I think it is the perfect answer. I have plenty of room now that Helen and Mark have moved out. I liked having them here, I don't mean to imply otherwise but both Clyde and Juliet are ready for a change."

"I have two young, active children. Are you sure that won't be a problem?"

"Not as long as their young, active mother looks after them. If you are thinking I shall be worn out, perish the thought. Juliet and Clyde keep me every bit as busy as children would. Perhaps more so. Last summer, I had five grandcoons underfoot. They made for a difficult but rewarding time. Clyde, what's your opinion?"

The dog woofed twice.

Charlotte looked at the raccoon on her shoulder. "Juliet, do you have an objection? No? There you have it. Clyde has said it is an excellent idea and Juliet has no objections."

"It's very kind of you, Charlotte," Clara said, "but Sophie needs to sleep under special lights and that requires electricity. Would you object to a generator being used for that?"

"I have no idea. Clyde, do we object to electricity?"

Clara didn't know how she felt about having a dog make this major decision. Clyde tipped his head to the side as if considering the idea. Then he got up and loped toward the children playing by the edge of the river.

"Well, there you have it." Charlotte grinned.

The women all glanced at each other. Helen leaned over and laid a hand on Charlotte's arm. "We didn't hear Clyde's decision."

"Really? I thought he was perfectly clear."

"Just so there is no misunderstanding, what did he say?"

"He said he did not care for the noise and smell of a generator but it would be a small inconvenience and having the children stay at the house would more than make up for it."

"He said all that?"

Charlotte patted Helen's hand. "I have often said that you are a lovely person but you don't listen well. I know people say that about me but I hear everything. Clara, how soon do you think you and your children can move in? Of course, you will want to see the house first. Why don't we run over there? It's only two miles. I don't really mean that we should run. I would fall over in a dead faint before I reached the covered bridge. The horse could run but I always say never run your horse unless you absolutely have to. Getting them to stop could be a problem."

Anna rose to her feet. "I think the house tour should be delayed until after we sing 'Happy Birthday' to Nicky and everyone has had their cake and ice cream. Charlotte, will you help me serve?"

"Indeed, I will." She got up and followed Anna into the house.

Helen patted Clara's shoulder. "I hope my aunt didn't scare you off, Clara. She really is a wonderful woman even if she is a little bit scatterbrained sometimes. It would relieve my mind to know someone was living with her. The house is quite nice, plain and roomy. She has a lovely flower garden, too."

Anna and Charlotte came out with a stack of plates and three tubs of ice cream. Anna called to the children, who came running for the treat. The men left their game and crowded around the table. After everyone sang to Nicky, he was allowed to grasp handfuls of his own cake and stuff them in his mouth. Charlotte began cutting the sheet cake while Anna topped each piece with the waiting child's preference of chocolate, strawberry or vanilla ice cream. The mothers in the group helped settle the youngest ones on the quilt while the cake and ice cream were being passed out.

Paul moved to stand beside Clara. "Are you enjoying yourself?"

"My head is spinning. I thought I was coming to let my children enjoy an afternoon of playing with new friends but it seems I have acquired new friends of my own, a place to live, a new treatment for Sophie's jaundice and I find the sheriff is willing to look into my cousin's dishonest dealing."

"So you are going to move in with Charlotte?"

"She has offered, and I'm hardly in a position to object. Apparently, Clyde is in favor of the idea, too. Juliet did not voice her opinion."

"That's great. Charlotte is a little odd but she's a wonderful person. You could do a lot worse. Would you like to take a walk with me?"

The offhand tone of his voice belied the intensity in his eyes. She wanted to hear what he had to say. She wanted to get to know him better but was she risking a heartache?

Chapter Ten

Paul held his breath as he waited for Clara's answer. Surrounded by his family and the happiness they all seemed to share, he became aware of how empty his own life seemed. His brother and all of his cousins were working to secure the future for their children and the children of others. How many good marriages had he seen in comparison to the one unhappy marriage that he remembered? He wondered if Clara's marriage had been happy. Was she still in love with her husband?

"I would love to see the inside of the covered bridge if you don't mind showing it to me," she said at last.

He smiled with relief. "I'll be happy to give you the tour."

Together they walked to the far side of the house and climbed up to the roadway. She paused. "Where does this road go?"

"The river makes a hairpin bend not far from here. There are farms, both Amish and *Englisch*, inside the bend. This bridge is the only way in or out. Actually, there is a place where a horse and buggy can cross the river if the water is low but it's seldom used. Our school sits inside the bend, as well. Timothy and Lillian both teach at the school."

"A man teaching school? A husband and wife both teaching? You have a very progressive congregation over here."

"I reckon that is true. We use a limited amount of solar energy. Some of our businesses use electricity from generators but no one is connected to the world by power lines."

She giggled. "I reckon you could say you are a wireless community."

He chuckled and started to relax. She didn't seem uneasy in his company, and that gave him the courage to continue their walk.

She glanced his way. "Tell me about your uncle's business."

"My uncle builds high-end furniture. It's sold in stores across several states. He has a business partner who is *Englisch*. He is the one who installed the computer for us and had a website built. He also pays for the upkeep of my uncle's website. It's a fine line we walk but our goal is to remain true to our Amish values and still provide employment for the young men and women in this area. Farming is becoming more difficult."

They entered the covered bridge. The sounds of the countryside became muted. He could hear the wind in the trees and the murmur of the water running under the bridge. It felt cozy and personal.

"I know how difficult farming has become for many Amish. My husband was unable to purchase farmland in our community. He ended up going to work for a carpet-manufacturing business. It wasn't ideal but it kept us fed. Eventually, he saved enough to start a part-time harness-making business."

"How did he die?" The Amish did not often talk about those that had passed on but he couldn't stem his curiosity about Clara's life and what made her who she was.

"It was an industrial accident. There was an explosion and fire at the factory. Three men were killed, including Lawrence."

"I'm sorry."

"*Danki*, it was God's will. I have learned to adjust because I had to."

"Why did you leave that community?"

She didn't seem to mind talking about herself. "Several reasons. There wasn't employment for me. My mother sold her house to help pay for Sophie's medical bills. She moved to Maryland with a friend. They are happy to be making quilts and exploring the beach. After Mamm left, I didn't feel connected to the people there. I knew Sophie would need more medical care. Our community was a poor one. They were unable to raise the money needed for Sophie's surgery. There were five children with severe genetic diseases in our church district alone. When my Uncle Eli wrote and invited me to stay with him, I was happy to come. I'm sure it must've been my mother's idea. Some people thought Eli was a grumpy old fellow but he was truly a kind man to me and my children. I'm happy I got to spend many of his last days with him. What about you? Did you grow up here?"

"*Nee*, like you, I am from Pennsylvania. My mother and stepfather still live there along with my five sisters." His words echoed back from the darkness overhead.

"Are you and Mark the only boys?"

"We call each other brother but we are not related. My

father died when I was six. My mother married Mark's father a few years later."

"Do you remember your father? I often wonder how much Toby will remember about his *daed*."

"I recall vague things. He wasn't a happy man. I don't think my parents had a good marriage. At least not according to him. I do remember he said we were like two peas in a pod." He stopped talking as an old memory surfaced. His mother scolding him for being just like his father. Never satisfied with what he had. Always looking for something better.

It wasn't that he was afraid to commit to a woman because she might not be what she seemed. He was the one who would never be satisfied.

Clara glanced at Paul from the corner of her eye. "What are your plans after the farm sale?"

They walked out into the sunshine on the other side. He drew a deep breath as he considered his answer. "I will pay back my brother and then the bank for the money I borrowed and invest the rest back into my business. Then I might sleep for a day or maybe go fishing."

"It has been ages since I've been fishing. You must go often with the river in your backyard."

He turned to the side and led the way to the narrow pedestrian walkway that ran the outside length of the bridge and started back across. It was easy to look over the railing and watch the water rolling beneath his feet.

"Not as often as I should. Why haven't you been fishing lately?"

"You'll laugh at me."

"I won't."

"I know you and you will. You are always looking for an excuse to laugh at me."

"That's not fair. I don't need an excuse to laugh with you, not at you. Tell me the reason you haven't been fishing."

"Forget I mentioned it."

"Now how can you say a thing like that? You know I can't let it go. I'll guess. You haven't been fishing because you hate to touch worms."

"Don't be silly. I don't mind worms."

He leaned back a little. "You don't have time because the children keep you too busy."

"They do keep me busy but that's not the reason."

"You haven't been fishing because you don't own a fishing license."

"I don't have a fishing license because I haven't been fishing. I don't see the point of paying for something I don't need."

"I've eliminated a lot of things. Is it because you don't own a fishing pole?"

"Now you're getting a little warmer."

"I know. You lost your bobber and you're afraid you'll never know if you have a fish on the line or not without it."

She chuckled. "Now you're very warm."

"Not a lost pole, not a lost bobber. I think I have to give up."

"I don't know how to put more line on my reel."

He sat forward to look at her more closely. "Are you serious?"

"Toby was playing with the rod and reel and he pulled all of the line out and it broke. I don't know how to put more line on it."

"It's a closed reel, right?"

"I guess. What other kinds are there? It has a compartment that the string goes into when you crank."

"You take hold of the front part and you unscrew the cap."

"It unscrews?"

He almost laughed at her shocked expression but he managed to keep a straight face. "*Ja*, the cap comes off and then you can see where to tie on the new string. Make sure you thread it through the hole in the cap before you tie it. Screw the cap back on and crank on your new line."

"Now I feel utterly foolish, and I give you permission to laugh at me."

He stopped walking and leaned on the railing to watch the water flowing underneath. "I don't want to laugh at you. I respect you too much for that."

"Now you're making me wonder where's the catch?"

"No catch. Can I ask you a personal question?"

She dropped a leaf into the water. "You can ask. I may not answer."

"Fair enough. Was your marriage happy?"

"I'm not sure how to judge happiness. Did I love my husband? I did. Was he a perfect man? He was not. He struggled with accepting Sophie's condition. Especially after we learned that more of our children could be born with the disease. He believed God was punishing him. Instead of embracing the marvelous gifts God had given us, he withdrew from the children. I don't think he meant to hurt them. I think he didn't want to be hurt when he lost them."

"It explains Toby's hero worship of me."

She chuckled. "I hoped that you hadn't noticed."

"He sometimes resents Sophie for the attention she gets from you, and he feels guilty about it."

"I don't know what I can do to change that."

"I'm sure you don't feel like taking advice on child rearing from someone who's never gone on more than three dates with anyone but I understand the need to have a parent's attention. Find something that you and he can do together."

"Like fishing?"

"That would be a wonderful starting place."

"How did you end up being an expert on children?"

"It's easy. I'm really just a big kid myself. My family will help you move to Charlotte's place whenever you want."

They started walking again and soon left the bridge. "I don't want to go but there is no reason to drag my feet. I will feel bad if you help me move and then must return all my things when it turns out that I do own the property."

He stopped to gaze at her. "We will all rejoice when that happens."

On Monday, at least half the people who had attended the party showed up to help Clara pack up and move to Charlotte's home. Her clothes, the children's clothes and Sophie's special canopy bed were all easy choices. The hard choices were the little things. Should she take the cookbook that had belonged to her grandmother or should it stay with the house? Her uncle's desk was hard to part with, as was the couch in the living room.

Clara sat down on the sofa and closed her eyes. "Are you all right?" Paul asked.

She looked over to see him watching her with the worried expression. She was the one who worried about everyone else. It was nice to have someone worry about her. "I'm fine."

"You don't look fine."

She ran her hands over the worn blue fabric. "This is where I read bible stories to my children every night. I have not lived here for that long but there are many good and tender memories here."

"Those you take with you. Ralph cannot sell memories. Have you heard from Opal Kauffman?"

"Only that her father is holding his own."

"He is still not able to communicate?"

"She says he is not. I can only pray that a few more weeks will make all the difference for him and for me."

"In the meantime, are there any of the books that belong to you?"

She smiled. "They all belong to me. Eli did not like reading except for his farm journals."

"Of course I would pick the heavy task."

"Never fear, I shall help you."

As they worked side by side, Clara was struck by how natural it felt. She was more at ease with Paul than with any man she could remember.

Charlotte was as excited as a small child on Christmas morning when Paul stopped the wagon in front of her house. She clapped her hands with delight. "I'm so glad you are here. I do hope you'll be happy with Juliet, Clyde and me."

"I'm sure I will be. Let us put Sophie's room together first since getting her lights set up and working are the priority." It turned out to be easy enough. Samuel and Paul had the bed moved in without any trouble while Luke worked on a stepladder to secure the hooks in the ceiling that would hold the light canopy. The long lights were unpacked and installed one by one. Isaac and Mark set up the generator on the back porch, where the fumes wouldn't be drawn into the house. When they started it, Clara held her breath as she flipped the switch and all the lights came on. A small cheer went around the room.

"Ooh, they are so pretty." Charlotte held her hands clasped beneath her chin.

Clara and Paul shared a speaking glance as they both struggled not to laugh out loud.

Paul's smile faded as his expression grew serious. Clara looked away first. She recognized the look of longing in his eyes, and she didn't know how to respond.

Two days later, Paul decided to see how Clara and the children were getting along with Charlotte. He had avoided seeing them sooner because he wanted to give them time to settle in and because he needed time to examine his changing feelings toward Clara. He was falling for the widow and her family but he wasn't ready to admit it out loud.

As he approached, he saw Clara wrestling with a large sheet of plastic film and something that looked like a frame for a greenhouse. He stepped down from his buggy. "What are you doing?"

"I'm building a playhouse for Sophie out of some lumber Charlotte had in a shed and this special plastic sheeting. It's a way to let the sun lower her bilirubin levels without giving her a sunburn."

"Interesting. Your carpentry skills are impressive. Where is Charlotte?"

"Baking cookies."

"Can I give you a hand?"

"I thought you would never ask."

He began to clap loudly.

She rolled her eyes. "Paul, help or go away."

"Okay." Paul took the roll of plastic film from her. "Let's get Sophie's new playhouse finished. You are blessed to have me as a friend."

"I do know that. Your friendship has been an unexpected gift, and I cherish it and you."

"That's good to know. I didn't want you to think I was interested in…wow, this is more awkward than I thought it would be."

"In courting me?" she offered.

"Yeah."

"Paul, I am older than you are."

"A couple of years. That doesn't matter."

She arched an eyebrow. "You didn't let me finish. I am older than you are. I have a child with a serious illness to care for. I am not looking for a man to court me. That is the furthest thing from my mind. If I can somehow arrange the surgery and know that Sophie has a chance at a normal life, then maybe I will think about myself. Maybe. So you don't need to tippy-toe around me."

"I figured that you would understand."

Clara was grateful for his candor even as she struggled to hide her disappointment. Her attraction to him wasn't returned. That was a good thing. She needed a friend more than she needed a boyfriend.

"It can't go in the shade." Clara walked ahead of him to the backyard and surveyed the grounds. An old tree held a tire swing and four railroad ties formed the border for a sandbox. The children came running outside to greet him.

He looked at Sophie. "Where do you like to play?"

"I like the sandbox. Toby likes the swing."

"What do you think, Clara. Shall we put it over the sandbox?"

"If she is occupied, she will be more likely to remain outside in it."

"Over the sandbox it is."

It took them an hour to put the frame together. Stretching the plastic film over it was easier. When they were done, all of them stepped inside. Sophie immediately sat down in the sand and began to scoop it into a toy wagon. After about five minutes, Clara and Paul looked at each other. She said, "It's too hot in here."

"You're right. Shall we leave the ends open? Or should we leave the sides open?" He walked outside and studied the frame.

Clara joined him. "I say leave the ends open."

He cupped a hand over his chin. "I think keeping the sides open all the way around will provide better ventilation. Plus, we can cut a small opening in the roof to allow hot air to escape."

"As long as the unfiltered sun doesn't shine directly on her skin I think we will be okay."

"This spot is going to be in the shade until ten or eleven in the morning." He glanced at the sun and judged its position. "It will get hot fast."

"Maybe moving it to the other side of the house would work better. That way, it will get sun all morning and shade in the afternoon."

"I was going to attach it to the railroad ties so it wouldn't blow over."

"There's nothing preventing you from moving the railroad ties to the other side of the house."

He made a disgusted face. "Do you know how much these things weigh?"

"You have big horses. I'm sure they can move four railroad ties."

"Very well. I will move the ties and you can move the sand."

She placed her hands on her hips. "How am I going to move all this sand by myself?"

"You'll come up with something. You're pretty smart."

She chuckled. "I'm glad you have confidence in me. I sometimes wonder if people don't see me as a hopeless case."

"Not hopeless but you have room for improvement."

"Look who's talking."

He pressed a hand to his chest. "Me? I have room for improvement? You are mistaken. I'm charming, I'm talented. I can sell the shirt off someone's back before he notices. Hey, bidder, bidder."

Sophie came out of the plastic playhouse to stand between them. Clara looked at her daughter. "Do you see that? There he goes again. Loving the sound of his own voice. He is a vain man and not Amish at all."

"Hey, bidder, bidder, bidder. Who'll give me a penny for this opinionated woman's opinion?"

"Opinionated?" Her voice rose in mock outrage. She struggled to ignore the laughter lurking in his eyes.

Sophie tugged on Clara's apron. She looked down to discover her daughter's eyes wide in her worried face. "Are you and Paul arguing?"

"*Nee*, little one. We aren't. We are only teasing each other."

"Are you sure?" Her tiny voice quivered as a tear trickled down her cheek.

Paul dropped to one knee. "Don't cry, *liebschen*. We aren't mad at each other."

"Mamm sounded mad."

Clara sank to her knees and pulled Sophie into her

arms. "I was just playacting. You know how Toby pretends to be a pirate sometimes? I was playacting like that."

Paul laid a hand on Sophie's head and wobbled it back and forth. "No more frowning. You need to smile or I will think you are mad at me."

She hid her face against her mother's dress. "I'm not mad at you. I like you."

"Only because I let you sit on Gracie."

Sophie glanced at him from the corner of her eye. "Are you going to bring her over today? That would make me feel better."

He burst into laughter. "You are a wheedler."

"*Nee*, I'm a Fisher."

Clara scooped her up and stood. "You are a Fisher who knows how to wheedle."

"A talent I suspect she gets from her mother." Paul rose to his feet. "Let's put the playhouse here temporarily and move it when we can decide which area gets the best light."

Clara nodded. "I think that's a good idea." She put Sophie down and the girl went back to playing inside the tent.

He grinned. "I have them sometimes. Good ideas, that is. How is life with Charlotte?"

Clara chuckled. "She has been as charming and as accommodating as possible. We are all settling in."

"That's good to hear."

"What's the news on the auction?"

"Ralph is happy that you have moved out. No surprise there. I've started on the inside of the house, and I have most of the items sorted into bundles."

"I don't suppose that you uncovered some critical documents?"

"I wish I had. Have you heard anything from Nick?"

Clara shook her head. "It has only been a few days." She walked into the garden and sat on the wicker bench beneath the rose arbor. The last of the midsummer blooms were fading but they still scented the air with their rich perfume. "The time is slipping away so quickly. Every day my hope fades a little more. Why is God doing this to me?"

He sat down beside her. "Don't despair."

"It's hard to accept that Ralph has cheated my daughter out of her chance for a normal life." Clara covered her face with her hand. "I can't forgive that and it's wrong of me."

Paul hated to see her so upset. He laid a hand on her shoulder. She leaned her head over and pressed her cheek against his fingers. "I wish I could take it all away."

She managed a wry smile. "I would let you."

He bent to place a kiss on her forehead. She sighed and lifted her face to his. He couldn't resist the temptation. He gently kissed her lips. She didn't pull away. He cupped her head and deepened the kiss, awestruck by the surge of tenderness that filled his soul.

Chapter Eleven

Clara turned her face away and Paul released her. She touched her mouth with her fingertips and drew a ragged breath. "You're going to tell me this shouldn't have happened."

"I thought about saying that but it would be a lie."

"It won't happen again."

"I'm not going to promise that, either."

She cast him a sidelong glance. "You're flirting with me."

"It's what I do."

She wanted to be angry with him but she couldn't. "Are you going to tell me that you have fallen madly in love with me?"

"Are you going to believe me if I do?"

"*Nee*. I think you decided to distract me from my self-pity."

He cocked his head to the side. "Did it work?"

"Are you ever serious?"

"I can't remember a time."

She smoothed the ribbons of her *kapp*. "*Danki*, my friend."

"For what?" He reached out and wound one ribbon around his finger.

"For reminding me that I am more than the mother of a sick child."

He tugged on her ribbon. "Yes, you are. Much, much more. Don't forget it."

"If I do, my dear friend will be here to remind me." She turned her head to the right. "We have a visitor."

Paul had to lean to see around her. Clyde sat looking up at them with a doggy grin on his face. He stood, woofed once and trotted away.

Clara looked at Paul. "I thought you said he liked to jump on people."

"Only people who aren't paying attention," Charlotte said as she came out the back door with a plate full of cookies. "You two are very attuned to one another. Oatmeal or peanut butter?"

Paul scooted away from Clara's side. She missed his warmth and the comfort his nearness gave her. "Nothing for me," she said.

Paul rose to his feet. "I love oatmeal cookies."

Charlotte smiled at him. "Among other things."

He took two from her plate. "I have to get going. I won't be around for a few days. I have a lot to do."

As he hurried away, Clara had the impression that he was running away from her.

Charlotte sat and took a bite of an oatmeal cookie. "I think I may have left out the cinnamon. How long have you known that you're falling in love with him?"

Clara took a cookie and sampled it. "You forgot the nutmeg. About five minutes."

"I believe you're right. It is missing the nutmeg. What are you going to do about it?"

Clara leaned a shoulder against Charlotte. "You can't add the nutmeg after the cookie dough has been baked."

And she couldn't force Paul into anything more than a flirtatious friendship. She would have to be content with that. Somehow.

"I have got to do something more for her. I feel like I'm helping steal Sophie's chance for a normal life." Paul paced in his uncle's living room while his brother and several of his cousins sat around him. He couldn't get the kiss out of his mind, or the overwhelming need to go kiss her again. It was ridiculous, and he knew it but he didn't know how to fight it.

He was grateful she hadn't taken it seriously. If only he could be so flippant.

Samuel stood by the back door watching the children playing with Clyde. "You are right about the fact that you can't just cancel your contract with Hobson. He will simply get someone else to sell the farm for him."

"Then someone else would have to deal with their conscience." And lose sleep over it.

"It might make you feel better but it won't improve Sophie's chances of getting a transplant." Samuel left the back door and came to sit in one of the chairs by the fireplace.

"I know. That's why I asked all of you here. I need your help. What can I do? Timothy, there has to be a way to raise the money for her."

"Holding a fund-raiser is not a problem," Isaac said. "Setting up to raise half a million dollars will take time and a lot of work."

"I don't mind the hard work. I'll do whatever it takes."

"The annual county firefighters fair is on next week.

They raise a lot of money for the volunteer fire department." Timothy sat opposite of Noah at the chess table.

"What of it?" Paul asked.

"If we could add Sophie's name to the fund-raiser and say we are splitting the funds, most folks would give to her cause as well and it will bring attention to her plight. A lot of people will already be coming to the fair. I'm sure they'll be willing to support two good causes."

"You could take up a collection at the auction," Noah suggested.

"That's an idea." At least one good thing would come out of the day. "Timothy, can I leave the details of the fund-raising to you?"

"Sure. Do you need help the day of the sale?"

"I do."

"Count on me," Samuel said.

"Me, too," Noah and Timothy said together.

"Thanks. I don't know what I would do without this family."

"When is the date again?" Noah asked.

"Three weeks from Saturday."

"Got it. Don't worry. We will see that little Sophie gets all the help she needs."

"When were you going to tell me about this?" Clara shook a newspaper in Paul's face before he'd had his first cup of coffee. Thankfully, no one else was in his uncle's kitchen.

He pulled away from her. "Tell you about what?"

"About this." She stabbed a finger at an article in the paper.

"You knew the sale was going to be advertised in the paper. You knew that from the beginning."

"I'm not talking about the sale. I'm talking about the date. This is next week."

Paul frowned and pulled the paper from her hand. "Let me see that."

He studied the farm sale announcement. It included all the things he had told the paper about the sale. They had the right farm. But the date was two weeks earlier than he had planned. "This isn't right. It's some kind of mix-up. They will have to print a retraction and include the right date."

She fisted her hands on her hips. "They had better print a retraction."

"Calm down. I'm going over to the shop and call them right now. We can't have people showing up two weeks ahead of time. I won't be ready."

"I'm coming with you."

"Let me handle this. I thought you trusted me by now."

"I do. I'm sorry I got so angry. Opal sent a note to say Dan is making a recovery but it's slow. He may not be able to tell me anything before the auction, especially if it's held early."

"There is no guarantee he can tell you anything about the trust even if he does recover enough to speak."

She seemed to deflate before Paul's eyes. "I know. But he is my only hope. I have talked to everyone else who knew my uncle and none of them can help me."

He reached out and took her hand. "Clara, you have to have faith that things will work out. Maybe not the way you thought they would."

"Call the paper right away and make them change the date to the original one we decided on. I need more time, Paul. Sophie won't be able to use the lights forever. She needs that surgery. I can accept it if God calls her home before He calls me but I couldn't live with myself if I hadn't done everything possible to give her a chance at life."

He squeezed her hand. "I know. I want her to have that chance, too. Never believe that I am against you."

"I'm sorry. I accused you without thinking. It was such a shock to see it in black-and-white."

"Let me go over to the workshop and straighten this out. It was a simple mistake, and I'm sure they will fix it. I've arranged for flyers to be put up in the shops and stores. I've ordered roadside signs made with the right date. You will have your extra two weeks. I wish I could give you more time."

"I know you do and I appreciate all you have done so far."

When she looked at him like that, with unshed tears glistening in her eyes, he couldn't resist pulling her into his arms to give her the comfort she desperately needed. She melted against him as though she couldn't stay upright without him.

"*Danki*, Paul Bowman. You are a dear friend."

He wanted to be more than her friend. He wanted to be the man who had the right to hold her every day but he wasn't the fellow she needed. She needed someone she could build a future with. He had nothing but an overpriced van, the ability to make people laugh and buy items they didn't really need.

She raised her face to look at him. "I don't know how I would've managed without your help."

It took every ounce of willpower that he possessed not to kiss her. "You would have managed just fine. I have never met a stronger woman or a more amazing mother. I am honored to be your friend."

She dropped her gaze and sighed gently. "You think too highly of me."

He forced himself to let her go as she stepped back. He didn't know his heart could ache so much or that his arms could feel so empty. "I'd better get going and call the paper so they have time to get the changes in for tomorrow."

He walked out the door and he didn't look back because he was afraid she would read the longing on his face. She needed a friend and he would be her friend no matter what it cost him.

Clara watched him until he was out of sight. She was a fool for throwing herself at Paul in such a wanton fashion. It had been a moment of weakness and nothing more. Not so long ago she would have heeded her common sense and kept her distance from him. Recently, her common sense had taken a back seat to her loneliness and the desire to be held. Not just by anyone but by Paul.

She had been warned that he wasn't the marrying type. She thought she wasn't, either. Her children demanded all her time and energy, she needed a way to support them, a way to keep a roof over their heads but the more she was around Paul, the more willing she was to share those burdens with him. He liked her children and they adored him. Simply being able to talk about her fears and her hopes helped to ease those very fears. And Paul was very easy to talk to.

She went back into the house. Twenty minutes later, she heard Paul come in. She braced herself to act normal and not seek his embrace again. One look at his face sent thoughts of furthering their relationship out the window. "What is it, Paul? What's wrong?"

"Ralph called the paper and had them change the date. He called the printer and told him to change the flyers, too. He also made sure that they wouldn't listen to me when I insisted the dates be changed back."

"How can he expect you to get everything done in such a short amount of time?"

"I don't know what he's thinking. Maybe he thinks I have been stalling because of you. Maybe he wants to hire a new auctioneer, and he's trying to make me quit. I won't know until I can speak to him."

"That's it then. The farm is going to be his."

"He will sell it without my help. As far as I'm concerned, this is a breach of contract on his part. I'm out. I should have been since the start. I can't profit while you suffer."

"Don't do it, Paul. Don't withdraw."

"I don't understand. I thought you hated the idea that I was working for him."

"Originally, I did. But I was being selfish. I know that you need the commission from the sale to get your business underway and to pay back your brother. I know all that is important to you."

"Being fair and just is more important to me. Mark will understand."

"I believe that but only one of us should end up a loser because of Ralph's scheme. You have put so much work into this already and you deserve to be paid. 'For the scripture saith, thou shalt not muzzle the ox that treadeth out the corn. And, the labourer is worthy of his reward.' Timothy 5:18. It was one of my uncle's favorite passages."

"I can't put a financial reward ahead of you and your children."

"You aren't. If Ralph has someone else take over, that

person may not be as kind to me and the children as you have been. The best way to protect us is to stay employed by Ralph. I know you don't feel right doing so but I want you to handle the sale of this place. You know it's more than a plot of dirt and an old house. It was a home and a man's life's work. It's important to me that it be handled with respect."

"Clara, I can't."

"I want you to do it."

"I wish there was another way."

She cupped his face. "I wish there was, too, but I don't want you to lose what you have worked so hard for. If you quit now, Ralph wins more than the farm."

"If you feel strongly about it."

"I do. I honestly do." Maybe her reasons were more selfish than she let on. She did want him to prosper but she couldn't tell him that seeing him every day was the real reason behind her suggestion.

The outside door opened and Jessica came in. "I'm glad I caught you, Paul. There is a voice-mail message for you from Opal Kauffman. She says her father would like to see you."

Chapter Twelve

Clara kept a tight grip on Paul's hand as Jessica drove them to the hospital. She tried not to get her hopes up but this was what she had been waiting for. Dan Kauffman had been Eli's best friend. She couldn't imagine anyone else he would've trusted with his last wishes.

Jessica pulled into the parking lot and stopped. She turned around. "I'll wait here for you."

Paul opened the door and helped Clara out. Together they hurried into the hospital lobby and took the elevator to the rehabilitation floor. At the nurse's station, they were directed to Dan Kauffman's room. Opal was sitting in a chair at the foot of his bed. She rose when they came in. "I'm glad to see you got my message."

Clara advanced to the side of Dan's bed. She was shocked at the physical changes to the once strong and outspoken man. "Hello, Dan."

He opened his eyes and stared at her. He looked to his daughter. She smiled at him. "This is Eli's niece. This is Clara. You remember her, Dad."

Recognition dawned in his eyes. He motioned with his right hand. His daughter brought around a dry-erase board and marker. He wrote on the board and Opal held it up for Clara to read.

I miss Eli. He was a good friend.

Clara grasped his hand. "You were as dear to Eli as a brother."

He nodded. A tear welled in his eye and trickled down his cheek. Opal dabbed it away. "Clara has something she wants to ask you, Dad."

Clara squeezed his hand. "Eli gave an important document to you. It contained his final wishes. Can you tell me where it is?"

Dan shook his head back and forth. Clara tried again. "Try and remember where you put it. It was important, so I know you took care of it."

Dan continued to shake his head. He pulled his hand from Clara's grasp and reached for the marker and board. Opal held it still while he wrote. When he was finished, he pushed it toward Clara. She picked it up. *Never gave me anything.*

Her heart sank. "Are you sure? It would've just been a couple sheets of paper. You might not think they were important unless you knew what they were."

He shook his head and wrote on the board again. This time, he wrote *Nothing.*

Clara struggled to hide her disappointment. She patted Dan's hand. "Thank you. You get well right quick. I'm praying for you."

He shrugged. Clara surmised that he didn't expect a full recovery. She thanked Opal and then walked out into the hall with Paul. He said, "Now what?"

"Unless the sheriff comes up with something, we are going to let Ralph sell the farm."

"Why don't we call and see if he has come up with any information?"

To Clara's dismay, Nick Bradley had been unable to turn up anything new on Ralph. Ralph's attorney was blocking their moves. He had located Eli's attorney but the man did not possess a copy of Eli's original trust. Eli held the only copy.

She hung up the phone and turned to Paul. "That's it. It's over."

Clara sat in Charlotte's kitchen with Charlotte, Anna and Helen. Charlotte was busy sweeping the floor.

Clara's heart was almost too heavy for words. "That is the end of it. No one knows who my uncle was talking about. Dan Kauffman was my last hope, and he says Eli did not give the documents to him. Ralph owns the farm, and I can't afford Sophie's surgery." Clara squeezed her eyes shut to stem the flow of tears.

"Do not despair," Anna said. "Your church will help pay for her medical care."

"We are a small congregation. I can't ask them to carry such a burden."

"So you are too proud to ask for help?" Charlotte continued with her sweeping.

"My pride has nothing to do with this. The surgery will cost many hundreds of thousands of dollars. We are a poor community. How can I ask this for my child when others may go without shoes for their children?"

"That's pride," Charlotte said flatly as she opened the door and swept the dust outside.

"How so?" Clara demanded.

Charlotte turned around with one hand on her hip. She shook the broom handle at Clara. "Because you believe you are the only one who should bear this unbearable burden. We are commanded by God to care for one another. You would take away another's chance to do as the Lord bids because you do not think it is fair to ask. Are you the judge of right and wrong in the world?"

"You know I am not." Charlotte's word bit into Clara's self-pity.

"When a man has only two loaves of bread in his house, and he gives one to a person in need, is he not more pleasing in the eyes of the Lord than a person who has many loaves and gives only one? If you believe you cannot ask your fellow Christians to comfort the sick, to care for widows and orphans or provide a child with lifesaving surgery because they are too poor, are you not saying that your judgment is greater than God's? I would call that pride." Charlotte turned to the refrigerator. "Are there any cinnamon rolls left? I believe Juliet would like to sample one."

Anna and Helen exchanged smiles. Helen pulled a plastic bag down off the refrigerator. "Juliet is welcome to sample these."

"*Danki*. Is your mother coming to the sale? Juliet and Clyde would like to meet her. As would I."

"I told her not to come. I think it would be too upsetting for her."

"You make up the minds of a lot of people, don't you?" Charlotte took the bag of rolls and went outside.

Anna smiled at Clara. "Charlotte has a unique way of looking at the world but in one thing she is right. You should not take away the chance for people to do something good for others because you think they are too poor. Those that can give will give. Those that cannot may find other ways to aid you. Stop trying to carry this burden alone. It will take longer but we will raise the money you and Sophie need."

"If only I can be sure she will have that extra time."

"You will speak to Bishop Barkman about joining us in our plans for fund-raising?" Helen asked.

"I will," Clara answered.

Charlotte came back inside. "Juliet took it down to the river to wash and it fell apart in her hands. The look she gave me was quite a scold. Have you offered your cousin your forgiveness, Clara?"

"I have not," Clara said bitterly. "I know that is wrong with me but I can't forgive him for making my baby suffer."

"That is very small-minded of you, and not very Amish. Jesus forgave the men who nailed him to the cross. Anna, are there some grapes that Juliet might enjoy? They don't fall apart in the water when she washes them."

"You will find some on the bottom shelf in the refrigerator. I hope she likes the red ones."

"I don't know. I will have to ask her. Holding bitterness in your heart is a lot like filling it with hot tar, Clara. It spreads easily but it is very hard to remove and nothing good can grow where it exists." Charlotte took a few grapes and went out the door again.

Clara shook her head, amazed at Charlotte's ability to make her point in the most roundabout fashion. "I'd like to go back to Eli's house one last time. Helen, can you watch the children?"

"Of course."

When Clara entered her uncle's house later that afternoon, she found Paul sitting in the living room. A single lamp glowed on the table beside him. He had her family bible on his lap. "What are you doing here, Paul?"

"Finishing up some last-minute details. I'm wondering who I can ask to buy your bible cabinet for you. I'll be happy to reimburse them. It shouldn't be separated from your family or from this bible."

She sat down in the chair beside him. "Having the bible is enough."

"Do you know these verses by heart?" he asked as he ran his fingers over the carvings.

She looked at the beautifully crafted cabinet. "Some of them."

"They must have meant something special to the man who carved out those letters. I wish I knew who he was."

"He must've been a man of faith."

"Genesis 1:1," Paul said.

"'In the beginning God created the heaven and the earth,'—I know that one." She also knew Paul was feeling low on her account. She wanted to see him smile.

"The next panel on the front says Isaiah 26:3."

She shook her head. "I'm not sure of that one. Will you look it up for me?"

He thumbed his way through the book until he found what he was looking for. "'Thou wilt keep him in perfect peace, whose mind is stayed on thee—because he trusteth in thee.'"

Clara tried to absorb the words. "It's hard sometimes to keep our minds on Him when there is so much going on in our lives."

Paul nodded. "I need to work on that, too. The left side is inscribed with John 3:16."

"That is one we all keep in our hearts. 'For God so loved the world, that he gave his only begotten Son, that whosoever believeth in him should not perish, but have everlasting life.'"

"Matthew 5:44." Paul spoke so softly she had trouble hearing him.

"I don't believe I can quote that one." She waited until he found the proper page.

"'But I say unto you, Love your enemies, bless them that curse you, do good to them that hate you, and pray for them which despitefully use you, and persecute you.' Makes a man wonder if the craftsman knew Ralph would fulfill that description."

"This one I have not lived up to," she said quietly. "I have not blessed him, I have not done good to him nor have I prayed for him. Perhaps all this trial is God's way of pointing out the error of my ways. I'm ashamed to admit that I have been a poor Christian. I have not held true to my promise to forgive others."

"Philippians 4:13."

She knew that one. "'I can do all things through Christ which strengtheneth me.' You would think the bible was talking about Sophie's illness but I think this one is meant for me. It will take more strength than I have without God's help to forgive Ralph."

She read the next one off the cabinet. "Proverbs 22:6."

Paul smiled. "My aunt's favorite. 'Train up a child in the way he should go, and when he is old, he will not depart from it.' Daniel 6:22," he said.

Her gaze snapped to Paul's face. "Daniel? Oh, Paul, you don't think that's what Eli meant?" Clara moved to the edge of her seat.

"Why didn't we think of this before?" He quickly found the book of Daniel and leafed through it. Nothing. He held the book up and shook it. No loose papers fell out.

Clara sank back in her chair. "Read what it says."

"'My God hath sent his angel, and hath shut the lions' mouths, that they have not hurt me—forasmuch as before him innocency was found in me, and also before thee, O king, have I done no hurt.'"

"I want to believe that I haven't hurt anyone but how can I ever be sure?" she asked, looking at Paul.

"The bishop says only God is perfect. We are not— but we must strive to be. He says we are not judged on our success, only on the efforts we make."

"What is the last scripture?"

"Romans 12:2."

"'And be not conformed to this world—but be ye transformed by the renewing of your mind, that ye may prove what is that good, and acceptable, and perfect will of God.'" He closed the book. "I should get going. It's going to be a long day tomorrow."

"I hope you know none of this is your fault."

"Knowing it and feeling it are two different emotions." He rose, placed the bible in the cabinet and lowered the lid. "Don't forget to take it out before the bidding starts."

"I won't." They walked together to the front door and out onto the porch. Clara gazed at Paul, wishing he would offer her the comfort of his arms. She knew the longing must be written on her face. If it was, he chose to ignore it, and he walked away.

Chapter Thirteen

The morning of the auction, Clara saw Paul's entire family pitch in to help him. Two of his cousins, wearing vests with yellow stripes, began directing traffic into the farm. Buggies, pickups and automobiles soon lined the lane and spilled over into fields beside it. Clara couldn't imagine so many people would be interested in her uncle's machinery and household items. More members of the Bowman family carried out beds, tables and chairs. Her family's beautiful bible cabinet was carried out last. The sight of it sitting on the grass was the last straw for her. She couldn't stop the tears that ran down her cheeks.

Toby grabbed her hand. "Don't cry."

"I can't help it. I know they are only things with no true value but they are things I wanted you and Sophie to have. They are part of the history of our family."

"Don't worry." Paul spoke from behind her. She didn't turn around. She didn't want him to see her this upset.

"I'm okay." Her voice quavered and she knew she hadn't fooled him.

He laid a hand on her shoulder. "I have asked my uncle

to purchase the bible cabinet for you to keep. It's my way of apologizing for this."

She turned around then. "I was going to bid on it but I doubt I have enough money to purchase it."

"It will belong to you and your children once again. It will be the last item for sale."

"*Danki*, Paul."

"I wanted to do something."

"None of this was your fault. I don't blame you for doing your job. I hope my uncle's things bring a fine price so that you can collect a good commission. You have earned it."

"Not yet I haven't. I'll get started in ten more minutes. I would give anything not to have to go through this. Are you sure you want to stay and watch?"

She heard the pain in his voice and knew how badly he felt. His hands still rested on her shoulder. She tipped her head to press her cheek against his fingers. "'Not my will, oh, Lord, but Your will be done.' I want to stay. I want to hear this speaker system you value so highly. I want to see if you are as good an auctioneer as you claim to be."

"I have never met a stronger woman than you are, Clara Fisher."

She managed to smile at him. "Clearly, you have been associating with the wrong kind of women, because I am nothing special."

"I happen to disagree with that statement. We can argue about it later. I have to go." He left her and made his way through the crowd to his van, which had been set up in front of the barn.

Toby jerked on her arm and pointed. "Mamm, I see Grossmammi."

Clara looked in the direction he indicated. Her mother

was walking up the drive with her friend Stella. With a glad cry, Clara rushed to embrace them. "What are you doing here? How did you get here? I'm so glad to see you. Why didn't you tell me you were coming?"

Her mother laughed softly. "One question at a time." She gestured to two Amish men standing behind Stella. "I'd like you to meet Alvin and Orrin Mast. They arranged for a driver to bring us here. I couldn't let my brother's belongings go into the hands of strangers without being here to support you. I know how much his gift meant to you and I know how bitterly we all regret that it has been stolen from us. We will raise the funds for Sophie's surgery some other way. Now where is my little girl? And who is this big strong boy beside you?"

"I'm Toby, Grossmammi. Don't you remember me?"

"Toby? Why, you have grown a foot since the last time I saw you."

"I can't believe you are here. Would you like some coffee and rolls?" Clara asked. "Paul's family is providing the refreshments."

"We stopped on the road for breakfast," Stella said. "I'm sorry Ralph has stolen your property. We must pray all the harder that he sees the error of his ways and repents before he is called to meet his maker. Is he here? Perhaps if I spoke to him."

"I saw him arrive a few minutes ago. I knew he would be here to collect his money before the day is over."

"I know this is disappointing but you must not let bitterness take root in your heart. I'm sure that Eli intended to provide for you and the children."

"I am sure, too. But we were never able to locate the document. Eli said in his last letter that he had given it to Daniel for safekeeping but Dan Kauffman knew nothing about it."

Her mother's eyes widened. "He said he gave it to Daniel for safekeeping?"

"Ja."

"Was that in the letter I forwarded to you?"

"It was."

"No wonder Eli didn't explain what he meant. He thought you would still be with me when you read it." A slow smile appeared on her mother's face. "Toby, run and tell the auctioneer to delay starting the sale."

The boy took off. Clara stared at her mother. "Do you know the Daniel he meant?"

"I believe I do. Where is Ralph? I'd like to speak to him."

Clara looked over the crowd. Ralph stood beside Paul's trailer. Toby opened the back door and climbed inside. Ralph must've heard what the boy said because he turned a fierce scowl in Clara's direction. She motioned for him to come over. He tromped toward them, looking angrier than she had ever seen him. Paul and Toby followed him.

"What is the meaning of this delay?" Ralph demanded.

"Hello, Ralph." Clara's mother looked him up and down. "You have created a great deal of trouble for your cousin and her children. You should be ashamed of yourself. What would your mother say if she were alive to see this?"

"I'm not causing trouble for anyone. Eli signed the farm over to me. Clara is the troublemaker. She brought the sheriff into this. The Amish don't invite the *Englisch* law into their business."

"But you are not Amish," Paul reminded him. He stood with his hand on Toby's shoulder.

Ralph rounded on him. "Get this auction started."

"Are you Paul Bowman?" Clara's mother asked.

He nodded once. "I am."

"My daughter has told me many good things about you." She glanced between Clara and Paul. "I can see for myself that she was right. Before the auction gets started, Ralph, I want you to know I forgive you."

Clara swallowed hard and closed her eyes. She had to mean it if she said the words. She waited for God's presence to fill her heart. "I forgive you, Ralph. I pray you will see the error of your ways and mend them."

"Fine. I'm forgiven." His voice wavered. Clara knew he had been affected by her and her mother's words.

Clara's mother turned to Paul. "There is one more place we must look for my brother's trust document."

Paul's eyes brightened. "You know where it is?"

"These are just stalling tactics," Ralph said. "I have the only valid copy."

Their conversation had attracted the attention of Paul's family. Sheriff Bradley made his way through the crowd and stopped beside Paul. "What's going on?"

Clara tried to hold back her growing excitement. She didn't want to be disappointed again. "Sheriff, this is my mother. She believes she knows who Eli gave the documents to."

Her mother smiled brightly. "Daniel isn't a person. It is a bible verse. Daniel 6." She walked over to the bible cabinet.

Paul's heart sank. "We have already looked through the bible. It isn't in there."

"Not in the bible. In the cabinet." Clara's mother pushed on the panel with the inscription and it slid open to reveal a hidden compartment. "My brother and I discovered it when we were little. We hid many things from our parents that we thought were valuable, like our comic books and a transistor radio. Our father heard us listening to the radio one night. The next morning, he asked us both where it was. Eli said with a straight face, 'I gave it to Daniel for safekeeping.' I almost gave him away by laughing."

The mine owner, Alan Calder, came up to them with a fierce frown on his face. "I thought we were having an auction today, Bowman. Let's get started. I don't have all day to waste."

The sheriff ignored him and stepped up beside the cabinet. He glanced at Clara's mother. "May I?"

She nodded and moved back.

"What is going on here?" Calder demanded.

"We are getting to the truth." Nick bent to look inside and pulled out a tightly rolled-up sheet of paper and an envelope stuffed with cash.

"This is ridiculous," shouted Ralph. "You don't believe this last-minute charade, do you, Sheriff? This is just a stunt to delay the sale." He began backing away.

"Stay where you are, Mr. Hobson." The sheriff nodded to someone in the crowd and one of his deputies moved to block Ralph's retreat.

The sheriff then carefully unrolled the document. "This appears to be the original trust drafted by Eli along with a notarized amendment naming Clara Fisher as his beneficiary."

"It's a fake," Ralph said, looking wide-eyed and frantic.

The sheriff fixed his steely gaze on Ralph. "I happen to know the man who drafted the original document for

Eli. He's here today. It will only take a few minutes to have him verify that this is the original. I strongly suspect the fake is in your possession, Mr. Hobson. You're looking at some very serious charges."

"You aren't going to pin this on me. It was their idea." He pointed to Calder. "Eli wouldn't sell the mineral rights. That's all he had to do—let them mine the coal under his farm ground. He would have made more money in a year than he ever made from growing corn."

"Shut up, Hobson," Calder muttered.

"Are you saying that the New Ohio Mining Company was directly involved?" Nick eyed the man.

Paul had suspected that Ralph was a coward behind his bullying exterior. There was fear in his eyes. "Yes. Calder came up with the whole plan. He knew the land was in a trust when he checked to see who owned it at the courthouse. He said all I had to do was claim Eli made me the new trustee and then lease the mineral rights to them."

Calder leveled his angry gaze at Sheriff Bradley. "If you have any questions for me, speak to my lawyer." He turned away.

Ralph caught his sleeve and stopped him. "I'm going to need your lawyer, too."

"I'm afraid that presents a conflict of interest for him. You'll get a public defender." He jerked away from Ralph and left.

"I don't understand," Clara said. "Why go to all this trouble? My uncle didn't have long to live. Why not wait and make the offer to me? I would have gladly sold the mineral rights."

Jeffrey Jones joined the group and tipped his hat to Clara and her mother. "Because they needed to be sure the new owner wouldn't start asking a lot of hard questions."

Paul started to see the picture. "The new fence on the east side of the property. It wasn't on the original boundary line. It had been moved to make it look like the mine owned more land."

The sheriff shook his head. "Seems like a lot of trouble just to hide a few extra acres."

"It wasn't the acres on top that they wanted to hide," Jeffrey said. "They discovered a large coal vein that travels due west of the main mine. They started mining it without checking to see if they held the mineral rights. Most of the mineral rights in this area were sold to the mining companies back at the turn of the century so they assumed they were within their rights. When they discovered their mistake, they had to take action."

"That's when they started pressuring my uncle about selling the property," Clara said.

Sheriff Bradley eyed Jeffrey closely. "Who are you exactly?"

"Jeffrey R. Jones." He handed over his identification and a letter. "I'm an investigative reporter. I've been looking into the New Ohio Mining Company for the last eighteen months and I have found a lot of dirt."

Ralph folded his arms over his chest. "I'm not saying another word without an attorney."

Jeffrey smiled. "Your attorney is going to make a ton of money off you, Ralph. I have had you under surveillance for quite some time, too. As a person of interest in several insurance scams in the past, I thought that's why you were here, to pull another scam. But when you wouldn't even hear my offer for the property, I knew you were onto something bigger."

Sheriff Bradley handed back Jeffrey's credentials. "If he wasn't pulling an insurance scam, what was he doing?"

"New Ohio Mining Company had been illegally taking coal out from under this farm for at least a year. If that had become known, the company would have had to pay millions in fines and legal fees. When Eli King wouldn't sell and then passed away, they still didn't know who owned the land. A little background checking would have shown them there were two contenders. An upright, law-abiding Amish woman and a less-than-upright swindler. They saw their chance to quietly get the mineral rights by making Ralph the new owner."

"I'm willing to testify against them if you cut me a deal," Ralph said. "They supplied the attorney, the notary and the forged document after Eli's death. No one knew Eli had amended the original trust until Clara told me."

Clara had moved closer to Paul. He took her hand in his. Her fingers were ice-cold. "I still don't see why Ralph needed to auction off the property. Why didn't he just sell it to them? No one would have been the wiser to the moved boundaries."

Jeffrey took his hat off and smoothed his hair. "Unfortunately, Ralph got greedy."

Paul remembered their first conversation. "They gave you a lowball offer."

"They thought I was stupid. They had a lot more to lose than I did."

Clara squeezed Paul's hand. "What does he mean?"

He gave her a comforting squeeze in return. "The mining company would have to buy the place no matter how high the bidding war went. Any other buyer would want a boundary survey done and the questions would start rolling in."

Ralph chuckled. "I thought they needed to sweat for underestimating me."

"Who was your accomplice?" the sheriff asked.

Jeffrey tipped his hat to Ralph. "I'm sure he or she is long gone. It was a clever plan but you were toying with some really bad characters. You got off easy. Calder's company has popped up and folded a half dozen times under different names. Two people who opposed him went missing. It will be interesting to see how it all washes out in court. I expect a lot of finger pointing and that will make my story worth even more."

"Ralph Hobson, you are under arrest for forgery, fraud and attempted grand theft." Sheriff Bradley read Ralph his rights as he led him away.

Paul took both of Clara's hands in his. "As the rightful owner of Eli King's estate, what are your wishes?"

"I want you to hold a farm sale. I will match the commission offered by Ralph if that is agreeable to you."

"I accept your offer. When would you like me to hold the sale?"

"Would today be too soon?"

"I think today would be perfect. I'd better get started before the crowd gets restless."

Hours later, the western sky was aglow with beautiful orange and gold colors painted across a few clouds above the horizon. Paul and Clara both paused to take in the beauty after the crowds had gone home with their treasures.

Paul gestured toward the beautiful sky. "My sister-in-law, Helen, says, 'Peace is seeing a beautiful sunset and knowing who to thank.'"

Clara knew she couldn't let one more sunset fade into night without telling Paul what was in her heart. Life was too short and too unpredictable not to tell him what he had come to mean to her and her children.

"Paul Bowman, I love you," she said softly.

She felt him stiffen beside her. "You are just caught up in the joy of having things turn out as they did."

"That's true but it doesn't change the fact that I'm in love with you." She wanted to be held in his arms and feel the touch of his lips on hers.

He shoved his hands in his pockets and looked at the ground. He kicked a small stone and sent it flying. "Now you think I should declare my love, ask for your hand in marriage and we will live happily ever after, is that it?"

"I was hoping for something like that."

"I care for you, I do but I'm not the kind of man you need. With me, you'd be getting another kid."

She squeezed her hands together until her fingers ached. She may have made the biggest mistake of her life. "You are selling yourself short, Mr. Auctioneer. I've seen how you are with my children. I've seen how happy you make them and how happy they make you. I think you are exactly the kind of man I need and want."

"Now see, that's where you're wrong. Your kids are wonderful. You're a beautiful and amazing woman but…"

When she realized what he couldn't say, her heart overflowed with love for him. "But? You were about to tell me you don't love me. You can't say it, can you?"

"Clara, I think you just like to argue. I can't give you the things you need. You know that."

"I don't. What is it that you think I need?"

"You need a serious and steadfast man as your helpmate. I'm not serious. No one would call me steadfast. You deserve far better, and as much as I admire you, I can't let you make this mistake."

She took his face between her hands. "Honestly, Paul. Why don't you just say what is in your heart? Stop denying it."

"I don't know what you mean."

She rose on her tiptoes and slipped her arms around his neck. "Say you love me." Then she kissed him.

It took every ounce of willpower Paul possessed not to gather Clara close and kiss her. He loved her with all his heart and soul. He had nearly robbed her of her inheritance and her chance to see Sophie well and whole. It was only by God's grace that the truth came out.

Just when he thought he would break, she stepped back. He saw the confusion in her eyes and hated himself for causing it.

She didn't need a joker making her laugh. She needed a man who would believe in her completely, and not allow his own wants to blind him to her needs. Everything that led to the happy outcome for her today had been done by others. They were the ones who saved her, not him. "You deserve a better man than I am."

"I don't want a better man. I want you. Faults and all."

"You need to aim higher, Clara. Your children deserve better. Think of them. Find someone who isn't in love with the sound of his own voice. Find someone who loves you and you alone."

"I have, only he's too stubborn to admit that."

"I care about you, Clara, I do. And about your children, and that's why I have to stand aside."

·He walked to his trailer, climbed in and turned his horses for home.

Clara ran after him. "You're not making this easy for me, Paul Bowman, but if you think I'm going to give you up because you didn't get to play the hero you are sadly mistaken!"

Two long, lonely weeks later, Paul stood on the banks of the river tossing pebbles in the water and watching the ripples spread out until they disappeared.

"That's a slow way to build a dam."

Paul turned to see his cousin Samuel walking toward him. Paul turned back to the water and tossed in one more stone. "It helps pass the time."

"Until when?" Samuel stopped at his side.

"Until I grow up and stop being a restless kid."

"I hope that never happens. I like you the way you are."

"I think I made a big mistake, Samuel. I don't know how to fix it."

Samuel reached down and picked up a handful of pebbles. He tossed one into the water. "I assume you are talking about Clara and her children? What kind of mistake did you make?"

"I think I fell in love with her. Worse yet, I let her fall in love with me."

"So you love each other. That's not a mistake, Paul. It is God working in your life for the good of you both."

"Now see, that's where you're wrong." Paul heaved the last pebble as far out into the river as he could. "I'm not husband material. I'm sure not husband and father material rolled into one."

Samuel chose a flat rock and sent it skipping across

the surface before it sank. "Exactly what is husband and father material?"

"You are. Joshua is. Luke is. You guys aren't insecure about taking care of a family. You know what to do and you do it. I don't have a clue where to start taking care of someone else. I can barely take care of me."

Samuel chuckled, causing Paul to frown at him. "What?"

"Paul, none of us had an idea of how to be a good husband and a good father. I pray for guidance every night and every morning. Raising a child is the most important task God has ever given me. Of course I am afraid I will make mistakes. But I trust in the Lord to guide me. As does Joshua and Luke. A man can't do the job alone."

"I guess I'm scared."

"As are a lot of men who stand in front of the bishop and promise to love, honor and cherish a woman for the rest of their lives but they stand there anyway."

"And if I fail at the most important task of my life?"

"Then you must pray that your spouse is strong enough to help you get up and go forward again. Life is not stagnant. It's not a stone." Samuel tossed the pebbles in his hand into the river. "Life is like the water out there. It keeps moving forward. It flows around the stone. Build a dam and the water will stay still until it gets deep enough to flow over or around the dam and cut a new path. You have to ask yourself if Clara can be strong for you and if you can be strong for her."

"She's the strongest woman I have ever met."

"*Goot*, because I suspect you will be a challenging husband but a fine one in the end. When is her surgery?"

"Tomorrow morning."

"Then you should see about getting a driver to take

you to Pittsburgh. I heard Abner Stutzman was looking for more work."

"Do you really think I can do it?"

"It doesn't matter what I think. What matters is that you and Clara love each other. Support each other and the rest of life will work itself out like water flowing around a stone."

Samuel began walking back to the house. Paul dropped his handful of pebbles, dusted his palms together and went to use the phone.

Early the next morning, Paul entered the hospital in Pittsburgh and learned that Clara and Sophie were already in surgery. He chastised himself for failing her yet again. He wanted to tell her how much he loved her before she went into surgery but he was too late.

He was directed to a waiting room. As he entered the room, he saw Clara's mother, Betty, and her friend talking to a woman in blue scrubs. They all looked worried. A television played in the corner of the room but he paid no attention to it.

When the woman in scrubs left, Paul took a seat beside Betty. She smiled at him. "I'm so glad to see you, Paul. Thank you for coming."

"Have you heard anything?"

"The doctor who spoke to us said Sophie is doing great but they are having trouble keeping Clara's blood pressure stable."

Paul shivered against the chill that touched his soul. "She'll be okay, won't she?"

"We must pray for her and for the people caring for her. She is in God's hands. Sophie is doing fine and that is what Clara wanted more than anything. She is grateful to you, Paul, for earning enough money at the sale to pay for this surgery."

If all his efforts only led to her death, he wasn't sure he could live with that. He rose to his feet and paced the length of the room and back. "Where's Toby?"

"Bishop Barkman and his wife are looking after the boy until Clara comes home."

"It's good that the church is helping." He should have offered to watch Toby.

Paul crossed the room to look out the window. His last conversation with Clara played over and over in his mind. She had been right. He was in love with her but he had been too afraid of failing her to admit it.

A phone rang and the receptionist at the desk answered. After speaking softly with the caller, she put her hand over the receiver. "I have a call for anyone here with Clara Fisher."

Betty said, "You take it, Paul. I'm afraid I'll just start crying."

He took a deep breath. "Sure."

The receptionist gestured to a small cubicle. "I'll transfer the call over there where you can have some privacy. Just pick up the receiver when the red light comes on."

"*Danki.* Thank you."

He did as she instructed. When the red light came on, he picked up the handset. "This is Paul Bowman."

"Paul, I didn't know you were going to be there." It was Toby on the other end of the line.

Just the sound of the boy's voice lifted Paul's spirit. "How you doing, kid?"

"I'm fine. Velda Barkman makes great oatmeal-chocolate-chip cookies, and the bishop let me drive his buggy to the phone shack."

"All by yourself?"

"He came along just to watch. How is my *mamm*?"

"She and Sophie are still in surgery. I haven't seen her yet."

"I hope Sophie doesn't have yellow eyes anymore. Sometimes kids make fun of her and it hurts her feelings."

"I don't think they will make fun of her anymore."

"I wish I could be there, too."

He gripped the phone harder. "I know you do. I'll tell Sophie and your mother that when I see them."

"Okay."

"Toby, you are the *goot* brother. I love you, kid."

"Really?"

"Really and truly."

"*Danki*, Paul. Love you, too. The bishop says I have to get off the phone now. Bye." The boy hung up before Paul could say anything else. It was a good thing because he couldn't speak past the lump in his throat. He loved Clara's children and he loved her.

Please, Lord, give me a chance to tell her that.

Agonizingly long hours later, a young man in blue scrubs came into the waiting room. "Is there anyone here for Clara Fisher?"

Paul and Betty rose quickly to their feet. The tired-looking doctor smiled at them. "Sophie and Clara are both doing fine. They have gone into the recovery room and you will be able to see them in an hour or so."

Betty pressed her hand to her chest. "That is wonderful news, thank you."

Paul's knees gave out and he dropped back into his chair. *She's doing fine.* They were the most beautiful words he had ever hoped to hear. He covered his face with his hands as tears of joy ran down his cheeks.

Clara struggled to open her eyes but her eyelids weighed a hundred pounds apiece. She couldn't lift them. A woman's voice said, "Wake up, Clara. There is someone here to see you."

"Are you sure she's doing okay?"

It was Paul's voice. How did he get here? Was she dreaming?

"She's doing much better now."

"Thank God for that." Clara heard the relief ripple through Paul's voice. Was he really here?

She tried harder to open her eyes and finally succeeded. His wonderful face swam into focus. She wanted to say hello but nothing came out of her mouth but a croaking sound.

"Try some of these ice chips," the nurse said as she placed a plastic spoon to Clara's lips.

Clara took the cold chunks, amazed at how wonderful they felt in her dry mouth. When they had melted away, she opened her eyes again.

Paul was bending over her. He laid a hand on her forehead and then moved to cup her cheek. "Hello, sleepyhead. It's about time you got up."

"How is Sophie?"

"She's fine," Paul assured her.

"She's right beside you." The nurse pointed and Clara turned her head to see her baby sleeping peacefully without the blue lights. *Thank You, dear Jesus.*

The nurse pumped up the blood-pressure cuff on Clara's arm. "You are in the recovery room. We'll be moving you to a room in the ICU in about an hour. On a

scale of one to ten, ten being the worst pain you can imagine, how would you score the pain you are having now?"

Clara shifted in bed. "Five."

"I'll give you something to help with that."

"Will Sophie come to the ICU with me?"

"No, she is going to the pediatric ward. But we'll arrange for you to see each other often."

"Sleep," Paul said. "I'll be right here for both of you."

"See how well I know you already? I knew you
couldn't stay away," Clara whispered. She smiled as she
closed her eyes and drifted off to sleep without hearing
his reply.

Sometime later, she heard Paul's voice again. He was
speaking to Sophie. "And the baby bear said, 'Someone
has been sleeping in my bed and there she is.'"

"I like this story," Sophie said. "I have yellow hair,
too. Will it change colors now that I have part of Mamm's
liver in me?"

"*Nee*, it will not change," Paul said, laying a hand on
her head. "You will always be my Goldilocks."

Clara turned her head and found her mother close at
hand. "May I have some more ice chips?"

"Certainly. I will tell your nurse." Her mother rose
and walked away.

A few minutes later, a nurse came in with a plastic cup
full of ice and a spoon. She glanced toward Paul. "Your
husband is very good with your little girl. It's nice to see
such an involved father."

Clara didn't correct her. She liked the idea that the
woman mistook the Amish auctioneer for her husband.
If only it was true.

The next time she opened her eyes, she saw she was
in a different room. Paul sat beside her slumped in a

chair. "I'm not the only sleepyhead," she muttered. He heard her and sat up, rubbing his eyes. She wished she wasn't so groggy.

"Can I get you anything?"

"A kiss would be nice," she thought and then realized she'd said it out loud.

"That's easy." He leaned in and placed a gentle kiss on her lips.

Astonished, she raised a hand to touch his face. "Why did you do that?"

"Because I love you."

She dozed off for a second or two but forced her eyes open. "What did I just say?"

"You said you needed a kiss. I gave you one."

"That's what I thought. Why are you here?"

He smiled softly. "Because you needed me to be here."

"I did. I'm very glad you came." She reached out her hand and he clasped it between his own.

"I will always be here for you and the children for as long as God will let me."

"What changed your mind?"

He smiled. "I can't live without you. I tried but I can't."

"How is Sophie?"

"She's doing fine. I took Toby in to visit with her for a few minutes. He told her he would feed the cat for her until she got home. I sent your mother to lie down for a while. She has been sitting with Sophie but I could see she was getting tired."

"I can't keep my eyes open. I'm sorry. I need to tell you something. I need to tell you…something."

"They just gave you something for pain. Rest now and talk later. I'll be here."

"Danki."

"You're welcome, my love."

"I like that."

The next time Clara roused, she was in a different room. A nurse was taking her blood pressure. "I need to get your vital signs. What is your pain level?"

"I'm fine." She ached but she didn't want to sleep anymore. "Where am I?"

"In your room on the surgical floor."

"Can I go see my daughter?"

"The doctor wants you on bed rest for another twelve hours. Maybe she can come down here. I'll check with the pediatric floor."

Paul rose from a chair in the corner of the room when the nurse left and came to the bedside. "You look like you are feeling better."

"Maybe a little. I'll be better yet when I can see Sophie."

"She was sitting up eating Jell-O when I was there a half hour ago. Your mother is staying with her. You told me once that you loved me and I told you I wasn't the man you needed."

"I remember?"

"I was lying to myself. I love you, Clara Fisher, more than I thought it was possible to love another human being. And I love your children, too. I want us to be a new family."

She was afraid to hope that he meant it. "That would be the answer to my prayers."

"I love you. Please say you will marry me."

"Of all the ridiculous places to propose, this takes the cake, little brother." Mark walked in with Helen by his side.

"I think it's very romantic," Helen said.

Paul left Clara's side. "I don't have an answer yet so you will have to wait outside in the hall until I get one." He put his hand on his brother's chest.

Mark backed up. "Okay. Okay. Clara, put this fellow out of his misery." Paul closed the door in Mark's face.

"I will."

Paul spun around to face her. "You will put me out of my misery or you will marry me, which question did you answer?"

She smiled. "Both of them. Yes, I will put you out of your misery and yes, I will marry you. And yes, your brother is right—this was a terrible place to make a proposal."

"I will ask you again when we are on a quilt under the shade of a chestnut tree watching the children play by the river."

"That will be a much better place."

"Only if the answer is the same."

She smiled. "It will be. I'm never letting you off the hook."

"*Goot*, because I need a strong woman to keep me in line."

"And I need a funny husband who will make me laugh."

"We will make a good team, won't we?"

She nodded. "We will. I will ask for kisses and you will oblige me."

"Absolutely, starting right now." He bent over the hospital bed railing and brushed her lips gently with his own.

There was a knock at the door and it opened to reveal her mother pushing Sophie in a wheelchair. Her daughter's bright smile was exactly what Clara needed to see. A group of people crowded in behind her—all the Bowman brothers and their wives, Isaac and Anna, Mark and Helen, and even Charlotte came in pulling a large suitcase on wheels.

Paul dropped to his knees beside Sophie as Clara's mother pushed her up beside the bed. Clara reached through the rails to squeeze her daughter's hand. "How are you?"

"I'm *goot*. My eyes aren't yellow anymore."

"I'm so glad." Tears of joy gathered in Clara's eyes. God was good indeed.

Paul took Sophie's other hand. "I have a question to ask you, Goldilocks. Can I marry your mother?"

"Does that mean I can ride Gracie whenever I want?"

"No, it does not. You can only ride her when I am with you."

Sophie gave a deep sigh. "Okay, you can marry Mamm. Will that make you my *daed*? Will I be a Bowman now?"

"*Ja*, I will be your *daed* and you will be a member of the Bowman family."

Sophie gave a quick nod. "I think I'll like that."

Charlotte clapped her hands. "Oh, Clyde was right again. I can't wait to tell him."

She unzipped her suitcase and Clyde stuck his head out. Charlotte grasped his face between her hands. "Did your big ears hear that? These two are going to get married, just as you predicted. You are such a smart dog."

The door opened behind the crowd. "I'm sorry, folks, but only four visitors at a time. Some of you will have to leave now," an annoyed nurse said but Clara couldn't see her.

Charlotte pushed Clyde's head back in the suitcase and folded in his ears before zipping it shut. "We're leaving," she said as she made her way through the group. It wasn't until Clara saw the back of the suitcase that she noticed it was full of holes. Charlotte had discovered a way to sneak her beloved dog in after all.

"We'll see you later," Anna said and pulled Isaac toward the door. One by one the Bowmans all wished her well.

From her bed, Clara surveyed the people who had come to mean so much to her and her children. When they left, she gazed at Paul with all the love in her heart. "I'm going to enjoy being part of the Bowman family."

"Not as much as I will enjoy having you and the children as my family."

"Could I have another kiss?"

"Yes, my love, you may. All the kisses you want." He leaned over the bed rail and tenderly kissed her forehead and her cheeks, then settled on her lips. When he drew away he smiled at her. "I'm the most blessed man in the world."

* * * * *

THEIR AMISH REUNION

Lenora Worth

To Marta Perry, a mentor and friend
and incredible writer. Thank you, Marta,
for your encouragement and support.

And ye shall seek me, and find me,
when ye shall search for me with all your heart.
—*Jeremiah* 29:13

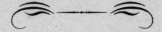

Chapter One

He thought of Ava Jane.

The memory of her sweet smile had held him together for so long, Jeremiah wondered if he'd ever be able to face her again. The real *her*. The one he'd left behind. Remembering her pretty smile was one thing. Coming face-to-face with her and seeing the hurt and condemnation in her eyes would be another.

Something he'd dreaded during the long bus trip across the country from California to Pennsylvania.

But he wasn't here today to meet with the bishop about Ava Jane. He'd lost her and he'd accepted that long ago. He didn't deserve her anymore. Twelve years was a long time. She'd made a good life with a good man. Or so he'd heard.

She had not waited for Jeremiah to come home because all indications had shown he never would come home again. At times, he'd thought that same thing. Thought he was surely going to die a world away from the one he'd left. At those times, he'd think of her rich strawberry blonde curls and her light-as-air blue eyes.

And her wide, glowing smile. And he'd wish he'd never left her.

But he was here now, waiting inside the bishop's home to speak to him. Here and needing to find some solace. He came back to help his family, whether they wanted him to or not. His younger sister, Beth, had tried to keep in touch, but her last letter had been full of fear and grief.

"Daed is dying, Jeremiah. Please come quickly."

Bishop King walked into the sparsely decorated parlor where Jeremiah waited and stood for a moment. The man's gaze was solemn and unreadable, but his dark eyes held a glimmer of hope.

"Young Jeremiah Weaver," the bishop said before he took his time settling down in a high-back walnut chair across from Jeremiah. "Have you *kumm* back to your faith?"

Jeremiah held his head down and studied his hands, horrible memories of rapid gunfire and grown men moaning in pain filling his brain. Studied his hands and wished he could change them, take away the scars and calluses of war and replace them with the blisters and calluses of good, honest work.

He needed to find some peace.

That was why he'd come home to Lancaster County and his Amish roots. So he looked the bishop in the eyes and nodded.

"*Ja*, Bishop King, I've *kumm* home. For *gut*."

Home for good. One of the hardest things he'd ever had to do in his life. Because the hardest thing he'd ever done was leave Ava Jane crying in the dark.

Ava Jane Graber grabbed her ten-year-old son, Eli, by the collar of his shirt and shook her head. "Eli, please stop picking up things, *alleweil*." Right now. "You might break something."

"Sorry, Mamm," Eli replied, his mischievous brown eyes reminding her of her late husband, Jacob.

Jacob had drowned two years ago while trying to save a calf during a storm, but he used to love teasing her. Eli had inherited his father's gift of mirth and his gift of getting into trouble.

Sarah Rose, soon turning seven, seemed to have Ava Jane's sensibilities and logical nature. Her blue eyes grew as she twisted her brow. "Eli, you know Mamm doesn't like it when we break things." Putting her little hands on her hips, the child added, "And you break things all the time."

Hmm. Her young daughter could also be a tad judgmental at times. Had she also inherited that from Ava Jane?

Ava Jane shook her head and gathered the few supplies she'd come into town to buy. "No, Mamm does not like it when you misbehave and accidentally break things."

Smiling at Mr. Hartford, the general store owner, she paid for her items and said, *"Denke."*

"You're welcome, Ava Jane, and thank you for the fresh apple muffins," the Englisch manager said with a wide grin. "Good to see you out and about today."

"It's a fine spring morning," Ava Jane replied, her items and her children in tow. Mr. Hartford loved it when she brought him fresh baked goods to sell, but he also liked that she saved a couple of choices just for him. "A wonderful, beautiful day."

"One of the Lord's best," Mr. Hartford said with a nod.

But when she walked out onto the sidewalk toward her

waiting horse and buggy, her beautiful morning turned into something she couldn't explain.

She looked up and into the deep blue eyes of the man walking toward them, her bag of groceries slipping right out of her grip. The paper bag tore and all her purchases crashed down, the sound of shattering glass echoing off the pavement.

"I think Mamm just broke something," Eli pointed out, his gaze moving from her to the hard-edged man wearing a T-shirt and jeans, his dark hair curling around his face and neck.

"Who is that, Mamm?" Sarah Rose asked, her distinctive intuition shining brightly as her gaze moved from Ava Jane to the man.

Ava Jane couldn't speak, couldn't elaborate. But inside, she was shouting and screaming and wishing she could take her children and run away. Her heart had shattered right along with the jar of fresh honey she'd purchased.

She knew this man. Had thought about him time and again over the years.

Jeremiah Weaver.

The man who'd left her behind.

Jeremiah couldn't stop himself. He rushed toward Ava Jane and the *kinder* with all the might he'd used to charge against the enemy while wearing heavy tactical gear.

"Ava Jane?" he called, fearful that she was going to pass out. Her skin, always as fresh as new peaches, turned pale, her sky blue eyes filled with shock, the pupils dilating.

He'd startled her. He had not meant to let her see him this way, here on the street in the small town of Campton

Creek, where everyone talked too much about things of which they knew nothing. Wishing he'd had more time to prepare, Jeremiah couldn't hide from her now.

"Ava Jane?" he said again when he'd made it to her side. "Are you all right?"

"Was denkscht?" she asked, anger in the phrase, her heart-shaped face dark with confusion.

What do you think?

Jeremiah saw a bench. *"Kumm,* sit."

"Mamm?" the little girl said on a wail, fright clear in her eyes. "May we go home?"

Ava Jane looked from her confused daughter back to Jeremiah. "In a minute, Sarah Rose. Go with your brother to the buggy and wait for me."

"You made a mess," the boy pointed out, love for his *mamm* shining in his eyes. "I can clean it for you."

Jeremiah could see Jacob in the boy's eyes. Jacob, one of his best friends. Married to the woman he'd loved.

"I'll clean it up in a bit," Jeremiah offered, taking Ava Jane by the arm to guide her to the bench. Few people were out and about but those who were, including some Amish, had stopped to stare.

She pulled away. "I'll get Mr. Hartford. Go now, Eli, and wait by the horses."

The *kinder* did as she requested. Only when they were out of earshot did she turn back to him, her eyes blazing like a hot sky. "What are you doing here, Jeremiah?"

"I didn't want you to see me yet," he tried to explain.

"Too late." She adjusted her white *kapp* with shaking hands. "I need to go."

"Please don't," he said. "I'm not going to bother you. I…I saw you and I didn't have time to—"

"To leave again?" she asked, her tone full of more

venom than he could ever imagine coming from such a sweet soul.

"I'm not leaving," he said. "I'm here to stay. I've come back to Campton Creek to help my family. But I had planned on coming to pay you and Jacob a visit, to let you know that…I understand how things are now. You're married—"

"I'm a widow now," she blurted, two bright spots forming on her cheeks. "And I have to get my children home."

Kneeling, she tried to pick up her groceries but his hand on her arm stopped her. Jeremiah took the torn bag and placed the thread, spices and canned goods at the bottom, the feel of sticky honey on his fingers merging with the memory of her dainty arm. But the shock of her words made him numb with regret.

I'm a widow now.

"I'm sorry," Jeremiah said in a whisper. "Beth never told me."

"You couldn't be reached."

Ah, so Beth had tried but he'd been on a mission.

"I wish I'd known. I'm so sorry."

Ava Jane kept her eyes downcast while she tried to gather the rest of her groceries and toss them in the torn bag.

"Here you go," he said, the bag tightly rolled while her news echoed through his mind and left him stunned. "I'll go inside and get something to clean the honey."

Their eyes met while his hand brushed over hers.

A rush of deep longing shot through her eyes, jagged and fractured, and hit Jeremiah straight in his heart.

Ava Jane recoiled and stood. *"Denke."*

Then she turned and hurried toward the buggy. Just

before she lifted her skirts to get inside, she pivoted back
to give him one last glaring appraisal. "I wonder why you
came back at all."

He watched as she got in the buggy and sat for a moment before she gave the reins to her son. Without a back-
ward glance, Ava Jane held her head high. Then Jeremiah
hurried into Hartford's and asked for a wet mop to clean
the stains from the sidewalk. He only wished he could
clean away the stains inside of his heart.

And just like her, he wondered why he'd returned to
Campton Creek.

Ava Jane didn't know how she'd made it the two miles
home. She'd been so shaken that she'd allowed Eli to
guide the buggy. Knowing that their docile roan mare,
Matilda, would get them home safely, Ava Jane watched
her son handling the reins, her sight blurred by an ache
that caught her at the oddest of times.

Well, seeing Jeremiah in *Englisch* clothes had certainly been odd. Seeing him, his blue-black eyes holding hers, so many unspoken things between them, had
certainly been confusing and overwhelming. His hand
brushing against hers had brought back memories of how
they used to hold hands and sneak chaste kisses. She felt
a headache coming on.

Why was he back?

Twelve years had passed since he'd awakened her in
the middle of the night and asked her to come out onto
the porch between the main house and the *grossdaadi
haus* where her grandparents lived.

Twelve years since Jeremiah had taken his *rumspringa*
to a whole new level while she'd barely done anything

different during her own. Her heart was here in Campton Creek while his heart had longed for adventure and...war.

War. He'd become a warrior, hardened and battle scarred and unyielding. A Navy warrior. SEALs, they called themselves. In desperation, she'd gone to the library and found all kinds of articles that explained things much too clearly to her. He'd gone against the Amish way and joined the military.

What had he done and seen out there?

"I have to go, Ava Jane," he said that night so long ago, tears in his eyes. "I can't explain it but...something has happened. Something bad."

"Was ist letz?" she asked, her heart pumping too fast. "What's the matter?"

"Edward is dead."

She knew Edward Campton, ten years older at the time than Jeremiah's seventeen. He and Jeremiah became good friends when Mr. Weaver and Jeremiah went to the stately Campton mansion centered in the heart of Campton Creek to build some new cabinets in the kitchen. Edward, a Navy SEAL, was home on leave for a couple of months and, for some reason, he'd told Jeremiah things he wasn't supposed to tell anyone.

But then, Jeremiah always had a rough streak. He loved to wrestle and fight, to swim as fast as he could, to be the first to win in any game. And he often talked about things of the world, hunting and fishing, which the Amish did only for food. Jeremiah became fascinated with battles and war games and sailing the open seas, things their kind did not condone.

During his second year of *rumspringa*, the time all Amish teens and young adults had a chance to run around before they settled down and became baptized, Jeremiah became enamored of Edward. Edward's Englisch ways and military talk swayed Jeremiah and changed him. Soon, Jeremiah began to spend more and more time with Edward, running and exercising with him, swimming in the big pool behind the Campton mansion, learning all about dangerous weapons and listening to Edward's stories of valor. Even learning how to scuba dive, of all things.

Edward loaned him history books full of stories of valor, which Jeremiah read late at night after his chores were done. After he came by to see her and tell her he loved her which he often did back then.

Why, she'd never understand. *Why, Jeremiah?* Why had he felt the need to run away and join the Navy?

She heard talk in town about the Campton family. Their roots stretched back to the American Revolution and the town was named for them. They were rich and had a house full of material things. The minute Jeremiah met Edward, she'd felt him slipping away from her. All his talk about history and battles and honoring the country that protected and sheltered him.

He'd been almost eighteen and able to make his own decisions. Finally, he'd told her he wasn't sure he wanted to be baptized. He wasn't sure he wanted to stay Amish. Jeremiah had always been adventurous and he'd often talked about things of the world, but he changed right before her eyes. She saw the change the last time they'd talked.

"Jeremiah, what are you saying? Your place is here, with me. This is our life. The life God gave us."

But that night she'd lost him completely. His friend who'd gone back to his duties had been on a dangerous mission to find and kill a known terrorist, he explained.

"I was at the Campton place a few hours ago, helping Mr. Campton with replacing some worn floors. They were watching a news report on television about a secretive raid that happened a few days ago. I could tell they were concerned. Then these two men in uniform showed up at the door. Mrs. Campton screamed out and we ran to her. Mr. Campton saw the two men and started to cry. It was horrible. They'd come to tell them that Edward was dead. Killed in the raid. Killed, Ava Jane."

Once Ava Jane heard that and after Jeremiah told her he'd been there when they'd received the terrible news, she knew she'd lost Jeremiah.

His friend who'd served his country as a Navy SEAL had died, and now Jeremiah wanted to join up and fight an unspeakable enemy to avenge that death. That went against the tenets of their faith.

"No, Jeremiah, no," she cried. "I beg you, don't do this. We don't get involved in these things. We don't fight wars. Stay with me. We have plans, remember? Our own home, children. A life together. We've talked about it since we were thirteen."

"I want that life," he said, tears streaming down his face. "But I have to do this now, while I'm young. I'll come back one day. Soon." His hands on her face, he looked into her eyes, torment twisting his expression. "I can't explain it, but I have to go."

"No." She didn't agree with him, did not agree with how he followed Edward around, always asking questions and trying to be Englisch. He'd spent his *rumspringa* trying to be someone he wasn't and now he'd become someone she didn't know.

Blinking away tears, she came back to the present, focused on her children and tried to take a breath.

But he's back.

He'd said he'd come home to help his family. True, his *daed* was ill, first from a broken hip and now with an infection that wouldn't heal. After many weeks in a nearby hospital, Isaac had requested he be brought home. He now lay, in and out of consciousness. It was just a matter of time.

But who had summoned Jeremiah home?

Surely not his stubborn, hard *daed*, who'd banned Jeremiah from their home. Probably not his *mamm*. She'd never go against her husband's wishes. Probably his sister, Beth.

The siblings had managed to stay close through the years. Beth often gave Ava Jane updates, even when she'd never asked for them. Sometimes, he couldn't be located, such as when Jacob had died. His life had become so secretive and covert. Because it had become a dangerous life. Ava Jane had prayed for Jeremiah so many times. That was her duty. She prayed for everyone she knew. But she'd never prayed him home. Not once.

She wanted no part of the man.

She wanted to go back to that night and hear him say instead, "I'll stay, Ava Jane. For you. Only you."

Stop it, she told herself. *Think of Jacob. You can have no betrayal of your husband in your thoughts.*

So now while her children did their chores and ran around in the sunshine, chasing butterflies, Ava Jane sat in Jacob's rocking chair and cried for her husband, her head pounding with both physical and mental pain. She needed his warmth right now. She needed him here with her in their safe, comfortable beloved world. Jacob would hold her close and tell her he'd protect her and take care of her. No matter what.

Her husband had tried to show her the love that Jeremiah had thrown away and, in turn, she'd tried to be a good wife to Jacob. They had truly grown to love each other. They'd been together through the loss of both of Jacob's parents, first his mother and then, a year later, his father. Jacob never quite got over losing his parents. But then he'd died five years later.

Now, struggling on her small farm, she didn't have Jacob to shield her from the pain of seeing Jeremiah again. Jeremiah, the same but so different.

Ava Jane tugged her shawl tightly around her as the gloaming fell across the green grass and newly budding fruit trees, the last of the sun's rays covering the hills and valleys and rooftops like a light linen veil. She wondered how she'd ever be able to accept Jeremiah being back in Campton Creek. No matter that she was allowed to speak to him since he'd never been baptized and there was no ban on him. No matter that she might not see him every day anyway. No matter that his family needed him and he'd heeded that call. None of it mattered and she shouldn't even fret about these things.

Just knowing he was nearby—that would be the hard thing.

Ava Jane rubbed her aching temples and sipped the tea she hoped would subdue the agony attacking her brain.

Dear Lord, give me the strength to go about my life. He has no meaning to me now. I have to forget he's back.

She would. She'd go on the way she'd been doing. She was blessed and, while she grieved the loss of her husband, she had to consider her children. They had kept her going these past two years. She'd concentrate on them and their needs.

But, even through her fervent prayers, Ava Jane knew that trying to put Jeremiah Weaver out of her mind would be like trying not to breathe.

Impossible.

Chapter Two

News traveled fast in the Amish community. Jeremiah knew before he approached the dirt lane leading up to his family home that they would be expecting him, even if they probably dreaded him being here. Bishop King had offered to come and talk to them, but Jeremiah wasn't sure if he indeed had made it by yet or how well that visit had gone. Maybe they could all meet with the bishop as a family. The bishop and the ministers had given Jeremiah their blessings to go through the eighteen required weeks of lessons he'd need before he could be baptized.

He'd already started on that at least, and he'd kept in touch with Beth so she'd know he was close by in case his father took a turn for the worse.

"When are you coming home to us?" his sister had asked when he'd sent her word to call him at the Campton estate.

"After I take care of a few things."

Things such as transferring the money he'd saved to a bank here so he could help his family financially and set up provisions for his mother and sister.

He'd wanted to talk to Ava Jane, too, but he'd never

found the courage. So now, she knew he was back. Soon the whole community would know he'd returned. He'd stalled long enough.

These last few weeks, he'd been staying in the guest-house at Campton House and working for the now-elderly Camptons. But after seeing Ava Jane yesterday outside Hartford's General Store, he knew it was time to do what he'd set out to do.

He had to face his family.

Beth had faithfully written to him through the years. That was allowed at least. He knew a lot of Amish who kept in touch with relatives who'd gone out into the Englisch world.

Mamm always sent her love but even now she wouldn't talk to him if his *daed* was alert and aware. But Daed. That was another matter. While he had not officially been shunned since he'd never been baptized, Jeremiah knew he'd been gone a long time. His *daed* had made it clear he was not welcome back in the Weaver house, unless he was willing to give his confession and be baptized. Then Jeremiah would be welcomed back and forgiven, and the past would be the past.

Only, he'd brought his past with him. Not willing to think about that now, he made his way up to the wide, welcoming porch that his *mamm* and sister kept swept and spotless. Already, a riotous bed of flowers bloomed in shades of purple, red and blue all along the porch border. Two potted plants graced each side of the front door. His mother and sister loved their gardens. Daed frowned on such frivolous colors, but Jeremiah knew his father well enough to know Isaac Weaver would do anything to make his wife smile.

Anything but forgive his only son for leaving. His father might accept him back, but Jeremiah wondered if that wound could ever be completely healed. He'd deserted his family.

The bishop had given Jeremiah some advice to help him get started on the process of attending baptism sessions, which happened an hour before church on every other Sunday. Then he needed to get right with his family. The bishop had prayed with him about that, too. And, while Jeremiah had not been ready to share everything he'd seen and done, Bishop King had offered him some hope. "You can talk to me, Jeremiah. Anytime, about anything. *Wilkum* home."

Thankful for that, Jeremiah had asked, "Where do I start?"

Rubbing his silver beard, Bishop King had lowered his head. "Your *daed* is gravely ill. He might not ever know you are home but Isaac will be glad in his heart to see you return. I encourage you to talk to him, even if he seems to be sleeping. Your *mamm* and sister need a strong man about. The place is going down in spite of neighbors pitching in to help. You will step up, Jeremiah. And in time you'll begin to heal."

He was about to step up, all right. He might not be able to truly be a part of this family but he'd do the right thing because he was ready now. Ready to settle down and give his life back to the Lord. Jeremiah would do whatever it took to find his way back to God.

And to Ava Jane.

He hadn't planned on trying to win her back but...she was alone now. She needed him and, even though she'd acted afraid and angry, he'd seen the truth when he'd touched her hand and looked into her eyes. She could love him again with time and forgiveness. Now he had a wonderful reason to work hard to prove his intentions. He'd make things right with God and his family and then he'd win Ava Jane back. It would be the toughest battle of his life.

Now he stood at the steps of the home where he'd been raised, memories coloring his mind in the same way those flowers colored the yard. But the pretty flowers couldn't hide the gloomy facade surrounding the big rectangular two-story house. One of the porch posts needed replacing, and the whole place could use a good coat of paint. The house contained four big bedrooms and a large open kitchen and dining area with a cozy sitting area by the woodstove. Big enough to hold church services, if need be. A large basement for storage and summer use. And the *grossdaadi haus* where his grandparents had lived before their deaths.

A lot needed to be done around here.

Jeremiah closed his eyes and thought about growing up on this vast farm. The laughter, the discussions, the prayers before each meal, the hard work. A heavy mist filled his eyes. He opened them and took a deep breath to calm himself.

Home.

Before he could take another step, his younger sister, Beth, rushed out the door and flung herself into his arms.

"Jeremiah, you're home! *Gott segen eich.*"

God bless you.

Jeremiah held her close, the scent of lavender and fresh soap cleansing away the ugliness of what he'd seen on the battlefield.

He held her for only a second and then stepped back. "Shh, now. You know Daed wouldn't want you touching me."

She blinked back tears, her dark hair spilling around her white *kapp* like smooth chocolate. "Daed doesn't wake up much anymore. We need you home and I need a hug from my big brother, *ja*."

"Where's Mamm?" he asked, his voice clogged with emotion. He smelled pot roast and gravy, maybe even biscuits. His mouth watered just thinking about his mother's cooking.

"Seeing to Daed in the downstairs room," Beth replied. "*Kumm*, we have a grand feast for you."

"A feast for the prodigal?"

Beth gave him a solid stare, her blue eyes bright. "*Ja*. And glad to have him home at that."

Ava Jane sat down next to her sister. Once or twice a week, she and her sister and some other friends got together to quilt and bake, taking turns to host. Some might call this time together a frolic and they did frolic, but they also worked and prayed and shared common joys and concerns.

Her friends had seen her through two babies and the loss of her in-laws and her husband. She loved them dearly and counted her sister, Deborah, as a friend, too. Deborah had been eight years old when Jeremiah had left. Ava Jane remembered her little sister crawling into her bed and snuggling close to her while she cried. Deborah remembered how Ava Jane had suffered.

Today, they were at Ava Jane's house finishing up a quilt she was making for Sarah Rose. The women had been working on the intricate appliquéd patterns all winter and now they needed to complete it before the spring chores, such as planting, gardening and canning, took over.

"Beautiful," Deborah said, her green eyes searching Ava Jane's face. "I think Sarah Rose will love this so much. The rose in the center is precious. It will make a wonderful present for her seventh birthday."

Ava Jane continued to stitch one of the black squares with white backings that would frame a colorful flower, bird or butterfly. "*Ja*, I'm thankful for the help. I have to work on it when the *kinder* are with Mamm and Daed." She glanced at the big-faced clock in the kitchen. Eleven in the morning. "We have a couple more hours. Daed is supervising the pony rides today."

Both of her children were learning about chores and responsibility thanks to help from her parents. Daed provided a good male influence that helped to discipline them properly, but he couldn't be with them all the time.

Jacob. She always thought of what a good father he'd been.

"*Gut*," her sister said in a conspiring tone, bringing her back to the task at hand. "Now you can tell us what you think about Jeremiah Weaver coming back to Campton Creek."

Ava Jane missed a stitch and pricked her finger.

Which her shrewd and overly curious sister saw right away.

With a soft yelp, she dropped her needle and held her finger to her lips, the metallic taste of blood making her wince. But she didn't dare look at her sister or her suddenly quiet friends.

Deborah handed her an old remnant of fabric to hold over her finger. "You've talked to him?"

Ava Jane held the fabric to her skin, the pain of the tiny cut stinging through her with a warning while the pressure she put on the wound only reinforced her anxiety. "Not intentionally, *ne*."

Why did she feel the need to defend herself and him?

"Then how?" Deborah asked, concern mixed with hurt in her eyes that her sister had not confided in her.

Ava Jane glanced at the two other women watching her with a ridiculous intensity that made her want to laugh. But she couldn't laugh. "I was coming out of Hartford's and he was there on the street, loading some lumber into a truck."

"Lumber, on the street? And a truck at that?" her friend Hannah asked, her brown-eyed expression full of awe. "What does he look like now?"

Did her friends think Jeremiah had grown two heads and now breathed fire? Well, remembering how she'd recoiled at first, she'd probably acted the same.

Ava Jane swallowed and wished she hadn't been so transparent here today or with Jeremiah yesterday. She never could hide her emotions. Tenderhearted, her *mamm* called her.

Holding her head up, she said, "He looks healthy." *And hardened and world-weary.*

Jeremiah had always been formidable, but now his shoulders seemed to be even wider than she remembered. Strong shoulders.

Her sister made a groaning sound. "*Ja*, I suppose he would at that."

"I've heard things," Hannah said, speaking in a rush. "Heard he looks like a different man now. Englisch, my *daed* says."

"Does everyone know he's back?" Ava Jane asked, unable to stop her own curiosity.

"*Ja*, and that he talked to you on the street," Hannah

replied. "Grossmammi heard it from Rebecca Lantz. She said he's been taking baptism classes already."

Ava Jane shook her head. "No wonder it's all over the place." Rebecca Lantz loved to gossip and she'd also had a severe crush on Jeremiah at one time. Now at least, she was married and settled. But she still didn't know when to stay quiet. "Rebecca likes to prattle too much," she blurted.

She also told herself that if Jeremiah was attending baptism sessions, he must be back for good.

"We are not to judge," Leah, older and married with six children, said while she cast her gaze across the creamy quilt backing. "Ava Jane might rather not talk about this."

"He looked fine," Ava Jane said to show them she was unaffected and that she, for one, wouldn't judge. "We spoke briefly and I left."

She didn't go into detail about dropping her groceries or how Jeremiah had helped her salvage what she could. Nor did she tell them that seeing him had shattered *her* into a million pieces. She'd thought her grief was becoming better but now she mourned Jacob's death in a raw, fresh way. She blamed Jeremiah for that. He'd brought out too many emotions in her.

"Has he returned for *gut* then?" Leah asked, sympathy and understanding in her brown eyes.

"I didn't ask. And it's not my concern."

Hannah supplied the rest, her brown eyes settling on Ava Jane. "According to what I'm hearing, he's come home because Isaac is dying. Jeremiah will take over the farm chores and continue the carpentry work he and his father used to do together. His father needed him a long time ago. At least he's home now. Beth is happy. She never gave up on her brother."

This time, when her friend looked at Ava Jane, there was a trace of regret and condemnation in Hannah's expression.

What did she know about heartache? She had yet to find a husband.

Ava Jane went back to stitching her daughter's quilt, her face burning, her eyes misting. She was pretty sure she made a mistake in laying the pattern, but then some believed no quilt should be perfect anyway. Only God held perfection.

A good reason to remember she shouldn't judge.

The women went on to other topics such as the upcoming Campton Creek Spring Festival to be held next month. The Amish had always participated in the fair. They took their wares into town and held a sidewalk sale in the park by the creek and across from Hartford's. But her sister's hand over hers brought her head up.

Deborah gave her a quick, quiet smile and then went back to stitching a yellow-and-white butterfly.

Her sister knew her so well, Ava Jane thought. Well enough to know Jeremiah being home *was* a concern. A big concern.

A few days later, Ava Jane's mother and sister came for an early-morning visit. *"Wilkum,"* she said, surprised to see both of them there on a fine Friday morning. "Come in."

Her family lived just around the curve, close enough that she could walk across the field and then take the covered bridge over the big creek between her land and theirs. She sometimes avoided going that way, though, and instead took the lane that wound away from the deep creek that held the same name as the town.

She visited with them weekly and her folks often stopped by to check on her. But usually that occurred when the children were just returning from school up the road. They loved their grandchildren.

This was an unusual visit.

"We need your help," Martha Troyer said, giving Ava Jane a quick hug. "We dropped by to see if you'd like to ride over to the Weaver place with us. Moselle is having a hard time of trying to take care of Isaac, and we've brought food to take." Then Mamm gave a little shrug, but her intent was soon clear. "I just felt that I needed to visit with Moselle this morning."

"And she felt that *we* both also needed to be there with her," Deborah said, giving Ava Jane an eyebrow lift that warned her this was not Deborah's idea. "Are you busy?"

Her dear sister was trying to give her an out.

Ava Jane searched to find an excuse. She'd already worked in the garden, swept the porch, hung some laundry on the line out back and made two chocolate pies. *"Ne,"* she finally said. "But why do I need to come along?"

Her mother gave her a soft smile. "I thought it might cheer up Beth. We haven't had a good housecleaning frolic in a long time, and Beth's been working by her *mamm's* side day and night for the last few weeks, helping to take care of Isaac. You two can distract her while I help Moselle with whatever needs doing. It'll be *gut* for Beth to talk to women close to her age."

Ava Jane couldn't say no. And besides, she wasn't sure Jeremiah's parents even knew he was back. But they'd have to know if he'd come back to help out. Everyone must have heard by now. He might be living here again, but he'd been using a truck in town when she'd seen him several days ago. That meant he might prefer life with the Englisch. But he must be living somewhere near here, at least. She wondered if he'd decided to stay out there in the world, after all.

But either way, surely he wouldn't be at his parents' place. He was no longer welcome there, from what Beth had said about their father's wrath.

Of course, Ava Jane hadn't been the best of friends with Beth through the years. Their friendship had been tested mightily. Maybe a visit could help that.

"Let me freshen up and get my bonnet," she said, already tugging at her work apron. "I made two chocolate pies. I can take one of those to go along with what you've provided."

Deborah gave her another meaningful glance and stepped back to mouth, "Sorry." Martha's all-knowing gaze moved between the two of them.

Did Mamm know what she was asking of Ava Jane?

Chapter Three

"I appreciate everything you've done for me," Jeremiah said, his hand over Mrs. Campton's, while they sat in the stately den of the big house he remembered so well.

Judy Campton smiled over at him and shook her head, her misty green eyes centered on Jeremiah. "No, son, we are the thankful ones. You made a great sacrifice, doing what you did after our Edward died. He would be so proud of you."

Jeremiah didn't feel proud. He'd done his duty and he'd followed orders, but he didn't know how he could ever wipe the stench of death and destruction off of his body.

"I did what I had to do at the time. I thought I'd make a difference, but so many died. So many. In spite of being wounded I managed to be whole and survive. I got to come home."

Judy nodded and patted his hand before she sat back in her comfortable chair and took a sip of tea, her faithful housekeeper and assistant, Bettye, hovering nearby. Looking into Jeremiah's eyes before skimming her gaze over his blue cotton shirt and broadcloth pants held up by black suspenders, she said, "But you're not really home quite yet, are you?"

"No, ma'am," Jeremiah said, his coffee growing cold on the Queen Anne table centered between the two chairs. "I wanted to thank you and the Admiral for allowing me to stay in the guesthouse for this past couple of weeks. I needed to get my bearings and being here helped."

"I wish the Admiral felt like sitting here with us this morning," she replied. "He so loves talking to you. Makes him feel close to our Edward."

Admiral Campton had taken a turn for the worse over the last year. He had a private nurse and was resting in his bed now, but some days he managed to get up and sit out in the garden he'd always loved. It was a garden Jeremiah had helped landscape and plant all those years ago, he and Edward working side by side with the hired yardman.

"I'll go up and see him before I leave," he finally said. "I won't be that far away. You can get in touch with me if you need anything."

Mrs. Campton nodded, her pearl earrings shimmering along with her short white hair. "I know you'd come immediately, Jeremiah. But your family is depending on you. I think God's timing is always perfect, so you go on and get settled. But I expect you to visit whenever you're in town. Please."

Jeremiah saw the anguish on her face and heard it in that plea. They'd lost their only son and now they had no grandchildren to carry on the Campton name. When he'd called and asked to come by for a short visit, they had immediately taken him in and sheltered him, because they understood what he'd been through. He loved them like he loved his own family but he couldn't be a substitute for their son. And they couldn't fill the void inside his heart, kind as they were to him.

"I will always come and see you," he said, getting up to stand in front of the empty fireplace. Staring up at the portrait of Edward in his dress uniform hanging over the mantel, he said, "I only knew him for a year or so but he changed my life forever."

"Do you regret knowing him?" Judy asked, her tone without judgment.

"No," Jeremiah said, turning to smile at her. "He was one of the best friends I've ever had, and he did not pressure me in any way to join up. I regret that I didn't understand exactly what I'd be getting into. I don't mind having been a SEAL. But the torment of war will never leave me."

"You have PTSD, don't you? Post-traumatic stress disorder is a hard thing to shake and I suspect you, of all people, know that."

Judy Campton was a wise and shrewd woman who'd been a military spouse for close to forty years. She and Ed, as the Admiral liked to be called, married late in life and had Edward a few years later. Like his father, Edward had lived and breathed the military. And he'd given his life for that loyalty.

"Jeremiah?"

He looked around the big rambling room with the grand piano, the exquisite antique furnishings and the rare artifacts from all over the world. This place brought him both peace and despair. "I have nightmares, yes. Bad memories. Moments where I have flashbacks of the heat of battle. But I'm hoping that will improve now that I'm home."

"Or it could get worse," Judy replied. "I can give you the names of some good counselors."

Surprised, he shook his head. "I don't need that right now."

"I see." Mrs. Campton didn't look convinced. "There is no shame in getting help. I used to volunteer at the veteran's hospital about thirty miles from here. I've seen a lot of men and women improve by just talking about things."

"I'll be fine," Jeremiah said, "once I'm back where I belong."

"As you wish," Mrs. Campton replied. "But call me if you ever need me. I'll be right here."

With that, he made his way to her. When she tried to stand, he said, "Don't get up. I only wanted to tell you *denke*. I owe both of you so much."

She gripped his arm and pushed with a feeble determination, so he helped her up. "And as I said, *we* owe *you*. Having you home brings a little bit of Edward back to us. Now, you go to be with those waiting to see you again."

"I'll tell the Admiral goodbye before I leave."

He helped her back into her chair and alerted the nearby housekeeper that he was going upstairs. Then he turned and headed toward the curving staircase.

"Jeremiah," Judy Campton called, her gaze lifting to him. "Don't tell him goodbye. Tell him you'll be nearby."

Jeremiah nodded and took the stairs in a rush.

Once he left here, he'd head straight back to his parents' house and he'd be living there from now until...

Until he could make amends, prove himself worthy and...maybe one day ask Ava Jane to marry him.

His sister, Beth, and his mother, Moselle, had welcomed him with open arms the other day since the bishop *had* told them of Jeremiah's wish to come home and help out. The bishop had talked this over with the ministers, too. They were all in agreement that as long as he followed the rules of the Ordnung and worked toward being baptized, he would be accepted back.

"Du bliebst Deitsch," the bishop had warned him. You must keep the ways of your people.

Mamm, perhaps too tired to turn down the help of her only son, had rushed into his arms the minute he'd walked into the familiar house two days ago. Then she'd stood back and said, "Go and see your *daed.*"

"He doesn't want to see me," Jeremiah replied, every pore of his body working up a cold sweat, his too-tight shirt straining at his shoulders.

His mother put her hands in Jeremiah's. "He needs to know his son made it home."

When he hesitated still, she added, "Do this for me."

Jeremiah couldn't deny his *mamm.* So he nodded and made his way into the hallway that lead to what used to be a sewing room in the back. His father lay there in a hospital bed, his body gaunt and pale, his once-thick dark hair now thin and streaked with gray. A shroud of sickness hovered over him, but with his eyes closed, he looked at peace and as if he was only napping.

Jeremiah blinked away the hot tears piercing like swords in his eyes. Had he caused this in his *daed*? Standing at the foot of the bed, he remained silent and asked God to give him the strength he needed.

I need forgiveness, Lord. I need my earthly father to know that I made it back to him. And You.

Now this morning, as he stood in the same spot and again prayed about how to approach his father, he could at least know that he'd never turned away from God. God had been there with him in the raging seas when he'd swum through treacherous waters and on the smoke-covered battlefields when he'd crawled with the snakes. God had been there when he'd held a buddy in his arms and watched the life leaving his eyes. God had been there when Jeremiah had woken up in a hospital and cried out for home. And for his God.

He had scars on his body and scars in his soul.

But how did he heal this rift that had separated him from this man? The man who'd loved him and taught him all the ways of being a real man. The man who'd cried out in anger that Jeremiah was never to enter this house again.

Talk to him.

Both the bishop and his mother had said the same thing.

So Jeremiah took a deep breath and used his military training to focus. And then he sat down in the hickory rocking chair beside the bed and let out a long shuddering sigh of both relief and regret.

"I'm home, Daed. I'm home for *gut*."

Isaac Weaver didn't respond. He kept right on sleeping in that deceptively peaceful way. But Jeremiah talked to him anyway, in gentle, hushed tones that held both respect and sadness.

He began to tell his story of taking a bus across the country and finding a job in Coronado, California, where the US Naval Special Warfare Command was located. He'd lived in a hut of an apartment with two other roommates who were planning to join up, and he had worked at restaurants and on farms while studying to get his GED. He'd saved up some money and passed the test, thanks to the books Edward had encouraged him to read and to his well-educated and worldly roommates who to this day still called him Amish. He'd then joined the Navy and immediately asked to enter the SEAL Challenge Program. He'd entered the Delayed Entry Program as an enlistee, so he could be sure he knew what he was doing and get some extra training and instructions before the real stuff began.

The instructors and counselors had warned him that training and duty would wipe out everything about him and change him. And still, he had insisted he was ready.

"No one can ever be ready for such a thing," he whispered in anguish. "But I couldn't fail. I would have had to go back to fleet—regular Navy for two years—that is." He stopped, shuddered a breath. "I didn't fail. In spite of everything, I made it through."

His father never moved, seemed to barely be breathing.

Jeremiah sat quiet for a while, his prayers centered on his father and this farm. He made a list in his head of all he needed to do. And he was just about to go on to explain boot camp and how the grueling training he'd undergone in a facility in Illinois, known as The Quarterdeck, had just about done him in. So close to his home and yet he couldn't reach out or visit.

He never got that far, however.

Because he heard feminine laughter in the front of the house…and smelled lavender and fresh soap.

Standing, he peeked up the narrow hallway to the front of the house and saw three women hugging his mother and sister.

And one of those women was Ava Jane Graber.

Ava Jane glanced up and into the other room.

Jeremiah stood staring at her, his expression full of

surprise and hope. He looked so different today. He was wearing the standard uniform of an Amish man: work shirt, broadcloth pants and dark work boots. He pushed the straw hat back, as if he'd become irritated with wearing it again.

Ava Jane couldn't move, couldn't breathe. This had been a very bad idea. She should have stayed at home, where she belonged.

Jeremiah started toward her and then halted, his boots creaking against the hardwood floors.

Her mother and sister stopped talking and stared at her, and then they both glanced to the end of the hallway.

Deborah's curious stare held shock. "So, Jeremiah is back."

Beth nodded, her glance dancing over Ava Jane before settling on the others. "*Ja*, indeed he is. Home to help out."

"I'm glad to hear that," Mamm said, patting Mrs. Weaver's hand. "And to see that he's visiting with his *daed*." She sent Ava Jane an apologetic smile tempered with a motherly warning.

"Isaac rarely responds to anyone these days," Moselle Weaver said. "We hoped Jeremiah might bring him back."

Ah, that explained why Jeremiah was in his *daed's* room. But Ava Jane wondered what would happen if Isaac Weaver should wake and find his wayward son sitting there.

Dear Lord, help me to be kind. Help me to find grace.

Jeremiah was now coming toward her, determination gathering like a thunderstorm in his eyes. He made it a few feet into the room and stood firm, his expression almost serene. "Hello, Mrs. Troyer. Deborah." His eyes moved from them to her. "Ava Jane."

Mamm hurriedly greeted him and turned back to Beth and Mrs. Weaver.

But both Beth and Deborah stood mystified by this encounter, knowing expressions passing between them like *kinder* playing volleyball.

"We only came to drop off this food and offer our help," Mamm said, holding up the baking dish full of chicken potpie. "I believe Ava Jane has a chocolate pie for you, too."

Ava Jane's hands were shaking so much she thought she'd drop the pie.

But before that could happen, two strong hands took the dish right out of her grip. "My favorite," Jeremiah said, his smile soft, his tone quiet. *"Denke."*

The rest of the women started scurrying here and there like squirrels after acorns. Nervous chatter filled the big room and echoed off the crossbeams, but Ava Jane couldn't hear what the women were talking about. She only heard the roar of her pulse pumping against her temples.

So she stood there like a ninny, wondering what to say or do. Ava Jane needed the floor to open up and swallow her. Needed the wind to lift her up and out into the wide-open spring sky. Neither of those things happened.

"How are you?" Jeremiah asked, true concern in his eyes.

"Fine, thank you," she managed to say. "And how are you?"

A loaded question. *What are you doing here? How did this happen? Explain everything to me and help me to understand.*

His smile reminded her of the old Jeremiah. Her Jeremiah.

"I'm *gut*. Better than when I first arrived."

"So…you're going to stay here with your family now?"

"*Ja.* I was staying with the Camptons in their guest-house."

The Camptons.

Like a cold splash of water, sharp-edged anger hit her in the face. "That makes perfect sense," she said, regaining her equilibrium and her strength. "Why didn't you continue to stay with them?"

Jeremiah's expression shifted and went dark. "Because they are not my family. I belong here. And I'm going to prove that to everyone, Ava Jane. Especially to you."

Shocked at his blunt words, she ignored the rush of embarrassment surging through her and accepted that he held bitterness in his heart, too. *Gut.* She hoped he had a lot of guilt and bitterness left to deal with.

Regretting her harsh wishes, she nodded and swallowed her pride. "Your *mamm* needs you now. But you don't need to prove anything to me, Jeremiah. Nothing at all."

Praying they could leave now, she turned to face her mother. But before Ava Jane could form a good excuse, her mother announced, "We've been invited to stay for dinner. I've accepted only because after we eat, we are going to give Moselle and Beth a rest while we clean the house and wash up the laundry."

Her mother's tone brooked no argument. Ava Jane took a long breath and reminded herself that she had come here for Beth and Mrs. Weaver. Not for him. She could share a meal with these two friends. She'd be just fine because she would not let Jeremiah's presence affect her. At all.

But before she could hurry into the kitchen, Jeremiah

moved closer. "I have everything to prove to you. But mostly, I have everything that is left in me to give to God."

With that, he spoke briefly to his mother, then nodded to the other women and turned to walk out the back door.

Ava Jane's face burned with shame.

She'd never once stopped to wonder about what he'd been through out there. And she had to consider—did he truly have anything left to give to God? Or her?

Chapter Four

The women ate a quick dinner, and then Ava Jane, her mother and Deborah did a thorough cleaning of the Weaver house while Moselle and Beth tended to and then sat with Isaac. After an hour or so of sweeping, dusting and freshening up, the smell of lemon-scented furniture polish and bleach gave the whole place a clean springtime freshness. They'd thrown open all of the windows, and a gentle breeze cooled the entire house and cleared away some of the gloom of medicine and sickness.

The whole time Ava Jane's nerves were on edge. She kept expecting Jeremiah to come through the door and glare at her again. She didn't belong here but she was having a hard time seeing *him* here. He didn't belong and he stood out like a mighty oak in a field of corn.

Father, help me to overcome this resentment. I know he means well but he left us. He left all of us.

Her prayers didn't calm her, and yet Ava Jane tried to wipe the bitterness out of her mind and go about the task of helping friends in need. Since Jeremiah had left, she'd stayed away from the Weaver house. But she'd been friends with Beth since they were close in age and had attended school together, even if Ava Jane had let things lapse in that friendship. Civil. She'd been civil to his family and she'd been sympathetic to their pain. *Ja*, she felt that same pain to the core.

Maybe that was why her mother had forced her to face the entire family head-on. So she'd see her own bitterness and work to overcome it. Her parents had a way of embracing adversity instead of turning from it. Her mother was forcing her to face her worst fears and work through them with prayer and guidance.

Indeed, she had to put her raw feelings aside. Isaac was dying. And his only son had come home to help out and be with him. Maybe she should talk to the bishop and get some advice on how to handle things better.

"I can't thank you enough," Moselle said over and over after Mamm had told her they were done. Coming out of the sick room, she'd gasped in surprise at the fresh flowers on the table and the sparkling clean kitchen and sitting area, her eyes as blue as her son's. Patting her *kapp*, she added, "I've neglected so much around here."

"Mamm and I try," Beth explained with an embarrassed blush. "We hurry through chores because we want to sit with Daadi as often as we can."

"Of course you want to spend time with him," Mamm said with a sympathetic smile. "That's why we came to help."

"We're blessed to have *gut* neighbors who do the outside chores," Moselle said, grief in every word. "I'm thankful Isaac is home with us and we can be near him."

Not to mention cleaning him and bathing him, Ava Jane surmised from hearing their conversations. No wonder the two of them looked so withered and exhausted. And no wonder they'd welcomed Jeremiah back with open arms. He was needed and she had to admire his stepping up to do the right thing.

That took courage, considering how he'd been gone for so long. Considering how he'd left and what he had become.

Father, can I ever forgive him? How can I even start?

Beth had voluntarily filled them in on the details earlier, her voice hushed and whispery. Ava Jane hadn't wanted to hear it but she'd held her breath with each revelation Beth brought out.

"He is staying in the *grossdaadi haus* for now. The bishop approved that. He takes his meals with Mamm and me, but doesn't sit with us." She shrugged. "His choice, out of respect for Daed."

He was here to work hard and help his family, she explained. In the meantime, he planned to make things right with the church. With God.

"He started the baptism sessions weeks ago."

Deborah glanced at Ava Jane during these tidbits of information regarding Jeremiah. "Where has he been for so long?" Deborah asked, her innocent tone barely masking her inquisitive nature.

"Out in California," Beth said. "At least that's the address he sent me a year ago, after he'd finished his duty. But I didn't tell anyone except Mamm." She shrugged. "He joined the Navy and went on some sort of secretive missions. I don't ask for details. I think whatever he did out there must have changed him. He needed to come home."

She shot Ava Jane a beseeching, hopeful smile.

Ava Jane didn't tell Jeremiah's sister or mother that she'd searched in the library to learn about the Navy and the SEALs. Why bring that up now? She hadn't asked any questions while Beth talked either, but now she tried not to think about Jeremiah being out in the world alone. She only knew he'd have to make a lot right in order to be brought back into the fold. That was the Amish way. The bishop and ministers had obviously approved of him coming back. He'd have to study and understand adult baptism, discipline, shunning and separation to see where he fit in and to accept that once he committed and was baptized, he'd be expected to stay here and follow the church rules.

Once Jeremiah confessed his sins in front of the church and asked forgiveness and was baptized, he would be accepted. They would not mention his past again. And he would become Amish again. For good.

Could he do that? Could he confess what he'd done all these years, just forget all about it? How did a man forget about killing and war? What if he wanted to go back out there into the world or go back into the fray? What about that *duty* Beth had mentioned?

If he left again after he'd pledged to serve God and return to the tenets of the Ordnung, which consisted of a district-wide set of rules and regulations they were all expected to observe, Jeremiah could never return.

Please, Father, I pray he means to stay.

She refused to feel anything beyond that hope, but her heart hurt for what he must have done in the name of war. He had courage, too much courage. He'd always had a reckless, rebellious side and he defended his friends, no matter what.

Honoring a friend was why he'd left in the first place.

But he was back and he was indeed trying to make amends. Ava Jane knew she wasn't to judge. That didn't mean she could forget either.

She could only pray for Jeremiah and hope for the best for him.

The shining thankfulness in Moselle Weaver's eyes told Ava Jane one thing. He was still very much loved. And love could heal a multitude of sins.

"I think that's it," her mother announced from behind where Ava Jane stood by the sink, staring out toward the fields.

They'd finished in time for Ava Jane to make it home to greet her children after school. "*Gut.* I need to get back before the *kinder* put out a search party."

She was about to turn to leave when she saw Jeremiah plowing, his broad shoulders firm and solid, his big hands working the reins with a seasoned knowledge, as he urged the two big Belgian draft horses through the hard dirt. Growing up, he'd been muscular and big boned, his upper body full of strength because he managed to sneak off and swim in the creek all summer long. He'd had a natural grace about him. He'd been the kind of man who could take on any task and make it look easy. A smart learner, her *daed* used to say. Now that muscle was solid and fully matured and that grace fell across his broad shoulders like a mantle. He would farm this land and make it good again.

She didn't want to accept how natural he did look, back in the fields, his hair long and curling around his hat, his face bare to mark him as unmarried. When she thought of that and of all the unmarried friends she had, a streak of fierce jealousy shot through her like a spark of fire.

She would not be jealous. She had no right to be jealous of anyone who might be interested in Jeremiah.

Behind him in the far distance, the covered bridge

stood solid and firm, a glisten of water peeking through
in diamond-like sparkles. Beyond that, far on the other
side of the big creek that ran deep and wide, stood Campton House. The huge Georgian-style mansion had always
fascinated Ava Jane. But the house held bad memories
for her, too. Jeremiah spent a lot of his *rumspringa* at
that house.

Something fluttered inside her heart. A memory of
Jeremiah and Jacob laughing and playing in the body
of water centered in their community. Jeremiah loved
to swim since the day his *daed* had begun teaching him.
He'd glide through the water like a fish. Jacob hadn't
been quite as strong but he tried to keep up. She'd watch
them from the covered bridge, her fear of water too pro-
nounced to allow her to join them. Jeremiah coaxed her
to join even though girls didn't swim with boys.

"I'll teach you how to swim, Ava Jane," he'd said.

She'd never learned. And she'd never told him that she
was terrified of the water.

Why had she remembered that now, when the man she
watched was deep in rich dirt and misty dust?

"He's going to plant our spring garden even though
it's late in the season," Beth said from behind, causing
Ava Jane to come out of her stupor. "He's trying so hard,
Ava Jane."

"I can see that," she said to Beth, meaning it. "I'm
glad for him. You need him home, *ja*?"

"Ja," Beth replied. "God brought him home. Our
prayers have been answered."

Thinking of the Biblical story of the prodigal and how
his father had welcomed him with open arms, Ava Jane
touched Beth's hand but didn't speak. Then she turned to
her mother and sister. "I need to go now please."

She almost ran out of the room, her heart betraying her every step. She had to stay away from Jeremiah Weaver. He'd broken her heart once…and she was still mourning the loss of her husband. But she was still mourning the loss of Jeremiah, too. It was wrong to think of another man when she ached for Jacob every day.

Jacob had drowned down in the creek, trying to save a hurt calf. He'd slipped on some rocks and old limbs, fallen and hit his head. A neighbor had heard the little calf crying out and had found Jacob.

The prodigal might be home but her husband was gone forever. That didn't seem fair to Ava Jane. Not at all.

She would try her best to forgive Jeremiah for leaving her but she couldn't forget how badly he'd hurt her. The guilt of loving him haunted her. Even now.

Jeremiah stayed away from the house long after he was sure Ava Jane and her mother and sister were gone. He couldn't be around her right now. It hurt too much to see the disappointment in her eyes, to read the judgment in her expression.

Coming back here had been hard. He'd been prepared for the curious stares and the condemning whispers. He'd also been prepared to work hard toward forgiveness and baptism. But he'd blocked out everything else. Or he'd tried. He thought he could get on with things if he avoided Ava Jane. Campton Creek was a small community and the Amish community within the tiny hamlet was even smaller. People knew he was back and, while most had been kind if not standoffish, everyone was watching him as if he were a deadly bug.

Shunned but not really shunned.

Alone in the middle of the world he'd loved and left.

Longing for a woman he'd loved and left.

Dear Father, I don't think I can do this.

"Jeremiah?"

He whirled, hoping.

But it wasn't Ava Jane walking toward him with a tall glass of lemonade. His sister, Beth, came up to the fence he'd been working on. "I reckoned you'd be thirsty."

"Ja." He took a long swig of the cool tart liquid. *"Denke."* His little sister gave him the curious expression he remembered so well. "Is there something else you need to say, Beth?"

Beth watched as the big Belgian geldings munched on their evening hay. "You stayed out here all day. You must be exhausted."

"I'm used to hard work." He glanced back toward the house.

"They have left, Jeremiah. You can come inside now."

"I'm used to being outside, too," he replied. "It's nice to be back on the land."

Again, that curious stare. "What was it like, Jeremiah? Out there, I mean."

His gut clenched. He didn't talk about such things. None of them ever did. For one thing, his team members were trained to stay quiet about their missions. But then, how could he explain it to innocent, pure Beth? Or anyone for that matter. The brutality of being in such a secretive, demanding career changed some men in ways that could never be explained. But he had refused to let it change him.

He did not want to talk about it either.

Instead, he did a scan of the landscape, his gaze hitting the big creek where he'd frolicked and played with Jacob, with Ava Jane sometimes watching from the shore or the bridge. "What happened to Jacob?" he asked.

Beth shot him a disappointed frown. "Did you not hear? I thought I told you in one of my letters."

"No. I didn't even know she…Ava Jane…was a widow. You never mentioned *that* in your letters."

"I did try to contact you, but later I tried not to mention *her* in my letters," Beth replied, guilt coloring her pretty eyes. "I didn't want you to think of a married woman, and then I only wrote about our family, since I didn't want to gossip or hurt you."

"I thought of her every day," he admitted. "Now, tell me what happened to Jacob."

Beth swallowed and held on to the weathered fence post. "He drowned down in the creek."

Jeremiah flinched and closed his eyes. "How? He was a fair swimmer."

"He went in after a trapped calf and, from what the sheriff could put together, he must have fallen and hit his head. They found a deep gash over his left temple. He was knocked out and went underwater. Just a foot or so of water."

Jeremiah hit a hand against the fence, causing the old wood to crack. Beth stepped back, shock in her eyes.

"I'm sorry," he said in a gravelly whisper, his heart rate accelerating. "I…I had to learn to swim one thousand yards in twenty minutes and to hold my breath for at least two minutes underwater. I mastered scuba diving, underwater demolition and swimming for miles at a time. I could have… I could have saved him."

Beth's expression filled with shock at what he'd blurted out, but she shook her head, a hand on his arm. "You weren't here, Jeremiah. And even if you had been, the fall caused him to go underwater. No amount of training or ability can change that."

"I should have been here," Jeremiah said, the rage at what he'd done bubbling up inside of him. "I should have been here."

He tried to move away but Beth held him still. "If you had been here, you would have been married to Ava Jane, and Jacob would have been somewhere else that day."

"Ja," he said, nodding in a rapid-fire gesture of anger. "Exactly."

Then he did pull away, leaving his confused, frightened sister to stare after him.

If he'd been here, everything would have been different.

But now that he was back, so many things had changed forever.

Chapter Five

A week later, Jeremiah stood in the hardware aisle at Hartford's General Store when Ava Jane came in, carrying a basket of muffins. Everyone praised her muffins and pastries, and he noticed Mr. Hartford kept a supply in stock at the store, which meant she was earning money by selling them there. Jeremiah had bought a couple. Good, sturdy muffins full of oatmeal, nuts and fruits. Carrot muffins, banana muffins, pumpkin, too. He even got ahold of a zucchini one and he didn't even like zucchini.

No fancy cupcakes for Ava Jane. She believed in hearty, stick-to-the-ribs food.

He watched now as she smiled shyly while Mr. Hartford bragged about her cooking skills to a couple of giggly female tourists out for a day of "experiencing all things Amish."

Ava Jane listened and smiled and answered their questions with grace and patience. After the women bought a bagful of the baked goods right out of her basket, Mr. Hartford took the rest and placed them near the register.

Then Ava Jane turned to shop, her eyes meeting Jeremiah's, her serene smile fading into a wisp of air.

He caught up with her in the produce aisle, where tender seedling plants lined the bins near the fresh produce. "Hi."

"Hello, Jeremiah," she said, her dainty hand patting her bonnet. "How are you?"

"Gut," he said. "Just gathering some supplies to fix things around the place."

Sympathy colored her eyes a sad blue. "It must be hard, seeing your *daed* like this. He was such a fine, strong man. I'm so sorry."

Jeremiah had to swallow the lump in his throat. "He hasn't woken once since I've been home. I talk to him but…"

"He hears you," she said, something shifting in her attitude, her eyes softening, almost as if a wall had crashed down around her. "He hears you. It's *gut* you came home."

"Is it?" he asked, wishing it so. Wishing he could have come home to friendly greetings and a welcoming community. Everyone tolerated him, but Jeremiah wasn't sure he'd ever belong here again. The bishop and the ministers and the deacons were all probably shaking their heads about what to do with him.

He had to stay on course, stay on the straight and narrow. Surprisingly, his military training was coming in handy. He could focus. He could go into a zone and see things through to the finish. Because he wanted *this* now as much as he'd wanted *that* then.

He prayed every night. He prayed while he sat with his father. He prayed when he looked into Ava Jane's eyes.

Ava Jane looked shocked at his question. "It can be good, *ja.* Isn't that why you came back? To make things right again?"

He nodded and wished he could snap his fingers and fix everything. But the bishop had warned him this would be a long, hard journey. "I have a lot of work to do yet," he said. "I guess I'd better get going."

"Not all of your work will be out in the fields, Jeremiah," she said. Could she see into his heart?

He nodded, understanding. He had a lot to work through and most of it revolved around his feelings for her.

He was almost to the door when Mr. Hartford called out to him. "Jeremiah, you've been doing a lot of carpentry work since you returned. Ava Jane was just asking me yesterday about someone to help repair her back porch. What did you say, Ava Jane? A couple of rotten boards?"

Ava Jane turned pale, panic frozen on her face. Mr. Hartford had no idea about her relationship with Jeremiah. "It's nothing, really. I can find someone else. I shouldn't have even brought it up."

"I don't mind," Jeremiah said, sending Mr. Hartford a nod. "I'll come by later this week to see what needs to be done," he said to Ava Jane. "If that's all right with you."

She lowered her head and fidgeted with her apron. "That is fine. Mamm has been complaining about it and Daed keeps forgetting to fix it. Besides, I try to do things on my own and not run to my parents for every little thing."

Jeremiah's heart hurt for her. A woman alone with two growing children, trying to keep things together. She probably got up early to get her baking done.

"You don't have to run to anyone," he said. "I'll be by to look at your porch first thing next week."

He turned to leave before she could tell him no.

* * *

Sunday morning dawned bright and sunny with a slight crispness in the wind. But springtime freshness filled that same wind with various scents rising up: herbs and baked bread, bacon frying, the earthy scents of hay and animals and trees blossoming.

Ava Jane stood at her favorite spot in front of the kitchen sink, where the view of the valley and the water beyond always took her breath away. The sun peeked out over the rolling hills and winked through the newly budding trees. She remembered so many mornings waking up to this. Jacob would come up behind her and tug her close, his chin against her hair.

The water reminded her of two men. Jacob and Jeremiah. In a way, she'd lost them both to water.

Dear Father, how do I remember one when I'm trying to forget the other?

Ava Jane finished washing the breakfast dishes and called to the *kinder*, *"Kumm."*

Sarah Rose came rushing down the stairs, chattering like a magpie. "Eli won't hurry, Mamm. He's got one boot on and one in his hand. His hair needs combing—"

"Stop spluttering so," Ava Jane said with a smile. "Eli, what's taking so long?"

Her son seemed to move at a slow pace at times. He was a good boy but he did tend to get into trouble a lot.

She added one more prayer to her morning list. She needed strength to raise her children. Strength and wisdom and purpose. She needed to teach her *kinder* obedience first and foremost.

Her parents were so good with the children, but Ava Jane knew she had to be tough on them in order to teach them the right paths in life. Eli was a constant challenge and Sarah Rose had a strong-willed personality.

Ava Jane might have softened since Jacob's death but she was gaining strength every day. Hadn't she managed to be kind to Jeremiah the other day at the general store?

And she'd be kind to him if he showed up to fix her porch. But that would be an uncomfortable situation.

At least it would save her having to pester her *daadi* about it. He had a bad back and she wouldn't have to add to that.

"Eli!" she called, frustration edging her tone.

Her son ambled down the stairs, his dark hair flying out in shiny clusters around his head. "I forgot my hat," he said, turning to head back up the stairs.

Sarah Rose shook her head and put her little arms across her midsection in frustration. "I don't like being late."

"Nor do I," Ava Jane confirmed. "Eli, you have sixty seconds. Sarah Rose will count."

She knew Sarah Rose could only make it to fifty, but Eli came rushing down the stairs, his black felt hat crooked. "Here, Mamm."

"I'm not finished counting," Sarah Rose whined, her eyes going big and misty.

"You can finish counting on the walk over to the Miller place," Ava Jane said. "Now, let's gather our things and get on the road. It's a nice Sunday morning."

The Millers held services in their big barn. Jacob and most of the other men of the district had helped them build it a few years ago. The women had gathered and made food for the event. Barn buildings were always an event to see.

Now the tall, sturdy building had weathered a bit but it would stand the test of time. Not like her old farmhouse. Jacob had tried to keep up with the many repairs around the twenty-acre farm, but he'd never been able to get the place the way he wanted. He loved working the land and they'd made a passable income selling produce and grain, but in spite of her family's best efforts, she'd been forced to let some of the field go fallow. Now she sold baked goods, eggs and canned goods to make a living and tended a small garden so she could sell fresh produce and fruit at the local farmers market. She also made quilts, doilies, pot holders and aprons to help bring in extra income.

It wasn't a bad life, but it was a tiring life. Constant worry nagged at her. She had two children to feed and clothe and, while her parents helped, she could never catch up.

Ava Jane waved to a family passing in a buggy but her thoughts went back to the day she'd seen Jeremiah in the general store. Why she'd agreed to let him come to fix her porch was beyond her. She couldn't stop him now. She'd seen the determination in his deep blue eyes. There was something commanding about him that frightened her and made her wonder what he'd seen and done out there.

Steel. His gaze held a sliver of steel.

That had to have come from being trained to…fight and kill.

She couldn't think beyond that. She couldn't imagine what he'd been forced to endure in the name of justice and democracy. And yet, beyond that steel, she'd also seen a brokenness, a crack in the armor he'd had to put on.

That armor would have to be pulled away, piece by piece, if he wanted to become Amish again.

When she looked up to find the crowd gathering at the open barn, she saw Jeremiah standing alone, away from the friendly chatter and greetings and hugs. Her heart stalled to the point that she stumbled and almost dropped the apple pie she'd made yesterday.

"Mamm?" Both of her children stared up at her in surprise.

"I'm fine. Just hit a rough patch."

That was the truth. She'd been limping along, coming to terms with her grief, that never-ending grief that tore at her soul and woke her up at night in a cold sweat. But she'd begun to see some light in all the darkness of her grief.

Until now. Now she stumbled forward, caught in the grip of despair all over again. Jeremiah not only reminded her of how much she missed Jacob, but Jeremiah brought back all the pain and grief she'd suffered through when he'd left her in the middle of the night.

Twelve years gone and now back here in the flesh. Back with so much between them, so many changes in his appearance and in his heart.

But she'd changed, too. Or had she, after all?

How would she come to terms with the not knowing, with the still wanting? With the guilt and fear and thoughts of him rushing over her like a spring flood?

"Are you all right, Mamm?" Sarah Rose asked, true concern in her eyes.

"Of course I am," she said, smiling down at her daughter. "Just clumsy is all."

Ava Jane lifted her spine and declared that she would make it through somehow. She always had. Obedience first. Obedience to God and the tenets of her faith.

She told herself that she had to keep moving. So she carefully made her way toward the sanctuary of the barn. With each footstep she took toward the man standing there, looking as lost as a puppy in the middle of the road, Ava Jane's fear diminished, to be replaced with a determination to obey God and show compassion for someone who was once lost but had now been found.

She owed Jeremiah that much, didn't she?

* * *

Jeremiah could feel the stares being shot like arrows toward his back. His sense of his surroundings had been hewn to the point that he knew when someone was watching him or approaching him. Even now, he stood with his back against the wall so no one could sneak up on him. Not that they could, but he didn't want to whirl in defense and send young children screaming in the other direction.

So he stood silent and still as Eli Graber approached him with a serious expression on his face.

"Hey," Eli said, his eyes piercing Jeremiah with so many memories. The boy looked a lot like Jacob.

"Hey, yourself," Jeremiah replied, nodding. "How are you this fine morning?"

"Gut," the boy replied. "My friends told me you know how to shoot guns."

Jeremiah lifted away from the wall. "I do. Why are you asking me about that?"

"Just curious," Eli replied. "My *daed* had a squirrel rifle, 'cause they were messing in the corn bin."

Jeremiah squatted so he could be at eye level with the boy. "You do know to never touch a weapon without an adult supervising, don't you?"

Eli bobbed his head. "Yes, sir. Mamm won't allow that either. Only when Grossdaadi is around."

"What's this all about?"

Jeremiah stood to find Ava Jane glaring at him, anger tinging her pretty eyes.

"The boy is curious. He's heard talk about me."

Ava Jane's eyes went wide. "Eli, go find your sister."

Eli took off like a missile launching, leaving Jeremiah to face the protective fury he saw in Ava Jane's eyes. "I didn't encourage him. He mentioned a squirrel rifle."

"I hid it away from him," she replied, fear mixing with her anger. "Why would he ask you about that?"

Jeremiah had to be honest with her. "He asked me if I know how to use a gun and I told him yes, since his friends had already informed him of certain things regarding me. But I also told him he should never touch a weapon without an adult nearby."

He expected her to reprimand him but, instead, Ava Jane shook her head and let out a sigh. Glancing around, she said, "People will talk, Jeremiah. I'll speak to Eli and explain to him he is not to listen to gossip. No matter that it has a thread of truth in it."

With that, she turned and marched away, her head and her bonnet high, still in a tiff.

Progress, he thought with grim amusement. It was a start.

And now he had to face the rest of them. Inside during the service. Another step he had to take after already getting curious stares from the young adults in baptism classes with him.

He'd always considered himself courageous, but now he was quaking in his boots. Maybe he should wait awhile before attending church.

Then Jeremiah felt a hand on his shoulder. Ava Jane's *daed*, Samuel Troyer, stood there with a slight smile and what looked like expectation in his wise hazel eyes. Mr. Troyer was a minister. He'd had to approve Jeremiah's return.

"*Kumm*, Jeremiah. You don't want to miss the first sermon."

"No, sir," Jeremiah said, his head down. This would be the beginning of his redemption.

But he wouldn't have true redemption until Ava Jane forgave him.

Chapter Six

Dawn crested over the pasture, the sun's early rays as muted and soft as the gentle cooing of the mourning doves strolling underneath the old live oak.

Jeremiah sat down in the chair beside his father's sick bed and took a deep breath. His father's once-virile, strong body had sunk into itself. Isaac's jawline lay slack and withered, and his once-thick, dark hair had now turned thin and streaked with gray. Labored breaths lifted and lowered his frail chest enough that Jeremiah could see the outline of his ribs underneath the night-shirt he wore.

"*Gut* morning, Daed," he said, his voice low but sure. He grew stronger each day while he had to watch his father grow weaker. "I tended the livestock. We have two fine new baby lambs, two growing pigs, and our milk cows are hearty. We are up to ten now. Mamm and Beth have chickens now. And ducks, too. The fields are tended, too. The garden is planted with tomatoes, corn, lettuce, beans and peas, and your favorite, brussels sprouts. The seedlings are that beautiful fresh green that signals spring. We're a bit behind but we'll catch up. I'll make sure of that."

Isaac continued to sleep, his breath the only sign that he was still on this earth.

His *daed* hated brussels sprouts.

Jeremiah swallowed and held his hands together. He'd been back at home a couple of weeks now and the quiet, steady routine had helped him keep things in perspective. He cherished these times with his father. "I attended services yesterday. Sang the old hymns, listened to the sermons and the Scriptures. Prayed. Had another lesson on being baptized. I'm going to do it, Daed. I'll be the oldest to be baptized this year, but my *rumspringa* is finally over." He chuckled. "The young kids look at me with a mixture of curiosity and aversion. They don't know what to make of a grown man sitting there with them."

He wished his father would respond. Open his eyes and touch Jeremiah's hand. But the doctors didn't hold out much hope that Isaac would ever wake again.

So Jeremiah lowered his head and prayed. He thought about the tenets of his faith: obedience, humility, following the Ordnung. He'd listened, and after the service, he'd been more at peace but still at odds. Where did he belong? He hadn't been able to sit and eat dinner with his sister since the men and women ate separately. His mother had stayed home with his *daed* so he hadn't been able to look to her for encouragement.

He almost left after the service, but this time Ava Jane blocked his path.

"You must be hungry," she said, a bit of mirth in her words. "The ministers went on a bit today."

Jeremiah's back ached from sitting on the hard bench. "*Ja*, but I felt the emotions in the words. Even the High

German ones that I don't really understand." Staring over at where the long tables were filling with people, he said, "I've truly missed all of this."

She smiled at that. "You need to stay and eat. There's a spot beside my *daed*."

Jeremiah followed the direction of her pointing finger. "I sat by him during the service. He might be tired of babysitting me."

"He's not babysitting a grown man, Jeremiah," she replied, true kindness in her eyes. "He's encouraging and standing with someone he cares about. He approved your return and he will stand by that. Go and have some food."

"Someone he cares about," Jeremiah said now, after telling Isaac the whole story. "Samuel Troyer is a *gut* man. He could have turned away from me, because of who I was before. But he didn't. I'm thankful for that kindness."

And he had a kind daughter. But would she always be so kind? Or had she felt obligated to show him compassion since they'd just attended church?

He wondered about her changing moods toward him, but he also understood the battle she fought against.

Jeremiah kept that notion to himself.

He'd see her today. This morning. He'd be near Ava Jane while he repaired her porch. He could enjoy that, at least.

For now, just being near her would have to suffice.

He had to get his head on straight and stay focused on the task ahead. He knew the bishop and the ministers were watching him. He couldn't mess this up. So he treated this new training in the same way he'd treated training to become a Navy SEAL: with the dignity and respect it merited. Failure was not an option. In both cases, one slipup meant you were out for good.

Jeremiah took in a deep breath and then went back to talking to his father.

"I think I told you about how I made it into basic training. But getting to that point was hard. First, I had to find work and study to get my GED. I had a little money tucked away, and I answered an ad for a roommate and wound up sharing an apartment with two other boys. They helped me get a job washing dishes at a nearby restaurant and, I think I told you, they helped me to get my high school equivalent degree. I passed on the first try, mainly because of all the books Edward had told me I needed to read, but those two helped me a lot, too. *Gut* men who also planned to join up. During my downtime, I swam in the apartment building's pool and out in the Pacific Ocean. It never gets too cold in California, but I swam even when it was chilly. I wanted to pass all the necessary tests."

Hadn't he already explained all of this to his father?

He stopped, remembering how he'd been probed and checked and questioned over and over. They'd done a background check on him and he'd had to do some tall talking to show the Navy that he was serious. He'd been so afraid they'd turn him away. But one personal reference had cleared him. Edward Campton's parents had vouched for him. That and he'd worked hard to make sure he had everything in order, even taking courses in mechanics and shop and talking with counselors and instructors about the reality of his decision.

"I worked hard, Daed, and made it through the first draft," he whispered. "I showed my Dive Motivators that I was committed. But that is nothing compared to coming home and facing the people of Campton Creek. Nothing compared to sitting here with you. I love you so. I want you to know that. I came back for you and our family and our faith. I will make this right."

He lifted his head and watched his father for signs of acceptance. Signs of life.

Just that ragged, harsh breathing, that sinking in and out of his father's once powerful body.

Jeremiah stood. He wanted to touch his father and hold him close but...he didn't feel quite that worthy yet.

Wiping his eyes, he turned and put on his hat. He would get through this. He'd made it through yesterday's whispers and stares. Ava Jane and her family had made sure he would.

Jeremiah didn't understand why her family had been so kind to him when he'd broken her heart and gone against his faith. They could have chosen to shun him, but the Troyers had always been looked up to in the community. Her *daed* was a minister. Maybe he had to set an example. Maybe that was all. If the Troyers set the standard, the rest of the community should follow suit. Their compassion touched him and burned him to the core. Did he truly deserve it?

Jeremiah would accept that bit of kindness and compassion. In the meantime, he'd show all of them that he was worthy. He'd fix her porch and make that right. One step at a time.

God had a way of showing the signs of life to those who were out on the road. Especially to those on the road toward home.

Ava Jane kept checking the road. Jeremiah said he'd be by today and she was as wired as one of the barn cats trying to chase a broom. Her children were in school and she was alone.

Always alone.

The acceptance that she'd worked so hard to create, that illusion that she could do this on her own, she wore now like a frayed quilt. Jeremiah's coming home had magnified her loneliness and made her bitter and antsy.

"I don't want to be bitter and antsy," she said to the wind. "I want to be gracious and secure in my faith."

When she heard a buggy jingling up the drive, all thoughts of remaining calm lifted out the window on the billowing lace curtains.

Jeremiah was here.

She watched as he stopped the buggy and secured the petite carriage mare near a grassy area by the barn. Then he gathered his tools and stood for a minute, his gaze moving over the barn and fields.

What did he see out there? Her father had helped her plant a small vegetable garden and she had chickens and two milk cows. She canned food and made quilts and baked breads to make a living, and her parents helped out with offerings of meals and labor. But her little farm always looked forlorn in her eyes.

Did he see it the same way?

Ava Jane swallowed her trepidations and went out on the porch, her *kapp* fresh and her apron clean. Not that she'd gussied up for Jeremiah. No. She just liked to start a new day with crisp possibilities.

"*Gut* morning," he called from the barn, his smile tentative. Tentative and shattered as if he, too, were afraid to be here.

Was he as nervous as she felt? Were his big, sturdy hands trembling and his heart pumping too fast?

"*Gut* morning to you," she managed, gaining strength with each deep breath. "A fine April day, isn't it?"

"*Ja,*" he replied. "Easter is coming."

"Easter." A few weeks away now. A new beginning, a fresh start. Maybe she should consider what Easter could mean for her and Jeremiah. Maybe she could be kind to him, just kind.

Kindness cost nothing, after all. Civility could hide all the hurt in the world. She could be cordial and civil.

But her heart bumped a longing that went deeper than kindness. Ignoring that longing, she nodded toward the rotten porch floor. "Daed's back has been bothering him something awful, so I've managed to hide this with rugs and such, until Eli slid on the rug and sent it flying. Then my parents saw the damage. I told them not to fret, but Daed keeps promising he'll fix it. And then he gets busy and forgets."

"He'll see it fixed next time he comes," Jeremiah said, his gaze awash in so many emotions that it reminded her of a storm cloud. "I've brought lumber and tools, so I'll get started."

"Yes, of course," she replied. "I'm sure you have lots of work back home, so you'll want to get this done and over."

He nodded while he sorted his tools. "Always. But the planting is done and the milk cows are healthy. I've cleaned out the barn and made repairs there. I have ideas for some improvements, too. One day."

"Modern improvements?" she said, wondering if he'd try to add in technology and the things of the world since he'd been out there and experienced such things.

"Maybe a tractor," he replied. "But I haven't decided yet."

"A tractor?" She didn't mean to sound so judgmental. She knew some Amish used tractors around their barns to help run things.

"Don't worry. I won't force you to go joyriding with me. The tractor would stay off-road."

She almost laughed but caught herself. Giving him a huffy glance, she whirled. "I can't stand here sputtering all morning. I've got chores. It's laundry day."

She could feel his gaze on her departing back. "So instead of sputtering about you'll be wringing out?"

"Something like that, *ja,*" she retorted. At least he couldn't see her smile. But in spite of frowning on the tractor idea, smiling at his jokes felt good. Too good.

An hour later, Ava Jane ventured toward the sawing and hammering noises to check on Jeremiah's progress. He'd gone about his work with quiet intention, not bothering her one bit.

Well, he was bothering her but he didn't know that.

She'd tried to get the wash done and hung on the line that wasn't far from where he'd busied himself with tearing out old porch planks and replacing them with new ones. Ignoring Jeremiah had proved to be harder than she'd imagined. She'd gone out the front door and around the house so she wouldn't have to step near where he worked. But he'd noticed that and shot her a questioning stare to show she wasn't fooling him.

Not an easy morning.

Now each time she glanced toward him with shy precision, Jeremiah worked on as if he didn't have a care in the world. His focus on his task was impressive. He walked to the buggy and picked out a couple of boards, measured, sawed, pondered, his brow furrowing into ruts as deep as the plowed ones in the field.

What was the man thinking anyway?

He was thinking how natural she looked there, hanging clothes on the line. The sunshine hit the sheets and towels and allowed the fresh-scented, clean items to send a sweet perfume his way. The perfume of home and family and happiness and a kind of normalcy he'd missed these many years.

He watched with a covert control honed by years of stealth and wished he could go to her and take her into his arms and spin her around. The ache of knowing that would be wrong nagged him like a wound that wouldn't heal.

He had so many of those kinds of wounds. But being here, his lungs filling with the clean, clear essence of Ava Jane, his senses remembering the peace of this valley and this place, helped to soothe the parts of him that were still broken and aching.

So he worked and pretended not to notice the woman who worked beside him, yet away from him. He worked and he watched and he calculated and he measured and he wondered and he prayed.

This morning, right now, this was what faith and hope were all about. In his world, the only easy day was yesterday.

Today was for hard work, the work that required doing even better than yesterday.

At least, with this work here right now, he was near her.

Just near her.

Jeremiah was so lost in his thankfulness he didn't

even realize she'd gone back inside. But when the back door opened again and he looked up and into her eyes, he smiled.

"I have lemonade and a blueberry muffin…or two."

"Two should do it," he said with a grin. "I think once I've eaten those, I'll be up to finishing this porch."

After placing a tray with two large glasses full of the icy liquid and a plate with two muffins on a small wooden table between two rocking chairs, she said, "*Kumm* and rest a bit, Jeremiah."

Such simple words but to Jeremiah they sounded like a request from heaven.

Nodding, he placed his saw on the porch railing. "*Ja*, I think I will at that."

This was the kind of rest that could save a man's soul.

Chapter Seven

A week later, Ava Jane sat in the rocking chair on the back porch, waiting for Sarah Rose and Eli to come home from school. Admiring the fresh planks and new coat of paint underneath her feet, she held Callie, her favorite calico cat, and allowed her mind to wander back to having Jeremiah here. After they'd sat and shared the muffins and lemonade, small talk about life in general keeping them on safe topics, he'd gone right back to work and she'd gone about her chores inside.

"You don't have to repaint the whole porch," she had said later when coming out to wait for the children to return from school. Noticing he'd found a broom and swept the porch clean and that a can of whitewash and a brush sat at the ready, she had to argue a bit. The new boards did stick out in a very noticeable way but she hadn't expected him to paint, too.

Jeremiah shrugged off her protests. "No bother. Won't take long. I had the paint left from some touch-ups I did for Mamm. The old place needed some spring freshening, too. And I thank you and your family for helping with that. So this is my way to return the favor."

Deciding not to nag him about the extra work, Ava Jane nodded instead. "You mean the day we came and cleaned for your *mamm*? That's what friends are for, Jeremiah." Hesitating, she added, "Although they had to twist my arm a bit to get me to come along."

He finished sweeping the porch and put the broom away. "Because you didn't want to see me?"

"I was afraid to see you," she admitted, steeling herself for his reaction.

"I think I can understand that. I was shocked to find you standing inside the house." He reached for the broom again and held it like a sword, his eyes dark with regret. "And now?"

She took a breath, so many emotions converging inside her head like a river stream flowing straight to her heart. "Now I've accepted that you're back."

"But you still don't want me here, right?"

"It's not up to me to want you here or not," she replied, the tone of that declaration softer than she'd planned. "You are here now and you have good reasons for returning."

"But you don't think I should be here at all."

"So you can tell that just from being around me?"

"I can see it in your eyes."

Deciding they needed to let this subject go, Ava Jane stood to stare down at where he propped a brogan-covered foot on the bottom step. "No matter how I feel, my duty is to accept you and not judge you."

He stared at her with eyes that held so many secrets but with a connection that could not be denied. "I want you to forgive me, Ava Jane."

How should she respond to that gentle plea? "I'm trying, Jeremiah. I pray for you on a daily basis."

"*Gut*, because I'm not going anywhere, ever again," he responded, propping the broom against the porch railing. Then he gave her another soulful stare. "Are you afraid of me, Ava Jane?"

"Should I be?" she countered, thinking by the way her heart was pumping, she ought to be afraid. Truth be told, he scared her in more ways than one.

"No," he replied. "You don't ever have to be afraid of me. Whatever I became out there," he said, waving his hand in the air, "I left behind out there."

"Are you sure about that?"

He stopped and stared off into the distance, giving her an answer loud and clear. "I can never be sure of anything except that God brought me home and I'm sure in my faith. My faith never wavered, but I did."

He sure did. He wavered enough to leave her sobbing in the night to go off on some dark duty that only he could understand and she needed to remember that. But she didn't tell Jeremiah her thoughts.

Instead, she said, "I'm not afraid but I don't want you feeling that it's necessary to make amends to me."

"Isn't that what friends are for," he echoed, "to help others and make amends when needed?"

"Okay, we'll stop on that note," she replied, more frightened of the conversation than she was of him. "We can agree that we have to make the best of things, so I'm making it a point to accept you back into this community."

But it ended there.

He nodded as if he knew exactly what she was thinking. "I'm going to paint the porch on either side and leave the middle open. If it's okay with you, I thought I'd ask Eli if he'd like to help with that part."

"He'd be happy to dabble in paint, I'm sure," she said, thinking Eli needed a strong male to influence him. Only she still wasn't so sure that person should be Jeremiah. Eli was already far too fascinated with him, so she'd warned the boy not to pester Jeremiah. She hoped Jeremiah wouldn't pester her boy either. "But you've been here all day. Shouldn't you go?"

Jeremiah stood up straight and looked into her eyes again in a way she both remembered and now found different—stronger, hard-edged and way too determined, his expression cut in stone. "Do you want me to go?"

Yes. No. She didn't want to delve into the strange feelings he provoked in her. "I'm not trying to get rid of you. I just don't want you to neglect your own family in order to help mine."

"You, you mean," he said. "You don't want me to help *you.*"

He was messing with her head. "I didn't say that either."

"Then what are you trying to say?"

Lifting her hand out of frustration, Ava Jane said, "Fine. Stay as long as you want. Stay past dark if you need to. But don't expect supper."

He laughed and kept right on at his work.

And now here she sat a week later, rocking away, her thoughts as jumbled and tangled as new barbed wire. Jeremiah had finished the painting, along with Eli, well before supper. She could still hear the echo of their masculine banter, Eli asking rapid-fire questions and Jeremiah patiently answering with care and consideration. Not a word about weapons or war had come up, thanks to his easy way of steering the conversation back to the chore they were finishing together. He'd left with a wave and a smile.

Which had been a shame. She'd made fried chicken and had planned to set an extra plate.

Jeremiah sat by his father's bed, wondering if he had the energy to stay awake much longer. The work didn't bother him so much. He was used to hard work and discipline. But being back in a community where every move he made was scrutinized and measured caused him a lot of anxiety and discomfort. He remembered feeling that way growing up and it had got worse once he became friends with Edward Campton.

Why had he been so tempted by the world out there? *Maybe I deserve to be judged and criticized.*

Now, however, he wanted to be here. Right here. He'd told Ava Jane he'd left all of that behind him. He wouldn't make the mistake of running away again. He'd have to take whatever came his way and deal with it based on the rule of surrendering his will to God. In the Navy, he'd had to surrender himself to his instructors and superiors to be broken down and made new again—stronger, more dedicated, more demanding and completely compliant. It was the same here, only this time his will was being softened and measured and renewed with hope and love instead of death and despair.

He honestly didn't know which was harder. This soft breaking could tear him apart much more than being a warrior ever had. If he lost her again...

"I can do this, Father," he said to the Lord. "I will do this for You." He'd put God first and hope the rest would fall into place, the Lord willing.

He often read to his *daed* from the Scriptures at times

such as this, when the doubt and shame covered him like a tattered blanket, revealing all of his flaws.

"I carried this Bible with me, Daed." Jeremiah rubbed his hand over the worn leather volume that Mrs. Campton had insisted he take when he'd gone to tell the Admiral and her goodbye.

"You'll need God's word now more than ever, Jeremiah," she told him in her calm cultured voice. "Edward always had his Bible with him and now we want you to accept this as our gift to you."

They'd had it engraved with his name. "Because the Lord named you before you were even born," she reminded him.

"Do you think the Lord had this in mind for me then?" he asked, wanting to know he'd made the right choice.

She smiled up at him. "I think we have to take many paths before we find the way home. God knows your heart. No matter what, as long as you keep your faith, no matter how many right or wrong turns you take, you will find the right path. And you will come back home again."

She hadn't needed to add that sometimes that meant in a body bag or inside a flag-draped coffin.

Jeremiah had never been without this Bible. It was worn, scarred, battered, the pages dog-eared and stained from battle and from his fingers moving over them and turning them.

He opened the book at random and landed on Psalms. And so he read to his unconscious father. When Beth and Mamm came in and quietly took their seats, Jeremiah kept on reading, his mind on the words of the beautiful lamenting prayers, his head cast down as he remembered the whispers and stares each time he came upon a group of Amish men. Some, such as Ava Jane's father and the bishop, had been kind to him. Others not so much.

He thought about Ava Jane and the wonderful day he'd spent at her home last week. Since then, he'd tried to avoid her because it just hurt too much. He'd thought being near her would cure him. But this malady couldn't be cured by nearness. He wanted all of her. Her forgiveness, her love, and her in his arms.

That would help take away the sting of judgment and curiosity that others cast upon him. But he couldn't expect that. Not now. He still had to earn the Father's love and forgiveness and he still had to earn his dying *daadi's* love and forgiveness.

He finished the chapter and looked at his father and then he looked over at his mother and sister. "I'm sorry, Mamm," he said. "So sorry."

His mother pushed out of her chair and came to his side, her hand on his arm. Jeremiah stood and she took him into her arms and held him. "You know I've already forgiven you, son."

"I want Daed to know, to hear my pleas just as David wanted the Lord to hear him."

"Your *daadi* hears you," she said, her hand touching Jeremiah's hair. "He knows just as the Lord knows."

Beth stood by their mother, tears in her eyes. "Jeremiah, would it help if we listen to you and let you tell us what you've been through?"

Jeremiah pulled away and shook his head. "No. I'm not ready for that. You're not ready for that. I…I need to check the livestock."

With that, he turned and hurried from the room, that feeling of being unable to breathe overtaking him. He could hear the choppers overhead, could hear the screams of women and children and the rapid fire of machine guns, could see the startled faces of the enemy being taken down. Those sights and sounds moved through his dreams with an echo of sorrow and urgency. Two of his team members had gone down. He'd had to get to them. He'd tried to save them.

He'd failed.

No, he wasn't ready to share the horror of what he'd seen with his precious sister and mother.

Maybe not even with his father.

Only the Lord above knew that story and knew his heart.

When he reached the barn, the misty night air hitting his feverish skin, Jeremiah stopped and held tight to one of the big, heavy doors.

Maybe he should start this healing journey by trying to figure out how to forgive himself? How could he expect true forgiveness from others if he didn't have the courage to look himself in the eye and offer forgiveness to the man he'd become?

Leaning against the solid door, Jeremiah looked toward the heavens. He'd often lain on his rucksack in the middle of the desolate mountains and looked up at the stars. On those nights, he'd wondered about Ava Jane and missed her with each rush of pulse that moved through his temples.

He missed her still, under this sky, the same sky but different now. A peaceful night sky with only the sound of animals settling in and the wind whistling like a hymn against his skin. He was safe here. His pulse slowed, his mind calmed.

A horse whinnied nearby, bringing him out of his musings.

Jeremiah looked up at the crescent moon. "I have to make it all right before I can even think of a future with Ava Jane. She's still not sure of me. I'm still not sure of myself."

And he wanted to be sure, very sure, this time. Because once he had her back, he would not leave her side again.

So he did the deep breathing he'd learned to keep calm in battle and he focused on what was coming next.

The spring festival was coming up. His mother and sister were excited about displaying the quilts they'd worked on all winter and possibly selling a couple, but they weren't sure they both could attend. Ava Jane had mentioned she would be selling her baked goods—muffins and pies and cakes and bread—to make extra money, along with some other wares she and her sister and fiends had been working on. Her friends would set up booths at the festival, too. Raesha Bawell and her mother-in-law would be selling hats they designed and made by hand for both the Amish and the Englisch. They'd all need help with moving and setting up in the big town square.

Jeremiah would volunteer where he could and do whatever needed to be done. The spring festival always brought large crowds of locals and tourists, too. He could blend in and still be a part of things without feeling as if he were on display for everyone to ponder and whisper about.

Deciding he'd talk to Mr. Hartford, this year's festival chairperson, first thing in the morning, he went about checking the animals and thanked God for presenting him with enough tasks to keep him busy and tired.

The more he worked, the less time he'd have to dwell on what might have been and what could still come to be.

Today. He'd take each day at a time and concentrate on today only. Because every SEAL knew the only easy day was yesterday. And Jeremiah was pretty sure the good Lord knew that, too.

Chapter Eight

A‌va Jane had lots to keep her occupied and she was very glad for that. These past few days had whizzed by with a busy-bee buzz, giving her plenty to keep her mind off of Jeremiah.

She and her friends had finally finished the rose-patterned quilt for Sarah Rose. She planned to give it to her on her upcoming birthday, which was about a month away. Sarah Rose would have a small party here in the backyard, complete with cake, cookies, lemonade and tea. Her friends would bring small gifts but Ava Jane couldn't wait to give her daughter the child-sized quilt, made especially for her little bed. She hoped Sarah Rose would cherish it in the same way she cherished quilts from her mother.

Today, however, Ava Jane focused on the many treats she hoped to sell at the spring festival this weekend. She'd made dozens of cookies, including every kind from chocolate chip to snickerdoodles to peanut butter. She'd made breads and rolls and pies, enough so that her gas-powered refrigerator was becoming completely full. Today, she planned to take a batch of her creations into town to store in Mr. Hartford's big refrigerator since the festival was only a couple of days away.

The back screen door opened with a squeak. "Hello, I'm here to help."

"In the kitchen, Deborah," Ava Jane called to her sister. Deborah loved to help her bake and they often talked about opening a café together, but her nineteen-year-old sister insisted she wasn't ready to get married and settle down.

Ava Jane figured that would change in a couple of years. Deborah already had her eye on Matthew Miller. Just like Ava Jane and Jeremiah, Deborah and Matthew had grown up together and were about to go through *rumspringa* together.

Ava Jane said a quick prayer for a better outcome for her sister. She'd lost Jeremiah during his *rumspringa* but…she'd found Jacob. They'd soothed each other after he'd abandoned them and one thing had led to another. They married a year and a half after Jeremiah left. Now even though she'd lost him, she had two beautiful children, thank the Lord.

I waited for you, Jeremiah. She had waited, at first hoping and praying that he'd change his mind and come home. Then she'd waited because she hadn't known what else to do.

Her family had sustained her, telling her she'd be okay, telling her that Jeremiah had to find his own way. They'd been as surprised and shocked as she when she'd finally managed to explain. Deborah had been so young, only eight years old at the time. But Ava Jane remembered her little sister crawling into her lap and hugging her tight.

When things between Jacob and her had changed from friendship to more, Ava Jane hadn't waited any longer.

Was I meant to be with Jacob all along? she wondered silently while her sister prattled on about the weather and the garden and—

"—four horns and two goatees," Deborah finished rather loudly.

"What?" Ava Jane squinted and blinked. "What are you talking about?"

Deborah put down the bag of baking supplies she'd brought and grinned over at Ava Jane. "I've been talking about this goat I saw down the road, but you weren't listening so I added a few details."

"Four horns?" Ava Jane asked, rolling her eyes. "Are you sure about that?"

"No, just checking to see if you heard a word I said." Deborah adjusted her work apron and moved around the wide, clean kitchen, her green eyes as bright as the corn popping up in the field beyond the yard. "Are you okay? You look tired."

Ava Jane lifted her hand in the air. "Of course I'm tired. I've been baking double time for a week now and putting the finishing touches on Sarah Rose's quilt and trying to keep things going. I've got gardening and flower beds and weeds and the chickens—they lay a lot of eggs. You know how busy planting season can be."

"Don't I," Deborah said, finding the coffeepot right away. "Mamm's pulling out her hair with her own crafts for our booth and tending the gardens. Daed seems to be slowing down a bit." She stopped and shook her head. "He's been so forgetful lately."

Ava Jane had noticed her father's slower gait lately and agreed. It wasn't just his physical appearance. His mind drifted a lot, too. "He's getting older but he doesn't want to admit that."

"His back is really bothering him," Deborah said. "Mamm stays on him to see about it but he doesn't like going to the doctor."

"No man does," Ava Jane said, remembering how Jacob would fight her tooth and nail whenever he had an ache, even a cold.

How she missed him. When her thoughts turned from Jacob back to Jeremiah she blinked and tried not to think about the time she and Jeremiah had spent together last week. *Forced* time. She'd only sat and talked with him to be kind, but now she wished she hadn't encouraged so much as a friendship between them. But…she had to wonder if he had scars that were hidden and if he refused to get help for those scars.

"There you go again," Deborah said, poking at Ava Jane. *"Was der schinner is letz?"*

At her sister's concerned expression, Ava Jane shook her head. "Nothing is wrong, I promise. Now, can we get to work?"

"It's Jeremiah, isn't it?" Deborah said with a note of persistence. "I heard he was here last week."

Ava Jane tried to frame her response in a neutral tone. *"Ja,* he fixed that bad spot on the back porch."

"And painted it, according to my sources," Deborah said on a smug note.

"And just who are your sources, sister?"

Deborah shook her index finger in the air. "You don't need to know that, but your *kinder* have eyes in their heads, in case you haven't noticed." Then her green eyes went dark and soft. "I worry about you. He broke your heart. Why is he hanging around?"

"I hired him to fix the porch so Daadi wouldn't have to do it," Ava Jane said on a determined but defensive note, thinking she'd be wise to heed Deborah's observation regarding what her children saw, heard and repeated. "Our parents have been kind to him and I'm trying to follow their example."

Deborah snorted. "Right. Daed has a duty to be kind to a prodigal. You don't." Leaning over the big table, she stared at Ava Jane. "Is there something more between you two?"

"Nothing else, sister," Ava Jane said, meaning it. "You know how much I loved Jacob. But I can't turn away from Jeremiah."

"So you're trying to honor both of them by letting Jeremiah work on this farm?"

Ava Jane set down the milk she'd pulled from the refrigerator. "He was Jacob's best friend. He's trying to prove his worth and make amends. And besides, Mr. Hartford suggested him and it was hard to turn him down right there in the general store." Shrugging, she added, "He wouldn't let me pay him in cash. Instead, he only asked for a pound cake for his family. Said it was his *daed's* favorite. But we both knew Ike wouldn't be able to eat the cake. I made it anyway."

"And had someone else deliver it?"

"Yes, but then you probably already knew that."

"So how do you really feel about him?" Deborah asked, her hand on Ava Jane's arm.

Ava Jane gave up and blinked back tears. "Honestly, I don't know. One day I'm okay with him being back and the next I wish he'd go away. It's been so hard. I don't know what to do."

Deborah took Ava Jane into her arms and held her close. "We pray. I'm sorry. I shouldn't have forced this issue but I know you so well."

"Too well," Ava Jane said through her tears. "But I'll be all right. God brought him home. He will have to answer to a higher calling. I'm not to judge but I can't forgive him solely based on his offer to repair some things for me."

"*Ja*, and he'll have to make greater amends—and repairs—than just touching up a porch," Deborah replied, stepping back to let go of Ava Jane. "But I'll go by your example and pray for him. I just don't want him to hurt you again."

Ava Jane nodded and quickly wiped her tears. "You were so young when he left that I'm surprised you'd remember anything about Jeremiah. Why are you so fierce about this?"

"I was young," Deborah said, her gaze on Ava Jane, "but I remember hearing you cry at night. And you know me. I listened when you poured your heart out to Mamm. It's hard to forget that kind of anguish even if I didn't quite understand it at the time. But all these years I've heard the story of what happened between you two. Makes me not want to fall in love."

Ava Jane had never stopped to think about the ripple effect of her misery or about what others might have been spreading all this time. "I don't want you to think that way. I was happy with Jacob and I have the *kinder*. I'm happy now. You'll find someone one day and you won't have to pour your heart out to anyone."

"Except my sister," Deborah said, smiling over at her.

"Always," Ava Jane replied. "Now, enough of this pity party. We have work to do."

Her sister went off to fetch more bowls and baking dishes.

Ava Jane stood there with her heart raw and frazzled and wondered how she'd ever get through this.

Trust in the Lord.

She clung to that remembrance and prayed the prayer from Proverbs 3:5 that taught her to lean not on her own understanding. And with each blueberry muffin she made, she tried not to dwell on how much Jeremiah had enjoyed eating blueberry muffins with her last week.

He now made it a point to look for the blueberry muffins each time he entered Hartford's General Store. That day last week with Ava Jane had sustained Jeremiah over the past hectic days.

His father was getting worse. The home health-care nurse told them it wouldn't be much longer. Jeremiah sat with him as often as possible, until late into the night and sometimes in the early dawn. He'd told his father things he'd never tell another living human being. But then his father probably didn't even hear him.

With some of the savings he'd set aside while he was in the military, Jeremiah hired a day nurse to help his mother and Beth. They both looked haggard and exhausted and neither was able to turn his father or change the bedding. The male nurse was strong and a good worker. He and Jeremiah could get the work done in record time. With the added home health care, his mother could get some rest and his sister could go back to being young and visiting more with her friends.

"Thank you, son," his mother had said, tears in her eyes. "Your father wants to die at home. I couldn't bring myself to put him in a nursing facility far away."

"Nor do you need to be going back and forth," Jeremiah had replied. "Don't worry, Mamm. I'm glad some good can come from the money I saved up."

"You might need it one day for yourself," Moselle had said, her gaze full of hope. "If you marry."

"We'll worry about that time when it comes," he'd told her with a quick hug and a peck on the cheek.

"I'll pray for that until the time comes," she'd responded.

In the meantime, he had the crops and livestock to tend, cows to milk and a dozen other things to keep him occupied. Helping set up for the festival had been a blessing, too. Mr. Hartford had recommended him for handiwork and so he had side jobs that should last through the summer. By then he should be done with his reintroduction to the church and he'd be ready to be baptized. Ready to start his life here all over again.

But until then, he had Ava Jane's rare smiles to spread warmth throughout his heart. While he prayed to the Lord to give him redemption, he also asked the Lord to bring him peace. In case Ava Jane couldn't forgive him. He would live the rest of his life right here with her nearby. He had to be able to accept that and let her go before he could bring himself completely back. But what if Ava Jane found someone else?

Either way, he had a tough row to hoe.

Now, after grabbing a muffin and a cup of coffee, he went back out onto the main street of Campton Creek and admired the hard work he and several other men had put forth.

Campton Creek was a beautiful little town anyway, but with newly blooming flowers he couldn't name cascading in bright reds, pinks, yellows and purples from huge sturdy clay pots that lined the quaint streets, it looked like the perfect picture of America.

The America he'd fought for, the home and town and people he'd defended. Why had he felt such a strong need to turn away from this simple, peaceful life and go into an unknown, dangerous world that had left him scarred and shattered?

Maybe because he wanted to preserve this and keep it just as beautiful as it looked this morning.

Standing here now in the midday sunshine, Jeremiah wondered how he'd ever made it home. Other dark thoughts pushed at his consciousness but he refused to let them in. He was here now and that had to count for something, didn't it?

He headed to help set up a big tent in the park by the creek when he heard a ruckus down the street. Turning, he spotted a group of Amish trying to get around several young men and women who looked like tourists—or maybe bored locals—with cameras and cell phones flashing while they laughed and made jokes. Jeremiah watched for a moment and then turned back in the other direction. Best to keep on walking when those kind were around.

Until he heard one of the Amish women cry out, "Stop that."

Jeremiah whirled back around and his chest tightened. Ava Jane and her sister, Deborah, along with two other women, were now cornered by two men from the group.

One of the men touched Deborah's bonnet and said something that made the others laugh. Deborah tried to go around but one of the girls stopped and blocked her path. "Why do you wear that funny thing anyway?"

Ava Jane grabbed her sister with one hand, her basket full of baked goods in the other, and tried to hurry away.

One of the men moved toward them again and pulled at the ties of Deborah's *kapp*.

As the women tried to step around, the man turned to his buddies. "Did you get that on the video?"

When he turned back to laugh at the women, he ran smack into Ava Jane and knocked her basket to the ground.

Jeremiah didn't think. With a red rage coloring his vision, he ran up the street and grabbed the brawny man and shoved him up against a wall, his arm pressed against the man's throat with enough pressure to cut off his breath. "You will respect these women, understand?"

The other Englisch parted and scattered, while the shocked man in his grip stared at him with a fear he'd seen over and over again in the enemy's eyes.

"Hey, we were just having some fun," the man said with a weak plea. "Let me go, man."

Jeremiah tightened his grip and flipped the man around to face the others. "Apologize."

But before the man could form a word, a gentle hand on Jeremiah's arm broke through the burning haze in his brain.

"Jeremiah, let him go please."

Ava Jane.

He backed away, still glowering at the red-faced, sweating man who now rubbed a shaky hand down his throat.

"I'm sorry," the man said, his nervous gaze moving over the four Amish women. Then he took off before Jeremiah made another move.

Jeremiah stared after the group that continued up the street and then turned to Ava Jane. If he'd thought he'd seen fear in the man's eyes, he was mistaken.

The fear and terror he saw in her eyes was real and alive and as shattered as his heart. He'd scared Ava Jane and her sister and friends. And he'd scared himself.

"I'm sorry, too," he managed to say through deep breaths, a cold sweat chilling his entire body. He tried to reach for her then dropped his hand. "Are you all right?"

She didn't speak. Shock colored her eyes and her skin had turned pale. She looked at him as if she didn't know who he was, fear and embarrassment clear in her misty eyes.

Jeremiah glanced at the other women but they, too, stood still and quiet, afraid to make a move. His head roared with that familiar dread, the kind he had when he awoke from the nightmare of reliving a battle. What did they see in him now?

Someone much more dangerous than a misguided Englisch man who didn't show respect?

Deborah stepped forward, her eyes wide and wary. "Thank you, Jeremiah. We're both okay."

Ava Jane whirled and dropped to her knees, trying to gather her damaged items, her hands shaking. The others followed suit, trying to salvage all of her hard work. Jeremiah wished the earth would swallow him. Everywhere he looked, people had stopped to stare. At him. At what he'd just done.

He bent down beside her and reached for a crushed loaf of what looked like nut bread.

"Stop it," she said in a heavy whisper. "Please, Jeremiah, don't help me again in that way. In any way."

Here they were, right back on the street, exactly in the same way as when she'd discovered he'd returned. She had that same shock and disgust in her eyes again.

They'd come so far and now he'd made a mess of things all over again.

He sank back, his hands on his knees, his gaze on her. But he saw it there, the shock, the rage, the confusion and the disapproval. She'd seen the worst of him right here today. He'd been fully prepared to rip that man's head off simply because he'd touched Ava Jane.

Jeremiah stood, every fiber of his being shaking and recoiling from what he'd become, while dark, horrible memories cackled through his head with a clarity that outstripped his nightmares. Sending her one last pleading glance, he turned and stalked away from the prying eyes of others and the crushing hurt in her ragged gaze.

His body coiled and tightened, his head pounded with each step, the rush of flashbacks almost overtaking him. But he didn't stop walking until he looked up and saw Campton House looming like a beacon over him.

And because he didn't have any other safe haven right now, he stalked up the steps and knocked on the door.

Chapter Nine

"Did you have a flashback?"

The quiet question didn't match the deep concern he could see in Judy Campton's still-sharp eyes.

Jeremiah took another drink of the water Bettye had brought him after Mrs. Campton had ushered him into the living room. He stared at the crystal goblet full of crushed ice and with a slice of lemon and strawberry. Mrs. Campton always believed in making her guests feel special.

"Jeremiah?"

Glancing up, he shook his head, his heart rate decreasing now, the cold sweat chilling him in the drafty old house. "No, ma'am. But I could feel that rage of battle overtaking me. I had to blink…and get a grip on things." Or he would have gone too far.

Thinking of Ava Jane's gentle hand on his arm, he finally faced the woman sitting across from him. "Ava Jane was there."

Looking confused, Judy put a pink-polished nail to her cheek, her diamond solitaire glistening in the soft light. "Oh, the girl you were to marry all those years ago. I see her sometimes in town. She's a marvelous cook. Bettye brings home her cakes and muffins all the time."

Standing, he took his water goblet with him to stare out at the bulging colors and fluffy blossoms of the formal garden in the sprawling backyard. "Yes, she makes extra income from her baking." He explained how he'd seen them with the young Englisch kids. "One of the young men insulted her sister and then almost knocked Ava Jane down. She dropped her basket of baked goods."

Judy tapped her fingernails against the brocade of her chair, her shrewd gaze moving over Jeremiah's face.

"So you wanted to defend her honor, of course." She waited a beat and then added, "Because you still love her."

"Yes." He turned back to her again, the relief of that confession lifting his shoulders and allowing him to breathe again. "But she saw my rage in my actions and she does not tolerate that. Ava Jane always was a gentle soul so it's hard for her to imagine me being a SEAL. I'm not sure she even knows what that means, but she knows enough to realize I have fought against others and…killed men in the line of duty. And she certainly remembers that I chose that over staying here to make a life with her."

He explained how Ava Jane had married his best friend and now was a widow with two children. "She resents me but things were getting better between us. We shared some pleasant time last week when I went to her house to repair some bad spots on the back porch. Now, after today, she doesn't want me around." Holding his straw hat in his hand, he added, "Today, she saw the real me."

Judy stared up at him with understanding. "She doesn't know what you've been through and she doesn't understand your reasons for doing what you did. Have you tried talking to her about it? About what your duties entailed?"

"No, ma'am. I don't want to frighten her even more and it's hard to talk about what I saw. What I had to do. Things I'm not ever supposed to repeat."

"Edward wouldn't talk much about what he'd done either. It's the SEAL code, of course, for reasons of national security and for protection of themselves and their families—never talk about the mission." She leaned forward. "However, I know Edward shared more with you than he ever did anyone else. Maybe because he trusted your dedication to your faith."

Jeremiah heard the irony in that statement. "A faith I left."

"Did he push you to join up?" she asked, the question rushing out in a way that made Jeremiah wonder how long she'd wanted to ask that question.

"No, he never revealed anything specific when he talked to me. He always stressed how tough it was to become a SEAL. So much so that I knew it all by heart. He gave me books to read and showed me the history of the Navy, but he was brutally honest about the hardness of it all. He never once suggested anything to me about joining. Edward thought he was safe with me and so he told me things he could never tell anyone else. And yet, the day he died I knew I had to go and fight in his honor. But I can't explain that to Ava Jane. I don't even understand it myself. And that might keep us apart forever."

Judy Campton shifted, her blue skirt crinkling. "But that rule of not talking makes it hard on everyone. We need to open our sorrows and our memories and be purged, so we can heal, so we can forgive, so others can forgive us."

Jeremiah sat down again. "Who do you talk to?"

"God," she said with a serene smile. "Ed would talk to me but only about his love for his work. But then, he never went through what you and Edward did. I think sometimes he wishes he had, so he'd have that bond with Edward. He so wanted our son to become a naval officer, but he respected Edward's choice to join the SEALs."

Jeremiah stared up at the portraits and medals lining the wall, wondering again about how much this precious woman held tightly inside her heart. "Your husband is a hero in his own right."

"Yes, but he's tired now and he wants to be with our son." She lowered her gaze, and Jeremiah saw a slight crack in her control. "Let's get back to you."

"I shouldn't have bothered you," he said, glancing at the clock. "I need to go back to work."

"You are never a bother," she said, waving him back down when he tried to stand. "Ed is sleeping but you are welcome to go up and say hello."

"I…I need to finish helping with the tents for the festival," he said, another kind of panic crashing around him. "I sit with my father almost every day and I don't think I have the strength to watch both of them die. I'm not ready to face that with the Admiral, too."

"You have more strength than you realize," Judy replied, her teacup rattling in her shaking hands. "We both do. Ed is ready to go. We've had a good full life, with both happiness and heartache. But that's what life is all about. It's also about second chances. You have the strength to stay the course, Jeremiah. Or you wouldn't have come back here."

Jeremiah hurried to help her set her empty cup back on the side table. "I thought I did. Thought I could do this. But today I realized I've got a long way to go. It takes more strength to walk away at times than it does to fight."

Judy puffed a weary breath. "Are you going to walk away, leave again?"

"No. I'm here to stay," he said, calmer now. Resolved. "But I might have to walk away from having Ava Jane back. I won't force things with her. If she doesn't want me then I have to find a way to accept that. But I'm not leaving again."

"I wouldn't give up completely on winning her back," Judy said, taking his hand before he could make it to his seat. "You might have scared her today, but you also came to her rescue. I know the *real* you and today was just a part of the goodness inside your heart. You meant well. She'll realize that after she's had time to absorb what happened. If she still cares, she won't be able to deny that you had the best of intentions even if you did lose control."

"Yes, but she might also realize that she doesn't want anything to do with me because she saw a side of me I've tried so hard to hide. She'll forgive me, Mrs. Campton. But she will never forget what I've done."

"No, but you can't give up on showing her what you can *become*, Jeremiah. God. Remember to talk to God. He brought you home and He'll see you through. God is never quite finished with us, you know."

Jeremiah didn't understand how she could be so sure of that when her own son hadn't come home in one piece. His remains were buried in the cemetery up the road but he was in heaven now.

How did she do it? How did she maintain such a solid, sure faith?

"Thank you," he said, instead of asking her that question.

"You can come to me anytime you need me," Judy said, lifting off her chair with wobbly dignity.

Jeremiah took her arm and allowed her to walk him to the door. "I appreciate you taking the time to talk to me."

She stopped at the open door where Bettye stood smiling at both of them. The loyal housekeeper and all-around helper took good care of the Camptons. Mrs. Campton nodded to Bettye and then walked out on the long, wide porch with Jeremiah. "I wish you'd consider going to counseling, Jeremiah. If you truly want to get through this and find some peace, it might help to talk to someone who is trained in dealing with PTSD."

Jeremiah wasn't ready for that again. He'd gone through some counseling after he'd recovered from his injuries, but he'd never been able to open up to anyone. It didn't sit right with him to bare his soul to a stranger. But wouldn't that be better than losing control the way he had today?

"I'll think about it, I promise. Right now, I have to get back and finish my tasks."

"Come back to see us," Judy Campton said. "And, Jeremiah, you'll be in my prayers."

"And you in mine," he responded, meaning it.

He'd finish his work and then he'd try to find Ava Jane and see if she'd calmed down. Maybe she'd listen to him now.

Or maybe he'd already lost her forever.

"Are you feeling better now?"

Ava Jane woke up to find her mother standing just

inside the bedroom door. "Mamm, what are you doing here? What time is it?"

Martha came and sat on the edge of the bed. "It's almost four in the afternoon. I came because your sister was worried about you. You never take to your bed in the middle of the day, not when you have so much baking to do."

"I'll get to it. I'll stay up late." She tried to sit up, but her body felt weighed down. "I...I had a headache."

The dull ache pulsed throughout her system and hit her right in the heart, while the scene there on the street played out like a bad dream. "I need to take care of the *kinder*. I slept right through them coming home from school."

"Deborah is playing stickball with them," her mother said, pushing her gently back down. "You've been working too hard. No wonder you got a headache. Always happens when you overdo it." Martha touched a hand to Ava Jane's forehead. "Or when you're fretting about something."

"I need to see—"

"Ava Jane, stop."

Recognizing that mother's voice, Ava Jane sat up and slid back against the wooden headboard. "I'm sorry. I'm okay. I drank some chamomile tea and my head is better now."

"Your sister told me what happened. She ran to the phone booth and got word to me to come soon."

"I was okay. I am okay," Ava Jane said, the sound of her children laughing outside the open window bringing her both joy and pain. "I just felt a bit dizzy after...after that man bothered us and..."

"After you witnessed Jeremiah attack the man."

Ava Jane blinked and stared into her mother's eyes, then burst into tears. Bobbing her head, she said, "Yes. Yes. I've never seen anything like it. He looked so angry. Such rage. And it scared me much more than what that Englisch did. It's like I never really knew him at all. Why, Mamm? Why does this hurt so much?"

Her mother gathered her into her arms and rocked her, patting her head and whispering into her ear. "You are in shock. You lost your husband and the man you tried to forget has come back. It's enough, daughter. More than enough to give you a headache. But I think your heart is hurting, too."

Ava Jane cried into her mother's apron, remembering how Deborah had hurried her to their buggy. Seeing Mr. Hartford standing there with worry on his face, hearing him ask if he could do anything to help. She'd seen the Englisch group moving on down the street, that one man turning around to glance over his shoulder. Scared. He'd been scared.

And he should have been. Jeremiah looked ready to tear his head off. She couldn't think past that image because her mind went to places she didn't want to take it. Places of war and pain and death and destruction.

Jeremiah had seen those places, had done that very thing to other men. Had probably killed other men.

She didn't know how she could feel this much hurt for someone she didn't want in her life. How she could pray so hard to get another person out of her system.

Today, she'd seen what he'd become. How could he ever return to what he'd left behind here when he still had such rage inside his heart?

But she's also seen something else after he'd let the man go. She'd seen the genuine anguish and regret in his tormented eyes. Yet, she couldn't forget the darkness of his anger.

Finally, her mother held her up and stared at her, her gentle expression full of compassion and concern. "You hurt because you love, daughter. I think you never stopped loving him."

"No, I loved Jacob. Only Jacob." Ava Jane shook her head but, inside, her heart screamed the truth.

She did love Jacob. Would always love him.

But she loved Jeremiah, too. And that scared her more than anything. No one could ever know that. And Jeremiah would never see that. Because she wouldn't show her feelings again.

Chapter Ten

Jeremiah sat near his father's bed. He'd volunteered to stay here today with Daed so his mom and sister could attend the festival in town. They had quilts and other items to sell—pot holders, pretty appliquéd clothes and other knickknacks they'd worked on since the last festival.

They needed the fresh air and light.

And he needed this solitude to keep his mind steady.

He'd come so close the other day to finding Ava Jane and telling her how sorry he was, but after talking to Mrs. Campton and then going back to finish up his work, he'd run into Mr. Hartford.

"Ava Jane and her sister went home after the ruckus. I told the sheriff about those kids. Always coming through here after the high school lets out. They like to tease the Amish. I ran 'em off the other day and I called the sheriff after what they did today." Patting Jeremiah on his arm, he had added, "I, for one, am glad you confronted them. Teach 'em to respect people."

Jeremiah heard all of that and wished he'd handled confronting them in a more peaceful way. "And Ava Jane? Was she all right when she left?"

Mr. Hartford gave him a sympathetic stare. "She was upset. Her sister took her home. I salvaged what I could of her breads and muffins but most of it got crushed and had to be thrown away." He shrugged and looked toward the road. "You know, she gets these bad headaches when she gets upset. Might want to give her a while before you try to talk to her."

Jeremiah came back to the present, remembering how she used to cry from the painful headaches. He couldn't forget how helpless he'd always felt when the pain would overtake her.

He felt that same helplessness now.

He'd stayed away. He couldn't add any more to her pain.

"I'm here, Daed," he said in a shaky whisper. "I've sent the women out for the day. Just you and me."

He'd given the day nurse the day off, too, since Derek had mentioned how his family loved to go to the festival. Derek had three children and a wife, who also worked at the hospital.

His father shrank into himself with each passing day. No hope. But Jeremiah hoped anyway. So he started talking.

"I made it to BUD/S—Basic Underwater Demolition/ SEAL training. I knew it would be tough and my instructors made sure I knew it. They never teased me about my background, but I knew they were aware of it every day and reminded all of us that we would belong to them for the next six months. Many weeks of preparations—orientation, they call it. In case any of us might change our minds. Some did. Some just up and quit—DORs, Drop on Requests. I couldn't do that. I'd already given up everything so I toughed it out. I prayed a lot. All the time.

I had to run for miles. I had to exercise on an obstacle course. Ironic, that, since we all had our own obstacles to overcome if we wanted to succeed. We had to be healthy, in top shape, so we worked all day long. Healthy in body and mind."

Jeremiah stared at his father and then glanced out at the foot-tall cornstalks. He had the window open to let in the fresh air. The swish of the cornstalks moving in the spring breeze made a nice lullaby. So peaceful, so comforting.

"My instructors figured my toughness came from all the hard work here on the farm. Swimming was the hardest. But I was gifted with loving the water and so I relished swimming, even two miles in the ocean, even loaded down with gear. Edward taught me how to do that, in that big pool at his house."

He stopped and took a breath. "I never knew what that would come to mean to me. I had a lot of resolve, a deep commitment, but there were times when I longed to be right here, sitting by the fire with you and Mamm."

He wanted to touch his father's hand, but shame kept him from doing it.

"That was our first phase of intense training. We all got pretty cocky and overconfident, but then we had to face what they call Dive Phase." He put his hands together, his elbows on his knees. "It's all about oxygen and spending most of your day emerged in water with a rebreather.

"A rebreather. I think that's what the good Lord is giving me right now, because sometimes when I look at Ava Jane I can't breathe.

"You're okay hooked up to the oxygen but the instructors don't let you enjoy that. They tie up your hose and take your regulator away and make sure you come close to drowning. That's when you really find the Lord, Daed."

His father sighed and let out a breath.

Jeremiah stopped, the memory cold and foggy in his mind of sinking to the bottom of the pool. That sensation of giving up overcame him with a frozen clarity. That floating against a weight so heavy he thought he'd never take another breath. His hands fighting against the knots, fighting against the weight, fighting against gravity and water and pressure and depth.

Jeremiah heard his father's staggering sigh while his own held breath caught against his throat like a chain, holding him back, holding him down. Drowning him.

He had to break free.

For a moment, he was back in that pool, his life flashing before him while he struggled to stay in control. He could see Ava Jane, see the tears in her sky blue eyes and remember the pain on her face the night she'd begged him to stay.

For just that instant, he wanted to push up and out of the water, to find the air he needed to breathe. He wanted so badly to come home. Just come home.

"Jeremiah?"

He turned to find Beth standing there, staring at him.

"Are you all right?"

Jeremiah stood and gulped in air. He hadn't even realized he'd been holding his breath. Glancing down at his father, he wondered how long he'd been sitting so stiff and cold, sweat beading on his brow.

And he wondered if he hadn't already been baptized. But by fire, not water.

* * *

Ava Jane smiled at the people milling past the booth she shared with her mother and sister. "We've had a *gut* crowd, for sure," she said, happy that the weather had cooperated.

The booth was full of baked goods, knickknacks and all kind of handmade items. Pot holders and aprons lined up one side while quilts lay folded for display on a big table on the other side. The smell of meat grilling wafted on the crisp breeze that filled the afternoon air.

Mamm had walked down the long alley of colorful booths to visit with friends, leaving the two of them in charge. Now they sat on stools and nibbled at the lunch they'd packed, enjoying a quiet moment before the next round of customers showed up.

"Ach," Deborah replied, her smile as bright as the sun. "And it's wonderfully *gut* to see my sister having fun for a change."

Ava Jane slapped at Deborah. "I know how to have fun."

"But you'd forgotten."

Seeing the seriousness behind her sister's lighthearted banner, Ava Jane pretended to straighten the already-straight row of banana, pumpkin and blueberry breads she'd made. The row was growing smaller as the day wore on. The oatmeal and full-grains had already sold out.

"I'm okay," she told Deborah. Two days ago, she'd been at one of the lowest points in her life. In pain both physically and mentally, she'd almost made herself sick.

But prayer and lots of talks with her parents and the bishop had helped her grow determined and strong again.

She'd get through this. The bishop had given her some good advice.

"These things take time, Ava Jane. Jeremiah has been through a lot and he has come home for more reasons than he's admitting. Mostly, he came home to heal," the bishop had said.

That would take time, considering how he'd reacted the other day. And considering how she'd reacted to him.

She had not seen Jeremiah since that day.

Thankful for that, she wondered if he'd leave her alone as she'd demanded in her shock and anger. She wasn't proud of how she'd reacted but she didn't want to ever go through that again.

"Forgive," the bishop had advised her. "If he confesses his sin before the church and becomes baptized, we will speak of this matter no more."

The bishop had also given her some other advice. Advice she wasn't sure she could follow.

"It's understandable to think fondly of Jeremiah and also to hold resentment toward him. You knew him in childhood and were close to him. You are alone now. He is alone, too. But let nature take its course. Jeremiah has a lot of healing to do and he has come home to do so. Let him heal and then you can consider whether you want to be a friend to him or not. Meantime, forgive him, Ava Jane. Forgive him so you can have some peace, too."

She might not speak of Jeremiah's sin again but she'd always think about him and what they'd been through. Now she had to decide if she could ever get past her own pent-up resentment and anger and learn to tolerate his presence here.

"Don't go getting glum on me now," Deborah said with a twirl of one of her bonnet strings. "We've at least two more hours. Aren't you hungry? You didn't eat much of your chicken salad sandwich. Or maybe you'd like some more lemonade?"

"I had the sandwich an hour ago," Ava Jane reminded her sister. "And in case you haven't noticed, I have food all around me."

"But you can't eat up the profits."

Laughing at Deborah's antics, she looked up to see her friend Leah strolling through the booths. Leah had sewn and crocheted some of the items in their booth, but with six children the woman barely had time to make clothes for her family and she couldn't help man the booth. But she crocheted beautiful bibs, baby hats and blankets. She kept saying one day she'd open a shop and call it Leah's Triple B Designs.

"Hi, Leah," Ava Jane called out, waving.

"Hello," Leah replied, two children in tow and her youngest in her arms. "Josiah has the other three," she explained. The other three were older and self-sufficient—two boys and the oldest girl. "I came to check on my items, but I have to buy some of that good fruit bread you make, Ava Jane."

"We have your favorites left," Ava Jane said, motioning to Leah to come over. "And I have one apple pie left. I know it's Josiah's favorite."

Leah hurried across to the booth. When she got there, Deborah took the babe in her arms and began to coo and sing to the little girl. One day she'd make a fine mother.

"Thank you for selling my wares for me," Leah said, noticing her pile of various handmade items had gone down considerably. "I can really use the income."

"Your things are very popular," Ava Jane said, straightening the little blankets, memories of her own children at that age comforting her. "We have enjoyed representing you."

Leah kept an eye on the other two children and then turned back to Ava Jane. "I heard about what happened in town the other day. That must have been terrifying."

Ava Jane steeled herself. But there was no way around it. "It was, but then sometimes the Englisch go out of their way to torment us, don't they?"

Leah looked confused and then nodded. "*Ja,* but it's even worse when one of our own reacts with anger."

Shocked, Ava Jane realized everyone would have heard about Jeremiah's reaction, too. Lifting her spine, she nodded. "He did overreact. But he also came to our defense."

"I'm glad he did," Leah said in a low voice. "Sometimes I wonder if slapping a cheek might work just as well as turning the other cheek."

"We aren't to do that," Ava Jane said, praying she wouldn't do that right now. Leah meant well but no one knew how much this had affected her and she wanted to keep it that way. "But sometimes we do have to bite our tongues, right?"

Leah paid for her bread and pie and nodded. "Right." Then she put a hand on Ava Jane's arm. "You know, I have an opinion regarding you and Jeremiah."

"Everyone does," Ava Jane said on a dry note while her heart pumped faster. No point in trying to stop her friend from giving that opinion.

"It's simple," Leah said. "You're a widow and he's unmarried. You cared about each other once. What's to stop you from doing that again?"

Ava Jane gasped. First the bishop had hinted at this and now one of her friends. "There is a lot to stop me," she said, lowering her voice. "He joined the Navy and fought against others, took up arms. It goes against everything I've ever been taught. It goes against our beliefs."

Leah grabbed one of her rambunctious children and reeled him in. "But we are to forgive him," she stressed. "He wants that. Josiah says Jeremiah is trying very hard to make things right."

Leah's husband was a kind, hardworking man with a big family. He wanted everyone to have the same.

"I know he's trying," Ava Jane said. "I wish everyone would stop telling me that. I'm trying, too. Trying to accept that he's back to stay, trying to accept that Jacob is gone. Trying to see the good and the right in all of this."

Leah's brown eyes widened in distress. "I did not mean to upset you. I'm sorry."

Ava Jane looked over at her friend, realizing she'd just overreacted again when she'd told herself she would not.

"It's all right. I'm dealing with Jeremiah in the only way I know how. Prayer."

Leah nodded and was about to respond but when she heard a crash and saw one of her sons running away, she shook her head. "I have to go but…Ava Jane, if you ever need to talk—"

"I know where to find you," Ava Jane said, forcing a smile.

Two hours later, while she was packing up tablecloths and the few leftovers, she looked up into the setting sun and saw the silhouette of a man walking up the street.

A strong man with broad shoulders and a steady, solid gait.

Jeremiah. Walking right toward her.

Chapter Eleven

Jeremiah watched her face for signs of fear.

Ava Jane appeared tired and nervous, but he didn't see any fear. More like a steely determination and resolve. She was much braver than he'd ever been. And much more forgiving. He hoped she'd forgive him yet again.

Deborah came around the booth and greeted him with a hands-on-her-hips pleasantness. "Jeremiah, what are you doing here?"

Glancing around, he saw others staring. What did they think of him? Would he ever fit in again, even after they'd forgiven his sins?

"I'm here to help with cleanup. Beth came home to sit with our father, and the home health-care nurse is there with her."

"That's *gut* then," Deborah said, her head held high. "Beth is a devoted daughter." Dropping the defense mode, she added, "Most of the crowds have come and gone and we had a fairly good turnout. Sold a lot of our baked good and other items." Staring down her nose at him, she added, "We hope to have a good end to the day."

Jeremiah ventured a glance at Ava Jane and then back to Deborah. "Are you warning me? Or trying to stop me?"

"Both," Deborah replied without skipping a beat.

The annoying little sister he remembered had turned into an annoying grown woman. With spunk.

Jeremiah turned to where Ava Jane stood behind the protection of the booth. "Do you want me to leave?"

She gave him a troubled stare, her heart in her eyes. He saw the answer. She wanted him to leave Campton Creek. Period.

"No," she finally said. "You did volunteer to help out. We're about to go home anyway."

He nodded and moved away. Then he pivoted back. "I'm sorry," he said, glancing between Deborah and her. "I apologize for my actions the other day. I've been away for a long time and I'm learning things all over again. I hope you will forgive my angry outburst."

Deborah went back inside the booth with Ava Jane but had the good sense to busy herself with packing up the remaining items.

Ava Jane rubbed her dainty hands down the front of her apron, two bright spots of color on her cheeks showing her discomfort. "You should work on controlling that anger you've brought back with you. Or at least let it go. But I wonder how you'll do that. You were trained to become an angry man, weren't you?"

Only she had the power to bring him to his knees with her curt, calm words. "No, Ava Jane, I was trained to be a fighting man, to attack any enemies and to do my job to the best of my ability. I had to learn to stay in control all the time."

She folded up towels and put tablecloths into a basket before turning to face him. "But that requires violence, doesn't it? Which is why you're probably out of control now."

Her words might be harsh but the guarded worry in her eyes told him everything. She *was* afraid of him, of what he might do if he lost his temper again. But he also saw a trace of tenderness there in her shimmering stare. She wanted to understand but how could she even begin to understand how much he'd endured?

"War is violent," he said. "I did what I was trained to do, and while I'm not proud to admit I had to use violence at times, I am proud that I protected this country that shelters us and allows us to practice our religion in our own way."

"Even though our beliefs dictate that we are not to raise a hand in violence, that we are pacifists and peace-makers, not fighters and killers?"

He took a long breath before he answered. She was a smart woman and she'd obviously somehow studied up on what being a SEAL meant. He would not lie to her. "Yes, even so. I went against our beliefs because, at the time, I felt this need to do something, to fight an unseen enemy in honor of a friend. But I'm done with that now. I came back here. Of all the places on earth, I came home. Because I needed to be here. Right here. And I will work until the day I die to prove that I'm returning to our ways and our beliefs and God's word."

Ava inhaled a breath that sounded like a sob.

"Sister?"

She turned her head toward Deborah. "I'm fine. Go and load the buggy please."

Deborah hurried out toward where the buggies were parked and placed some of their items inside. Then she found a friend and started chatting in her animated way, but she kept glancing back toward the booth.

Ava Jane kept busy, her lips pursed and pinched, a soft frown marring her smooth forehead. Her hand stilled on a baby bib appliquéd with blue butterflies that matched her eyes. "Did you kill people, Jeremiah?"

That question threw him. Swallowing hard, he closed his eyes, images of death surrounding him. "It was kill or be killed."

She went still her eyes wide. "So you did?"

He nodded, keeping his eyes on her. "I took lives, yes. It can't be changed. I can only ask for forgiveness and… learn to forgive myself."

"And what if you can't?"

He couldn't answer that so he began to ask his own questions. "What else is there then? Do I leave again and become the outcast forever? I don't want that. I wouldn't be here if I didn't mean what I say. This is much harder than anything I endured out there."

"Harder than fighting and killing?"

"Nothing can ever be that hard, but I was hoping maybe to find some kindness in your eyes and your words. That's the hard part about facing you—seeing the condemnation you feel for me."

She stared at him, her own anger simmering beneath her sweet, tormented face. "Why did you decide to come back?" she asked, her tone numb and quiet. "Beth said you were in California for a while before you returned here."

"I was," he said, coming around to help her with the baskets of wares that needed to be put away. "When my last tour of duty was over, I was afraid to return home. A coward, that's what I'd become. I did my time and left the military, and then I landed in California since that's where I'd started my training. I worked on the farms out there. Produce for miles and miles. Fields of fruit and rows of olive trees, almond trees and grapes that would make wine and jam and juices. I loved being out in the fields and being in a clean, calm place near the sea."

He thought about that vast ocean that he'd fallen in love with, thought about the crashing waves that he'd learned to maneuver. Sometimes late at night when he couldn't sleep, he'd remember that cool water flowing over him like a soothing balm.

Pushing away those memories, he continued. "But I missed home. I missed my family. And even though I knew you were married, I missed you and Jacob—and my life here. When Beth mailed me and said our father was dying, I took that as a sign that I needed to return."

Ava Jane's eyes held his but he couldn't read her thoughts. She was as closed off to him today as she had been for all these many years. Even way back, she'd always held a part of herself away. He hadn't minded it so much when they were young. But now it shouted at him loud and clear. He'd lost her. Or maybe he was just now seeing what he hadn't seen back then. Maybe she'd never been his at all.

"I have to tell you something," he finally said as he lifted a basket and started walking with her toward her buggy, glad at least that she didn't push him away. "I'm not going back out there. I am here to stay, receive my baptism, confess *all* of my sins and give my life over to the Lord. If you can't stand the sight of me, I will stay away from you. If you can't forgive me, I will accept that and I promise I won't bother you again. If we pass on the street, I will look the other way to save you the discomfort of speaking to me."

Setting the basket in her buggy, he turned and faced her again. "And if you can't forgive me, Ava Jane, I will understand and it will hurt for the rest of my life, more than any wounds I've suffered, but I'll have to learn how to handle that."

She stopped near the buggy, her surprised gaze full of questions and yet, she said nothing.

So he continued while he still had the strength.

Touching a hand to his forehead, he said, "One good thing I learned in the Navy—I learned how to focus and concentrate on what needs to be done, to block out all distractions. I'll do that here and probably for a long, long time. I am disciplined and I'm in good shape. Maybe I'll find a wife and settle down and have babies and finally be a happy man. Maybe. But then that wouldn't be fair to any woman I married because I'd always be pining for someone else."

Then he leaned close. "I will always be near *you* and I guess I'll have to take that as all I'll ever have of you. Just being near you. It will have to be enough."

He turned and left before he started begging her, before she could respond with more measured words. He wouldn't look back. He would not force her to see what little good he had left in him. If she found any good in him, it would have to be through her own actions and her own eyes. And the seeing and forgiving would have to come from within her heart.

Because he was badly wounded, in both spirit and in physical body, and not yet strong enough to force anyone to do anything. If she ever came to him, he wanted her to come of her own accord and because, at long last, she wanted to be with him again.

She almost called after him, but her sister's hand on her arm stopped her. "That was some show you two put on."

Ava Jane held Deborah's hand. "It wasn't a show. It was as if we were the only two people left in the world." She stared after Jeremiah, her heart hammering in her chest with such an intense pain she almost doubled over. "And I think this will be the last time Jeremiah ever bothers me. I've lost him for good this time."

"Lost him?" Deborah frowned and got into the buggy seat. "Did you ever have him?"

"No," she said, lifting up to sit beside her sister. "I meant I've lost a chance to at least be a friend to him. I haven't understood him at all and I never will. Looking back, I don't think we truly knew each other at all, even before he left. I'm not a very good Christian now because I'm having a hard time forgiving what he did. What he became." She inhaled a breath to keep from sobbing, but her grief would always be twofold. "He implied I'm a distraction and that he will ignore me from now on."

"You are the best distraction he's ever had," Deborah said, taking the reins as they headed toward home. "Don't let him do this to you."

"He's not doing this," she admitted. "I'm doing it to myself because I've wrestled with this since he left me. Now he has solved my dilemma. He has decided in his own way to shun me, to save grace and keep me from being uncomfortable, and I can't blame him. I've been horrible to him. He's taken the hint and he says he will stay away from me. So I won't have to fret about Jeremiah Weaver again. It will be as if I never existed for him."

He'd find someone else. Several of her single friends had eyed him outright at church. He didn't mean that part about never being able to marry another woman. "He'll move on now," she managed to whisper. "And I'm glad for it."

Deborah's derisive snort echoed out over the gloaming. "We'll have to see how that works for the two of you."

"It has to work," Ava Jane said. "We are both here and we can't avoid each other. But we can pretend to ignore each other and that means I won't have to deal with him in any personal way, at least."

"This is going to be hard for both of you from what I've seen," Deborah pointed out. "Campton Creek isn't big enough for the two of you trying to avoid each other."

But Ava Jane would do her best to avoid Jeremiah. And she knew, after today, he'd do his best to stay far away from her.

She'd hurt him.

Which brought her to the other nagging thought now centered in her mind. What kind of wounds had he suffered in fighting for his country? And would his wounds every truly heal?

Chapter Twelve

She'd spent the last two weeks trying to ignore Jeremiah Weaver. But the man seemed to pop up in the oddest places.

He always had business at the general store and Mr. Hartford didn't have a clue that Jeremiah and Ava Jane were at odds. Jeremiah had been long gone when Mr. Hartford inherited the store from his parents ten years ago. And besides, the kind Englisch man was not one to gossip or make observations. He respected the Amish. But he seemed determined to shove any single Amish man and woman together. So Ava Jane had taken to checking each aisle and even the hardware and lumberyard out back before she ventured past the produce section.

True to his word, Jeremiah did not approach her, even on the one day she came close to bumping into him. Before Mr. Hartford could gather them into his conversation, Ava Jane had taken off in the other direction.

But she saw Jeremiah's furtive glances and frowning expressions.

She'd stopped two days ago with her children in the

pretty park just past Campton House, hoping to give them
a few moments to walk the trails and enjoy the warm day.
The park had exploded with new fronds on the tall pines
and green shoots on the budding oak trees. A weathered
white gazebo stood at the center of the park and held a
perfect view of the water and woods. Nearby, a dogwood
promised to burst forth with white blooms.

It was peaceful and quiet until she looked up to find
Jeremiah walking along one of the winding, tree-shaded
trails. He kept his head down, his hat drawn low, probably because he didn't seem to like bringing attention to
himself. He hadn't even looked their way.

But she knew he was around. Always around. She'd
noticed his buggy going up and down the road in front
of her property. A buggy that never stopped in her yard.

He did work hard. She'd give him that. Beth went
on and on at their last frolic about how he'd painted the
house and cleaned out the barn and repaired everything
that creaked or squeaked.

"He sits with Daed every morning and every night,"
Beth divulged to the fascinated group of women who'd
gathered at Leah's big house. "Sometimes I hear him
talking about…things…he did out there. Sometimes I
hear him praying."

Praying. That notion had brought Ava Jane's head up
and got her heart beating too fast. She'd never pictured
Jeremiah praying. Not since he'd left, at least.

The man was a paradox. Too confusing for Ava Jane
to understand.

Now another Sunday had rolled around. As she worked
with the other ladies to serve dinner since the church service was over, she watched with a shuttered gaze as Jeremiah helped with putting out chairs and moving tables

and then assisted elderly Mrs. Knepp to a shaded bench underneath a towering oak.

When he turned, he caught Ava Jane staring and immediately hurried the other way.

In spite of the cool afternoon breeze, Ava Jane's skin burned hot. He was truly shunning her. No, avoiding her. Ignoring her. Hurting her.

As you've done to him. But she'd tried so hard to be kind and forgiving. Hadn't she?

Remembering the minister's message of doing unto others, she lifted her chin and continued with her work. Easter was coming, a day of resurrection and new beginnings. She'd be kind and civil to the man. If he ever looked at her again.

The weather was wonderful on this Sunday. One week before Easter and two weeks before Sarah Rose's seventh birthday. She could focus, too. *She* hadn't gone through some sort of rigorous physical training to do so. Ava Jane had her faith and the disciplines she'd learned from the Ordnung to train her in the ways of the church.

So why was she having such a hard time focusing these days? Why did it hurt that Jeremiah's beautiful smile was so rare? That his blue eyes looked so cloudy and tormented? That he walked among them as a man who'd gone cold and numb, tortured and stoic?

"He swaggers."

She whirled to find her friends Hannah and Leah glancing from her to Jeremiah. "What?"

"Jeremiah," dark-haired Hannah Smith said, her prim smile full of curiosity. "He swaggers. It's like he walks differently from most of our men. Have you noticed?"

Why did her friends always ask her to define Jeremiah? Had she noticed? *Yes.* His swagger was one of the things about him that both scared her and intrigued her. He moved in a way that showed too much confidence and made him too masculine. He might be world-weary and tired, but Jeremiah was still a handsome man.

A dangerous, handsome man.

"He's so different now," Leah said, adding to Hannah's remarks. "But then, I only remember him as a boy. He was always as cute as a button and stocky, but now..." She shrugged. "Josiah says it's the warrior in him. Might be hard to get rid of that."

Why was Leah so interested in this? Ava Jane's older friend usually didn't abide gossiping and ogling. Now she was discussing Jeremiah with her husband? Had Josiah warned her to stay away from him?

The warrior. Yes, she'd seen that warrior side of Jeremiah. And she was trying sorely to avoid him and his swagger.

"I haven't noticed," she told her fascinated friends before she hustled to put out tea jugs and then went to her buggy to get the three apple pies she'd made.

Just as she reached for the long flat woven basket holding the pies, two boys ran by and almost knocked her off her feet.

But a strong hand grabbed her before she lost both the tray of pies and her footing.

Her gaze on the long basket tray, she struggled to balance and said, "Thank you." And then she looked up and into Jeremiah's midnight blue eyes.

"You're welcome," he said, taking the basket right out of her hands. "Boys."

Her heart did the bump-bump that made her lose her breath. "Boys will be boys." She checked to make sure her Eli hadn't been in the unruly group.

"Remember when that was us?"

His quiet words touched her and stung her.

"You aren't supposed to be speaking to me or assisting me," she reminded him, a deliberate nip of chill in her words.

"I'm going to take these pies to the table over there," he said, indicating with his chin toward where several other desserts were already being displayed. "I wasn't trying to bother you. I just happened to be passing by."

Then he nodded again and hurried to deposit her load before he headed back inside the big, roomy barn where they'd held services for two hours.

So he *was* good at ignoring her, Ava Jane thought with a trace of despair and disappointment. She'd return the favor by not looking his way again.

No, she hadn't noticed Jeremiah or the changes that only made him more attractive and intriguing. She hadn't noticed his dark unruly hair or the scars on his hands and…one tiny crescent-shaped scar near his left temple. Nor had she noticed how he walked or talked or breathed.

Or prayed.

Not at all.

Jeremiah ate his meal in silence, the banter and easy conversation of the men around him only making him stand out even more than he already did. They treated him nicely enough but he didn't offer up much in the way of conversation, which made some of his old friends glance at him with uncertainty and maybe a little bit of judgment.

But he could handle that.

He'd learned how to make himself invisible. To blend in and sit so still that people would start talking over him and around him and through him. So he'd watch and listen and learn a few details that would help his team down the road. Details that could save lives.

Right now, he was keen on hearing the details of Eli Graber planning to sneak down to the creek with his friend Simon Kemp.

"My *mamm* doesn't like it when I go swimming. She's scared of the water," Eli said from the spot away from the table where he and Simon had clustered. "My *daed* drowned there and it makes her sad. It makes all of us sad. We miss him."

The other boy's fascination caused his freckled face to go blotchy. "That's a terrible way to die."

Eli nodded, his dark eyes so like Jacob's, casting up to make sure no one was listening. "Yes. It was bad. She won't even teach Sarah Rose how to swim. That's why I have to sneak down to the creek. Daed taught me. He said his best friend taught him. I'm pretty good. I'll show you."

Jeremiah remembered sneaking down to the creek with Jacob, remembered showing his friend how to hold his breath and go under. Ava Jane would find them and sit up on the bridge, because, for modesty's sake, girls weren't supposed to swim with boys. She'd been terrified of the water anyway.

Jeremiah took a breath and pushed the memories away. He missed Jacob, too. Why did his friend have to die there of all places?

Another irony between them that Jeremiah couldn't explain. Why had God given him such a keen love of water and made Ava Jane so scared of it, only to have her husband and his friend, Jacob, drown at the very creek where they used to hang out?

His father had taught him how to swim, telling him he'd never know when that ability might come in handy.

An understatement. And yet another irony. His father, whom he loved dearly and who now did not want Jeremiah in his house.

Jeremiah kept listening, just to silence all of his questions. It wasn't up to him to stop the boy. Ava Jane wouldn't like him interfering. But she wouldn't like it if Eli disobeyed her either.

Jeremiah lifted up off the bench without making a sound and casually walked past the boys, a solid smile on his face.

"Good day, Eli, Simon. What are you two cooking up over here?"

Guilt colored both of the boys in shades of red that matched the checkered tablecloths.

"Uh, hello, Mr. Jeremiah," Eli said, his gaze shifting out over the crowd. "We were talking about the creek."

Surprised that the boy had been honest, Jeremiah nodded and glanced off in the distance where he could see the water from the Bylers' hillside farmstead. "It's one of those spring days where you want to get your fishing pole out and bring home a nice trout or a mess of perch. You two thinking about going?"

Eli glanced at Simon. "Maybe. Either that or…swimming." He almost said something else but halted, his mouth shutting into a grim line.

"Water's still a bit chilly," Jeremiah said. He'd never admit he'd gone swimming since he'd been home. Usually late at night or early in the morning when no one was out and about. He also knew how to slide through the water without even making a splash. "Might want to wait a few more weeks."

"How do you know that?" Simon asked with a daring, shrill voice, accusation in his eyes.

Eli held quiet but looked as if he had a lot he wished he could say.

"I stuck my toes in," Jeremiah replied, leaving it at that. "Besides, you know how mothers can be about little boys sneaking away without permission. I'd think long and hard before I went swimming. Maybe talk to your *mamm* first."

Eli's eyes went dark with disappointment. "She does not like the creek."

"She has good reason," Jeremiah replied, giving the boy a steady stare. "You wouldn't want to hurt her feelings now, would you?"

"Eli!"

They all three whirled to find Ava Jane standing there with her hands on her hips, glaring at them. "Stop sputtering and help me load the buggy. It's time to go home and do chores."

Simon whirled and ran away while Eli stared at Jeremiah in obvious wonder and then stalked toward Ava Jane. She said something to him and then marched over to Jeremiah.

"So, you decide to avoid me but you manage to talk to my son? What was that all about, Jeremiah? More questions about guns and curiosity about your former life? Trying to turn my son into something he can never be by influencing and encouraging him?"

Hurt that she'd even consider such a thing, he shook his head. "That's not what it was about."

Her eyes wouldn't let go of their doubt. "Then what?"

Jeremiah wouldn't squeal on Eli. The boy had got the message. No need to fill her in on things. "That was boy stuff. Sometimes young boys need to talk to older men about things. We talked about fishing and swimming once the water is warm. Your son is interested in that, nothing more." Watching her confused reaction, he added, "And as far as I know, those are normal things that all young boys like to do."

He nodded to her before she could respond and then turned and headed home on foot. His sister had come to the service with a friend and his mother was home with his father.

Jeremiah needed some time alone to think about how much the effort of trying to avoid Ava Jane was exhausting him and confusing him.

Did she want him around?

Or was she just playing a game of her own to punish him and make him suffer before she finally allowed him fully back into her life?

Either way, his patience was running thin. He'd have to refocus and pray even more for the Lord to give him the strength he needed to keep his eyes on the prize. That prize would be God's grace. With or without Ava Jane's blessings.

Chapter Thirteen

"Ava Jane, you have a note here from Mrs. Campton."

Ava Jane whirled at Mr. Hartford's comment, her gaze falling on the fancy cream-colored envelope he held up.

"Are you sure?"

"Got your name right here in black ink," he said with a soft smile. "Her assistant person left it yesterday."

Ava Jane took the envelope and rubbed a finger over the scrolled lettering. "Someone has lovely handwriting."

Mr. Hartford nodded. "The Camptons do everything first-class."

"Yes, they sure do," she replied, careful to place the envelope in the pocket of her apron. "*Denke*, Mr. Hartford."

Hurrying away, she gathered the few items she needed and made sure she'd placed the money Mr. Hartford had given her for this week's supply of baked goods inside her other pocket.

No sign of Jeremiah, thankfully. But each time the bell on the door of the general store dinged she half expected to see him standing there. Even her weekly trips to this old-fashioned country store had been tarnished by memories of Jeremiah.

And from seeing the man himself here in front of her.

Still smarting from their encounter at church two days ago, she remembered having a talk with Eli yesterday.

"Why do you insist on talking to Jeremiah Weaver?"

"I don't, Mamm." But her son's eyes shone bright and he didn't look her in the eye. "I mean, not unless he talks to me. He's always kind to me."

"You don't know him."

Eli finally faced her, his expression pinched and guarded. "But you did. And so did Daed. I know he's the one who taught my *daadi* to swim."

Suddenly it all fell into place. Eli wasn't fascinated with Jeremiah because of where he'd been. He only wanted to know more about the man who'd been so close to his daddy.

"Who told you that?" she asked, her heart breaking for her boy. What kind of tales were people telling?

"I heard some of the men talking. Heard how they used to run around together and swim in the creek and hunt with Daed and Mr. Jeremiah. Is it true?"

"Yes, it's true. But that was a long time ago."

Eli's brown eyes went rich with unshed tears. "Is that why you get upset when he's around? 'Cause you miss Daed?"

Gathering her son into her arms, she'd kissed his unruly hair and said, "*Ja*, I get all emotional and want to have a good cry because of the memories and because I loved your father so much."

Then her son had asked yet another hard question. "Then why don't you like his friend?"

She hadn't been able to give a good answer to that one.

"I like him. But he's been gone a long time so I have to get to know him better."

"So you don't want me to talk to him?"

"I want you to be careful when you talk to all adults."

She wished she'd done better by her son, but here she stood with yet another reminder of all the ways Jeremiah Weaver had betrayed her and his faith.

She'd open the note from Mrs. Campton when she was alone back home. Ava Jane hurried about the store, grabbing her needed items and tried once again to forget about Jeremiah. She only saw a couple of people in the store and when she headed to her buggy parked in a designated spot in the lot beside the store, it looked as if she was one of few people out and about today.

The main street through the town, aptly named Creek Road, was nearly deserted. So she loaded her basket into the buggy and guided Matilda toward home, glad for the solitude.

Taking the buggy out onto the main road, she thought again about seeing Jeremiah at church. He'd looked good. Healthy and settled, some of the strain she'd noticed on his face a few weeks ago now replaced with a quiet reserve and a solid resolve. He'd always been stubborn and single-minded. He must truly be focusing on getting back right within the church. He didn't converse with the other men a lot, but he spoke when spoken to and he helped as needed. Now and then, she'd glance his way and actually see him smiling at a comment someone had made.

Jeremiah had a beautiful smile.

Urging Matilda on up the road, Ava Jane silently reprimanded herself and tried to find something else to occupy her mind.

Her mother and Deborah had come by early this morning to check on her, a sure sign that she was giving off some sort of distress signal.

"Any more headaches?" Mamm asked, concern in her question. "You were quiet at services on Sunday."

Ava Jane ignored that remark. She'd tried to stay busy after church. "No. I'm better. That last one was a doozy."

"You haven't suffered headaches in a while," her mother noted. "Remember to take care of yourself. Drink your chamomile tea and get some rest."

"I'm fine," Ava Jane replied. As fine as she could be, considering.

Deborah flittered around the spotless kitchen, picking up fruit and studying the contents of the cabinets. "I remember the bad attack you had after Jacob died. Understandable, of course."

Ava Jane barely remembered much from those dark days except the piercing pain inside her heart, but thinking about it gave her muscle memories of pain and despair all over her body and brought out a hazy dread inside her soul.

To lighten things, she asked, "Is that why you're both staring at me as if I have bugs crawling out of my *kapp*? Are you still concerned that I won't be able to handle things?"

"No," Deborah replied. "You look fairly normal this morning. You've always handled things just fine."

Ava Jane smiled at that. "I function most days and I'm okay, really. I think the worst of it is over."

"You mean the worst of having to accept Jeremiah being back in the community?" Mamm asked, her voice soft with compassion.

Ava Jane poured coffee and got out her notebook.

"Yes. We've reached a truce. We don't even notice each other anymore."

Her sister snorted and her mother frowned.

"That might be for the best," Mamm said while her frown turned to a neutral expression on her still-young face.

"Yes," Ava Jane agreed. So why was she so riled about it? She almost told them about finding him talking to Eli, but decided she'd given everyone enough fodder regarding her and Jeremiah. Instead, she added, "So let's change the subject and get down to the business of planning Sarah Rose's seventh birthday party."

Her mother and sister had the good grace to leave things at that, but she knew her family was worried about her. Daed came by most afternoons to check on her. Knowing how blessed she was to have such a loving family, she didn't begrudge them. Right now, they brought her comfort and kept her grounded.

Today the sun was bright on her garden so after she unhitched the buggy and took care of Matilda's needs, she went to work on hoeing weeds and pruning tender shoots. Her spring flowers were already blooming. Petunias, daisies and lilies colored the many groupings she'd worked on. Soon, she'd have tomatoes, onions, peas and beans and herbs in the little vegetable garden behind the house, too.

Bending over, she noticed something fluttering out of her pocket. The note from Mrs. Campton. She'd forgotten about it.

Ava Jane stared at her own name on the elegant paper, too many bitter memories warring inside her brain. What could Edward Campton's mother possibly want with her? And why such a formal way of reaching out to her?

Shoving the note back into her pocket, she finished up with her garden work and then washed her hands and made herself a quick dinner. The *kinder* would be home soon and, after hearing about Jeremiah's conversation with Eli last Sunday and then having her own talk with her son, she planned to take them for a walk down to the creek. It was painful to go there, but her children were getting older and more curious about their father and his death. She wouldn't bring it up unless one of them asked. But they should know their father and keep him in their memories. Maybe going there would help with that, at least. And she'd take Eli back to fish there, too.

Because seeing him seek advice from Jeremiah rubbed her the wrong way. It shouldn't. Her son was seeking answers she had not provided. She'd do better at that.

Thank You, Father, for allowing me to see this need. Jeremiah had been the one to point it out.

Thank You, Father, for allowing me to see that Jeremiah has some good traits.

She cleared away her dishes and then settled in a rocking chair with a cup of mint tea. Finally, she pulled the now-crumpled note out of her pocket.

Dear Ava Jane,
I was wondering if you'd come by to see me sometime this week. My husband's seventy-fifth birthday is coming up and I'd like to celebrate with a cake. I've sampled some of your baked goods from Hartford's and so I'd like to hire you to bake the cake. But we need to talk about what kind and such things. Can you come by on Wednesday morning?
Sincerely,
Judy Campton

Ava Jane didn't trust the Camptons. She knew they were good people but…they'd taken Jeremiah from her. How could she do this? Go and take a food order from a woman she didn't care to associate with?

You could use the money.

That was true. Judy Campton's influence stretched far and wide around here. Ava Jane might receive more orders from this one visit. Was she willing to do that? To go and talk to Mrs. Campton? The woman hadn't done anything to her and she knew the Camptons had been generous to the Amish community their ancestors had allowed to settle here. They'd lived together in peace for centuries and this generation could be the last of the Camptons, but one part of her wanted to ignore the formal request.

Manners dictated that she should visit the elderly woman. Mrs. Campton didn't venture out much these days. She seemed to prefer staying close to her husband, who had been in ill health for months now.

It would be rude not to show up, wouldn't it?

At least, she shouldn't have to worry about seeing Jeremiah there.

The next day, Ava Jane wore her best blue dress and a clean white *kapp*, her hair caught up in a bun underneath, her white apron crisp and fresh.

"Do you want me to wait for you?" her father asked, questions coloring his hazel eyes. Her father never brought up the subject of Jeremiah Weaver, but his need to protect his daughter shouted through his stoic silence.

"Why don't you park and go sit on that bench out in the front garden?" Ava Jane said. "I'm sure Mrs. Campton won't mind that."

"Will she mind if I fall asleep with the bees humming around me?" Daed asked with a teasing grin.

"She probably won't even notice." Ava Jane patted her father's sturdy arm, noting the fatigue that seemed to shadow him these days. "I won't be long, I promise."

Her father gave her a gentle gaze full of love. "If you need me…"

"I'll be fine, Daed."

Knowing he was nearby did bring her comfort.

She didn't know why she'd asked her father to bring her here, but she felt safe with him and she knew he'd intervene on her behalf if anything about this meeting upset her. Because Ava Jane figured this summons was about much more than baking a cake.

Nerves tingling like the silvery wind chimes she saw hanging on the rambling white-columned front porch, Ava Jane stood staring at the massive black front door. She'd never been to this house. Jeremiah had always wanted her to see it. Odd that now she was finally here.

Made of red bricks and trimmed in black shutters, the house welcomed with transoms over the heavy door and windows. Georgian style, she'd heard it called.

She lifted a hand to the brass door knocker and then waited for someone to answer, her heart beating like a trapped bird inside her chest. Ava Jane almost turned around to leave but the door creaked open before she could escape.

"Good morning." Bettye Byer, the widowed housekeeper who'd also become an assistant and lived on the estate since her husband had passed away twenty years ago, greeted Ava Jane with a welcoming smile.

"*Gut* day to you," Ava Jane said. "It's *gut* to see you

again, Bettye. I hope you found lots of buys at the spring festival."

"I did," Bettye said, guiding Ava Jane inside where a marble floor shimmered in the morning light. "I told Mrs. Campton she should get you to bake the cake for Mr. Campton's party. The blueberry pie I brought home went pretty fast."

Feeling more at ease, Ava Jane smiled. "I'm glad you enjoyed the pie and thank you for recommending me."

"Let's get you into Mrs. C's sitting room before she wonders if I've kidnapped you and taken you straight to the kitchen," Bettye said with a wink.

It was rumored that Bettye had once been Amish until she'd met an Englisch man and married him. They never had children, but because he was the caretaker of Campton House and took care of the expansive gardens, they'd lived here in the carriage house.

Romantic, but Ava Jane's hurt cut through that notion.

Jeremiah had been in this house, had enjoyed the graciousness that Bettye was now showing her. She had to stop thinking about that and concentrate on why she was here.

Ava Jane straightened her clothes and followed Bettye, noticing the other woman's gray bobbed hair and her creamy skin. Bettye looked young to have been around so long. Maybe her attitude made her seem carefree, but Ava Jane wondered what she'd sacrificed by leaving her family and faith to marry someone forbidden.

She prayed that Bettye and her husband had been happy here.

The house was impressive. Not as fancy as she'd imagined but comfortable and full of antiques and beautiful artwork. She passed a mirror and was shocked to see her own wide-eyed image there.

"Here we go," Bettye said. "I'll bring out some refreshments for you two."

She showed Ava Jane a cozy little room off the back of the house. "This is the sunroom. Mrs. C likes to sit here and read most mornings."

"Denke," Ava Jane said, glancing to where Mrs. Campton sat smiling over at them.

The room was filled with sunlight that glistened off the white wicker furniture and shot back out into the massive backyard, spreading all the way to the creek. She noticed a small dock with a rowboat nearby.

Out in the yard, old camellia bushes bustled together like ladies at a church meeting and massive azalea bushes held fresh pink- and salmon-hued buds that reminded her of quilt scraps. Beautiful.

But when she glanced to the left and saw the huge pool, her mind shifted back to the task ahead. She needed to get this over and done with.

"Ava Jane," Mrs. Campton said, holding out a hand. "I was afraid you wouldn't come." She patted the floral cushion of a high-backed wicker chair next to her own. "Please have a seat. I would stand to greet you, but it takes me too long to get up."

"Hello," Ava Jane said, sitting down on the edge of the chair. "It's good to see you, Mrs. Campton."

"I doubt that," the woman said, laughing. "I would imagine this is the last place on earth you'd want to be."

"You'd be right about that," Ava Jane said, surprising herself. "I almost didn't come."

Judy Campton gave her a shrewd once-over. "This

house held bad memories for you even before you entered it."

Since the woman seemed intent on getting to the bottom of things, Ava Jane nodded and took her time glancing around at the potted ferns and exotic houseplants. "I don't really know much about this house or you," she said, her voice calm in spite of her sweaty palms. "But Jeremiah holds you in high esteem."

Judy Campton's green eyes met hers with a focused appraisal. "He holds you in high esteem, too. That's why I thought it was time for us to meet."

Anger caused Ava Jane to sit up, her spine stiffening. "I didn't come here to talk about Jeremiah Weaver."

"No, we're here to discuss cake," Judy replied, her gaze never wavering. "But we'll get to that. I just wanted to meet you, dear, because…well…my husband and I won't be around forever. It's important to us that Jeremiah has someone he can turn to if he needs help."

"What do you mean?" Ava Jane asked, surprised yet again. "Is he ill?"

"Not in any physical way," Judy said. "But he's hurting inside. He gave up a lot to do what he did."

"I'm well aware of what he gave up," Ava Jane replied, keeping her tone kind.

"Then you should also be aware of what he might one day suffer, even more than he already has."

Now the woman had her worried. "What are you trying to say to me?"

Bettye came in before Mrs. Campton could reply. Carrying a tray complete with two floral-edged china cups and a dainty teapot, she set it on the oval table between them. "Tea and some snack cake. Not as good as yours, Ava Jane, but one of Mrs. C's favorites. Spice cake."

Ava Jane didn't think she could eat a bite of the dark pecan-crusted snack cake. Why did this woman bring her here?

And what was so wrong with Jeremiah that Mrs. Campton would demand that Ava Jane needed to know?

Chapter Fourteen

"What do you mean?" Ava Jane asked, her teacup halfway to her lips.

"Have you ever heard of PTSD?" Judy asked, her own tea forgotten on the table.

"No." Ava Jane put the delicate china cup and saucer down and stood. "I have to go. I'll be happy to bake your husband's birthday cake but you can have Bettye send me the details."

"Please," Judy said, trying to stand. "Don't go."

Ava Jane saw the worry and remorse in the woman's aged eyes and immediately guided Judy back into her chair and then sank down on her own. "I can't talk about Jeremiah. I won't."

"All right," Judy said. "I'm so sorry. I've said more than I intended. But he still cares for you and…I feel I need to warn you."

Ava Jane's heartbeat accelerated as she took in a deep breath. "You mean, to warn me about the anger he's holding inside, the kind he displayed on the street the other week?"

Judy nodded, clearly as rattled as Ava Jane. "I'm divulging subject matter that is very personal. I don't normally interfere in such things, but I love Jeremiah...like a son...and I deeply respect what you've had to deal with, too."

Feeling contrite, Ava Jane leaned forward. "I'm sorry. But you brought me here under false pretenses."

"No, I really do want that birthday cake. Bettye and I both are getting too old to spend a lot of time in the kitchen." Judy finally took a sip of her tea. "It's just that when I saw you I couldn't help but blurt that out. Someone needs to be aware."

Ava Jane took another breath and decided to listen to the woman's concerns. Curiosity and fear gave her the grace to do so. That and her burning need to understand Jeremiah. "Is he a danger to himself or others?"

"No." Judy Campton shook her head. "Not unless he is provoked by someone meaning to do harm. Did he tell you he was badly wounded?"

Ava Jane put a hand to her mouth, horrible images crowding her head. "No, but I've wondered."

"Jeremiah is a hero," Judy continued. "My husband doesn't have all the details, but he asked around and found out that during a mission that went bad, Jeremiah saved two of his team members and several civilians, even though he'd been shot. But something happened that he can't get over. Something he's locked inside himself. That's the thing that makes him angry sometimes. When he sees injustice of any kind, he reacts."

Ava Jane held her hands together, remembering how even growing up Jeremiah was always the first to defend those he loved. "The way he did with those young people. He was protecting my friends and my sister." She looked up at Judy. "And me."

"Especially you," Judy said. "When he came here right after he attacked that man, he was so shaken. I've seen it many times. Post-traumatic stress disorder is something that a lot of military men and women go through. Those who've been on the front lines suffer it the most. I have volunteered for many years at a nearby clinic where members of the military go to get help. I've encouraged Jeremiah to talk to the counselors there."

A clinic. Ava Jane had been only once to the big hospital about thirty miles away, when a distant family member had been ill. This clinic must be connected to that facility.

"But he refuses?" she asked Judy, her heart breaking apart.

"For now," Judy said. "I think he'll change his mind on that one day. I pray."

"Are you asking me to *not* provoke him or *to* protect him?"

"Neither of those things, dear," Judy replied on a soft note. "I'm explaining to you why he might lose his temper at times. He has flashbacks that can cause nightmares or cause him to withdraw. If I'm guessing correctly, he probably feels uncomfortable in a crowd, standoffish and silent. What I'm telling you has to remain confidential, but I think Jeremiah will recover with care and nurturing and some counseling. But, Ava Jane, he needs a friend."

Ava Jane put her hands in her lap, the image of Jeremiah standing away from the other men at church front and center in her mind. "And you think I should be his friend. Me, the woman he left to go and put himself through that kind of torture? You think I'm the one to help him heal when he and I can barely be near each other. He knows how I feel. I resent him going away and

I resent him returning here. I can't get past what he did, even though I know in my heart I have to find a way to forgive him."

Judy nodded, her eyes misty and full of understanding. "You're the only one who *can* calm him and help him to heal," Judy said. "I'm only asking you because I know how he feels about you. He was devastated the other day after he went after that misguided young man."

Ava Jane felt drained and even more concerned for Jeremiah. Only, she didn't have the strength to help him. "Thank you for telling me these things, Mrs. Campton," she said. "But I can't be responsible for healing Jeremiah. He will have to find a way to do that himself."

"Just consider what I've told you," Judy said, insistence in her voice. "Jeremiah is a good man. A kind, hardworking man. He needs his family and his community in his life, especially because of his emotional wounds."

Ava Jane wondered about that and tried to steel herself against feeling anything more than being sorry for him. "I needed him in my life," she said. "But he chose to leave me."

"Greater love has no one than this, that someone lay down his life for his friends," Judy said, her words floating out over the room in a whisper.

John 15:13. Ava Jane knew the verse.

She closed her eyes and fought back the tears. "Hasn't he given enough?"

"More than enough," Judy said. "That's why he's come home."

Ava Jane sat silent for a few moments. "I will do my best to be kind to him and to watch out for him. But I can't become involved with him, do you understand?"

Judy nodded, shrewdness bringing color back to her

eyes. "Yes, I'm beginning to understand so much more than I ever did."

Bettye walked in, right on cue. "Did you two decide what kind of cake we need?"

Judy gave Ava Jane a reassuring glance. "My husband loves carrot cake. Could you do a three-layer one with cream cheese icing?"

Ava Jane nodded, afraid to speak, amazed at how Judy Campton switched from an intense conversation to a lighthearted order with a blink of her intelligent eyes.

But finally she said, "I'd be glad to bake the cake. My father favors carrot cake, too."

"Then you should bring him to the party," Judy said. "In fact, I'd love to have you here at the party to help us serve. I'd pay you for your time, of course."

Feeling a bit put off, Ava Jane didn't want to come back to this house, especially since she might run into Jeremiah here, and she certainly didn't want to be bribed into working in this house. She had to make that clear. "I don't usually take on that kind of work. I have two children."

"I've insulted you," Judy said. "Bettye, help me to keep my mouth shut from now on."

Bettye shook her head and gave Ava Jane an apologetic smile.

"I'm not insulted," Ava Jane said. "My friends have mentioned working for you. I'd just prefer not to."

"Then come as my guest," Judy said, leaning forward. "I think you and I could become good friends."

Ava Jane didn't see that happening either but she finally let go of a smile. "Are you always this persuasive?"

"Yes, she is," Bettye said, laughing.

"Let's get that cake baked," Ava Jane finally said. "We'll let God take care of the rest."

"Good idea." Judy sat back and sipped her tea, a proud smile on her face.

Bettye told Ava Jane when they'd need the cake and gave her the time of the party. This coming Saturday afternoon. "You can deliver it earlier that day or we can pick it up."

"I'll pay extra if you deliver it," Judy added. "We don't drive very much anymore either." Then she grinned at Ava Jane. "Maybe then I can convince you to stay for a while."

"I thank you for the invitation," Ava Jane said, getting up to really leave this time. "I'll bring you the cake but I don't think attending the party would be wise on my part."

She turned and headed out of the room before Judy Campton could talk her into anything else.

"What took so long?" Samuel asked when she came rushing down the front steps.

"Too many cakes to make a rash decision," Ava Jane replied. "And too many cooks in that kitchen."

"Ach," her *daed* said with a soft smile. He didn't ask for any further explanation.

As they left the Campton estate, Ava Jane sent up a thankful prayer for her father's solemn quiet. She couldn't talk about what she'd heard at Campton House. But she could double up on her prayers for everyone involved, including herself and Jeremiah.

She needed prayer now more than ever.

Jeremiah had been wounded out there. Wounded by a gunshot and still he'd apparently saved others.

And he'd lived. He'd survived for a reason.

Dear Lord, thank You for bringing him home.

That unexpected prayer surprised her, especially when she realized she'd been in denial for weeks now. A gentle thankfulness filled her spirit and this time she didn't push it away.

If he hadn't been wounded, how long would he have stayed and fought? For a lifetime? She might not have ever seen him again.

That brought up a new revelation. She became glad in her *heart* that he'd made it home. Glad she'd had this second chance with him, to forgive him in person.

Too glad at this moment.

She didn't understand why that notion made her want to cry happy tears right along with her sad tears, but she had to blink to clear her eyes.

Had she been denying her true feelings for Jeremiah? Or were *these* feelings new and fresh and different because they were both changed and different now?

"You're mighty quiet," her father said as he clicked his tongue for Matilda to move along.

"I've got a lot on my mind."

"More than cake?"

"A lot more than cake," she said with a soft laugh that didn't ring sincere.

"You'll figure it out, daughter. You're smart, you know."

She wondered about that. Judy Campton was the smart one. Because she'd opened up that tiny hole in Ava Jane's heart and flooded it with compassion Ava Jane hadn't wanted to feel, and had made her see the truth she'd been trying so hard to deny.

Jeremiah had come home to stay. But he'd brought a lot of that world outside of Campton Creek with him.

Would he ever be able to let go of what he'd been trained to become?

And would she ever be able to let go of what she'd built up in her mind, the bitterness and resentment and unbreakable hurt of being rejected by the man she loved?

"Daadi," she said with a weak whisper, "your oldest daughter needs a lot of prayer."

"Daughter," Samuel said in return, glancing over at her briefly, his eyes full of compassion and love, "my oldest daughter is prayed for every day."

Ava Jane patted her father's arm and then looked out over the rolling hills and green valleys of spring.

A new beginning.

Maybe it *was* time to let go of the past.

Saturday morning, Jeremiah was back at Campton House helping to set up tables and chairs underneath a big catering tent. He'd been invited to attend the Admiral's party later today but had decided not to do so.

He was no longer part of that world, a world where he'd made money and put it in a savings account in case his family ever needed it, a world where he'd had to wear a dress uniform at times, his gold trident insignia shining brightly while he greeted high-ranking officers and politicians. A world where he'd watched two of his eight team members die on the battlefield.

Because he couldn't save them.

He'd let the Admiral enjoy his seventy-fifth birthday without having to endure the elite members of Campton Creek's social scene gawking at the Amish man who'd joined the Navy and was now home.

SEALs didn't like attention. They were trained to ignore honors and accolades and publicity. Secretive and covert, that's how they lived.

Now he wanted that but in a different way.

He wanted to be left alone with his family and his faith.

With his thoughts of the woman who could never return his love. A different kind of war raged inside his soul now.

And in hers, too. She was fighting against what they once had together because he'd left her and broken her heart.

He deserved her scorn and her condemnation.

But, oh, how he wanted, needed her love and forgiveness.

When he looked up from his work to find Ava Jane standing on the big back veranda of the house, staring down at him, Jeremiah wondered if he was having one of his dreams.

But when she waved and gave him a shy smile, he became fully awake and aware. So he walked toward her with a tentative smile of his own.

"What are you doing here?" he asked carefully.

"I baked the birthday cake," she said, her smile tight now and unsure. "I should have known you'd be helping out with the celebration."

No condemnation. More of a quiet resolve.

"Just setting up and taking down later. I seem to be a jack-of-all-trades and a master of none."

"You are a hard worker."

A compliment. He'd take it.

"I like to stay busy and I like this kind of work. Where I don't have to splutter along or make small talk."

Holding her hands together against her crisp white

apron, she watched him as if she were seeing him for the first time. "Like we're attempting to do right now?"

He laughed at that, a sound of relief in his own ears. "Are you speaking to me again?"

She nodded, something new and fresh in her gaze. "Yes." Then she came down the steps and stood a few feet away. "This is a lovely place. A peaceful place."

He couldn't deny that. "*Ja*. Quiet and secluded, pretty."

"I can see why you were drawn to it."

"But you're wondering why I keep coming back?"

She shook her head. "No, I'm beginning to understand, I think. Whatever happened to you here, Jeremiah, is now part of you. I'm truly trying to accept that."

He didn't dare break this tentative thread by asking what she meant by that statement. Could they be civil? Friends? More? "It's good to see your smile, Ava Jane."

She smiled again. "I must go. I brought the cake by while Mamm and Daed are at their house with the *kinder*. I hope the party goes well. I'm sure you'll be here so I hope you'll taste the carrot cake."

He couldn't take his eyes away from her, even when he saw Mrs. Campton watching them from the big bay window with unabashed interest. "No, I'm not attending. I'll visit with the Admiral later, when things are quiet." Then he grinned. "But I will tell Bettye to save me a slice."

Ava Jane moved a bit closer, her gaze flashing on the other workers around them. "Does it bother you then, to be around a lot of Englisch? A lot of people?"

He held tightly to a heavy white plastic chair, his knuckles almost the same pale white, because he didn't dare move toward her. "It bothers me to be around people, *ja*. But I can make an exception to that whenever *you* want to be around *me*."

She lowered her head and gave him that precious smile again. "I've been thinking about that. We have to find a way to be friends, Jeremiah. Everyone deserves a *gut* friend, don't they?"

He didn't want to hope because he wasn't sure they could stay *just* friends. "What made you change your opinion on that?"

She didn't answer right away. Instead, she put her hands into the pockets of her apron. "A lot of prayer and some wise advice from someone who made me see beyond my pain and judgment."

With that she turned and stared up at Mrs. Campton, gave her a wave and then hurried around the corner where the open gate let workers in and out.

"Ava Jane?" Jeremiah called after her.

She whirled at the gate. "Yes?"

He swallowed, then took in a gulp of air. "I could use a friend."

Nodding, she hurried away.

Jeremiah watched her go and then stared up at Judy Campton. The woman wore a serene smile, as if all was right in her world.

Jeremiah was left to wonder just how much that birthday cake had cost both the baker and the taker.

Chapter Fifteen

Easter morning.

Jeremiah sat with his father, his mind on the last week. "I've finally started feeling at home, Daed," he said. "Ava Jane has…changed. She's back to smiling at me and actually talking to me. She wants to be my friend."

Of course, that could go the other way in a hurry. He'd prepared for that but he was trying to be respectful about reining in his fighting side, about not allowing his anger to overcome this new mission. Would he always have to be careful around her? Around the entire community? Would he be able to let go of his nightmares and truly find peace?

"A couple more months before I confess all and go before the church to be baptized," he said now. "I've met with several of our leaders and told them I'm committed to returning for good. Eighteen weeks of training." He shrugged. "It's a lot like my SEAL training but more of a mental thing than physical. Although I've poured myself into learning the eighteen articles of the *Dordrecht Confession of Faith* in the same way I learned stamina in basic training."

During those meetings, Jeremiah had told the ministers some of the details of what he'd seen and done, but he had yet to open up to anyone other than his sleeping father. He'd been reading his Bible, as he always had, and they'd discussed the Ordnung with him, bringing him up to speed as his buddies used to say.

Now he understood why Edward Campton had felt safe in telling Jeremiah about being a SEAL. While Edward had never divulged top secret information, he had poured his heart out to Jeremiah. Because he had known he could trust him to never repeat their conversations.

Edward had been a godly man, a true believer. And he'd also believed his work was important. But he'd suffered greatly because of that work, too. Edward had never complained to his parents, but he'd given up a lot to be a good SEAL.

Jeremiah understood that same suffering now. He could talk to his dying father because no one was around to judge him.

"We had eight team members," he began. "And we all had nicknames. We were based out of Coronado, California. So I was called Amish, of course. Our commander was Mudbug, because he was from Louisiana. Then we had Rider—he loved motorcycles—and Cowboy-from Texas; Peanut—Georgia; Broadway Joe—New York; Hillbilly—Tennessee; and Gator from Florida.

"All good men. Strong men who gave it all to our missions. We trusted each other, although I had to earn their trust, you know. But once they saw I was all in, they had my back."

Jeremiah stared into the dawn, remembering other dawns, dark and dangerous and filled with smoke and heat, the smell of an acrid burning and the ear-piercing boom of an explosion.

"Remember how I used to love to run around and play with pretend guns and make-believe horses? Where did that come from? Why did I have this dark streak inside me? Why did I have to go away and become a machine instead of a man?"

His father sighed in his sleep. Now and then, he'd mumbled but never opened his eyes. His father's silence echoed out over the muted light from the kerosene lamp on the bedside table. Jeremiah had learned how to bathe him and change his soiled clothing, and he'd learned how to change out the feeding tubes that sustained his father's last days on earth. Thankful that he had the money to hire more nurses if needed, Jeremiah remembered happier times with his *daed*.

One of those times had been at Campton House, building and creating beautiful things for a family who had now become a part of his life. His father had conversed with the Admiral and Mrs. Campton and even Edward. They'd all laughed together.

But those good times could never be again.

Now Jeremiah said his usual morning prayers and then took a deep breath. "Gator and Cowboy didn't make it home alive."

He had to stop, to catch a hand to his stomach. That sick feeling hit him every time he thought about his two friends. And those women and children. He'd saved a lot of people that day, but he'd lost two people he loved dearly. And some people he'd never even known.

Collateral damage. Innocent human beings in the wrong place at the wrong time.

Unable to tell his father about that horrible day, he

stood and wiped his eyes. "That's all I've got today, Daed. Some things are too hard to speak about."

With that, he went into the kitchen to start the coffee and do what he could to help with breakfast.

"How many times have I told you that's my work?" his mother said when she came in from the little room she'd been sleeping in to be near her husband.

Jeremiah turned as she fussed with her bonnet strings. "I know it's odd, Mamm, but I've learned to fend for myself even in the kitchen. I don't mind helping wherever I'm needed."

Moselle stared at him in the same way she did every morning, as if she couldn't believe he was actually standing in her kitchen. "So much has changed through the years. You're all grown up and handsome and your sweet *daadi* is at the end of his days. I wish…"

Jeremiah knew what she wished. "Me, too," he said. "But I'm here and I'm not leaving again. *Sie Batt nemme duhn ich gern.*"

He would willingly take his father's part.

And he could see now what was eating at him and keeping him awake at night. He needed forgiveness for what he'd had to do in the name of duty. He needed forgiveness for leaving. He needed forgiveness for not being here to help his family and for Ava Jane. How could he ever accept that forgiveness when he didn't think he deserved it?

"I thank God for your return," his mother said as she busied herself with scrambling eggs and frying ham. But then she turned back and hurried to him. Putting a hand on his cheek, she said, "God's way, Jeremiah. God's time."

Then she went back to her work. Jeremiah felt something new and warm inside his heart. A touch of humanity, a touch of hope. His world brightened and the morning light shifted and poured through the lacy kitchen curtains like a stream of clear water.

Beth stumbled into the kitchen and hugged Jeremiah tight. "Happy Easter, brother."

"Same to you," Jeremiah said, noting her pretty dress and fresh *kapp*, his heart suddenly full. "How are things with you and Joseph Kemp?"

"What things?" Beth said with a warning glare and a glance at her mother.

"She's pretending," their mother said from her spot in front of the stove. "Joseph doesn't know it yet, but the rest of us do. I predict a proposal by summer's end."

"Mamm," Beth said with a giggle. "We are just friends."

"If you say so," her mother retorted. Then she eyed Jeremiah. "I know several single women who have inquired about my son, too."

Beth's eyes widened in surprise. "Really now? Most of them seem to run the other way." Her teasing giggles sounded like the wind chimes Mrs. Campton kept in her garden, dainty and tinkling.

Jeremiah couldn't deny he'd encountered some curious women since he'd returned home. They wanted a husband and he was as good as any to them. They had no idea. No idea at all of the kind of baggage he'd bring into a relationship. He thought of Ava Jane and knew he needed to stay away from her for that reason, if nothing else.

"I'm not looking," he said now, his words too sharp.

Both his mother and his sister turned to stare at him, shock and worry in their gazes.

"I'm not looking," he said again on a gentler note. "I think I'll remain a bachelor all of my life."

"I wouldn't count on that," his mother said, her knowing eyes going soft as she relaxed again. "You will make someone a fine husband one day, I pray to God."

Beth's glance shifted from her mother to Jeremiah. "*Ja*, and we all know who that someone might be."

Jeremiah grabbed some coffee and a ham biscuit and headed out the door to do chores. But he stopped on the porch steps and watched as the beautiful pink-and-salmon dawn crested to the east over the trees guarding the big creek. The sun's rays shot out in a golden slumber that left him breathless and hopeful.

He closed his eyes and felt the warmth of that rising sun on his skin and bones and imagined Ava Jane walking toward him, wearing a wedding dress, a sweet smile on her face.

When he opened his eyes, the sun was still there but the dream disappeared in a mist of reality. And off in the distance, gathering clouds promised rain on the way.

Too much to hope for.

Too hard to imagine.

He'd have to settle for being her friend. That way, he could at least watch out for her and help her if she needed him. *If* she needed him.

Draining his coffee, he went about his work so he could clean up and head to church.

To be near God's grace.

And to be near the woman he wanted in his life forever and yet couldn't have.

"Eli, straighten your shirt."

Ava Jane fussed with her son's clean clothes and tried

to tidy his dark hair. While the Amish didn't go all out for Easter, they still celebrated with a big meal and lots of fellowship. They'd had a somber Good Friday and a quiet Saturday and now, church on Sunday. Then tomorrow would be Easter Monday—more food and fellowship and family time.

In spite of the upheaval of having Jeremiah back over the last couple of weeks, Ava Jane accepted him more and more each day. But while they had developed a tentative friendship, she knew she had to avoid anything else.

So that meant she couldn't wake up thinking about him or wonder during the day how he was doing.

"How does my hair look, Mamm?" Sarah Rose asked, her long golden ponytail peeping out from her Sunday *kapp*.

Her daughter was growing up so fast. "You look pretty," she said, adjusting the ponytail a bit. "And your dress is just right."

"I like the blue," Sarah Rose said. "I can't wait to hide Easter eggs after services."

"That's always fun," Ava Jane replied, taking a deep breath. She'd see Jeremiah today. That would be her Easter treat for the day.

Then she shook her head and chastised herself again.

"Mamm, why are you shaking your head?" Eli asked, his lip jutting out. "I tucked in my shirt and straightened my suspenders."

Now she'd begun to do odd things in front of her children, too. "Just musing," she replied. "I wasn't shaking my head at you. You look handsome."

"Are we walking?" Sarah Rose asked, ready to go. Her good little daughter seemed so eager to please.

"Not today. Aunt Deborah and Mammi and Daadi are

going to pick us up." Glancing out the window, she noticed puffy clouds trying to shut out the sun. "Good thing since the sky can't make up its mind today."

"Can we go outside and wait on them?" Eli asked, always eager to be out of the house doing anything that could get him into trouble.

"Let me gather a few things and then, yes, we'll sit on the bench by the road and wait for our ride."

Ava Jane picked up her basket of cookies and two *snitz* pies, their aromatic mixture of dried apples, oranges and cinnamon wafting out into the crisp morning air. After they did one last check on their Sunday best, Ava Jane and the *kinder* headed down to the corner where someone had long ago erected a taxi bench near the phone booth. Sometimes, the Amish had to use modern means of getting to and fro for work or business in the nearby towns.

The old bench sat weathered and rickety but still sturdy. Ava Jane remembered other times, sitting here with her friends. The boys would run by and pull their hair.

The first time she noticed Jeremiah, really noticed him, she'd been sitting right here. He'd playfully tugged at her *kapp* strings, causing her white covering to go askew and fall right off her head.

A couple of years older than her, he'd seemed larger than life.

"I'm sorry," he'd said, running back to pick up the soiled *kapp*, a broad smile asking her to forgive him. His dark blue eyes had captivated her and her heart had done a funny little dance that day.

The same dance it did now, whenever she saw the man. Or thought about him, which seemed like every time she turned around lately. Why couldn't she get that image of him standing in the garden of Campton House out of her mind? Or the hope in his voice when he'd told her he could use a friend?

Eli's fingers tugging at her dress caused Ava Jane to come out of her musings. "What is it?"

"There's Mr. Jeremiah. He told me he'd take me fishing one day. May I go, Mamm?"

"What?" Ava Jane glanced up the lane and, sure enough, the very man she'd been thinking about appeared over the horizon. Beth sat next to him in the buggy, no doubt on her way to church with him.

"We'll talk about that later," she said to her son, her eyes on the approaching buggy. Taking a breath, she schooled her expression into something she hoped looked friendly.

Eli got up and waved to Jeremiah and Beth. "*Gut* morning."

Jeremiah brought the buggy to a halt, his gaze moving from her son to Ava Jane. "*Gut* morning to you, too. Are you waiting for a ride?"

Ava Jane stood and straightened her skirt. "*Ja*, my parents and sister should be here any minute now." She smiled at Beth. "Hello. How is Ike?"

Beth's blue eyes went misty. "About the same. Mamm insisted on staying there with him and the day nurse."

"We'll send her some food," Ava Jane said, wishing she could do more. Then she looked at Jeremiah, reminding herself of their new truce. "I'm glad you are here with your sister and mother."

"So am I," he replied. Then he smiled down at Eli since her son was hovering near the buggy. "How are you, Eli?"

"Will you take me fishing?" Eli blurted before Ava Jane could hold him back.

Jeremiah shot Ava Jane a questioning stare. "That depends on a lot of things. First, your mother has to give her consent."

Eli squinted up at her, the crinkles around his eyes reminding her of Jacob. "Mamm? Is it okay?"

Ava Jane's heart became at war with itself. She could be friendly to Jeremiah, but did she dare let her son grow close to him? "I told you we'd discuss this later."

When she heard another buggy coming up the road, she breathed a sigh of relief. Her parents had arrived.

Sarah Rose and Eli rushed to greet their grandparents while she stood silent and uncomfortable by Jeremiah's buggy.

"What if I went with them?" Beth asked, hope in the words. "You, too, Ava Jane. We could both go fishing with them. I haven't been fishing in a long time."

Jeremiah's serious gaze changed to a bemused half smile, but the steely, daring look in his eyes didn't die down. "Plenty of chaperones, since you obviously don't trust me to be alone with the boy."

"It's not that," Ava Jane said. Turning to gather her basket, she whirled back. "I don't like my children being near the water, is all."

With that declaration, she tried to push the sudden realization and hurt she saw in his eyes away and pivoted toward the buggy where her parents and sister sat, watching the whole interaction.

"Morning," Daed said, his gaze on the other buggy.

"*Gut* day," Ava Jane replied as she crawled inside and onto the back seat where her children huddled with Deborah under the heavy canvas covering.

"Mr. Jeremiah and me are gonna go fishing," Eli announced as her father waited for Jeremiah to go on ahead. "One day. After Mamm and I talk about it more."

Her mother glanced back at her with a raised furrow in her forehead and then turned back around.

Deborah poked Ava Jane in the ribs and whispered, "Is that true?"

"I haven't decided," Ava Jane said. "I'll have to consider that very carefully."

"Well, when you do consider that," Deborah whispered with a giggle, "I'd like to be a frog on a lily pad sitting nearby. Because that would be interesting to watch."

"Yes," Ava Jane retorted, "according to you and a whole lot of other people, too."

Seemed everyone around her was either pushing her toward him or warning her to be cautious.

Or maybe they were more afraid for Jeremiah to have to deal with her. After all, she had to be a source of great woe for the man.

Ava Jane sat back on the buggy seat and asked God to give her the strength of friendship.

Nothing more.

She wanted to be his friend.

But what if that could turn out to be the worst thing for both of them?

Chapter Sixteen

The nice Easter day soon turned from partly cloudy to fully dark. The egg hunt was winding down when the first lightning strike moved across the sky to the west.

"Kumm," Ava Jane called to her children as they ran by, looking for colored eggs. "We'd better get home before the storm hits."

Some people had left right after dinner on the grounds of the huge Schofield farm. Now everyone started scurrying when a clap of thunder followed the lightning. The horses neighed and began stomping, their dark eyes wild with anxiety. She hurried to where the buggies were lined up like gray-covered boxes, then turned to look for her parents. Her father was helping someone else and Mamm hurried around, gathering children still out looking for eggs.

Another bolt of lightning clashed through the gray sky, followed four heartbeats later by a boom of thunder. One of the horses near Ava Jane reared up, his nostrils flaring.

Glancing up, Ava Jane saw the big animal towering over her and reached up a hand to shield her face. She took a step, but the horse shot up again and she gasped, watching as his big hooves hovered in the air near her head.

Before she could move, a strong arm reached out and lifted her into the air. Startled, she whirled as Jeremiah sat her down three feet away and then rushed toward the frightened horse.

"There, there," he said, staying near the horse and slowly reaching out to soothe the animal. "*Gut, gut.* It's okay. Just a bad storm brewing."

His soothing voice soon had the animal calm again. The owner came over and took charge. "*Denke*, Jeremiah."

Jeremiah nodded to the other man, then straightened his dark vest and found the hat that had fallen off his head.

"Are you all right?" he asked Ava Jane, his dark hair curly in the wind.

"Yes, thanks to you," she replied, touched by how he'd handled the frantic horse and the man who had not spoken to him before today. Remembering being in his arms for those few seconds, she swallowed and tried to think of something to say.

"I don't know where this storm came from," he said before she could form any words. "But it is springtime."

"*Ja*, and we'd better get home before we're drenched."

"Today was nice," he said as he walked her back to her parents' buggy. "The service has a new meaning for me now, since I've been back."

"The resurrection is always moving and encouraging," she replied. "Such beautiful music and…knowing that Christ rose again after so much pain and anguish. That he went through that for us."

"He lives, so we can live."

Jeremiah was right, of course. The love of Christ shone through their faith. A deep warm feeling filled her heart, causing the layers of her pain to peel away bit by bit. "I'm sorry," she said, looking up at him.

His blue eyes went as dark as the sky. "For what?"

"For the way I've treated you. It's been confusing, I know."

"Ava Jane, I'm the one who's sorry. I can't begin to tell you—"

A commotion near the big barn caused them both to turn around. Men were running and a woman pointed to the east.

"Fire!" somebody shouted. "At the bishop's place!"

"I have to go," Jeremiah said, pushing past her.

"*Ja.* Of course." She watched him running out toward the road, where several other men were hopping onto buggies.

"He didn't even take his buggy," Deborah said from behind her. "Where is he headed?"

"Toward the fire," Ava Jane replied, worry suddenly filling her with dread. Running toward danger.

Daed rushed up to them. "He signed up last week for the volunteer fire department."

"What?" Ava Jane held her hands together, a silent prayer moving through her. True to his word, Jeremiah was doing his best to stay on the straight and narrow. But, true to his nature, he still had a need to seek out dangerous work, whether he got paid for it or not.

Daed urged her mother up onto the seat. "Let's get home. I think this one will give rain."

Martha looked toward the plumes of black smoke. "I know we're to stay out of the way, but we need to pray that Bishop King's home will survive this fire."

Ava Jane got into the buggy just as big fat drops of moisture hit her skin. But she wasn't sure if her wet cheeks were from the rain or the tears now falling down her face. She prayed for the bishop and his family and the firefighters. But mostly she prayed for Jeremiah. He still wasn't completely healed.

He fought against the wind and rain and tore through the billowing, suffocating smoke, his only goal to save Bishop King's barn and stables. The rain helped but the fire wasn't contained yet. Along with a dozen or so other men, some Amish and some Englisch, Jeremiah held up fire hoses, climbed ladders and broke through fallen walls to get to the source of the fire.

A lightning strike.

The smells and sounds shattered the shield he'd built to protect himself, and the shouts held him in a grip of flashbacks that he couldn't run from. So he kept working, harder than the others, fighting against the fatigue taking over his body. He'd pulled the horses out first. Made sure no humans were inside the barn. Now he worked the bucket line and helped the firemen from the nearby fire station move and shift the heavy hoses, water from the pump truck spraying up to meet the fire and the rain.

Everything had to be contained.

"Jeremiah?"

He turned and suddenly realized where he was.

Here, in Campton Creek.

The bishop pulled him away from the wet rubble, his own face smudged with dirt and grime.

"Jeremiah, *kumm*. The fire is put out. You can rest now."

Jeremiah stood, his whole body shaking, and saw the

other men staring at him, some with admiration and some with concern.

"I'm sorry," he whispered to the bishop.

"For what? You almost single-handedly saved my place. We owe you a great debt, my family and me."

"You owe me nothing," Jeremiah responded. "I need to get home now."

The bishop wiped at his soot-covered clothes and rubbed his silver beard. "*Ja*, go to your folks. They'll be worried."

Jeremiah started passing through the group of sweaty, dirty men, images of other tired, dirt-covered men assaulting him. Lowering his head, he refused to look anyone in the eye.

"Jeremiah?" the bishop called.

Jeremiah turned. "Yes, sir."

"You are home. You can rest now, son."

He nodded and kept walking, his silent tears leaving streaks of clean against the blackness that covered his clothes and body.

The rain and wind, so violent and unyielding before, now came down in a soft cold drenching that washed him and soothed him.

Almost.

Buggies passed. People waved. Yet another kind soul who at first had stood away from him stopped to offer him a ride.

"*Denke*, but I'm all wet and filthy. I'm almost home."

The man and woman and three teens all smiled at him and moved on.

He was dirty, chilled, soaked and still shaking but a warm spot formed inside his hardened heart. A sense of home filled him, a sense of being a part of a strong community where people looked out for each other. He and his father had helped to build the bishop's big barn over fifteen years ago. It was solid, built by men who knew exactly how to move in unison and make everything fit into place.

Now he'd been a part of saving something he'd helped create.

Is that the way with You, Father? You take something You created and save it over and over again, the way You are trying to save me. I want to be worthy. I need to be worthy again.

A small voice told him he'd always been worthy.

But he wasn't ready to respond to that voice yet.

When he made it to the drive up to his parents' house, he stopped and stood in the rain, taking in the sight of flowers in the mist and white curtains, crisp and clean. The old porch swing squeaked a welcoming melody and the scent of pure, fresh air assaulted him.

And pushed away the dark memories that haunted him so often.

Maybe it was time he stopped fighting. Against himself.

"It was a sight to see."

Ava Jane sat with her parents and some friends who'd come by to visit on Easter Monday, another day of rest before the workweek began again. The Millers and their three daughters along with Deborah's not-boyfriend— their big brother, Matthew—were gathered around Mamm's big table, munching on ham sandwiches and baked potato casserole left from yesterday.

Mr. Miller and Matthew, who kept casting glances

toward Deborah across the table, had seen the fire and gone to help out.

"I'm telling you, that man could move. Jeremiah is a strong one. He got six skittish horses and two milk cows out of that barn, with the roof over his head about to collapse."

"Then he ran back in and called out to make sure no one was trapped inside," Matthew added to his father's story.

"Organized the volunteers, too. And pretty much had things under control before the town fire truck arrived. Impressive, how he saved that barn by thinking on his feet."

Mamm sent Ava Jane a quick glance, probably checking to see how hearing about Jeremiah's heroic deeds was affecting her.

She was all right. She had to be all right. Jeremiah had done a good thing and all the people who'd witnessed it now held him in a higher esteem than they did yesterday before the fire.

He needed that kind of boost and acceptance.

"Maybe he learned some of that while he was away," Matthew offered up. Then realizing what he'd said, he turned red and lowered his gaze. "I mean, maybe he's just smart that way."

Daed, ever the diplomat, cleared his throat and scrubbed a hand down his gray beard. "We have to consider that some good has to come from Jeremiah being away. We don't know how and when that good will appear, but I think yesterday is an example."

"An example of what?" Ava Jane asked, the words hitting the air before she could pull them back.

Daed leaned up and placed his hands together on the

table. "An example of the best a man has to give, even after he's been through the worst."

Everyone became quiet for a few moments. Mamm offered more coffee and dessert. Finally, Matthew stood and looked at Deborah. "Want to go for a walk?"

"I'd enjoy that." She looked to her father.

Daed nodded and then gave her the behave-yourself stare.

After they hurried out to the back porch, Mrs. Miller shook her head. "Those two don't even know they are smitten, do they?"

"They are in denial," Mamm said with a soft smile. "Meantime, I'll be saving up material for a wedding dress."

They all laughed at that.

Ava Jane got up and began removing dishes to take to the big sink. Feeling a tug on her dress sleeve, she looked over at her mother.

"Daughter, did our talk upset you?"

Ava Jane cleaned off the dishes, her head down. "I have to accept that I'll hear things about him. And it's been better between us. We've both made our peace, but I still can't see any good in him going away to fight and harm others."

"What he did changed your life so it's hard to see past that," Martha said, patting her hand. "Remember the good in the life you have now. Your children, your family, people who care about you. You found a way to get over losing him. That hasn't changed."

"But I'm doing that without my husband," she replied, wishing Jeremiah hadn't become such a thorn in her side.

"Do you blame Jeremiah for Jacob's death, too?"

"No. But I have to question where the good is in his dying…when Jeremiah got to live."

Her mother readied the dishwater and took the rag from Ava Jane. "God will show you the answers one day, and maybe sooner than you think. But it is not up to us to question or doubt God's plan. You can't blame Jeremiah simply because he survived and Jacob died."

Ava Jane took that into consideration.

But in her heart she accepted that some things were too hard to bear and there were no answers for this kind of grief and torment. Prayers and reading the Scriptures might help but she'd never truly understand any of this.

She didn't want the burden of blaming others to weigh her down anymore. She didn't want the burden of the ache in her heart to turn her bitter and hateful.

"Jeremiah did a wonderful thing yesterday," she finally said. "He's courageous and honorable. But it seems there is a part of him that still craves that kind of danger." Then she turned to her mother, tears in her eyes. "He came back to us, but he could have been hurt or killed yesterday."

Martha's eyes filled with compassion and understanding.

"Ah, so that's it then."

"What?"

"You still love him. Even more so now than before."

Ava Jane shook her head. "*Ne*, I do not. I can't."

Martha held her dishrag still but she didn't respond.

Ava Jane could see what her mother was clearly thinking. Her sister and Matthew weren't the only ones in denial around here.

Chapter Seventeen

Jeremiah finished the day's work and headed toward the creek for a quick swim. It would be sunset soon, so no one should be about. Most folks would be retiring inside for the night, for supper and maybe some Bible reading and family time playing board games.

Derek was with Isaac since this was the time of day when his father seemed to slip away a little more with each sunset and the nurse stayed nearby to watch his vitals.

Until Mamm ran him out of the room, too.

"My time with him," his mother had explained to Jeremiah and Beth. "Just him and me, with me doing the Bible reading and talking, but it's precious time to me."

But she made sure Derek was nearby in the living room.

Jeremiah didn't like leaving the house but his mother probably wanted him and Beth to take some time to themselves, too. Especially Beth. They'd both insisted she go to the singing tonight with the rest of the young people.

And his mother had shooed him away. "Get a nice bath and read your Bible."

So now he stood underneath the bridge at the far corner of the big wide body of water. The long covered bridge had been built over a narrow stream that moved away from the expanding creek and into the hills and woods near his family's property. The red-colored bridge, trimmed in aged brown crossbeams and open underneath the center arch, had been built well over a hundred years ago to allow people a quick way across the water and woods, but a local gardening society had raised funds to preserve it and maintain it. He was pretty sure Mrs. Campton had spearheaded that.

Wearing an old work shirt and trousers, he took off his dusty black boots and socks and walked into the shallows. The water's cold wetness hit him, reminding him of the chilly rain on Easter Sunday. Reminding him of the cold against the heat, the fire against the water.

Things had changed somehow. People waved to him more and smiled at him. Asked him how he was doing, how were his father and mother. What was Beth up to?

Had his family been inadvertently shunned, too, because of him? If so, he'd somehow received a little bit of forgiveness for helping with the fire on Sunday. Even Mr. Hartford had praised him when he'd gone into the store earlier today to pick up some things for Beth and Mamm.

"Heard you saved the day."

"I didn't do anything more than the other volunteers and firemen."

"That's not what I was told," Mr. Hartford had replied with a knowing smile. "I always knew you were a good man, Jeremiah. Now they do, too."

He didn't want to be anyone's hero. Not anymore.

And he remembered the shock in Ava Jane's eyes when

he'd taken off to help with the fire. Had he lost her yet again?

He took another step or so into the water, the chill numbing his tired bones. That fire had brought out a lot of emotions but he'd managed to work through them without falling apart.

Before, he'd have had to go somewhere quiet and dark to hold himself close so he could become invisible. The memories and images of war and death would have pierced him like daggers and torn through him with the velocity of bullets. Would have wounded him all over again. But here, he could move away from the brutality that haunted him. Here, he was becoming whole again.

Chest deep in the chilly water, he lifted up and started a long lap across the water, following the bridge to the other shore and then moving back and forth, not bothering to count. He knew the feel of swimming a mile or two.

When he swam, his mind would calm and he'd drift into memories of the good times with his buddies. The laughter and camaraderie, the secrets revealed, the times of doubt and fear where he could at least share his faith with them.

"Pray for us, Amish," one of them had always asked right before a mission. Some were believers, others more skeptical. Cowboy had been a devout, faithful man. He had usually prayed right along with Jeremiah. Then he'd look Jeremiah in the eye and reassure him, "We're doing what we can to make a difference. Remember that."

Had he made a difference? He prayed so. Else, Cowboy and Gator had died in vain.

After several laps, he lifted up to tread water and admire the last of the sun's rays peeping over the trees to the west. Taking a deep, calming breath, he walked up on the bank and sat down, his muscles stretched, the kinks worked out of his joints.

When he heard laughter down the way, his whole body went on alert. Pushing his long, wet hair back, Jeremiah put on his hat and crept up the bank so he could see across the bridge.

Two boys walking toward the middle, carrying fishing poles.

Eli Graber and his friend Simon Kemp. They weren't wet so they hadn't been swimming, but he guessed they'd sneaked off to get in some evening fishing. Not much time left since the sun would be behind the trees in another half hour.

How should he handle this situation? He could sneak away and forget he ever saw the boys, or he could let them know he was here and go up there and fish with them for a few minutes before he made sure they got home safely.

He opted for the second choice. He'd never forgive himself if he left them here and then something happened.

Yes, he had that burden to carry, too. He needed to stay one step ahead of the people he cared about. He didn't want them getting hurt or worse.

"Hey," he called out, grabbing his shoes and heading up the earthy bank. "It's Jeremiah Weaver."

Eli and Simon both whipped around, looking surprised and a bit scared.

"Hi," Eli said before he and Simon gave each other furtive glances.

Then he looked over Jeremiah's wet clothes, his mouth dropping open. "You've been swimming?"

"Ja," Jeremiah said, taking one of the old poles to

check it out. "I can help you tighten the cork and put a better hook on this. Did you bring a tackle box?"

Eli shook his head. "No, sir. We left in a hurry."

"Is that water cold?" Simon asked, completely oblivious to being caught in the act.

"It's cool," Jeremiah said, finishing up with what he had on hand to make the pole and line work. "Here, Eli, try this."

"We have worms," Eli said. "Got 'em out behind the chicken coop."

"Smart move," Jeremiah said, watching the sky. "You two cast out and see what's out there and then I'm taking you home."

"You don't need to do that," Eli quickly replied.

"Yes, I do." Jeremiah worked on untangling Simon's line. "Your *mamm* will be worried, unless of course you cleared this with her first."

Eli kept his eyes on the cork floating through the dark water. The boys both went silent.

"I see," Jeremiah replied. "All the more reason I make sure you get home safely."

"We're not babies," Simon pointed out. "I drive the tractor and ride our plow horse."

"I did those things when I was your age," Jeremiah replied, showing Simon how to throw out his line so he wouldn't get it tangled in the beams at the top of the arch. "But usually I had adults nearby." He waited a few beats, then asked, "So, Eli, does your *mamm* even know you're gone?"

Eli pulled in his line. "I told her we were going to check out the new baby lamb."

"So she thinks you're behind the barn back home."

"*Ja.* She's visiting with Simon's *mamm* in the kitchen. They can chatter for hours and never miss us."

Jeremiah glanced at the gloaming. He was wet and starting to chill but he couldn't go home yet. "So that means when we get there, you have to be honest with her, okay?"

"I can't. She'll punish me."

"Better to be honest and take the punishment now than to hold a lie in your heart."

"What about me?" Simon asked with big brown eyes. "Can I just hold the lie in my heart?"

Jeremiah shook his head. "No, you are to go back to Eli's house with me and then face your own *mamm.*"

"And then I'll get in trouble, too."

"You're both already in trouble," Jeremiah said, wondering how much trouble he'd get into because of this. "But as infractions go, fishing isn't such a bad one."

"What's an infraction?" Simon asked as they rolled up their lines, fishing forgotten now.

"I think it means when we don't obey our parents… or anyone else," Eli added, staring at Jeremiah. Then he asked, "Did you get infracted a lot when you went away and shot people?"

Jeremiah didn't know how to answer that, but he went with the truth and left out the details. "Most people get in trouble now and then. I've had my fair share."

"Did you confess and take your punishment?" Eli asked, his eyes burning with the need to know.

"I did," Jeremiah replied. "We have to be men about these things. Take it and get on with life. Learn from our mistakes." Then he stopped as they came off the bridge. "I'm dealing with a big infraction right now because I left, but when I get baptized, I'll be forgiven and I won't have to worry about that again."

"You're kind of old for that," Simon pointed out.

"Never too old to turn my life over to God. I'm catching up and once it's done, I'll never leave again."

"Then can you take us fishing for real?" Eli asked, hopeful.

Jeremiah laughed and nodded. "Then, yes, we'll go fishing at a decent time of day and with the proper equipment and bait and *with permission*, for real. But right now, I need to get you two home so your mamas won't be worried."

"And to face our fate," Simon said in a somber tone.

"*Ja*, and my own, too," Jeremiah replied. He had a feeling that when Ava Jane saw him with the boys, it wouldn't go over very well.

Ava Jane laughed at another of Ruth Kemp's funny stories. Ruth could take an ordinary event and embellish it to the point of making everyone laugh. She had a great wit and a comic streak that made her bubbly and happy all the time.

"Oh, look at the time," Ruth said, hopping off her chair. "I've sputtered on so long that you must be starving for your supper."

"We're having more leftovers," Ava Jane said. "But, yes, I need to round up the *kinder*." She could hear Sarah Rose upstairs with Ruth's daughter, Rebecca, laughing and playing with their rag dolls and other toys. But Eli and Simon had been quiet. Too quiet.

"I'll call the boys back in," Ruth said, heading to the kitchen door. But she stopped with her hand on the screen. "Oh, my."

"Was der letz?"

Ava Jane followed Ruth to the door and stared out into the golden dusk. Then she saw Jeremiah walking along with Eli and Simon, his clothes and hair wet, the boys carrying fishing poles.

Pushing past Ruth with a building fear and anger, she rushed toward the boys and Jeremiah. "What have you been up to?" she said, directing her anger toward Jeremiah. "Did you take them swimming without even consulting me? Jeremiah, how could you?"

Jeremiah stood silent, his expression a stone wall of regret and disappointment. Eli looked from her to Jeremiah. Simon hung his head.

"Will someone please explain?" Ava Jane said, her voice rising, her pulse hammering. She'd never be able to trust him. Why had she even tried?

"Simon?" Ruth called, her hand out to her son. "*Kumm* and tell me what happened."

Jeremiah didn't speak. Didn't move.

Ava Jane didn't ask again. Instead, she let loose on him. "You know how I feel about this and yet you somehow take them off and with it growing dark, too. I don't understand how a grown man—"

"He didn't do it, Mamm," Eli shouted over her rant, his expression muddled with an anxiousness she'd never seen before. "He didn't do anything wrong. Me and Simon… We sneaked away. We weren't playing with the lambs. We went fishing."

Ava Jane gulped a breath, her eyes slamming into Jeremiah's. She saw the truth in his silence.

Glancing from him to her son, she asked, "Eli, you did this all on your own?"

Eli squinted and toed the dirt with one muddy boot,

his eyes downcast. "Yes, ma'am. Mr. Jeremiah had been swimming and he found us and told us we had to come home and tell the truth. So that's the truth. We have to own up and learn from our mistakes. He told us that, too." Lowering his head and adjusting his hat, he added, "We're sorry. Very sorry."

Simon bobbed his head. "We don't want to be infractioning again, ever." He glanced up at Jeremiah, admiration in his brown eyes. "Mr. Jeremiah said he'd teach us to fish, once he's baptized and forgiven, and if we get proper permission. Which we will, promise."

Ruth took Simon into her arms and then nodded toward Jeremiah before she lifted her son's chin with one hand. "*Denke* for being honest. We will discuss your punishment when we get home. Now, go and fetch your sister. We're leaving."

Simon nodded and took off.

Ruth turned back to Jeremiah. "*Denke* for watching out for the boys. Simon's father works long hours at a nearby lumberyard so he has little time to take the boy out fishing and hunting. I'm sorry for the inconvenience."

"No inconvenience," Jeremiah said, his eyes still on Ava Jane. "None at all."

Ava Jane's skin heated with a rush of regret and embarrassment. "Jeremiah…"

The other children came running out, the door's urgent slam causing Ava Jane to almost jump out of her skin.

"I'll talk to you later," Ruth said, before hurrying her children into their buggy.

Eli's gazed moved between Ava Jane and Jeremiah and then he took Sarah Rose by the hand and urged her into the house, ignoring her prattling and questions.

Ava Jane stood and watched to make sure they were

out of earshot and then turned back to Jeremiah. "Can we talk?"

He didn't speak at first. He only stared at her, a hard frown marring his beautiful face. Then he shook his head. "You will never forgive me. You'll pretend to care and you'll even try to convince yourself that you've let the past go. But if you can't trust me, especially with your children, then what is there left for us to talk about, Ava Jane?"

He pivoted to leave, a dark silhouette against the blood-orange sunset.

And her heart went with him.

"Jeremiah," she called. "Please come back."

He kept walking, his broad shoulders slumped in defeat.

Ava Jane sank down on the steps and watched him until her eyes burned from the fading brilliance of a beautiful sky.

Chapter Eighteen

A couple of days later, Jeremiah sat with his father, silent and waiting for the right words. He couldn't forget the other night and the anger and condemnation in Ava Jane's eyes.

The community might be slowly accepting him and forgiving him, but the woman he loved never would. He'd fought with his team members against massive enemies and learned how to compartmentalize his feelings. But he'd never fought anything that hurt him more than losing Ava Jane.

"I remember Gideon," he finally said to Isaac. "With the army of three hundred against all of those thousands of Midianites. That's what my team and I were constantly up against—the kind of enemy that always has more coming. But just like Gideon and his men, we were trained to use our own form of trumpets and torches. To be more than we seemed. That way we could take them down, one by one, with the right strategy and detailed plans. And with a level of trust among us that brooked no questions." Stopping, he held his hands together. "I trusted the Lord during those times. Don't get why some had to die, but I never wavered on trusting the Lord."

He thought about how hard he'd worked since coming home to win trust, to receive forgiveness. A weariness settled over him, heavy like combat gear. He'd hoped Ava Jane would come around.

The other night she'd made it clear she might not be able to truly forgive him or trust him.

"I'm searching for that kind of trust now, Daed. I want others to trust me and I want to be able to trust in return. But I don't know if I'll ever have anyone's trust again."

Jeremiah ran a hand over his hair. He'd let it grow when he'd returned stateside. It was longer now, thick. Beth had trimmed it for him. Soon, he hoped to have a beard to match. A beard that would signify him as a married man.

"I have to keep fighting, keep waiting on the Lord. I have to overcome the enemy, the doubt and the fear. I have to trick the enemy and win the battle. I'll keep pressing against the rock of her resistance, holding it steady, until I win her heart again."

One step forward. Two steps back. He'd regroup and start over. But there might come the time he dreaded. The time he'd finally give up and walk away.

"The enemy is my own doubt and fear, telling me to leave again. To just go away and never return." Leaning in, he whispered, his eyes on his father, "But I won't be a coward. I won't put down my armor until this final battle is over. I came back for God. His grace is sufficient."

His father sighed in his sleep.

Jeremiah closed his eyes and said his morning prayers, the silence of a quiet echo covering him in God's warmth. Then he looked at his father's gaunt, pale face and remembered the man he'd once been. Jeremiah turned and thought about the man *he'd* once been, too.

"I will be the man You need me to be, Father. I can do that, for You," he said as he looked upward.

He went into the kitchen and found some breakfast and headed out to do his day's work so he could keep his mind off the woman who had accused him of trying to lead her son astray.

Three hours into cleaning the barn, Jeremiah looked out the wide-open doors as he heard a buggy approaching the house.

His mother wasn't feeling well, so she was resting this morning while Derek stayed near Isaac. Beth had decided at the last minute to go next door to a quilting frolic since he or Derek could reach her there if anything changed with their father. So he wasn't expecting anyone and he really didn't want to see anyone.

He was covered with dust and cobwebs, and probably smelled worse than a billy goat. He prayed this wasn't some well-meaning mother bringing around yet another daughter to gawk at him.

But he couldn't ignore anyone's kindness, especially if they'd come to check on his *daed* and bring food. Wiping at his brow and arms with a cleaning rag, Jeremiah walked out and waited by the barn doors.

Then he recognized the woman driving the small open buggy.

Ava Jane Graber.

Ava Jane saw Jeremiah emerge from the barn and wondered if he'd ignore her. But he didn't do that. Instead, he started walking toward her. He'd show courtesy to a woman, even a woman who'd been cruel in assuming the worst about him. But after a couple of sleepless nights and a lot of Bible reading and praying, she hoped she could make that up to him today.

"Ava Jane," he said by way of a greeting. His rolled-up shirtsleeves showed off his impressive biceps while he wiped his face and hands with an old rag. "What are you doing here?"

Even though he was filthy and a dark scowl sat plastered across his face, he still made her heart jump too fast. *Swagger*, she reminded herself. That could get her in trouble.

She'd come here to apologize and make amends. Not stare at the man.

Hesitant now, she wished she'd thought this through a little more, but she straightened her spine as she started down out of the buggy. Jeremiah hurried to help her down and then stood back, stoic and still hurt from the look of the unyielding frown covering his face.

"I brought you some lunch," she said. "I thought we could visit for a spell."

She'd missed the quilting frolic because she wanted to talk to him. At the insistence of her coconspirator, Deborah, after she'd poured her heart out to Deborah a little while ago, they'd managed to coordinate this little excursion with sneaky precision. Beth was one farm over at the frolic. Deborah had convinced Beth to attend with her earlier today. And Moselle didn't want any visitors, also according to Deborah. Even if Moselle happened to see them out the window, Ava Jane figured Jeremiah's mother wouldn't interrupt them. So Ava Jane had to say a lot in a little amount of time.

He didn't move, so she turned to get the picnic basket she'd filled with chicken salad and chopped-ham sandwiches, boiled eggs and snickerdoodle cookies. She'd also brought a jug of fresh lemon-mint tea.

"I've got it," he finally said from behind her. Taking the basket before she could lift it, he held it and waited.

"I brought an old quilt. For us to sit on."

"Why don't you leave it and go?" he retorted. "I'll tell Mamm you brought food."

Ava Jane blinked back tears at his cold monotone response to her picnic idea. His eyes held a brittleness that she'd put there and his pulse throbbed a warning beat along his strong jawline.

"Jeremiah, I brought the food for you."

"Why?"

He wasn't making this easy. But then she had not made things easy for him since day one. Her turn to be strong and focused, as he'd taught her. "Because I wanted to apologize for assuming the worst. I was wrong."

He moved back a couple of feet, his stance softening. "Why is it that you *always* assume the worst when I'm around?"

"Can we sit and have a talk?" she asked. "A real talk?"

"Chatter all you want."

He pivoted with the basket, so she grabbed the quilt and headed toward the barn with him. Setting the basket down, he moved toward the old water pump and washed his face and hands and then did his best to damply comb his hair with his fingers.

Which only added to her attraction.

Then he turned to look at her. "So you want to talk to me now? After what you said last time you saw me?"

"Yes, I thought we'd decided to…be friends."

"*Ja*, I thought that, too. But you find fault with me at every turn, Ava Jane." When they reached the yard near the house, he turned and tugged the quilt out of her hand and motioned to a towering live oak. "I'll sit here with you. Derek, the nurse, is in with Daed and Mamm. He can see us out the window from the downstairs bedroom and, since he's twice my size and willing to help anyone in trouble, you can call out to him if you don't like the way I chew my food."

Offended and burning with embarrassment, Ava Jane nodded but refused to spar with him. "Okay, let's eat and then I'll let you get back to work. I have things to do myself today." Things she'd abandoned to come on this misguided attempt to fix what she'd messed up so badly.

He threw down the quilt and offered her his hand. Ava Jane took it for a brief moment and then settled across from him and passed him two sandwiches and an egg.

Her own appetite lost, Ava Jane looked out over the hills and valleys surrounding the creek. "This is a *gut* view you have here. I always did love this farm."

He chewed and drank. "I missed this place so much."

She heard the longing in his voice. "Jeremiah, I *am* sorry. I've been horrible to you and I keep making a mess of things, no matter how hard I pray to do better."

Putting down what used to be a sandwich and was now crumbs and a napkin, he stared out over the creek and hills with a scowl that took it's time turning soft. "I deserved your harsh treatment."

"No, what you deserve is my prayers and my hopes. It's always a celebration when someone is lost but returns home."

"Home. I missed that word and all it means to me."

She found the cookies and opened the container to place it between them. Just so she wouldn't reach out and push damp hair off his forehead. "Your home missed you. Your family missed you."

"Did *you* miss me, ever?"

"All the time." She could admit that now. It should hurt but it didn't. "I loved Jacob. He was a *gut* man, the best husband, and he loved me and our children."

"I believe that," Jeremiah said, turning to her, all traces of his anger gone now. "You'd be a devoted wife."

She nodded, tears forming again at the way he'd said that. Not *you were. You'd be.* "He courted me in a slow, gentle way and…I came to care about him very deeply. He never once asked about my feelings for you. Because he knew. He knew, Jeremiah."

"Knew what?"

She stilled, her heart beating so hard and fast she was sure Jeremiah could hear it. "That I still thought of you." She looked away and out over the distant water. "He thought about you a lot, too. It was like this unspoken rule, how we both thought about you but never talked about you."

Then the tears came because the guilt she'd held inside for so long now glared at her and, like the lesson Jeremiah had taught her son the other night, she knew she had to tell the truth.

"I…I didn't tell him enough that I loved him. I should have told him that…he was more than second best." Holding a hand to her lips, she said, "The day he died, I was angry that the calf had got out, that the fence hadn't been mended. He went after the calf because of me and I never stopped to think that anything bad could happen to him. I should have called after him or gone with him. I never got the chance to tell him I loved him. That he wasn't second best. He was *the* best."

Jeremiah's sharp intake of breath caused her to look his way. Silent tears streamed down his face. "Is this why you keep pushing me away, because you're punishing yourself instead of me? Or maybe as much as me?"

She couldn't speak. The acknowledgment of something she'd held inside for so long seemed to open the floodgates of her pain. Holding her hands in her lap, she lowered her head. "I should have loved him more."

Jeremiah reached across and took one of her hands in his. "And I should have never left you."

She shook her head. "My *daed* says there has to be some good in all of this. Maybe you had to leave in order to truly return."

He stared into her eyes, his heart revealed in the dark blue mist of his gaze. "I hope there is good. I want to find the good." His gaze moved over her face, his eyes going dark with a new raw emotion that left her longing and too aware of his closeness. "But, Ava Jane, you need to let go of that blame you've been holding for so long. You had no way of knowing what would happen that day. It's terrible and it hurts, I understand that. But it wasn't your fault. Let that go, okay?"

She took a breath, a great weight lifting off of her, releasing her. "I've never told anyone the truth, not even Deborah or Mamm." Her eyes holding his, she said, "You're the only one who can understand and, Jeremiah, on this I trust you. Only you."

He lifted his chin, his lips trembling. "I asked God to show me the way. You've trusted me with your deepest secret. I'll hold your words dear to my heart forever."

Jeremiah held tightly to her hand and nodded, too overcome to say much more. They sat that way for a while, their gazes on the ducks with new ducklings out in the creek and the birds that sang fresh songs through the trees.

Ava Jane felt a peace she hadn't felt in a long time. "I'm glad I came to see you today."

Jeremiah nodded and let go of her hand, then shot her a dazzling grin. He looked younger. "Me, too. I love snickerdoodles."

She laughed at that and handed him the rest of the food. "I have to go."

He got up with her. "I'm glad we're becoming friends again."

"*Ja*, me, too." She planned to trust him more from here on out. Hesitating, she said, "If you'd like, come to Sarah Rose's birthday party this Saturday. I made her a quilt and she'll have friends over. Maybe you could take her brother fishing so he won't antagonize the girls."

"Oh, so now I see the real reason you've plied me with food," he said, smiling.

Seeing the teasing gleam in his eyes, she relaxed. "I came to start over. Again." Then she shrugged. "But Eli needs to be doing more boy stuff. Daed tries but he's often tired. Eli seems to listen to you."

Jeremiah's eyes filled with humility. "I'm not a hero, Ava Jane. But I'd be honored to spend time with Eli. With all of you."

Ava Jane had to swallow the lump in her throat. "We're going to get through this, Jeremiah. With God's guidance."

When they heard female chattering coming up the lane in the front of the house, they parted and gathered up the lunch items.

"Deborah and Beth," he said. "*Gut* to hear them laughing together."

"Good to see you smiling," she said, meaning it. "I'll go and tell Beth hello and grab my sister, and I'll be on my way."

Jeremiah took the basket and the quilt. "I'll drop the quilt in the buggy and I'll bring the basket by later. You go on to them because you know they'll be curious."

At one time, Ava Jane would have run the other way. But she wasn't worried about assumptions anymore. On their part or hers.

"*Denke*, Jeremiah."

Giving him one last smile that came from her heart, she hurried to greet their giggling, curious sisters.

Chapter Nineteen

"This is an exciting day," Deborah said a few days later, standing in Ava Jane's fresh, clean kitchen. "Sarah Rose has grown so much in the last year. She's going to be as pretty as her *mamm*."

Ava Jane smiled at her sister and breathed in the fresh air from the open windows. "She's willful and stubborn but she's a *gut* girl."

"As I said, like her mother." Deborah checked the baked chicken with vegetables that they'd taken out of the stove to cool a bit and admired the strawberry cake with pink and white icing Ava Jane had made yesterday. "So Leah's bringing her two girls and Ruth will be here with Rebecca, right?"

Ava Jane nodded. "And two other girls her age. I also invited Jeremiah and Beth, too."

Deborah fluffed napkins and rearranged flowers, her eyes full of so many questions. "Beth told me about that. So going to visit him helped smooth things over between the two of you?"

"I told you that the other day when you and Beth came back to her house. You know, the day you two cornered me on the porch and made me give you all the details of our picnic."

Remembering that day, Ava Jane grew warm inside. She and Jeremiah had connected that day. A small thread of trust had been woven between them. After telling him about her guilt and agony over what had happened the day Jacob died, Ava Jane's yoke of burden had lightened. Jeremiah's whole stance had softened, too. She could see that in the way he'd looked at her. She prayed they could hold together that fragile thread.

Deborah slapped at her wrist. "*Ja*, because we found the two of you looking mighty close and chummy."

"Friends, Deborah. We are friends," Ava Jane pointed out yet again. Her sister waffled on wanting them together and wishing they'd stay apart. "We have to start somewhere."

"I'm glad you two are friends," Deborah said with a little eye roll. "So what else needs to be done around here?"

Ava Jane checked the kitchen. "We have the baked chicken and vegetables, rice and gravy, salad and cake. Tea is made and lemonade is freshly squeezed. Mamm is in charge of the cookie table. The volleyball net is set up and the rubber ball and bat are out for baseball."

Deborah clapped her hands like a little kid. "And Daed and some of the men are out there arranging tables and chairs. Oh, look. There's Jeremiah."

Ava Jane whirled so quickly she knocked a cutting board off the table. Vegetable scraps went flying all over the clean floor. Mortified, she bent to grab the cutting board.

"Seeing your friend sure does make you jittery," her sister said with a saucy grin while she went about, gathering scraps. "I'll clean this up. You'd better go out there and supervise setting up those tables and chairs and maybe offer Jeremiah a cookie."

Ava Jane took a deep breath. "What was I thinking? I shouldn't have invited him. His father is so ill. He should be with him."

"He can be reached if anything happens with Ike," Deborah said. "Having him here to keep the boys occupied is a *gut* idea. And it will be a signal to others that it's time to really forgive him."

Ava Jane's pulse raced in waves of awareness once she reached the backyard. He looked nice in his fresh broadcloth pants and white shirt, his dark hair curling around his face and neck. Jeremiah didn't stand around. He went to work on moving chairs and tables so they'd be in the shade later this afternoon. Eli and Simon, who'd come on foot ahead of his parents, followed Jeremiah around like two puppies, eager to help and learn. He put them to work, guiding them on how to arrange the tables and put on cloths, the lines of each straight and crisp.

She'd worried about him being a bad influence on her children and here he was, being a good encouraging adult, after all.

I needed to change more than he did, Father.

Ignoring her fascinated sister's covert stares, she straightened her dress and apron and went out to finish setting up for the party. When she saw her mother also helping, Ava Jane relaxed and went to say hello.

"Mamm, I didn't know you were already out here working."

Her mother whirled from placing a giant tray full of oatmeal cookies on the table. "Your *daed* put me to work before I ever made it into the house." Hugging Ava Jane close, she said, "*Gut* day, daughter."

"It's a perfect day," Ava Jane said, the light breeze lifting her *kapp* ties. "I'm so glad you're here."

Mamm glanced at Jeremiah. "I see you've invited extra help."

"Yes, but Beth was supposed to come, too. Let me go and find out why she didn't."

Martha's eyebrows shot up. "You and Jeremiah—"

"Are on friendly terms now. He's here to distract the boys." She explained about Eli wanting to go fishing and how Jeremiah had brought the boys home the other night. "I had to quit fighting against that and let someone else who knows how to fish take over that task. He took care of them the other night and I am grateful for that."

"Smart idea," her mother said. "I'm glad you've found it in your heart to be kind to him since he seems to know how to handle rambunctious boys. Kindness costs you nothing."

"Oh, it cost a lot," Ava Jane retorted. "But it's also taught me a lot. God uses our suffering to teach us, doesn't He?"

"Yes, sometimes He does indeed do that." Her mother stared after her but didn't respond any further.

Ava Jane got the feeling that her family had forgiven Jeremiah long before she'd even thought about doing so.

He looked up to find her coming toward him, a sight he'd often dreamed of but never hoped to witness again.

Seeing the tentative smile on her face, Jeremiah relaxed and hurried to meet Ava Jane. While he strolled toward her, he noticed her sparkling white apron and crisp blue dress. She was so pretty that it took his breath away. With each day, they moved closer to each other. He treasured these moments.

"Hello," he said, his hands at his side. Staying a respectable distance away, he added, "Is there something else I can do before the party starts?"

"No," Ava Jane said, checking the white cloths on the tables and the bounty of food being spread across the serving table. "We normally don't make big deals out of birthdays, but Sarah Rose is growing up and...I made her a special quilt. She misses her *daed* so much, I thought I'd pamper her this year. Now Eli will expect the same."

"I didn't know we could pamper each other," he said, half teasing. "It sounds nice."

"Every now and then," she replied. "And within reason."

He nodded. "So I have new fishing poles for the boys and lots of bait—worms and crickets. But I will not pamper them, I promise. They have to learn to bait their own hooks and remove the fish when they catch them. Which they will do."

She laughed at his blustering confidence. "Well, you have to eat first. We have plenty of food. Can't go fishing on an empty stomach."

"Is that my payment then? A good meal?"

"Is that a good enough payment?"

He nodded. "Better than enough." Then he lowered his voice. "I'll take it for now anyway."

Giving him a surprised wide-eyed stare, she blushed and went to work straightening an already-straight tablecloth. Then she turned and said, "After you and the boys eat, you can go ahead and take them fishing. We have games for the girls and then I'll give Sarah Rose her quilt."

He'd flirted and now she was in a huff. *Way to go, Amish.*

Out in the world, his buddies had taught him how to flirt and sometimes things like what he'd just said still slipped out.

"Ava Jane?"

She rearranged the flowers in the center of the table. For the third time. *"Ja?"*

"I didn't mean to sound disrespectful. I appreciate the meal and the chance to see you and go fishing with the boys. I won't linger long. I want to check on Daed, as I do every night."

Understanding filled her eyes. And regret. "I shouldn't have asked you here. You need to be with your father as much as possible."

"I don't mind," he said, thinking he was botching this whole thing. "Mamm wanted Beth to come, too. But Mamm's had a cold all week and Beth decided to stay there with her. She's so tired these days."

"I'll miss seeing Beth and I hope your mother will feel better soon. Thank you for coming. We will send them some food."

Relieved, he asked, "So, we're...still friends?"

She shot him a confused glance. *"Ja*, I thought we'd settled that."

"But my teasing and flirting just now—"

"Was funny and...confusing," she admitted. "I'm going to ignore it. But I'll be glad to cook you meals now and then. How's that?"

"That works," he said with a grin. "I never turn down a meal from a friend."

Ava Jane glanced around, taking in all the people who'd come to help her celebrate Sarah Rose's birthday.

Some would frown on making a fuss but this was like any other gathering, full of good fellowship and food, celebrating life and love. Sarah Rose and her friends were done with food and gifts and playing volleyball and baseball. They'd wandered toward the barns, probably to find a corner to chatter away in. Ava Jane's friends and family had insisted she sit and take a rest while they tidied things up in the kitchen. But she suspected all of the well-meaning matchmakers in her life hoped Jeremiah would come back and they'd have some quiet time together. She'd give them a few minutes to stew in their hope and then she'd clean her own kitchen, thank you.

She thought of Jeremiah and how she'd treated him with her high and mighty notions on how he should conduct his life. She still did not understand why he'd left and gone off to fight, but she could clearly see the warrior inside of him. It showed in his fierce need to do what was right, to be kind to others, to work hard to prove himself every day. Whatever influences had caused him to leave had been beyond her control. And maybe his, too. But God knew his heart. God had brought him home.

That was a cause for celebration. But her own bitterness had held her back from seeing that until now.

Things would be different now. She'd be kind to him. She'd visit his family more often and help them during this difficult time. She'd pray for him with a new spirit. Her emotions couldn't reach past that to anything more right now, even if her imagination had taken flight on too many what-ifs.

"You're sure in deep thought."

She looked up to see her *daed* smiling down at her. "I was counting my blessings," she said, searching the yard. "Where are the girls?"

"They ran off to check on the baby chicks and pick wildflowers out in the meadow," he said, sitting down beside her. "Sarah Rose sure did like the rose-patterned quilt you made for her."

Ava Jane glanced at the table where the quilt lay spread out in all of its glory, along with some books and a few other handmade items others had brought—dolls and shawls, a new bonnet. "She seemed glad, yes. I hope she will cherish it for a long time."

"I think she will," her father replied. "You seem happier today, daughter. More at peace."

"I am at peace," she said. "I have much to be at peace about. A *gut* life—one that I couldn't see for a while there."

"You and Jeremiah are getting along better?"

"Yes. We're friends. I want to put the past behind us."

"That's wonderful to my ears," her father said. "He has a couple more months before he is baptized. I believe he is sincere and he's ready to return to the fold."

"I'm glad to hear that and I believe that now, too," she replied. Getting up, she said, "I think I should go inside and see if Deborah has rearranged my whole kitchen."

Daed laughed at that. "That girl has a mind of her own."

Ava Jane started up the steps and then turned. "Will you check on the girls?" A memory of Eli telling her he'd be in the barn and winding up at the creek instead caused her heart to stop for a minute.

"On it," her *daed* replied. "They are as quiet as little mice, aren't they?"

"Too quiet," she said, a trace of worry clouding her peaceful mood.

* * *

Jeremiah helped Eli reel in the big bream, happy to see the boy's wide grin. "That's a fine one, Eli," he said. "And the third one you've caught."

"And Simon has two," Eli reminded him, sharing the bounty. The boy expertly held the flapping fish tight and removed the hook from his mouth. "I love fishing, Mr. Jeremiah."

"Well, you are good at it and we have a nice mess of bream," Jeremiah replied, his heart welling when he remembered fishing right here with Jacob. "We'll need to head home soon, but maybe a couple more casts."

The boys baited their hooks like pros and studied the water with the patience of Job for the next few minutes. Then they heard giggling and splashing around the bend, out in the wider part of the creek.

"Who is that?" Simon asked, craning his neck to see. Then he whirled toward Jeremiah. "That's my sister, Rebecca, and Sarah Rose, with their friends."

Jeremiah put down his pole and hurried to the other side of the bridge. "Sure is. How did they wind up down here?"

Eli came running, too. "I don't think Mamm would allow this. You know how she feels about us getting near the water."

"I don't like it either," Jeremiah said, concern filling his heart when he saw the girls wading in the shallows. The creek had a sharp drop-off in the middle.

"Should I go and get Mamm?" Eli asked.

"Not yet," Jeremiah replied. "But we're going down there to fetch them."

Leaving their poles and tackle box, they hurried off the bridge and rounded the path that ran by this part of the creek. Jeremiah searched and easily spotted the girls. "Hurry, boys." He called out, "Sarah Rose, Rebecca!"

But the chattering, splashing girls didn't hear him.

He called again. "Girls, come out of the water!"

Rebecca turned around and stepped toward the shore where the other girls were standing with their feet in the water.

Then he watched in horror as Sarah Rose took another step. Rebecca called her name. Sarah Rose looked around, stumbled.

And disappeared into the water.

Chapter Twenty

J̲eremiah went into action, untying his boots as he ran. "Eli, run and get help. Tell one of the adults to go to the phone booth and call 9-1-1 for help, okay?" He looked back as he called out. "Simon, stay on the shore with the other girls. Don't leave them and don't let them get in the water."

"Yessir." Simon ran behind him while Eli took off in the other direction.

Jeremiah ripped off his boots and socks and headed into the water. He had to find Sarah Rose.

A few minutes after she'd sent her father to check on the girls, Ava Jane wiped the kitchen table and turned to smile at Leah, Ruth and Deborah. "We are finished. Now we can go and sit under the oak tree and have some lemonade. *Denke* for the help. And thank you for coming to share in Sarah Rose's special day."

Mamm came in from the porch, carrying what was left of the cake. "The men are full and resting and your *daed* is still with the girls apparently. I saved Jeremiah a piece of this, and there is a plate on the stove for him to take home to Beth and Moselle."

Ava Jane smiled as she put a cover over the cake. Then she glanced outside. Jeremiah and the boys had wolfed down their food and left in a rush to get to the creek. "They should be back by now. Of course, if they're catching fish—"

Then she heard a shout. "Mamm! Mamm, hurry!"

Eli!

Pushing past the other women, she ran out the door and down the steps to where the men were gathering. "Eli, what is it? Where are Simon and Jeremiah?"

Daed hurried from the far side of the barn. "I can't find the girls."

Eli whirled to his grandfather. "They are all at the creek!" Then he ran to Ava Jane and buried his head in her apron. "We saw them and…they were in the water… and Sarah Rose—"

"What?" Ava Jane's heart stopped cold, a sick dread piercing the center of her being. "What?"

Eli's words came out in a breathless rush, his eyes red rimmed and wide. "She fell in. Jeremiah went in after her. He said call for help."

Ava Jane gasped and then she ran. Ran as fast as she could to the creek, her mind whirling with memories of another day and another horrible memory. *No, no!* her heart shouted while she couldn't find her next breath. *Not my baby. Not sweet Sarah Rose.*

Jeremiah had to help her. He had to save her little girl.

Weariness tugged at his body. The weight of the cold water covered him and forced him to remember being in underwater training, cold and tired and weighed down with dive gear and tactical gear, praying he'd make it to the top again. Only today, he wasn't wearing the armor of war. Today, his own failures and shortcomings were weighing him down. He only had a few more precious seconds. He could stay down here and let the weight take him away, but he had a reason for being here. He had so much to be thankful for, to hope for.

And he had to find Sarah Rose. The precious seconds belonged to her, not him. He was trained and equipped but he only needed one weapon right now. The armor of God.

Help me, Father. Give me the strength. I have failed everyone but I will not break Ava Jane's heart again. And I will not go against Your word again.

He went to the bottom of the sharp drop-off, about eight feet deep here, and tried to see through the murky depths, tried to focus and remember his training. He might have to try another spot, but she'd stepped off right here. She had to be near.

He turned, treaded, watched. Waited.

And then he saw a little dress billowing up like a blossoming flower, a bonnet wet and pulling at her beautiful face.

Jeremiah swam as hard as he could and grabbed the little girl into his arms and pushed up, up, toward the last of the sun's brilliant rays. He surfaced and took a deep, cleansing breath and then he swam until he could touch the bottom and run through the muck holding him back. Pushing at her bonnet, he managed to get her head up so he could start mouth-to-mouth.

Holding Sarah Rose close, he noted her closed eyes and the blue around her lips. Then he felt her neck.

A pulse. She still had a pulse. He wouldn't have to do cardiac compressions. Yet.

Quickly laying her down on the grass and leaves near the shore, he flipped her on her stomach to clear her lungs of water. When that didn't revive her, he turned her onto her back. Gulping air, Jeremiah told the others, "Stay back. I have to help her. I'm going to breathe into her mouth."

The girls cried and clutched each other.

Simon knelt beside him. "Should I help?"

Jeremiah looked up at the frightened boy. "No, keep the girls calm."

Then he went into combat mode and tried with all his might to save this life. This one life.

To make up for what he'd done out there.

To make up for what he'd done to Ava Jane.

To redeem himself at last and give his heart completely to God.

She saw him leaning over her child. A scream caught in her throat, a dark claw shredded her heart into little pieces.

"Sarah Rose!" she cried out. "Sarah Rose?"

Eli was right behind her, calling to her. But Ava Jane kept running, the sound of other voices echoing through the woods, the sound of a siren somewhere off in the distance.

"Jeremiah!" she called as she fell down beside Sarah Rose and tried to push him away. "Jeremiah, give me my child!"

"He's helping her," Simon said, grabbing Ava Jane's arm. "He knows what to do."

The boy's words halted her and she stared through her

tears at the man trying to revive her daughter. Jeremiah methodically and carefully breathed air back into Sarah Rose's still little body and pumped at her chest, trying to save her life.

Ava Jane put her hands together. "Jeremiah, don't let her die. Please don't let her die."

He never looked up, never responded. He just kept doing what he had to do, stopping to check her breath and her pulse and then starting all over again, his strong hands so big and yet so gentle.

Eli sank down beside Ava Jane, his breath coming in great huffs. "Mamm, I thought she might be cold."

Ava Jane turned to see the rose-patterned quilt in her son's hands and realized he'd run home to get it. Grabbing Eli and hugging him close, she rocked him there and then held to the quilt. They'd had such a sweet, beautiful day. Surely God wouldn't let it end in such a tragedy.

"Denke," she managed to say, tears streaming down her face. *"Denke."*

A silence fell over the woods. The birds hushed. The air held still. Ava Jane heard others come up behind her, felt someone touching her arm. But she held to the quilt and watched Jeremiah fight a battle, his face lined with fatigue and despair. And she could see it all there in the shadows around his eyes, in the pallor of his skin. He'd suffered out there. But here, right now, all of his torment had come back to war with him. If Sarah Rose died, he'd never recover.

And neither would Ava Jane.

She held her hands together and prayed.

Then she noticed others bowing their heads. Her parents, her sister, their friends, the children. They all seemed to be praying. While the one man she had not wanted near her children kept working, breathing, touching, whispering words of encouragement to her daughter.

He finally stopped and looked up and over at Ava Jane, a dark torment coloring his eyes, a single gruff sob escaping from his mouth. Touching three fingers to Sarah Rose's neck, he tried to speak.

And then they all heard it—a cough, a moan. Water came out of Sarah Rose's mouth. Her eyes flew open and she coughed again, causing a collective cry of joy to fill the gloaming.

Ava Jane heard a weak cry. "Mamm?"

Jeremiah fell back on his knees, exhaustion overtaking him.

Ava Jane lifted and then dropped down beside her daughter and wrapped the quilt over her trembling little body. "I'm here," she said. "I'm here. Help is on the way."

Hugging her scared, confused daughter close, Ava Jane looked up at Jeremiah, her eyes holding his, the love in her heart bursting forth at last. She'd always loved him. Now she knew she was *supposed* to love him. Later, she'd tell him her true feelings and make him see that he was worthy of so much more than her love alone.

So she gazed at him, gratitude in her heart, love in her soul, and prayed he'd see the truth.

He nodded at her, his eyes full of regret, and then got up and walked away.

Jeremiah needed to escape. He couldn't breathe, couldn't think. Everything he'd been through had erupted in those few minutes between finding Sarah Rose in the water and hearing her call out for her mother again. Now his life was all out there for him to see: the mistakes, the victories, the regret and the hope. His heart held too much weight, too much agony. The flashbacks came in great, shattering waves that blinded him.

Ava Jane's eyes had filled with gratitude and understanding and, instead of running to her, he'd walked away. He had to find a quiet spot and think things through. He couldn't accept her gratitude.

He wanted her love.

"Mr. Jeremiah?"

Jeremiah turned away from the lane that would take him home and saw Eli standing there. He couldn't run from the boy.

Eli stared up at him with dark, brooding eyes. "*Denke* for saving my sister."

Jeremiah held tightly to his tears and nodded down at the boy.

"Hey, I hear you're the one who rescued the girl?"

The paramedic hurried up to Jeremiah and shook his hand. "Good job. Her vitals are stable and she's alert. She should be fine but we're taking her to the hospital for overnight observation and to make sure her lungs are clear. Good thing you knew CPR, man."

Jeremiah still couldn't speak.

Eli gave him an admiring stare and told the paramedic, "He…he was trained that way."

Then Eli ran off to be with his mother and sister while the paramedic's eyes filled with realization. Shaking Jeremiah's hand again, he said, "Welcome home."

Ava Jane sat in the hospital room that night, watching her daughter sleep. Deborah was on the small settee by the window, sleeping under a white blanket. Sarah Rose's quilt lay over the bedding, keeping her warm. She had not let go of it since Ava Jane had wrapped her in it.

She'd sent her parents home with Eli, telling them to come back tomorrow. They'd all be home tomorrow, she hoped.

She had to see Jeremiah. To thank him and tell him how she felt. He had to know that she loved him. Why had it taken something so tragic to make her admit that to herself?

He'd left, disappeared while everyone clustered around Sarah Rose to wish her well. The ambulance had carried Sarah Rose and Ava Jane off, with Daed promising they'd call a cab to get them to the hospital.

Ava Jane had glanced around, hoping to see Jeremiah so she could thank him. But he was nowhere to be found.

Chapter Twenty-One

$\backsim$

He went to his father's side.

Jeremiah fell onto the chair and lowered his head.

"I…I need to talk to you, Daed."

It was late and his mother and sister were both asleep.

He'd walked until the moonlight covered him in shadows, until his wet clothes had turned to damp. Until the weariness crushing his soul had brought him home.

But he couldn't sleep. So he sat here and talked to his father. "I saved Sarah Rose tonight. She fell into the creek and almost drowned. Just like Jacob." He stopped, wiped at his eyes, took in a breath. "Just like me, Daed. I almost drowned in my own pain and sorrow. Funny how I could spend well over eighteen weeks training to become a SEAL and yet these last months of retraining myself to become Amish again have become the hardest test of my life. I still have some lessons to learn."

He sighed and laid his head in his hands on the bed. Prayers rattled through his head like tanks moving through a blown-up village. "I couldn't save them," he finally said. "Two children. Two little children who got caught in the cross fire. I lost Cowboy and Gator, I told you that. But I've never talked about the two little children. Villagers trying to get away. Somehow they'd got separated from their family and they got shot. I didn't shoot them but I tried to save them."

He stopped, his head down, tears soaking the blanket, the memory of those precious little faces so clear he could almost touch them. "The fear in their eyes, their cries, those things stay with me. Always."

Jeremiah's hands clutched the blanket. "I wanted to go back for them. I turned to run back and get them." And then another round of shots and he'd woken up in a hospital in Germany and refused to let anyone get in touch with his family. He had wanted to go back to sleep and never wake.

"I didn't save them. They told me I couldn't have saved them. That I almost died trying."

He remembered one of his buddies calling him. "Amish, you go home and start your life over. You did the best you could, man. You saved five of us. That counts for something."

"But I didn't save all of you," he'd replied.

Jeremiah kept his head down, confessing all now.

"Tonight, in that creek, I saw those innocent faces all over again. I could not have lived with myself if I'd failed Sarah Rose," he said to his father.

He lifted his head and wiped his eyes. Then he lowered his head again and sat silent, his prayers lifting up to God. He needed peace. He needed love. He needed forgiveness.

Jeremiah must have fallen asleep. For how long, he wasn't sure. But when he felt a hand on his head, he came awake and sat up to find his father's eyes on him.

"Daadi?"

Isaac's hand slipped down Jeremiah's arm. Jeremiah took his father's hand and held it, a soft, warm joy washing over his body. "I'm sorry, Daed."

Isaac nodded, a single tear moving down his skeletal face. Then, still holding Jeremiah's hand, he closed his eyes and took his last breath.

When Ava Jane and her parents brought Sarah Rose home the next afternoon, she was surprised to find a car waiting in her yard. A big black fancy car.

After they all unloaded and entered the house, her *daed* carrying a still-weak Sarah Rose, Deborah met them at the door.

"Who is here?" Ava Jane asked, wondering if someone from town had come to help out.

"It's me, dear."

Deborah turned and indicated the parlor.

Then Ava Jane saw her. Judy Campton sat in a high-backed chair, wearing a suit and pearls.

"How kind of you to come," Ava Jane said, turning to Judy. "If you let me get Sarah Rose situated, I'll be right back down."

Deborah shook her head. "Mamm and I will watch the *kinder*. You and Daed need to go with Mrs. Campton."

"Why?" Ava Jane asked, her heart too bruised to hear more bad news.

Judy Campton pushed off the chair. "Jeremiah's father died last night," she said. "And I'm afraid Jeremiah isn't taking it too well. I think he needs to see you."

Ava Jane whirled toward her parents.

"Go," Mamm said. "Sarah Rose will sleep most of the day and Deborah and I will make sure she is taken care of. Eli, too."

"He'll need a minister," Daed said. "And I agree with Mrs. Campton. He probably needs a friend."

Ava Jane hugged Moselle and Beth close. "I'm so sorry for your loss."

They both nodded and thanked her while Daed stood with the bishop and several other men. A few neighboring women worked the kitchen in a system as old as time. They knew funerals and weddings and births. They knew life and death and hurt and love.

She was one of them and right now Jeremiah needed her. The quick ride over had been quiet but now she needed to see him, to make sure he was all right.

Mrs. Campton had taken a spot in a comfortable chair, Bettye with her now since she seemed as tired as Ava Jane felt. She nodded to Ava Jane so Ava Jane went over to her.

"Where is Jeremiah?" Ava Jane asked.

"When they called me, he was out in the barn," Mrs. Campton said. "He didn't want to talk to me. I hope you can help him."

Ava Jane lifted her spine and went out the back door. The sun shone a creamy yellow light on the growing wheat in the field beyond the house and bounced off the tall silo behind the barn. But inside, the dark coolness contrasted sharply, the muted shadows causing her to blink.

The animals were out in the paddock, grazing. The big high barn was quiet.

"Jeremiah?"

"Ja?"

She heard him, felt him, ached for him. "Jeremiah, it's Ava Jane. Can I come back?"

"Yes."

Ava Jane followed the sound of his voice. But when she saw him, her heart tripped over itself to get to him. He sat huddled in a corner with his hands hiding his face, as if he'd tried to curl into a tight ball.

Sinking down beside him, she didn't flinch. Instead, she put her hands over his and forced them away from his face. "Jeremiah, I'm so sorry."

He held on to her hands, his red-rimmed eyes bright with something that broke her and scared her. Such a raw pain, she wanted to turn away. But she didn't.

"He touched me," he said, his eyes widening now. "My *daed* touched me, Ava Jane."

She leaned against the wall, her hands still holding his. "You were with him last night?"

Bobbing his head, he said, "*Ja*. Early this morning, really. I talked to him the way I always do. Told him about my life as a SEAL. The training, the doubts, what we all had to endure."

Swallowing, he looked away through a crack of light pushing through the ceiling beams. "I told him about the children. A girl and a boy. Dark haired and olive skinned. They…got separated from their family and they cried out. I heard them and turned. I had tried to save Cowboy and Gator, two of my teammates. But I could not get to the children. I tried and then there was a blast and shots fired and…I couldn't save them."

Ava Jane gasped and held tightly when he tried to pull away. This was what Mrs. Campton had seen and had warned her about. He carried this with him, all the time. What must have he gone through when he'd gone into that water to save her child?

She tried to form the right words, but he started talking again. "It all came back. Leaving you, training, fighting, killing. When I went into that water, it all came pouring back over me. I wanted to stay down there, safe and covered and washed clean, but I had to save Sarah Rose. You know, to balance what I'd done, to appease those I couldn't save." Shifting, he touched a hand to her face. "I had to get back to you. But I needed to get back to God."

Ava Jane's heart burst with love and pride. "Jeremiah, I'm here. I'm here. You found me again."

"But I want you to love me. And if what I saw in your eyes was just gratitude—"

"Yes, gratitude," she said, never letting his hands slip away from hers. "But more than gratitude. I saw it all, too, Jeremiah. If you hadn't come home, Sarah Rose might have died last night."

"But if I'd never left—"

She shook her head. "*Ne*, we can't say what would have happened if you'd stayed. We can't know God's will for us. But I do know that my daughter is alive and well today because of you, and that my son walks taller now and wants to do right by people, and that many of the people of our community have seen you in action, running toward the hard things that most people run from. That is who you are, Jeremiah. That is who you have always been. And that is what I love about you."

He moved away. "I don't deserve your love, but I want it. I so want it."

She wasn't afraid now. Ava Jane moved in front of him and pulled his head up with her hands. "I love you. I always loved you but I loved Jacob, too. He's gone and he'd want you and me together. He'd understand. Your *daed* is gone but he forgave you, Jeremiah. He loved you.

Don't push me away out of a sense of duty. Don't shut me out. Let me help you. Let me love you and give you that peace you seek." Kissing his tears again, she began to cry but through her tears she whispered, "Jeremiah, listen to me. I love you."

He stopped fighting against her and looked into her eyes. And then he pulled her close and shed all of the tears he'd held at bay for so long.

"I love you, too," he said, lifting his head to smile up at her. "And I'm going to prove that to you for the rest of my life."

One year later

Jeremiah walked into the parlor after doing the evening chores and found his wife asleep in her favorite rocking chair. He still couldn't believe that last fall Ava Jane had become his wife. She'd been so beautiful, walking toward him in the late-afternoon sunshine. He'd been so happy that day and he was even happier this evening.

Mrs. Campton had helped him find counseling and Ava Jane had waited for him to come back to her, but she'd also visited him and brought the children to see him.

"We'll be right here, when you are ready," she'd told him.

Now he'd been baptized and his beard was long. He was a married man. A happily married man.

When the nightmares tried to come, Ava Jane was there beside him. Mrs. Campton was always nearby. And the community stood solidly with him. He stayed busy teaching children to swim, and he still volunteered with the local fire department, farmed the land and did carpentry work on the side, while his amazing wife cooked and baked and gained a reputation for her wonderful cakes and muffins.

Now here he was, ready to rest at the end of the day, loving the beautiful routine of this quiet place that held his heart.

And now smiling at his beautiful wife.

As if sensing that, she opened her eyes and smiled back. "*Gut* evening, husband. You caught me taking a catnap."

"*Gut* evening, wife," he replied, kneeling to place a hand on her growing tummy. "I've been thinking. If it's a boy, we should name him Jacob."

Her eyes misty, she stared over at him. "Jacob Jeremiah Weaver. We can nickname him JJ."

"That's different," he said with a grin as the sunset washed over them in shades of burnished gold.

Slapping at his hand, she stood and tugged him close. "*Ja*, but then…so are we."

She was right about that. Different but the same. Because now God's light shone on their lives and brought the kind of warmth that sealed a man's soul.

Jeremiah Weaver, the Amish, was home at last.

* * * * *

WE HOPE YOU
ENJOYED THIS

LOVE
INSPIRED®
BOOK.

If you were **inspired** by this

uplifting, **heartwarming** romance,

be sure to look for all six Love

Inspired® books every month.

Love Inspired®

Save $1.00

on the purchase of ANY
Love Inspired® or
Love Inspired® Suspense book.

Available wherever books are sold,
including most bookstores, supermarkets,
drugstores and discount stores.

✂- -

Save $1.00

on the purchase of ANY Love Inspired® or Love Inspired® Suspense book.

Coupon valid until October 31, 2019.
Redeemable at participating retail outlets in the U.S. and Canada only.
Limit one coupon per customer.

52616440

Canadian Retailers: Harlequin Enterprises Limited will pay the face value of this coupon plus 10.25¢ if submitted by customer for this product only. Any other use constitutes fraud. Coupon is nonassignable. Void if taxed, prohibited or restricted by law. Consumer must pay any government taxes. Void if copied. Inmar Promotional Services ("IPS") customers submit coupons and proof of sales to Harlequin Enterprises Limited, P.O. Box 31000, Scarborough, ON M1R 0E7, Canada. Non-IPS retailer—for reimbursement submit coupons and proof of sales directly to Harlequin Enterprises Limited, Retail Marketing Department, Bay Adelaide Centre, East Tower, 22 Adelaide Street West, 40th Floor, Toronto, Ontario M5H 4E3, Canada.

U.S. Retailers: Harlequin Enterprises Limited will pay the face value of this coupon plus 8¢ if submitted by customer for this product only. Any other use constitutes fraud. Coupon is nonassignable. Void if taxed or restricted by law. Consumer must pay any government taxes. Void if copied. For reimbursement submit coupons and proof of sales directly to Harlequin Enterprises, Ltd 482, NCH Marketing Services, P.O. Box 880001, El Paso, TX 88588-0001, U.S.A. Cash value 1/100 cents.

® and ™ are trademarks owned and used by the trademark owner and/or its licensee.

© 2019 Harlequin Enterprises Limited

LICOUP47012

Paralyzed veteran Eve Vincent is happy with the life she's built for herself at Mercy Ranch—until her ex-fiancé shows up with a baby. Their best friends died and named Eve and Ethan Forester as guardians. But can they put their differences aside and build a future together?

Read on for a sneak preview of
Her Oklahoma Rancher *by Brenda Minton, available June 2019 from Love Inspired!*

"I'm sorry, Eve, but I had to do something to make you see how important this is. We can't just walk away from her. It might not be what we signed on for and I feel like I'm the last person who should be raising this little girl, but James and Hanna trusted us."

"But there is no *us*," she said with a lift of her chin, but he could see pain reflected in her dark eyes.

The pain he saw didn't bother him as much as what he didn't see in her eyes, in her expression. He didn't see the person he used to know, the woman he'd planned to marry.

He had noticed the same yesterday, and he guessed that was why he'd left Tori with her. He'd been sitting there looking at a woman he used to think he knew better than he knew himself, and he hadn't recognized her.

"There is no *us*, but we still exist, you and me, and Tori needs us." He said it softly because the little girl in his arms seemed to be drifting off, even with the occasional sob.

"There has to be another option. I obviously can't do this. Last night was proof."

"Last night meant nothing. You've always managed, Eve. You're strong and capable."

"Before, Ethan. I was that person before. This is me now, and I can't."

"I guess you have changed. I've never heard you say you can't do anything."

He sat down on a nearby chair. Isaac had left. The woman named Sierra had also disappeared. They were alone. When had they last been alone? The night he proposed? It had been the night she left for Afghanistan. He'd taken her to dinner in San Antonio and they'd walked along the riverfront surrounded by people, music and twinkling lights.

He'd dropped to one knee there in front of strangers passing by, seeing the sights. Dozens had stopped to watch as she cried and said yes. Later they'd made the drive to the airport, his ring glistening on her finger, planning a wedding that would never happen.

"Ethan?" Her voice was soft, quiet, questioning.

He glanced down at the little girl in his arms.

"What other option is there, Eve? Should we turn her over to the state, let her take her chances with whoever they choose? Should we find some distant relative? What do you recommend?"

He leaned back in the chair and studied her face, her expression. She was everything familiar. His childhood friend. The person he'd loved. *Had* loved. Past tense. The woman he'd wanted to spend his life with had been someone else, someone who never backed down. She looked as tough, as stubborn as ever, but there was something fragile in her expression.

Something in her expression made him recheck his feelings. He'd been bucked off horses, trampled by a bull, broken his arm jumping dirt bikes. She'd been his only broken heart. He didn't want another one.

Don't miss
Her Oklahoma Rancher *by Brenda Minton,*
available June 2019 wherever
Love Inspired® *books and ebooks are sold.*

www.LoveInspired.com

LIEXP0619

Looking for inspiration in tales
of hope, faith and heartfelt romance?

Check out **Love Inspired®** and
Love Inspired® Suspense books!

New books available every month!

CONNECT WITH US AT:

Facebook.com/groups/HarlequinConnection

 Facebook.com/HarlequinBooks

 Twitter.com/HarlequinBooks

 Instagram.com/HarlequinBooks

 Pinterest.com/HarlequinBooks

ReaderService.com

Love Inspired®

LIGENRE2018R2